# HEARTSONG
## APRIL ASHMORE

**ZEBRA BOOKS**
**KENSINGTON PUBLISHING CORP.**

ZEBRA BOOKS are published by

Kensington Publishing Corp.
475 Park Avenue South
New York, NY 10016

First Printing: February, 1994

Printed in the United States of America

# MI CORAZON

Savanna's thoughts reeled. "Don't call me that," she spat. Why were her knees turning to jelly now! Good God, she couldn't let him do this to her again. "I'm not your love."

He laughed deep in his throat and gave her folded arms a complaining look. "That isn't what the words mean." Fire leapt in his raven eyes, making her feverish and dizzy. "Mi corazon is 'my heart.'" He brushed a kiss across her lips.

She felt them tremble, an odd reaction for someone who didn't love him.

He traced her trembling underlip with his thumb. "Now, if I said 'mi amor mi corazon,' then you'd have cause for complaint." He breathed the word against her lips, kissed her again, then added, "Assuming, of course that you weren't my love."

She pressed away from him in a half-hearted protest. "I don't speak Spanish."

"Of course." He smiled, warm, seductive, irresistible like his kiss. "Spanish is a tongue for lovers, and, as you said, you are no man's love."

She didn't have to wonder how to reply—whether to confirm or deny it. His lips possessed her in the instant of silence that followed . . .

# CAPTURE THE GLOW OF
# ZEBRA'S *HEARTFIRES!*

*To my weekly buddies in the
Northwest Arkansas Fiction Writers Workshop;
And to the great ladies in the
Northeastern Oklahoma Romance Authors;
Writer friends are the best friends*

# One

Six men sat astride nervous, lathered horses staring at her like they'd seen a ghost. Raising her heavy rifle, Savanna strode down the veranda of the massive old adobe and took aim at the intruders on her lawn. Only her second night at the Vista Del Sol, and they were here already.

Her fingers trembled against the trigger as she tossed back her moon-gold hair and spoke. "You can tell this shadow man, or whatever he calls himself, he'll get nothing from me by sending kerchief-wearing hoodlums in the night." Her very proper English accent made the words seem less threatening than she would have liked. "I'll not succumb to extortion."

At that, she heard a gasp from the bunkhouse. She ignored it and squinted down the rifle barrel. "Now, I must insist that you leave Vista Del Sol and not return." She hoped her voice sounded steadier than it felt. "Your kind are hardly welcome here."

Slowly, the riders looked at each other, their confusion plain even through the bright-colored silk bandanas hiding their faces. Savanna bit her lip and willed her aching arms to hold the rifle up a few moments longer. Now was not the time to let them know tapestry hoops were more her custom.

With a helpless shrug, the foremost man backed his horse a few steps and whispered something to one of the others. Giving a quick wave of his arm, he started to turn his horse away.

"You shoult tell your patrona she ees a fool," he said to the dumbfounded cowhands assembled on the bunkhouse porch in their longjohns. "Venenoso expectz hees money. He will come in zee night and keel you one by one until he receif what is due."

Without another word, he spun his mount away, called "Vamos," to his cohorts, and they melted back into the darkness like shadows.

Frozen in place, the ranch hands watched them go, then slowly looked back at the woman on the veranda.

"Who the hell is she?" Brandt Wade whispered as he twisted the handles of his long moustache. It seemed like a strange question to ask, considering he was foreman of the Del Sol.

Beside him, his youngest rounder reeled up his bottom lip long enough to answer. "I ain't never seen her before." Waddie had that bubble-eyed look of a kid getting his first look at a woman. "She acts like she owns the place."

"She's Carver's kid," the cook settled it finally with a shrug of disgust. "Came in day 'afore yesterday while y'all was out at the Rocky Branch camp. Reckon the Vista Del Sol is hers now that the old bastard's dead." The tone of his voice made his opinion of the situation clear. Muffled grumbles from the crowd said the others agreed.

"I didn't know Carver had a kid," Waddie muttered.

Brandt stroked his moustache and thoughtfully looked back at the main house. There wasn't any point letting his crew get all stirred up in the middle of the night. Come morning, he could figure out what was going on.

"Hell, boys," he chuckled as he watched the woman walk calmly back into the ranch house, her shapely form dimly visible beneath the white nightdress, "that ain't no kid."


Inside the door, Savanna calmly replaced the rifle in the cabinet by the yawning half-moon fireplace. Numbly, she stared into the flames, ignoring the shocked gazes of the house cook and the housekeeper. One drew a long breath as if to say something. Spinning around, Savanna gave them a warning glance and headed for the stairs. The last thing she needed tonight was more of their petrified prattling about Venenoso and his hoodlums.

"Don't bother to make breakfast for me, Esperanza," she said as she passed them. "I'll be going to town early in the morning." Gripping the banister for support, she climbed the winding staircase on legs that felt like strings of wet dough. She could feel her house staff watching her from below as she crested the stairs and walked to her door.

It was all she could do not to run through and slam the door behind her. Leaning weakly against the heavy wood, she pushed it closed, letting out the breath she felt she'd held since the yells and shots woke her. How long ago was that? Probably not more than a half hour. It seemed like a lifetime. Strange how facing six loaded guns made the minutes seem endless. A chilling sweat broke over her as she thought about it. She might just do the ladylike thing and faint after all.

Slapping a hand over her racing heart, she stumbled to the bed and sat down. If she fainted there at least no one would know. Maybe they all knew already. Maybe they all saw right through her. Could they tell by the way she held the rifle she'd never shot at anything but a few clay pigeons?

She smoothed back the wild curls of her golden hair and allowed herself a trembling smile. How shocked the beau who had taught her to shoot would be if he knew how the lessons had come to be used! On the other hand, perhaps he wouldn't be shocked at all. Every warning he gave about coming to the wilds of America came true. The past weeks had been the worst in her life.

How foolishly excited she'd been about taking the rail to Saint Louis and then traveling overland to California! She envisioned all sorts of wild adventures—like in the tabloids—wild Indians and vast herds of free-roaming buffalo. The America she saw had none of those things. This America was built of endless prairies, barren sun-parched deserts, and mile after mile of empty stage road. Everything that crawled, crept, or slithered here was poisonous. It was no wonder those who made it to California called it the promised land. After Indian Territory and New Mexico, hell would look like the promised land.

So here she was in hell, and the devil was knocking at her door already. The strain of getting here aged her ten years. Being awakened by bandits added another ten. She was definitely not twenty-one any more.

A cool breeze slipped up her sleeve and touched her dampened breasts. Shuddering, she glanced down at herself, and her thoughts scattered like sparrows. Her nightdress! She was wearing her nightdress! What had been bad was now worse. She had just paraded in front of her employees nearly nude!

Groaning, she fell back against the bed and

snapped her violet eyes closed. Things could not possibly, possibly get any worse. She was an unwelcome resident in the only place she could call home, and she had made a fool of herself in front of her staff. How could she hope to convince them she could run the Vista Del Sol when she didn't even have enough sense to put on a bed jacket?

She pictured the combination of rifles and ruffles as the night ticked by to the muffled sound of the grandfather clock in the hallway. All she wanted to do was pack her bag and run away before morning came. But she had nowhere to run. This ranch on the edge of the world was her last island. She was going to have to pick up her oars and row.

The first rays of morning awoke her a few hours later. Stiffly, she rose from the bed and dressed in a crisp maroon riding skirt and jacket. Pulling on her high black leather riding boots, she looked in the dressing mirror with a frown. The outfit was old. Not worn out, but frightfully out of fashion. She'd purchased it several years before—in better times, when she'd never guessed her fortunes would turn. Fortunately, fashions lagged behind here in the colonies.

Taking an ivory-handled brush from the dressing table beside her, she combed the tangles from her hair. She drew the front back neatly with a clip before placing on her head the bolero-style hat she had purchased on a whim in the San Francisco market. It wasn't as fashionable as the riding hats brought from overseas, but with its broad brim, it was much more practical in the intense California sun.

The house was still silent as she opened the door and stepped into the hall. Perfect. She didn't want to see anyone this morning.

Careful to make no noise, she descended the stairs and slipped out the front door onto the veranda. The smoke from the bunkhouse chimney told her the ranch hands were at breakfast already. Feeling a little like a mouse among lions, she hurried to the stable to saddle a horse. Later, she'd force herself to gather the employees she'd not yet met and introduce herself—as if she hadn't last night. Right now, she had something more important to do if she was going to save the Del Sol.

The stable was mercifully unoccupied save for a good stock of palomino horses. Her father always had a weakness for horses—among other things he couldn't afford. These, as usual, looked to be the finest money could buy, which was amazing for a man who had none. Doubtless, like everything else, he won them in some game of chance or other. It turned her stomach to live off her father's ill-gotten gains, but any legitimate family fortune had been squandered long ago. It was just fortunate her father died while his luck was on an up streak.

She looked the horses over quickly and settled on a saucy-looking mare whose proud arched neck and long, thick, cream-colored mane testi-fied to her Spanish barb ancestry. She could only hope the mare was saddle broken, since she wasn't about to go ask. She also hoped she could figure out where her English-style saddles were stored. She hadn't the slightest idea how to use one of those barbaric cowboy saddles the Cali-fornians rode.

She found her own familiar tack looking strangely out of place beside the hands' rougher-looking gear. With a sigh, she passed her sidesaddle and took a plain saddle, one that belonged to her father many years ago. If the mare wasn't used to carrying a sidesaddle, putting her in one would be disastrous. Be-sides, proper or not, women in California rode astride quite often.

Women in California probably knew how to saddle their own horses also, but it was a first for Savanna. Tossing the saddle up was easy enough, but the rest required a little thought and study. It felt strange to be saddling her own mount—in the past she never would have con-sidered it. Now, it was an insignificant conces-sion compared to the sacrifices already made for her new life.

"That mare's likely to think she's got a gnat on her back with that lacy little saddle," a voice from the door caught her by surprise. "She's li-able to try to scratch you off on a low branch somewhere."

14

Unconsciously Savanna stiffened. The last thing she wanted this morning was company.

"I'm certain we'll manage." She turned to face a tall, dark-haired cow hand. He was smiling ever so slightly beneath the waxed handlebars of his thick moustache. The warm sparkle of humor in his blue eyes softened her instantly, and she added, "But thank you for your concern all the same."

"Goin' into town?" he asked. Somehow, the question didn't seem prying. His easy nature made it more like friendly curiosity.

Savanna couldn't help liking him. "Yes." She fought the urge to smile. After last night, she had to maintain her dignity. "I have some things to attend to this morning."

"Need some company?" he asked. "The roads aren't the safest."

She shook her head and led the mare to the doorway where he stood. He didn't move.

"No thank you," she replied, her tone definite, slightly cool. "I'm certain we can manage, mister . . . uh?" It seemed strange to be begging an introduction to someone who worked for her. It was unfortunate that some of the men had been away in cow camp when she arrived.

He smiled a wide easy smile, a light of good humor softening the sun-hardened lines of his face, making him look younger than he probably was. "I guess I should introduce myself," he extended his hand as though greeting another man. "I'm Brandt Wade—your cattle foreman. That is, assumin' you're Miss Storm."

Slipping out a hand tentatively, she accepted his greeting with a nod. How strange for a man to greet a woman with a handshake! America was stuffed like a feather mattress with strange customs.

"Savanna," she corrected with a smile. The glimmer in his eye said it wasn't wasted on him.

He released her hand and leaned against the side of the doorway. Crossing one long leg over the other, he waved a hand as if to usher her out. "Well, Savanna, it's been good to meet you, and I won't hold you from your travels any longer. It's time I dragged those lazy coyotes out of the bunk house and got 'em started on the day's work." Leaning over, he lowered a hand near the horse's knee. "Leg up?" he offered.

She accepted by cocking a boot into the outstretched palm. As if she were made of feathers, he lifted her onto her mount. He grinned and shook his head at the saddle as she righted herself in it.

"Damndest thing I ever saw," he chuckled. When Savanna shot him a surprised glance, he tucked his head and muttered, "Uh . . . pardon my language, ma'am."

She didn't reply, but smiled back over her shoulder and urged the uncertain mare forward. The mare snorted, jigged sideways, and humped up like a bristling cat. Savannah gave the reins a jerk and tried to ignore an unpleasant vision of herself sprawled in the stable yard for all to see.

"Stop that," she snapped under her breath, giving the palomino a solid kick. The mare tossed her head and jumped blindly through the open corral gate, then pranced up the road snorting and tossing her head. Savanna bit her lip and resisted the urge to say something unladylike. Barely dawn, and she'd already been faced with her first near disaster. Most certainly, that didn't bode well for the rest of the day.

The ride to town made the mare considerably more tractable. Except for an occasional toss of her head, she was acting like a respectable saddle horse by the time they reached the waking streets of Oro Grande. Around her hooves, miniature dust devils swept down the empty street. They gained strength as they passed the cross breezes of various alleyways, only to wither and die in the yard of the imposing adobe mission at the north end.

Framing the street and leading up to the mission was a row of carefully spaced trees, all dead now—the casualties of several seasons of drought and flood and drought and flood, and finally two years of drought. All around, there was evidence of things that had once been grand but were now in ruin, like the Del Sol.

A young man on the stage had told her about several seasons of devastating weather—floods which decimated cattle herds, some 150,000 drowned in the Sacramento valley alone, and then a long drought to starve many of those that remained. Given that, and her father's gambling tendencies, it was a wonder the Del Sol had any assets left at all. The man on the stage said his own uncle, like many old Spanish landholders, was forced to sell his cattle for thirty-seven cents a head and his land for ten cents an acre just to feed his family. It was, no doubt, that type of tale which attracted her father to California—like a vulture sneaking in to pick at the bones.

She stopped her horse in front of the sheriff's office, dismounted, and went in. The man inside, who unfortunately turned out to be the sheriff, looked sleepy, or drunk, or both. He watched her with pointed disinterest as she told him what had happened the night before, and he offered no help when she was finished.

Finally, she leaned forward and met his gaze with narrow determination. "Sheriff," she began again. "I don't think you understand." Obviously, he didn't or he wouldn't be sitting back calmly in his chair. "Thieves invaded my ranch last night demanding extortion money. Evidently, they have been victimizing the entire valley for quite some time. Perhaps everyone else is too afraid to stand up to them, but I will not bow to thievery!" She neglected to mention that paying the money was not an option for her. She didn't have any to give.

He leaned farther back in his chair, tipping it onto two legs so it squealed in protest. With a skeptical look, he crossed his arms over his chest and drew in a deep breath, rolling his eyes back like an uninterested basset hound being prodded toward the hunt.

"Well, that is a heck of a story," he remarked, "and I can see why a woman alone like yourself would get afraid. Ummm, these men you're talkin' about, did you get a good look at any of 'em?"

Her temper flared at the belittling tone of his voice, and she shot out of her chair. Leaning across the desk, she braced her palms against the clutter with a thud.

"Don't patronize me, Sheriff!" How dare he treat her as if she were some ignorant child! Did he think she was too stupid to know what he was doing? "I'm no fool, and I'm no helpless woman either. I want these thieves kept away from my ranch, which I believe, is your job. If you're not man enough to do it, sir, I would appreciate your just admitting it to me!"

This time the sheriff looked irate. Once again, her temper had goaded her into going too far. How did that saying go?—*You catch more flies with honey* . . .

"Listen, miss," his voice cracked as if he were on the verge of losing control. "I'm just one small-town lawman. I get paid twelve dollars a month, and I do what I can to earn it." His voice raised to a cannonlike boom. "But that doesn't include getting myself killed by going up against the Sombras." Giving a brazen look up and down Savanna's slender form, he shook a finger at her. "And the last thing I need is an uppity Brit telling me how to do my job."

She dragged her fingernails along the desktop as she stood back, plowing furrows through his loose papers, scattering them to the floor. Slowly, she nodded, trying to look sober and confident. She could feel her face going paler by the minute.

"I see," she said quietly. She placed her bolero back on her head and drew the stampede string under her chin as she met his gaze. "I appreciate your honesty. It is clear that I'll be forced to see to my problems myself. Perhaps there are some other ranchers in this valley with the courage to stand up against this injustice."

"Don't bank on it," the sheriff replied, apparently unashamed of his own cowardice. "They all have more sense than to go against Venenoso. They'd rather pay what's due and be left alone. It's cheaper than repairing the damage that gets caused otherwise, and better than winding up dead. That's the way things work here, and if you want to live in this valley, you'd be best to accept it."

"I think not," was the last thing she said as she turned and headed for the door. On her way out, she gave it a healthy slam, rattling the loose panes of glass.

On the boardwalk, she let out a long angry breath, clenching fists at her sides to keep from screaming. One thing she didn't count on when she stood against the bandits was a cowardly sheriff. Now that she was on her own, she'd have to come up with a plan . . .

Stepping to the edge of the walk, she stared narrow-eyed into the street, considering it. Around her, the sleepy Spanish town was coming to life. Its streets were slowly filling with brightly clad passersby, most of them dark-skinned, of Spanish or Indian descent.

Self-consciously, she looked down at her subdued burgundy riding suit, and the trails of pale hair falling forward over her shoulders. She was a strange contrast to the general citizenry of Oro Grande. No wonder she felt like someone was watching her.

She turned to one side then the other. No one was looking at her. The sidewalk was empty except for two gentlemen engaged in what looked like an argument in front of the cantina next door. Neither one appeared to notice her. She was just being silly—letting her nerves run away with her.

She shook her head at herself and started to step off the boardwalk. An explosion roared past her and sent her heart slamming into her throat. Unsteadily, she spun around. What was happening? She glanced at the men by the cantina. One grabbed his arm, gasped, and collapsed into a pool of blood on the walk. The second man, his back to her, holstered his pistol casually, then turned slowly around like he knew she was watching.

His gaze caught her and she stood frozen, her

mouth dropping open in shock, but not because of the dead man. A hot, dizzy feeling swept over her. She had to do something, say something, run away, but she couldn't. He held her fastened to the spot.

His dark eyes, as black as raven's wings, were incredibly powerful, set against ruddy cinnamon skin and framed by a crown of neatly groomed jet hair. Tall and solidly muscled, his air of power and confidence made him look danger-ous, frightening. Perhaps that was only because of the smoking gun at his hip.

Strong muscles coiled beneath the fabric of his white cotton shirt as he motioned to the dead man. "Small disagreement," he said with no hint of the Spanish accent she expected to hear. To her shock, he gave a gallant smile that would have been charming under different cir-cumstances. "But no need to worry, the problem is solved now."

Savanna choked on a breath of air. Didn't he know she just saw him commit murder? Perhaps he intended to shoot her too. Could he do that on the street in broad daylight? Of course. He had done it once already. What would he do if she turned away—just pretended nothing had happened and moved calmly to her horse?

But raven-wing eyes held her to the spot like shackles.

The sound of the sheriff's door opening be-hind her broke the spell. She spun around to see the lawman stepping out onto the walk.

"Monheno Devilla," he addressed the murderer, "I should have known it would be you."

Sweeping off his hat, the murderer made a slightly exaggerated bow. "At your service." There was a silent challenge in his voice. "Just doing your job for you again, Raymond. I believe this is another of our much-celebrated thieves." He replaced his hat and cast a roguish smile and a wink at Savanna before turning his gaze back to the sheriff. "I'll leave him to your charge. I don't think he'll cause any trouble you can't handle."

"You can't go shooting people in the street," the sheriff protested nervously. He took a step forward, then backed away at the murderer's steely look.

"It had to be done," he returned as he stepped past the sheriff to stand uncomfortably close to Savanna. "My only regret is that I seem to have upset the lady, and now I intend to make amends by helping her to a seat until she recovers."

Savanna opened her mouth and raised a hand to wave him away. Specks of blackness swam into her vision. Dear Lord, she was going to swoon! Weakly, she reached for the porch railing. Her hand landed instead on the strong arm of the stranger, and she felt his other hand slide around her waist. Helpless to protest, she let him lead her to the bench in front of the dress shop.

With hard-won determination, she took a deep breath and subdued her rising stomach.

"I'll be fine, I assure you," her voice came in a thin ribbon—hardly as convincing as she planned. She blinked her vision back into focus only to see the dark-eyed man looking down at her with concern. Hoping he would leave, she added, "I'll just sit here for a minute, then I'll be on my way."

"I'll sit with you." He was smiling now, like it was all a good joke.

"There's no need. I wouldn't want to burden you."

"Not at all," he slipped easily into the seat beside her. "After all, this was my fault. I never should have shot a man when there was a lady present—terrible manners, of course."

Her eyes widened and her stomach flipped back into her throat. She'd never heard anything so callous in her life! "I . . ." She didn't know what to say. "I shouldn't have been standing there. I should have been on about my b-business." Caught in his dark gaze, she paused for a moment, and then stumbled on. "I've never seen a man killed before." Good Lord, what a stupid thing to say! Now he knew she saw it all.

He looked confused, but only for a moment before his gallant mask returned. "Oh, he isn't dead, I assure you," he glanced back over his shoulder. "I only shot him in the arm, and that was accidental. I meant to knock him over the back of the head—but, well, accidents happen even to the best of us." He gave her a helpless

24

shrug. "Don't look so peaked. That's not blood, it's salsa. It seems I interrupted him in the middle of a meal. When he wakes up he'll have a patch on his arm and a headache."

Now she'd heard everything! She couldn't force herself to look at the body to see if what he said was true. She closed her eyes for a moment, drew a shuddering breath, then opened them again, hoping to suddenly be rid of the problem. Unfortunately, he was still there.

"I really must be . . . going," she muttered, trying not to look at him again. Somehow she couldn't help it. There was something . . . exotic about him that drew her in. "Um . . . if you'll . . . excuse me . . ." She stood up, a flush appearing on her granite-grey cheeks.

He stood also, a tempting sparkle in his eyes. "Of course," he took her hand before she could move away. With a slight bow, he kissed the back of it. "But tell me your name first. In case we should come across each other again on the street, I will be able to call you by name."

Taken aback, she withdrew her hand and took a step away. She hoped they wouldn't meet on the street again—ever. "Savanna," she replied. "Savanna Storm. If you'll excuse me."

She stepped off the porch and untied her mount from the hitch. Tossing the reins up over the mare's neck, she put a foot in the near stirrup and swung up. Unwillingly, she looked back to find Monheno Devilla grinning, an even row of teeth white against his dark skin.

"You're not from around here," he observed, looking at her saddle.

"No," she replied curtly, "I'm not." She didn't offer any more information about herself. She didn't want him to know where to find her, if he decided to try. An alarm was ringing in her head—the same one that warned her not to come to the colonies in the first place. She ignored it that time, but never again.

"Well, thank you for your help." Why in the world did she say that? She wouldn't have needed help in the first place if not for him.

He set his hat on his head and tipped it to her, then smiled from the shadow of the brim. "My pleasure," he said as she turned her horse around. "My pleasure, indeed."

Savanna spurred the mare into a trot as she made her way up the street and then into a lope once they were clear of the town. The mare, as it turned out, was smooth and swift, and the miles of grass and woodland rolled away at an easy pace. Against her skin, the warm summer wind was soothing, but it couldn't wash away her strange meeting in town.

Monheno Devilla. His name repeated, exploded in her mind. Warning chills screamed up and down her spine, and she shivered unwillingly. Who was he? Why had she lost her wits the minute she met those strange, dark eyes? True, he was handsome, exotic, a little dangerous, but she'd met many a handsome man in her life—smooth-talking rakes like Monheno Devilla. She'd always been able to put men like that in their place.

# Two

"Bail off, Waddie, he's a cinch-binder!" Brandt's voice rose above the noise as Savanna rode back into the yard of the Vista Del Sol. Where they had been empty in the morning, the cattle pens were now a chaos of steers running in all directions to escape a wildly bucking black horse. Astride it, a dark-headed youth clung to the saddle like an oversized rag doll.

"Bail off, damnit!" The foreman whipped his horse forward, pushing, battering a path through the surging cattle. "Bail off! Bail off!" Behind the dark moustache, his face went white as the socks on his horse.

The youth's mount reared onto its hind legs and let out an unearthly scream. For a fragmented second, horse and rider froze in mid-air. The horse scrambled for balance, screamed again, and fell backward. The boy cried out, tried to kick his feet out of the stirrups, but it was too late. He hit the ground with a sickening thud, and the horse crashed down on top of him, legs flailing in the air.

Savanna gasped in horror as the horse thrashed and rolled—pounding the fallen rider. Face-down in the dust, the youth didn't move, didn't react as the horse rolled over him again and climbed to its feet, running wildly away.

White-eyed steers bolted forward, spooked by the loose horse, and headed toward the fallen man. Desperately, Savanna kicked her horse toward them, pulling off her hat and swinging it wildly at the charging cattle. They kept coming, and her nervous palomino jumped sideways, tried to bolt. She swung the mare around and screamed at the cattle, throwing her hat at the lead steer. The steer ducked and swung around, ramming her horse in the shoulder as it pressed back into the herd. The mare stumbled to her knees, and Savanna gripped her saddle to keep from falling. Her heart stopped in her throat as a sea of horns waved under her chin. She snapped her eyes shut and prayed. Please don't fall. Please don't fall . . .

She felt the mare lurch back to her feet, and she opened her eyes to see the tide of cattle turning back. A huge gush of air passed her lips and her heart started beating again. Kicking her feet out of the stirrups, she jumped to the ground and ran the few steps to the fallen man. He lay motionless as she knelt and carefully turned him onto his back. Leaning over, she touched his bruised, muddied face. He was breathing!

"Waddie!" she heard Brandt holler as he slid his horse to a stop and jumped off. Kneeling down, he pressed an ear to the youth's chest. "Waddie, can you hear me, boy?"

"He's breathing," Savanna gasped. "We have to get him to a doctor."

Brandt glanced at her, his eyes wide with panic. "Santo, Rella," he called, "carry him to the bunkhouse and tell Cook to see to him. Patrick, ride to town and see if you can find that damned drunkard doc." He let out a long sigh and stood up as two men came forward and lifted Waddie. "God damnit, boy," he muttered. "I told you to bail off."

Savanna stepped in front of the men as they started to carry the boy away. "Wait," she directed. "Take him to the house. He'll be more comfortable there."

They stopped and looked at the foreman uncertainly. He glanced at her as if the offer surprised him, then nodded toward the house. The men shrugged at each other and started toward Del Sol house, the limp boy supported carefully between them.

Brandt watched them go, then sighed and rolled his eyes heavenward. "You'd best go on up to the house with him, miss." He sounded tired, but there was a steely, purposeful look in his blue eyes as he started toward the black horse, now recaptured by two stone-faced cow-hands.

"Take that lucifer's saddle off and tie him to my horse," he ordered, his voice tight with anger. "I'll take him out and be done with him."

I'll take him out and be done with him. The words repeated in Savanna's head as she watched them unsaddle the black gelding and bind his reins to Brandt's saddle. I'll take him out and be done . . . What did that mean? Were they going to punish the horse? It wouldn't do any good now.

"What are you going to do?" She was almost afraid to ask. The grey looks on the men's faces said she wasn't going to like the answer.

Brandt grimaced as if he didn't want to give her an answer. He looked angry, murderous even, but maybe just a little regretful also. "It'd be best if you went to the house," he said flatly. "I'm going to have to put that horse down."

Her eyes flew wide and she choked on a breath of air. "You're going to shoot the horse for tossing someone off?" She couldn't believe her ears! "You can't be serious."

He nodded gravely.

She blinked hard at him, certain he'd lost him mind. "That is the most preposterous thing I've ever heard!" She couldn't let this go on another minute! "You don't shoot a perfectly good horse for throwing a rider!"

"That isn't a perfectly good horse." Brandt waved a finger angrily toward the barn. "That

31

worthless son-of-a-bitch is a cinch-binder. One that'll flip himself to throw a rider is no good. Sooner or later he'll get someone killed. We can take him to town and sell him if you want, but that's just passing the problem along to someone else. It'll be on your conscience when somebody finally gets killed or crippled." He pulled his hat off and wiped his forehead with his sleeve, then rammed the hat on again. "I should never have let the kid ride him in the first place."

She shifted uncomfortably from one foot to the other, looking at the exhausted, trembling horse, then back at her foreman. He was right in a way, but she couldn't let him shoot the animal.

"Put him in the barn with the palominos," she said in a tone she hoped was authoritative. The horse did belong to her, after all. "We can decide what to do with him later. Perhaps he can be broken for a buggy horse."

The foreman opened his mouth, then closed it, then opened it again, his face blazing angry red. Savanna swallowed hard and forced herself to stand a little straighter and look him in the eye. She was going to have this her way no matter what.

Finally Brandt threw his hands up. "I'll tell the boys to put him up," he ground out, "but there's not a soul on this ranch who'll ride him. Unless you sell him off, you'll be feeding him till the day he dies for nothing. It's bad enough we've got a whole barn of useless palominos too high in the knee to last through a day's work. If you're going to live out here, *Miss* Storm, you'll have to face the hard facts of life." He turned and strode angrily away toward the barn, leaving her standing alone in the yard.

Savanna waited for him to disappear before she let out a long breath and swallowed the lump in her throat. She'd just made an enormous mistake. Men like Brandt didn't like being told what to do by a woman. She hoped she hadn't pushed him too far.

She was pacing the veranda worrying about it an hour later as the doctor's buggy rushed up in front of Del Sol house.

"He's in here!" she called. Without waiting for the doctor to get out, she turned and hurried through the front door.

Esperanza looked up as Savanna came into the downstairs bedroom. "Oh, *Dios mio,* he is bad," she whispered. "He does not wake up."

Savanna nodded and took the housekeeper's hand, moving her away from the bed as the doctor came in. "We should get out of the doctor's way," she said quietly. Esperanza looked like she was on the verge of falling apart. "Why don't you go and sit down. I'll call you when the doctor is . . ." The last word halted in her throat as a second man strode into the room behind the doctor and bent over Waddie's bed. *It couldn't be . . .*

Unconsciously, she backed out the door as Esperanza threw her hands over her face and stumbled down the hall sobbing. Numbly, Savanna stood to the side watching the man helping the doctor. Blood rushed painfully into her ears, and her stomach swirled like a whirlpool. *It couldn't be* . . .

But it was. She knew it the minute raven-wing eyes turned to meet hers. His gaze held her frozen as he whispered something to the doctor and started toward her. She had the ridiculous urge to run, but she pushed it away. What was she thinking? This was *her* house.

She narrowed her eyes at him. "Monheno Devilla," she ground out. The last thing she needed now was an encounter with him. "What are *you* doing here?"

He looked disgustingly unaffected by the cool reception. "Helping the doctor," he waved a hand toward the bed. "He and I happened to be . . . together when your man came to town."

"Oh," she pursed her lips suspiciously. "You needn't have interrupted your day to come along."

Those raven eyes sparkled and his lips curved into a sensuous hint of a smile. "I wouldn't have missed it."

Her heart fluttered against her chest like a caged bird and an unwanted flush prickled into her cheeks. What was wrong with her? "Really?" she challenged. "You seem more the type for killing men than curing them."

"Me?" He slapped a spread-fingered palm to his chest and had the nerve to look offended.

He took a step closer and she backed against the wall. His dark gaze burned into hers with deadly intensity. "Madam, I'm afraid you have me all wrong."

She gripped the folds of her skirt and tried not to waver. "No, Mister Devilla. I'm sure I have you quite right."

The doctor called him from the room, and he glanced over his shoulder. He held both hands palm up, a slow smile spreading over his face. "Don't look so worried, Miss Storm." His voice was low, steady, seductive. "As you can see, I am unarmed."

She swallowed hard as she watched him turn and stride back into the room. Why did he come here? Was he looking for her, or was it merely a coincidence? Why did she feel like she was going to faint?

She bit her lip and forced herself to wait as the doctor finished with Waddie, gathered his things, and came with Monheno into the hall.

"No broken ribs, no sign that he's bleeding inside." The scent of whiskey floated into the air as the doctor spoke. "Stay with him overnight. Have one of your men come for me if he doesn't come out of it in a day or so."

Savanna winced at the smell of his breath and moved back a step. "I will." She pointedly ignored Monheno. She wasn't in the mood for another sparring match with him. She could feel his eyes tugging at her . . .

The doctor nodded, stumbled to the side,

then turned and started unsteadily down the hall. "Come on, Devilla," he called back. "I recall we have a game to finish."

Monheno glanced back at Waddie as the doctor stumbled away. "Come for the doctor in the morning if there's no improvement," he contradicted the doctor's orders. "By morning Doc should be a little more sober." The concern in his face seemed genuine, and Savanna's resolve melted like butter.

"I will," she heard herself mutter. "Thank you."

As quickly as his softness came, it was gone—replaced by that roguish grin. "It has been a pleasure, Miss Storm," he said. "I will see you again soon."

*I hope not.* She thought as she watched him stride confidently down *her* hallway like he owned it. Rubbing her hands up and down her arms, she walked back into the bedroom and sat in the chair beside Waddie's bed.

*Madam, I'm afraid have me all wrong.* Did she have Monheno all wrong? *As you can see, I am unarmed.* Hardly. Just those eyes were weapon enough. He was about as innocent as a rattlesnake.

Combing her hands through her hair, she lay back in the chair and closed her eyes. She didn't have time to waste thinking about Monheno Devilla. She had to think about the Del Sol. How much trouble had she caused by going against Brandt about the black horse? What were the

36

men saying about her? Were they in the bunk-house right now packing their things? Oh, God, what if her foreman left? How would she find another? What was she going to do? What was she going to do? What . . .

She drifted off to sleep worrying about it. In the morning, she awoke with a stiff neck and a headache. Her patient was still silent, but breathing easily and seemed comfortable. Finally, she left him in the care of the housekeeper and went to her bedroom to clean up and change clothes. When she was finished, she headed down the kitchen stairs and out the back door. It was time she stopped hiding inside and took this situation in hand.

She found her crew at breakfast in the huge mess hall. Perfect, since it was the only time of the day everyone was together. Now was the time to show them all she was here, and here to stay.

A low thunder of voices and laughter rumbled past her as she stepped into the mess hall door-way. Seventy-some amazed faces looked up suddenly, and silence fell like a lead weight.

She stood there looking back at them and felt herself growing smaller, and smaller, and smaller. Oh, God, this was a big mistake. To begin with, there was the problem of where to sit. The crew was carefully segregated at a number of long wood tables—cow crew next to the stove, the preferred location, sheep crew a safe distance away near the door, the orchardmen and the gardener at a small table in the back corner, and beside that another table for the ranch's game hunters, who were afield. Along the far back wall squatted twenty peons, mostly Mexicans, held by debt to the Vista Del Sol.

Her foreman was the first to rise and offer her a chair. If he was still mad about the day before, it didn't show in his face. "Guess no one can stay away from cookie's grub," he joked, and the members of the crew laughed uncomfortably as the cook served her a plate.

"I suppose you're all wondering why I'm here," she said as she looked up from her plate. "I suspect all of you know by now who I am. I would like to know each of your names." She forced a smile—the only one in the room.

The introductions started with a tall, raw-boned man who spoke with a slight southern accent from beneath a blond moustache so long it hid his lips completely. "Name's Hal Calfort." He didn't look at her as he spoke, but watched his hands like a shy boy. "I'm a pretty fair hand with a rope and a decent drover, but Hailey and me," he nodded toward the end of the table, where one of the black men raised a hand slightly to identify himself, "spends most of our time bustin' out new horses for the remuda."

And so the introductions continued down the table, through the cowboys first, then the vaqueros in Spanish. Everyone at the table looked like they'd been staked to an ant hill, so Savanna cut the ill-conceived encounter short by standing up as soon as they were finished.

"I will let you finish your breakfast in peace." She couldn't help feeling disappointed by the relief on their faces. "But I did want to tell you Waddie seems a little better this morning, although he hasn't come to yet."

She left without waiting for any questions, or for anyone to bring up the subject of the black gelding. She wasn't prepared to handle that issue yet this morning.

She rubbed her throbbing forehead as she walked slowly toward the house. "No danger of this day going from bad to worse," she muttered to herself. That was the truth. Short of an earthquake, or another meeting with that murderer Monheno Devilla, nothing could be worse than breakfast.

She found Waddie not only awake, but seated over a breakfast tray in bed.

"Good morning, ma'am," he greeted her with a charmingly sheepish smile as she stepped into the room.

She couldn't help smiling in return. There was something about Waddie's sparkling green eyes, framed with girlish black lashes, that made him instantly likable. Besides, it was just plain good that someone was glad to see her.

"Good morning." She glanced at the pile of dirty dishes he had generated in the very short time she was away, and added, "I'm not certain we can afford to keep you."

"Knockin' your head against the ground is hard work." He pointed to a bump visible even

39

through his thick mop of black hair. "Tain't every guy who can ride one all the way to the ground."

She giggled. "No doubt. But I think you'd feel better if you would dismount before your horse lands on you."

"Reckon," he agreed. His grin faded suddenly. "I heard you wouldn't let 'em put Nantucket down."

"Nantucket?"

"The black horse," he explained. "I heard you wouldn't let them put him down."

She sat down in the chair beside the bed and masked her irritation. It galled her to know tongues were wagging behind her back. She could only imagine what they were saying.

"That is true," she said finally. "The horse is in the barn, where he will stay until *I* decide what to do with him."

He ducked his head like a scolded child. "Yes ma'am," he muttered. "But I . . . I hope you'll give him another chance. He's sort of a . . . well, a pet, ya' see. I raised him on a bottle because his ma' was got by a mountain cat. He ain't cut out for workin' cattle, that's all. He's too spooky, but he'd make a good saddle mount."

She raised a finger to her chin and looked out the window toward the barn. "I suppose," she muttered more to herself than to him, "the only thing for me to do is to try the horse myself."

"Ma'am?" He looked at her like she'd just grown horns. "I . . . I don't think that's such a good idea. He'll make a good saddle horse, sure enough, but he ain't gentle for a lady."

"Don't worry." She was amazed how confident the words sounded. "I'm nearly as good with a horse as I am with a rifle."

He grinned. "Well, that makes me feel a heap better. I imagine if you can handle the Sombras, you can handle Nantucket, but if you'll pardon me saying so, both ain't very good ideas."

She shrugged to let him know she wasn't going to be told what to do. "You're probably right about that," she agreed noncommittally. "But I don't regret driving off those bandits, if that is what you're hinting at. What amazes me is that I had to do it by myself when I have seventy able-bodied men working for me."

"Everyone here knows the way it is with the Sombras," he lowered his voice like the walls had ears, "and they know better than to mess with things."

She smacked her lips and rolled her eyes irritably. "Are you telling me everyone on this ranch will let those thieves bleed the Vista Del Sol dry?" She stood up, waving a hand toward the bunkhouse.

"Th-they don't take so much," Waddie stammered. "They don't take more than the Del Sol can pay."

"Anything is more than we can pay!" she exploded. "I don't think you understand. The

Vista Del Sol is broke—bankrupt—bled dry—like everything else my father ever laid his hands on. What you see here is all there is. There isn't any surplus to give to bandits or anyone else. We'll be lucky just to make it until the next crop of steers is ready to sell!"

She slapped a hand to her parted lips. What was she doing? Was she out of her mind? She couldn't let her crew find out she might not be able to make the payroll! "Perhaps I exaggerate a little," she tried to cover her tracks. "I'd appreciate your not telling anyone."

He combed back the thick strands of dark hair in his face. "Oh, no ma'am." He shook his head vigorously. "I wouldn't say nothin'. You have my word on that."

She breathed a sigh of relief. "Thank you." She just hoped she could trust him. "Now tell me how you know so much about the Sombras."

He shifted in the bed and looked nervously around the room. "I've been here on the Del Sol for six years—came here when I was nine," he replied. "The Sombras have always been here since I can remember. Your father paid 'em their dues, and the man before your father, he did, I expect. Del Sol ain't never had any trouble with them, but a few years back the Camino Del Rey said they wouldn't pay—hired on a crew of vigilantes to fight if the bandits came after 'em for it—fifteen good guns, I heard tell, plus the men who worked for the Camino already." He paused, his eyes growing wide with boyish excitement. "It didn't help a bit, though, Venenoso came in the night and killed five of the hired guns. Then he burnt down the house and the barns, stole the remuda and five-hundred head of cattle, and made off with the owner's daughter." He leaned close to her. "No one on the Camino ever saw him during the whole time, and when they went out to track him, it was like he'd disappeared into the air—six hundred head of livestock gone and not one print left in the dust anywhere."

She crossed her arms over her chest and cocked one arched brow. This was all a little hard to swallow. "Amazing," she said flatly. "Now why do you suppose a man capable of disappearing into thin air with six-hundred head of livestock needs to extort money for a living? Why, a man with those amazing abilities could certainly earn a living for himself, don't you think?"

His face drained to grey, and he crossed his arms over himself. "You shouldn't joke about him, ma'am. It ain't a laughin' matter," he scolded as if she had just blasphemed. "At least it won't be when he does the same thing to the Del Sol." He said it with unnerving certainty.

She rolled her eyes and threw her hands up helplessly. "I cannot believe this!" She truly couldn't. "Adults believing in this nonsense! If this Venenoso does exist at all, he certainly can't walk on water or disappear into thin air."

"We've seen it!" Waddie looked younger than

ever as his eyes went wide and his mouth went slack. "I seen him once myself at the cantina in Oro Grande. He shot a man and then just walked out the front door, but when we got up and looked out at the street, he was gone," he met her gaze intensely, and whispered, "into thin air."

"Well, we shall see." Savanna gave up. She hoped all her neighbors weren't as foolish as Waddie. "Take care of yourself, Waddie, and don't you dare try getting out of this bed today. I'll be back later to see you."

"Yes ma'am," he gave her a mock salute and a devilish grin.

She shook her head and left the room. She had a feeling he'd be out of the bed before she got to the stairs. "Esperanza, please look after Waddie," she called as she passed the kitchen. "I will be in my room seeing to the books if you need me."

She spent the rest of the day trying to make sense of her father's sketchy paperwork. When evening came, she paused to check on Waddie and pick up a tray of food, then went back to her work. The Del Sol's finances did a lot to ruin her appetite.

Finally, she set her the books aside and fell into her bed, exhausted. She couldn't look at the figures any longer. They kept telling her the same thing. It wasn't possible to keep the Del Sol alive until fall, when the next crop of steers, wool, and produce would be ready to sell. There was no money in the till. Until fall, there would be none coming except a small amount from the orchard and some hide money from the game traps.

Even with all the Del Sol's enterprises, summer was a dry season for income. She'd have to figure something out and cut staff. God, how was she going to do that? How could she show up on the ranch one day and tell men who had been there for years they would have to leave? Growing up at Miss Culpet's Preparatory for Young Ladies might have taught her how to sew pillow cases, speak Latin, and balance household finances, but it did nothing to prepare her for this.

"Somehow . . ." she whispered as her lashes drifted heavily to her cheeks. "Somehow . . ." but she never finished the thought.

Her mind was foggy with sleep when she awoke again. Was that thunder outside? No, no, someone was running horses!

The Sombras! She started to reality and her eyes flew open to the dimly lit room. She jerked back the coverlet and threw her legs over the side of the bed. Blindly, she reached for the pistol hidden behind the lamp on her night table. Where was it? The lamp had burned down so far she couldn't see. It had to be there!

The sound of a voice froze her.

"I do not think you'll find it, senorita." The words came in a low, liquid tone smooth as fine wine and tinged ever so slightly with a Spanish accent.

"Who is there?" She spun toward the voice. Outrage turned her cold, then hot. How dare someone come into her bedroom! Angrily, she reached to turn up the wick on the lamp.

"I would not do that." The unmistakable click of a pistol.

She jerked her fingers back and stared into the darkness beyond the faded lamplight. Where was he?

"Who is there?" Her voice came in a sleepy crackle that sounded more frightened than she felt. What did she have to be frightened of? She was in her own house. She had only to scream to bring the staff running. "I insist that you tell me who you are and what you are doing in my room." She squinted into the darkness, leaning first to one side and then the other. "Please come forward!" The silence was fast becoming frightening. She clasped her arms in front of herself to hide the all-too-obvious outline of her breasts against her nightdress.

"Far be it from me to deny the wishes of a beautiful lady." Again, the voice washed across the space between them like liquid. A dark figure stepped into the light and stood there like a shadow come alive—clad entirely in black and somehow larger than life. The face was hidden by a bandana, and his hat pulled down low, casting an eerie shadow across his eyes.

She stumbled backward, grasped the edge of

46

her dressing table. "How—how dare you!" All the warnings about the Sombras came back to her, and her body went cold. "How did you get in here?"

"Ah," he whispered, stepping closer and giving an elegant bow in her direction. "Don't you know, madam? Shadows can go anywhere." He moved closer still, the uneven lamplight catching the strongly chisled line of his cheekbones, but leaving his eyes hidden in two pits of darkness.

She slid away from him. "Go . . . go away," she stammered, her heart hammering like it would jump through her chest. "I'll . . . I'll call the staff."

Even in the dim light, she could see his face lift into a smile. Above the bandana, the line of his cheeks rose, casting his eyes deeper into shadow. "Feel free." He sounded relaxed, confident, deadly. "but I don't think they will be quick in coming. You see, they're preoccupied. Your remuda seems to have broken loose."

She gasped, her hand flying to her throat.

He stepped closer again, leaving her no escape. "So if you do scream," his voice lowered as he came closer, within inches, "there isn't much chance of your disturbing anyone."

She swallowed her pounding heart and tried to push the terrible pictures from her mind. "I demand to know why you are here."

"Well," he began, his tone light, as if they were conversing over Sunday tea, "it seems you and I have a problem. My men returned from here last week with a fantastic tale but no money."

"Your men," she gasped. Her problems just grew by tenfold. "Then you are . . ."

He leaned so close she could feel his breath on her cheek. A single word brushed past her like the touch of death. "Venenoso."

# Three

Venenoso! The name rang in her ears like the tolling of a warning bell. "You!"

"In the flesh," his tone was cordial, mocking, but there was a threat beneath it.

"How did you get in here?"

Casually, he clasped his hands behind his back and bent forward at the waist as if to get a better view of her. "Ah, you asked that already. You'll accept my apologies if I do not answer it again."

Caught between fear and the seductive lure of his voice, she pressed closer to the wall, leaning away from him. A thief with manners of all things. She forced herself to meet the shadows that hid his eyes. "What is it that you want?"

He turned to the side for an instant as if listening for something. His form stiffened. "We seem to be going around in circles here." He sounded suddenly impatient. "As I said before, there is the problem of your dues being in arrears."

Her temper boiled up like a bulging volcano, but she clenched her fists to control it. He has a gun. Don't let yourself get out of control. "My dues?" She tried to sound cool, but her voice sizzled with indignation. "My, what an interesting word for it—my extortion money, you mean?"

"As you like." He didn't seem bothered. In fact, he smiled again. "In any case, the Del Sol is two months behind in payment. I have let it go because there has been no one in charge here to pay since your father's . . . disappearance. Now that you're here, I assume you will pick up where he left off."

A hot flush poured through her, and the hairs on the back of her neck raised like quills on a porcupine. She narrowed her eyes and leaned forward. "You assume too much. I'll not pay a cent." She heard herself say. Her temper was running away with her. She could feel it.

He sighed and scratched his forehead with a darkly gloved hand. "I have in the past encountered dissenters much stronger than you, Miss Storm. I can, of course, force you to pay or see the Del Sol destroyed acre by acre." He repositioned his hat and then added tiredly, "I would prefer to save us both the trouble."

"Savanna—Miss Storm?" A voice from the hall snapped them both around. "Ma'am, is everything all right?"

Savanna's heart leapt. Waddie! She'd forgotten he was in the house. She opened her mouth to call to him, then stopped. Waddie was unarmed, injured, certainly no match for the man beside her now.

She shrugged back the fallen tendrils of her hair and tried to look confident. "I think you'd better leave. That is, unless bullets pass through you as easily as words."

He clasped a hand over his heart and laughed quietly, looking more amused than worried. "Ah, such touching concern." A speculative glance toward the door. "Savanna . . ." he said as if considering the word, "Savanna Storm, what an interesting name, and so . . . appropriate."

Before she could move, he leaned forward, caught her chin in his strong hand, tilted it upward, his eyes looking into hers from the shadows. "Take care, Savanna Storm, I like a woman with spirit."

Her blood turned to ice. They both knew his meaning. The door handle clicked and he released her. In two able strides, he crossed the distance to the window. "Adios for now, my dear." There was laughter in his voice. "We shall meet again."

Savanna stood frozen. A thousand insults ran through her mind, but she couldn't choke one out. Her body tingled with a mixture of horror and fascination as he stepped to the open window and slipped through. He jumped two stories and landed without a sound.

Gathering her wits, she ran to the balcony door, threw it open, and dashed to the rail. She braced her hands on it and leaned out into the night. In the moonlight, she could see him crossing the yard, his dark knee-length saddle coat spreading behind him like a flowing cape.

He reached his mount and swung aboard in one fluid motion. Gathering his reins, he looked at her balcony as if he knew she would be there. He whisked his hat from his head and waved it at her as his men gathered around him. She thought she could see him smiling as he spun the dark horse around and charged from the yard.

There was no reason for his haste. Once again, her cowboys were gathered on the bunkhouse porch, and not one of them bothered to bring a gun. As before, they were watching her, and as before, she was in her nightdress. If it hadn't been so embarrassing, it would have been funny. Worse yet, when she hurried back into her room Waddie was standing in the doorway looking at her like he'd never seen a woman before.

She didn't say a word, just glared at him until he choked on his tongue, muttered something, and left the room. When he was gone, she closed the door, the window, and the balcony door, pulled all the curtains and climbed into bed. Shivering, she pulled the blankets up to her chin and clamped her eyes shut. She wasn't going to think about this tonight. She couldn't. Let her so-called cowboys worry about gathering the loose horses and repairing whatever damage had been done. She was going to forget all about this and go to sleep.

But she couldn't forget. A nightmarish intruder haunted her dreams. Take care, Savanna Storm. I like a woman with spirit, he whispered. We shall meet again.

She awoke hungry and exhausted, as if she hadn't slept at all and hadn't eaten in a week. She dressed, combed her hair, and gathered her books wearily, then headed for the east parlor where Esperanza always set her breakfast tray.

She was halfway through her meal when she looked up as she heard the unmistakable jingle of spurs outside the door. She set it aside when she saw her foreman in the doorway.

"I came up to check on Waddie," he said, stepping into the room as though he felt awkward being there. "That boy seems to be pretty well rooted in here at the big house. You may have a hel . . . uh . . . hard time getting rid of him."

She forced a tired smile. Obviously Brandt was trying to lighten the mood before he went into the grim realities of the midnight attack. "Actually, we're having a hard time keeping him here until he's allowed to go back to work."

Brandt's grin straightened and he let out a long sigh. "I hope not. It looks like we're going to need all the hands we've got." He twisted the ends of his moustache between two fingers thoughtfully, his clear blue eyes hidden beneath lowered brows as he looked toward the glass veranda doors. "The Sombras's little raid seems to have made an impression. I lost two of my crew and four good horses this morning."

I lost two of my crew and four good horses . . . She felt the blood drain from her face. Things were worse than she'd even imagined. "Lost . . . lost two of the crew?" she choked.

He nodded gravely. "I'm sorry. I'm sure this isn't the kind of news you wanted first thing in the morning."

She closed her eyes and scratched her forehead. "No time like the present," she muttered, but that wasn't true. She didn't want to talk about the raid yet, so she changed the subject. "I want to talk about my father's palominos." She realized instantly she'd said the wrong thing.

One side of his mouth curled into a sneer. "You're talking to the wrong person," he warned. "I don't want anything to do with those damned Spanish horses. I told your father the same thing."

She nodded, feeling more confident about what she was about to do. "It is your opinion that they are of no use for ranch work?"

He cocked a quizzical brow like he was trying to figure her out. "It's not an opinion," he said flatly. "It's a fact. They're useless for ranch work. They're high steppers so they can't make it more than a few hours under hard use. They've got no sense about where they land their feet. A man would be like to get killed on

54

them in the hills. And," he raised a finger into the air like a preacher bringing down brimstone. "They haven't got a lick of sense about cattle."

Savanna couldn't keep satisfaction from showing in her face as she stood up. "Sell them." Saying it was almost as good as dancing on her father's grave. If those fine horses were his pride and joy, it would give her particular satisfaction to dispose of them.

Brandt blinked at her in obvious shock. "Ma'am?"

She lowered her eyes coolly. "Given those facts about the horses, I want them sold." She tipped her chin up and looked out the window, then back at him. "The Del Sol has no use for animals that can't pull their own weight." That was true, but the real fact was she needed the money.

He met her eyes, and there was a new look of respect in him. "Does that include Waddie's black?"

She winced and pretended to be occupied with smoothing her skirt over her petticoats. She felt like a guilty child caught in a lie. "No, I intend to keep him." She didn't look at him, but she could imagine what he was thinking. "It's Waddie's opinion that he will make a good saddle mount. I intend to try him out myself."

He coughed in disbelief, and she forced herself to face him.

"You what!" He looked like he was about to blow steam out his ears. "Are you gone in the

55

head? The horse is a cinch-binder. He'll do it again, and this time it'll be your neck!"

She faced his fury with a stoney look. She swallowed an outraged retort and narrowed her eyes at him. It was time he learned who was in charge here, but she had to handle this carefully. Good men were hard to find. The Del Sol would fall apart if he left.

She took a breath and let it out, then tilted her chin to one side. "There you've hit on it," she leveled a narrow stare. "It's *my* neck."

He threw up his hands and let them fall to his leather chaps with a hollow slap that echoed through the room like a clap of thunder. "We have a remuda full of good horses. Hell, even one of the palominos would be better than him—they may be useless, but at least they're not crazy!"

She crossed her arms over her chest obstinately and gave an impatient tilt of her lashes.

He clenched his teeth and growled, "Have it your way then, but that horse will prove you wrong. There ain't enough good blood in him to fill a hoof print."

She rolled her eyes, an old habit from preparatory school. She wasn't interested in being told how to behave—then or now. "Yes, yes, I know. You're right I'm sure, but I have to learn these things for myself." She could see him getting angrier by the minute. Now was probably a good time to change the subject. "You said we lost two of your crew?"

He seemed confused for a minute. "Appears so." The fiery color faded from his cheeks, and grey anger came in its place. "Lars Mathes turned in his leave this morning. Now it looks like Bo Silvas is gone too, probably on one of our horses. He left behind that broken-down roan he tramped in here on. I sent Benjamin to report him to the sheriff for horse stealing."

She scoffed at that. "I am sure our illustrious sheriff will be tripping over himself to help." Just thinking about that poor excuse for a lawman made her blood boil. She clenched her fists over the folds of her skirt and tried to push it out of her mind. "How long will it take to replace the men we lost?"

Brandt looked out the window and shook his head gravely. "I'm not sure we can."

Savanna drew back, eyes widening. Why couldn't he replace the men? Did he know about the Del Sol's finances? Did Waddie tell him? Be calm. Be calm. "Why is that?" She sounded anything but calm.

He stroked his moustache and met her eyes quizzically, as if he suspected she was hiding something. "Well, I won't lie to you," he said finally. "You've made a heck of a mess by taking on the Sombras. Word is all over. There probably isn't a decent hand around that'll work for us. Nobody wants to sign on to that kind of trouble."

Savanna threw up her hands and spun away, golden hair flying in all directions. "Good God, you people are cowards!" Now she'd come to the end of her rope. "Are you telling me the Del Sol is unable to find help because of a half-dozen nightriders? Doesn't anybody in this valley have a backbone?"

He didn't seem offended. He shrugged the words off like harmless drops of water. "Everyone knows how things work around here, that's all. The Sombras have been here a lot longer than all of us foreigners, and they won't give up their hold because one more Brit moves into town."

Heat rose on the back of her neck until she felt like she was boiling—or exploding. "I'm going to town," she growled, narrow eyed. "To find someone with the courage to help."

The foreman frowned and gave a noncommittal shrug that said the effort was futile. "And I suppose you're going to ride that cinch-binding lucifer, too."

She started toward the door, then spun back to face him. "I wasn't," she bit out with vindictive satisfaction. "But now that you've given me the idea, I think I shall."

She threw her chin up, grabbed her hat from the peg, and headed for the barn, long, determined strides whisking the folds of her heavy cotton riding skirt, and her small English-style bob spurs clicking on the terracotta walkway.

I'm going to town to find someone with the courage to help. She heard her own words over and over as she took the black horse from his stall and saddled him. Going to town . . . She was? To find someone with the courage to help. Who in heaven could that be? No one in this valley had courage where the Sombras were concerned.

Take care, Miss Storm. I like a woman with spirit. Did she have the courage to face Venenoso again? What if he was there in town when she went? What if . . . what if Monheno Devilla was there? God, that was a worse prospect yet.

Or was it . . . ?

Hadn't Monheno Devilla called the man he shot one of those thieves? Didn't he turn the man over to the sheriff? Maybe there was someone in Oro Grande with the courage to go against the Sombras. Maybe, she had a hope after all . . .

Riding Nantucket hadn't turned out to be too difficult, but finding Monheno Devilla turned out to be more of a task than she bargained for. Everyone in town seemed reluctant to give information to a stranger. Finally, one of the padres at the mission took pity and directed her to a house of low repute at the end of the street. He warned her it was no place for a respectable woman, but she hiked her skirt up with determination and headed there anyway.

The padre's opinion was nothing compared to the surprise on the cantina man's face when she stepped through the open doorway into the dim interior. Clearly, he was shocked. Everyone was shocked. In the past, she would have been shocked herself, but her standards had come down a long way since her arrival in America.

She hardly even blushed as she crossed through the tables of leering, muttering men and giggling women whose occupations she didn't want to think about. Now was no time to give in to her sensibilities. She had to find Monheno Devilla. She should have expected to find him in a place like this.

He was seated at a table with a deck of cards, and, of course, a woman, when she spotted him. Drawing a breath of the dank, tobacco-scented air, she braced herself and headed purposefully for his table.

The woman met her gaze as she stopped beside the table, a wicked expression in her dark eyes.

Devilla stood up and extended a hand to her graciously. "Miss Storm." There was a wicked twinkle in his eye, as he took her hand, bowed and kissed it before she could react. "How nice to see you again. Come here often?"

She blushed from her hair to her toes and all points in between. What would the girls at Miss Culpet's school think if they could see her now? Coming alone into a dirty Mexican pub! Consorting with a man she had never formally met! This uncivilized country was turning her into something she scarcely even recognized!

"No." She finally managed an answer to his insulting question. "It is hardly my sort of place . . ." She glanced down at the woman still seated there and cut the sentence off. "I actually came here to speak to you."

He looked completely taken by surprise. It was a pleasant turnabout. "How fortunate for me." He narrowed his eyes with mild suspicion, then stepped to the side and drew out a chair for her. "Please sit down."

For an uncomfortable moment, Savanna sat staring into dark, very pretty female eyes that looked like they wanted to kill her. Monheno leaned down, improperly close to the woman's ear, and whispered something in Spanish. She threw him a seething glare, then stood up and left the table.

"My sister," he said watching the woman leave with a look that was anything but brotherly.

Savanna pursed her lips and nodded, lifting the bolero from her head and setting it in her lap. Her heart danced up into her throat as she gripped both hands over the brim, twisting it nervously. She hoped she could go through with this.

His raven gaze came slowly back to her, slid across the table, up her arms, over her breasts, up her neck, past her lips, caught her eyes. She shivered unwillingly, her skin tingling as if he'd done more than just look.

"Now then, Miss Storm." He leaned forward a bit, the dark arch of his brows lifting into a question. "Or may I call you Savanna?" She nodded, and he went on, "Savanna, what is it that I can do for you?"

She squirmed uncomfortably in her chair, her body burning, tingling, her thoughts spinning. This was all a very, very bad idea. She should never have come here.

Even as she thought it, she heard a plea tumble from her mouth. "I need someone to help me defend the Del Sol against the Sombras." She watched for a reaction. He gave none. "I have been having trouble finding men of courage in this town."

Still no reaction. "I'm not surprised." He looked completely impassive. "People around here know better than to try." He took his eyes from her and smiled at some private thought. When he looked back, his raven eyes were frighteningly intense. "But what makes you think I want to get involved in that mess?"

She popped back in her chair, her eyes widening with shock. Wasn't he the same man who shot one of them only days before? "But I . . ." She had to gather her thoughts. "I saw you shoot one of them. I assumed you were already involved."

He didn't say yes or no, just watched her with that bewitching gaze until she almost forgot what she came for.

"N-never mind." She stood up so quickly the chair fell over with a crash. The pressure of a dozen pairs of eyes made her leave it and head for the door.

She was out before he caught up with her. She spun about to face him. "I do not think we have anything left to discuss." Coward! Rake! "I am sorry to have troubled you." She should turn away—go home.

She just stood there as a slow smile creased his lips. "Don't leave in such a hurry." The words slid over her like warm honey. "I didn't say I wouldn't help you."

"You said you didn't want to involve yourself."

"Not exactly."

"Then what did you say?"

He laughed, his eyes dancing with sunlight. "Nothing you need have taken so . . . seriously."

She twisted her brows into a confused, perplexed, irritated knot. "I beg your pardon?" She braced her hands on her hips and leaned forward. "How did you intend me to . . . take it?"

"Savanna Storm," he took her hand, captured it in one of his. "If you knew me at all, you'd know that I am not a serious man."

"I see." A warm shiver ran from her hand, up her arm, and settled finally in her stomach. Things were going too far. It was time she put an end to it. She pulled her hand away and fastened it on the brim of the hat she held. "Mister Devilla, I have no time for jokes. I'll be on my way."

She didn't wait for a reply. Knees quaking, she stepped from the walk and crossed the street to her horse. Her hands trembled as she untied the reins. In frustration, she jammed her hat on her head and worked the knot with both hands. The hat flew off and landed at her feet, spooking Nantucket and pulling the knot tighter.

"Oooohhhhh!" she growled, bracing a foot against the boardwalk and tugging at the reins.

"Need help?" she heard him call from across the street.

She didn't look at him, just kept working. "No!" She hoped she never saw Monheno Devilla again as long as she lived. She hoped someone shot him tomorrow—today—this minute. She might do it herself!

"You certain?"

She could tell he was coming closer.

# Four

"Yes!" she shot back. Nantucket spooked to the end of his reins again, pinching her fingers just as she was freeing the knot. "Ooowww!" She jerked her hands away and Nantucket balked onto his hind legs. Impatiently, she caught at the reins, but the horse jerked them from her fingers, sending her sprawling backward.

The hitching rail caught her in the waist so hard the breath rushed from her lungs. Dazed, she clasped the rail and tried to regain her footing. Something wasn't right. The rail had fingers. Broad, strong fingers holding her frightfully close to her breast. Her heart lurched into action and pounded against them.

Good God, what did she do now? She grabbed a breath of air and turned around to face him. The look of chivalrous concern on his face was disgusting, patronizing . . . absolutely, positively melting. He adjusted his hand ever so slightly and her stomach quivered. She gasped and swallowed hard.

"Let go of me." She meant it. She couldn't let this go on another minute! It was horrid! Improper! It was making her ache all over. "I said, I want you to release me."

He gave that slow, devilish grin that told her he knew differently. "I'd rather not." There was laughter in his voice. "This is so . . . cozy—don't you think?"

She bit her lip, gripped his white cotton shirt, and gave it the hardest tug she could in her cramped position. "I said unhand me." It sounded so convincing even she was impressed. "Now."

He released her, just slightly, then grabbed her back and pressed his lips to hers before she could protest.

It wasn't as if she'd never been kissed before—kisses stolen behind the backs of negligent chaperones. It wasn't as if she'd never been cornered by an attractive man. It wasn't as if she didn't have a mind of her own. It wasn't . . .

It wasn't like anything that had ever happened to her.

Desire rushed through her like wildfire. Her mind spun until she wasn't even sure where she was. Her lips burned as he parted them, tasted her, drew her out of herself. Her breasts hardened, swelled against her chemise, begged for . . . . Would he dare touch her there?

She felt dizzy . . .

She swayed against him, felt her body press against the solid muscles of his chest, felt her hands slide over the starched cotton of his shirt.

The mission bell tolled, ringing in her ear like the rebuke of God. What was she doing? Scooping her wits into a pile, she pulled her lips from his and pushed out of his arms. She stumbled backward dizzily, caught her balance, and rescued the remains of her squashed hat from the ground.

Raising an arm, she pointed an arresting finger at him. "Don't even come near me!" She waved the finger like a gun. If only it were! Monheno Devilla would be dead where he stood.

He raised both hands as if in surrender. "You wouldn't shoot an unarmed man."

"You're lucky *I'm* unarmed." She spun around and stalked off after her horse. He started to follow, but she wheeled around and gave him a murderous glare. "Leave me alone!" Her voice raised to a shrill yell. Here and there, people came to their doorways to see about the commotion.

She flushed from head to toe and spun away, leaving him standing in the street. Fastening her gaze to her shoes, she tried to ignore the curious eyes watching her from the sidewalk. She didn't want to attract any more attention. Had anyone seen what happened between her and Monheno? It was too horrid to even consider. What would people think? What would they say?

She caught Nantucket, mounted, and headed out of town without a look back. She wasn't going to Oro Grande again—ever. Monheno Devilla was definitely not the answer to her problems. She'd just have to go home and think of something else . . . or start to pray.

The answer to her prayers came the next day in the form of an invitation to a wedding. She knew the minute she read the parchment the Baca-Garza wedding was exactly the opportunity she'd been looking for. According to Esperanza, every landowner in the valley would be there. It would be the perfect place to bring her neighbors together against the Sombras. The question now was could she do it?

She felt better about the plan when her foreman came to her study to ask her if he might have time off to go to the wedding. At least she wouldn't be going alone.

"I'm an . . . uh . . . old friend of the family," he explained. "Do you think you can get along without me for a few days?"

She couldn't help smiling. "I won't have to." Apparently, it hadn't even occurred to him that she might go to the wedding too. "I'll be going to the wedding also."

He blinked hard, like he couldn't believe his ears. "You're . . . going to the wedding?"

She straightened a little. "I am." Why should that be such a shock to him?

"*Que es eso?*" Esperanza came through the parlor door with a dust mop in her hand. "Jou are going to de wedding?"

Savanna braced her hands on her hips defensively. "Yes, I am." Why was everyone acting so strangely? They looked like she just told them hell froze over.

Esperanza propped the dust mop on her shoulder and strode across the room like a sergeant-at-arms. "Why jou decite to go to dees wedding?" She looked suspicious and a little worried. "De Baca-Garza wedding ees for de Californios."

Savanna raised her chin defensively. "I was invited." She'd had enough of her staff bossing her around. "*Brandt* is going." Why was she defending herself? "I'll need your help packing so we can leave tomorrow." She looked back at Brandt. "Could you see that there is a buggy ready in the morning?"

He exchanged a covert glance with Esperanza and shrugged. "Will do." He started toward the door. "Anything else?"

She nodded. "I'll want to take my saddle horse along also. In case . . ." She stopped short of saying in case there was more trouble with the Sombras. "In case I have to return home in a hurry."

He cocked a questioning brow at her, then nodded, and walked on out the door.

Savanna headed toward the stairway. "I'll need your help packing, Esperanza."

The housekeeper set the feather duster on a table and followed her. "Are jou sure . . . ?"

"Yes," Savanna cut her off. "I am sure I'm going. Please don't ask me again. Can you please tell me what to pack? The invitation said to be prepared for an overnight stay."

Esperanza gave a resigned sigh. "De wedding can go on for two days or three," she said. "Jou will need that many clothes to wear."

Savanna dropped her mouth open in surprise. "Two or three days?" She hadn't planned on being away from the Del Sol that long. "How can they accommodate so many guests? Where do people sleep?"

The housekeeper lowered one brow and shook her head as if Savanna was an idiot. "Wherefer dey fin' a place." She shrugged her shoulders up and down. "But most don' sleep. Dey dance and dey drink and seeng de songs."

"All night?" Surely Esperanza was exaggerating. "But that's . . ." She tried to think of the right word for it, "vulgar!" which was exactly what she meant.

Esperanza looked surprised, then started to grin. Doubling forward, she clapped her hands to her knees and burst out laughing.

Savanna felt ridiculous. Vulgar! Of all the stupid things to say! No wonder Esperanza didn't think she should go to the wedding.

By the time she and Brandt arrived at the wedding the next day, she was beginning to wish she'd taken the older woman's advice. The Baca-

Garza wedding looked like much more of an event than she'd anticipated.

The sun was just rising to its height as she drove her buggy up to the Dos Rios Rohos hacienda. Along the drive, at least thirty buggies were parked, and two dozen or more saddle horses were tied in among them. From behind the house, the sounds of music, singing, and cheering voices told her the party was already in full swing.

Brandt pulled his horse up behind the buggy, dismounted, and tied his mount beside Nantucket. "One thing I always liked about the Roho." A smile curved his moustache. "They know how to throw a party."

Savanna reached up secretly and pinched color into her cheeks as her foreman came around to help her down. She hoped she didn't look as worried and out of place as she felt. Tossing her hair back, she took a deep breath of the warm air. It smelled of cooking fires, sage, and chiles, and rang with the gaudy sound of guitars, mandolins, and castanets.

"Esperanza told me you once worked here," she said as he helped her down.

He shrugged noncommittally. "Esperanza talks too much." He gave her a sly sideways grin. "I've worked for just about every spread in this valley."

She drew back in surprise. "I didn't know that."

71

He grinned again. "That is, of course, before I got settled in at the Del Sol."

She smiled back at him. "That's a good thing." She meant it. He was the lifeline holding the Del Sol above water. "I don't know what the Del Sol would do without you."

He met her eyes as if he knew what she was thinking. "The Del Sol doesn't have to worry about that," he promised. "If you came to this wedding because you were afraid I'd find another job here, you can go home."

The thought had crossed her mind, but she tried not to let it show. "Of course not." She looked away from him. "I came here because I wanted to see a Californio wedding." She slanted him a wry glance. "If you came here because you thought I needed looking after, you can go home."

He shook his head and placed a broad hand on the small of her back, ushering her toward the festivities. "Your first time at a Mexican wedding." He tipped his hat to a hefty Spaniard as they passed. "Are you in for a few surprises."

She wasn't sure she liked the sound of that. The only surprise she wanted here was to find that her neighbors weren't all as cowardly as they seemed.

She forgot all about her plan as they rounded the hedge and came within full view of the party. Nothing Esperanza told her prepared her for the spectacle on the patio and lawns of the Dos Rios Rohos. The tiled patio was alive with loudly colored banners and swirling dancers in bright skirts. Even the men were colorfully arrayed for the event, most in trim-fitting suits decorated with brightly beaded and stitched patterns that made each of their skillful dances even more flamboyant.

One of the most skillful she recognized immediately—Monheno Devilla—neatly clad in a short black jacket trimmed with intricate red and black beadwork, black breeches, and oiled black knee boots. On his arm danced the young woman from the cantina. Her choice of a partner was obviously the envy of the women who stood cooling themselves with lace fans at the edge of the floor.

Savanna narrowed her eyes as the girl leaned close to his ear, whispered something, and burst into a gale of laughter. She was beautiful—perhaps his flame, or even his wife for all Savanna knew. She was clinging to him with all the signs of ownership.

Savanna rolled her eyes privately as the girl stood on tiptoe and kissed him flirtatiously on the cheek as the dance ended. That poor girl needed a few lessons in proper behavior. She probably wasn't more than sixteen—too young to be acting so experienced. She was . . .

She realized suddenly that Devilla was turning around—looking at her. She'd been caught! She flushed and tipped her sky-blue hat downward to hide her face. Good Lord, how embarrassing!

Now he would think she was . . . heaven forbid . . . flirting with him.

From beneath her hat, she saw black boots coming closer. She ducked to the side and started to walk away like she hadn't noticed him.

Brandt foiled her maneuver. "Monheno Devilla." He stepped forward and extended his hand to Devilla. "I didn't get a chance to thank you for bringing the doc out to see about Waddie. Doesn't sound like he was in any shape to do it himself."

"Glad to hear your young hand's doing better," Monheno returned cordially and shook the foreman's hand. "Haven't seen you since . . ." he paused abruptly, as if suddenly realizing what he was saying. "Well, I'm sure it's been too long."

Brandt nodded. "I'd have to agree with you there, Monheno," he reached out and clapped Devilla on the shoulder. "I know it's been too long since I've seen a good poker game. Ain't one decent player in that shaggy bunch of pups at the Del Sol. Suppose you could oblige me later?"

Monheno laughed, his ebony eyes like shining bits of stone beneath thick straight brows and dark lashes. "It would be my pleasure." With an inquiring look, he turned the subject about again. "So you're at the Del Sol now?" He glanced at Savanna. "That explains how you have managed to bring the prettiest lady of all to the dance."

74

Brandt stood back, looking vaguely embarrassed. "This is Miss Savanna Storm." He introduced her as if she were the queen of England, and stressed the "miss." "She owns the Del Sol now."

Monheno nodded, and started to say something, but Savanna cut him off curtly.

"Mister Devilla and I have already met," she said flatly, "when he brought the doctor."

Monheno laughed—a low infectious sound. "True," a wisp of thick dark hair fell onto his forehead as he leaned forward into a slight bow. "But the last time our dance was cut short." He captured her hand before she could move away. "Perhaps we could finish it now?"

She gave him a stiff nod. Short of causing a scene or admitting what was really going on between her and Monheno Devilla, she couldn't refuse. He, of course, knew that very well.

Savanna kept herself stiff as a steel shaft as he led her in the dance. It was either that or melt into his arms like a lump of wet dough. "Why is it that you insist on tormenting me, Mister Devilla?" she demanded. "I thought I made it clear that I want nothing more to do with you."

"Did you?" He wore that damnable grin again—like a cat taunting a captured grasshopper. "It must have slipped my mind. The last time we talked, I thought I remembered your asking for my help."

She delivered him a frigid glare. "Which you

promptly refused." What game was he playing now? "I believe you said you didn't want to get involved. So, by all means, stay out of the matter!"

His eyes sparkled darkly as he leaned closer to her. The pace of her heart quickened, and her skin tingled where his fingers touched her back. Not five minutes at the party, and she'd already managed to fall into trouble. She should have known better than to come here. She should have . . . how long was this cursed waltz going to last?

He made a lamenting tsk-tsk sound. "I've tried, I've tried." He threw up his free hand. "But, you see, I'm a fool for a hard luck case."

The indignity of his remark straightened her spine even more. "I beg your pardon," she gasped, outraged. "You may be a fool, but I am not a hard luck case. I do *not* need your help. I don't want it. In fact, I don't want anything to do with you at all."

She looked impatiently toward the musicians. How much longer was this damnable music going to go on? She could see Devilla plotting his next move behind those dark eyes. Why? Why was he bothering to pursue her? He had no interest in the Del Sol. Quite obviously, he was in no need of female companionship—there were at least a dozen watching him wistfully now, including the pretty girl from the cantina. How was she different from those women?

It hit her in a moment of eureka. *Those*

women were pursuing him. She was not. So the quickest way to solve this problem was to do a turnabout. She braced herself and forced what she hoped was a comely smile.

"Very well, Mister Devilla." She tilted her eyes up from beneath her lashes. "Since you insist on my company, we might as well be cordial. Tell me, do you live in Carlos's Cantina, or do you have a home somewhere? And what is it you do with your time when you're not shooting men over their salsa?"

He looked shocked. Good. Let him be shocked. This would be easier than she thought. She'd be rid of him inside of an hour.

"I keep a ranch on the other side of Canyon de Casas," he replied finally. "Nothing so grand as the Vista Del Sol of course, but it keeps me occupied. A man cannot spend all of his time shooting thieves over their salsa, now can he?"

"No, I suppose not." Her mind wasn't on the conversation. She had somehow slipped to contemplating the incredible depth of his eyes. They seemed endless—like the space in a room where there was no hint of light. She couldn't imagine what might lie within.

The music stopped, and he held her closer than ever.

She gave herself a mental kick. "The dance is over." She was losing sight of her plan already. She had to try harder to keep her wits.

"Ummm," he agreed. "I don't suppose you would surrender to a walk in the garden. The

77

garden during a Californio wedding is . . . magic."

She glanced into his eyes and was ready to surrender to anything. "I wouldn't know," she whispered. Was she really considering going to the garden with him . . . alone? "I've never been to a Spanish wedding. My housekeeper was of the opinion that I shouldn't come to this one. Her thought was that it was only for Californios."

He grinned broadly. "Ah, but being a Californio is only a state of mind." He took her hand in his and led her from the dance floor just as the music started up again. "You see, your bright eyes tell me you're halfway there already," He touched the stray curls that spilled from beneath her hat. "But I have to warn you, my pretty Brit, spend an hour as a Californio, and you'll never go back to the world you came from."

She had a terrible, sinking feeling he was right. Perhaps it was the music, or the gentle heat of the day, but she felt giddy—as if her feet weren't quite touching the ground—as if she didn't want to think about anything, or worry about anything, or wonder about anything.

"Where do we start?" she heard herself ask. The real question was where would it all end.

He gave that warm, seductive grin that said he knew exactly where they were headed. "The garden." He led her from the patio and down a tile walkway. "And then to the rodeo."

"The rodeo?" The word sounded silly in her accent. "I've never seen one, but I hear they are grand. Esperanza was telling me just this morning. Is it true that they ride wild horses?"

"That is so." He glanced toward the rodeo grounds, in a shallow valley below and gave her a roguish wink. "Wish me luck."

She drew back. "Luck?" she gasped in amazement. "You are riding in the rodeo?" Why did that idea send a bolt of apprehension through her? Why was she picturing him having some terrible accident?

He gave her that damnable grin, as if he saw right through her question and knew what she was thinking. Maybe an accident wouldn't be such a terrible thing after all.

"Of course," he said. "Everyone rides in the rodeo."

Her heart fluttered. "Not the women."

Monheno let her squirm for a minute before he answered. She looked astounded, worried, completely aghast. It was absolutely charming. "No," he told her finally. "Of course, not the women."

The color came back into her pretty face. "Oh," she breathed. "For a moment, I thought. . . . Well, I really have no idea about these Californio weddings."

He held back a chuckle. She didn't know how right she was. She had absolutely no idea—about the wedding or about anything else in this valley. She was so completely out of her element here.

79

He had to admire her for giving it such a determined effort. Amazing that bastard Carver could produce a daughter with so much spunk. Too bad her survival here in California was so much in question.

They stopped walking. He captured her hand and gazed down into those fantastic eyes that had captivated him the first time he saw her—violet like an evening sky. There was an innocence there with all that bluster and determination, like she'd never been out on her own before. He reached out, combed a golden strand of hair from her face without thinking. She delivered a threatening glare that made him laugh. Not quite so sweet and innocent, after all.

"I think I've a lot to learn about California if I'm going to live here." Her voice broke into his thoughts. She pulled her hand away and started walking again.

He shook his head and gave her back a one-sided smile. "So you plan to live at Del Sol house for good then?" Now was as good a time as any to find out what a rich little English girl wanted with a ranch so far from her own kind.

She turned around, looked him straight in the eye with a stare that could have turned back a charging bull. "Yes." She was daring him to tell her differently. "I will be making my home at Del Sol . . . for good."

He catalogued the determined, almost desperate look on her face with the other things he couldn't figure out about her. "I see." But he didn't see. "You won't be going back to England?"

"No."

He shrugged. She would, of course. When the time came, he'd help her pack her pretty little dressing trunk and get on the stage. In the meantime, she was his favorite kind of diversion . . . the female kind.

# Five

She'd had about enough of Monheno's questions. She walked a few steps down the garden path and took a deep breath of the rose-scented air. The garden was spectacular, with its neatly groomed rows of blooming roses and azaleas. Lengths of ribbon and bright yardage had been threaded among the bushes to match the colors of the flowers. Atop the waist-high bushes ran rows of banners, swaying lazily in the sweet-scented breeze.

"The garden is beautiful." She changed the subject. "I must admit I've never seen such revelry for a wedding." Weddings were never her favorite thing. "But I'm told Californios do everything in a big way."

He raised a brow quizzically. "I gather you're not a fanatic about weddings. I thought all women liked them."

"Most do, I suppose." She didn't want to go into detail, particularly not with him.

"But not you," he pressed.

"No."

"You never plan on having one of your own, I take it?"

"No." That was the truth. Hell or wild horses couldn't drag her into a marriage. She wasn't ashamed of it, either. Independence was something to be proud of.

He caught up with her and faced her with a puzzled expression. "And why is that?"

He said it like she just told him the world was flat and dragons lived at the edge. His reaction was strangely pleasing. It was nice to catch him by surprise for a change.

She gave him a sly tilt of lashes. "I'm firmly committed to spinsterhood." That ought to send his jaw dropping down to his knees. Pah on him if he didn't believe her. She knew she'd never marry, and she knew why.

"That," he took a step closer, "would be a shame." His gaze drifted down to her lips, then back to her eyes.

Her heart fluttered and she swallowed hard. The look on his face was different now, intense, and she knew what was coming. Things were going too far again. She had to stop it . . .

The words stopped in her throat as he caught a stray tendril of her hair, tucked it behind her shoulder, slid his hand to her waist. That slight touch struck her like lightning, made her skin tingle with fire.

He leaned closer to her, almost close enough

to kiss her, those raven eyes showing nothing but her own reflection. "In fact," he whispered, "it would be a tragedy."

His touch, those eyes. She was convinced—convinced, at least, it would be a tragedy if he didn't kiss her. Every inch of her wanted it.

She closed her eyes as his lips brushed hers. She was dizzy, felt herself falling. His arm caught her like a steel circle, pulling her closer.

His kiss was light at first—like the soft touch of the azalea-scented breeze. Slowly, carefully, he parted her trembling lips, tasted her, coaxed a response from her. She replied without thinking, without wanting to, knowing she shouldn't. Nothing in her past prepared her to resist. His was the kiss of the devil, something wild, forbidden, and tantalizing.

His fingers slowly moved along her back, burning through her thick day dress like hot coals. She felt hot, feverish. Her breasts hardened against his chest, throbbed with a painful ache.

A foreign sound pierced the swirling fog in her head. Voices! Someone coming!

She parted her lips from his and pushed away from him. Eyes wide, she slapped a hand to the racing pulse at her throat and stood there dizzy, confused. She was shocked, not at him but at herself. She had more resolve than this!

She had to say something. "You take too many liberties, sir!" was the first thing that came out. How completely ridiculous.

He seemed to think so too. "The response of a truly proper young English lady." He cocked his head back a little, his eyes sparkling with challenge. A quick step brought him within reach again, and he touched her cheek, tracing the line of her parted lips with his thumb. "But you kiss like a Californio. Perhaps you're not as proper as you pretend to be."

She raised her chin and faced him with wide-eyed indignance. "I beg your pardon!" How dare he! She'd spent ten years in preparatory school learning how to be proper. "You, sir, are not much of a gentleman." That had to be the understatement of the century.

He gave a wicked nod, "My apologies. Perhaps we should finish our tour of the garden. The rodeo will be starting soon."

"I think that would be a good idea." Was it? Her oatmeal knees might not cooperate. The last thing she wanted to do was fall back into his arms. Or did she? She pressed her lips together and tried to blot away the tingling memory of his kiss.

She clasped her hands in front of her so tightly the knuckles turned white, and started walking. From the shadow of her lashes, she watched him as he fell into step beside her. What was it about him that made him so tempting? He had wonderful eyes, true—dark and mysterious. He was strong, well-built, disgustingly handsome. He knew that, of course. It showed in his smooth manner, his arrogant grin, and his overconfident swagger. He was a rake and a gambler, and not the least bit ashamed of it. He was a womanizer every chance he got.

He was everything she despised in a man. So why was she walking in the garden with him? Why did she let him kiss her—good God—*twice*?

She realized he had asked her a question. "Pardon?" She couldn't even look at him. What if he could read her thoughts?

"I asked how it was that you came to California."

So he was on that subject again. She glanced at him, and suspicion ignited in the back of her mind. His expression was more than casually curious. Why was he so determined to know about her?

She thought about her answer carefully. She didn't want to give any information that wasn't already common knowledge. "I inherited the Vista Del Sol when my father died."

"So I've heard." He looked over at a bush of red roses, as if he were trying to seem casual. "But why did you leave your comfortable British school to come all the way to California?"

So he knew more about her than she thought. Talk must be going around—talk that was starting somewhere in her own household. When she got home, she would find out to whom those loose tongues belonged . . .

"You seem to feel I am not suited for life here." She skirted the subject as cleverly as she could. In the pit of her stomach, an indignant anger boiled up. She'd had enough of everyone telling her who she was and what she should do. She wasn't the pampered miss they all thought. She knew how to take care of herself. She was twenty-one, for heaven's sake. Most women her age were married and raising children.

"I should tell you that I lived on a ranch in Africa when I was young—before my poor mother died." She didn't know why she was defending herself. "And it was much more primitive than California could even begin to be. I liked it there very much, and I most certainly would have stayed, but for . . ." She caught herself in time, and finished lamely, "If my mother hadn't died."

She looked back down at her hands and clenched her fingers a little tighter. She had to be more careful. She'd almost blurted out the truth of how her father gambled away their lives in Africa.

"Ummm." He sounded more interested than ever. "Is that how you came by your name?"

She winced and rolled her eyes. She couldn't help it. It was a lifelong habit. "Yes," she admitted. Getting rid of Savanna Storm was the only reason she'd ever wanted to marry. "Rather a cruel joke to play on a child, isn't it?"

He seemed surprised. Of course he would. What would a man like him know of good Christian names?

"It's beautiful," he flattered. "Who chose it?"

"My father." It was the only thing he ever gave her he didn't take back. "I am told I was born during a terrible deluge. It was inconvenient timing for my father, so he cursed me for life with this name." She tried to smile as she said it, to make it sound light so he wouldn't guess the very real hatred in her heart.

He gave a wry twist of his lips that told her he hadn't guessed the truth. "You could marry."

She couldn't help grinning. "Humph. I told you, I am firmly committed to spinsterhood. I'd rather be saddled with the name than a husband." Cursed was a better word for it, really.

He laughed, the arch of his cheekbones making the slightest wrinkles at the corners of his eyes. "Saddled?" He raised one brow and lowered the other. "I thought you might have changed your opinion."

Savanna felt a faint quiver in the bottom of her stomach. "From just one kiss?" She couldn't believe her own boldness. "I think not."

That light of challenge sparked in his eyes. "Perhaps I should try again . . ."

She stepped out of reach in case he decided to try it. "Perhaps not." She didn't feel so bold now—not with that smoky look in his eye.

He held her gaze for a moment, stepped closer as if to show her he could, then threw his hands up and broke the spell. "So," he sounded completely unaffected, "you still haven't answered my question about what brought you to California."

She crossed her arms over her flip-flopping stomach. It was hard to say which was worse—talking to him or kissing him. He was an expert at both, dangerous in both.

"I simply felt the need for a change of life-style." She tried to sound matter-of-fact. "My inheritance of the Del Sol provided the opportunity."

"I see." The look in his eye said he knew she was lying. "And how have you found it so far?"

She came up with the best description she could. "Challenging," was the only word for it. "But I intend to . . ." she pushed her shoulders back, "stick to it like a burr on a cat's tail."

He laughed. "And what about the Sombras?" His eyes weren't laughing. They were deadly serious.

It was surprising to have him bring that up. "I'll stand against them." She didn't have much other choice. "Together with my neighbors if I can. Alone if I must."

"Mmmm," was the only reply he gave. He hid his reaction by looking toward the rodeo grounds. "I think things are about to begin." His voice was absent, as though something else was in his thoughts. "We'd best be heading that way."

She watched him suspiciously as they walked to the rodeo grounds, where crowds were already beginning to gather. He looked thoughtful, pre-occupied. What was in his thoughts? The Sombras? Was he considering helping her? Did she want him to? How could she possibly have him at her home for days, even weeks, when she couldn't even resist his advances for a few hours?

Neighbors stopped him with greetings at least a dozen times as they moved through the crowds to the arena. For an owner of a modest ranch, he was certainly well-known, and, it would seem, well-liked. Men greeted him with respect, women with adoration. She could see why. He had a way of looking each one in the eye, joking with them, asking small questions about their families that made him seem genuinely concerned. He went about drawing people in, just as he had done to her.

But there was one decided benefit. She was meeting her neighbors, which was going to come in handy later when she tried to enlist their help.

Monheno helped her onto a buckboard with several other onlookers before he slipped into the plank-fenced rodeo corral. Feeling out of place and embarrassed, she took a seat among them and waited for the events to begin. The women, mostly older motherly looking ladies, gave her little notice, and probably would have given her none at all if she hadn't arrived with Monheno Devilla. She heard his name at least a half-dozen times as they chattered in rapid Spanish around her.

The first event, a cow-penning contest, had already started when an elderly lady hurried up and climbed onto the buckboard next to Savanna. She greeted the women around her in Spanish, and Monheno's name came up five or six more times. When the conversation was over, the woman looked over at Savanna with interests.

"Que buena dia!" she exclaimed enthusiastically.

Savanna blushed. "Si, es buena." Which was about all the Spanish she knew. The woman giggled good-naturedly at her attempt, and Savanna raised her hands in a helpless gesture. The woman wasn't making fun of her really. She seemed rather sweet, in a grandmotherly way.

"El Devilla es muy guapo, eh?" She elbowed Savanna in the ribs and pointed to Monheno standing on the other side of the corral.

Savanna flushed down to her toes and tried to pretend she didn't understand the words. She wasn't about to admit to anything.

The woman narrowed her eyes slyly and motioned to Monheno again. "Mi cou-sin," she sounded out carefully. "No es mar-ried, eh? Muy, muy guapo."

Savanna just sat there turning deeper and deeper red until her cheeks felt like they were on fire.

The woman grinned and patted Savanna's hand like she'd found out what she wanted to know. She started to say something else, but a horn blew on the field and drowned her out. An impromptu horse race started before she could say anything else.

Several more events went on one after another. Most tested skills used daily on the ranch, such as roping, tying down and branding a calf, as well as riding bucking horses. There was a demonstration of cutting calves from the herd on horseback by Señor Baca himself. Savanna took note of him so she would know how to find him later. The Dos Rios Rohos was one of the biggest ranches in the valley. If she could get him on her side . . .

Following the cutting, there were several displays of trick riding. Monheno's was one of the best, all the way down to scooping a coin from the ground while riding at a full gallop. He then did the same maneuver with five coins, scooping them up like child's jacks as his horse thundered by. When he stopped, he flung them into the air like raindrops, and eager children raced to scoop them up.

The matchmaker squealed with delight and elbowed Savanna in the ribs. "Muy guapo, eh, muy fuerte!"

She blushed again, wishing she could sink into the loose hay and never reappear.

Several other displays of horse trickery followed Monheno's. He stood coolly by, leaning up against the betting table on the other side of the field. Powerful arms crossed in front of him and full lips showing the faintest hint of a smile at the corners, he looked mildly pleased as others tried to match his feat.

Savanna rolled her eyes disgustedly. No doubt

he had money wagered on this. Probably a lot of money. He gambled like a man who didn't have to worry about his finances. But then, so did her father . . .

"And where have you been hidin' yourself?" Brandt's voice surprised her from behind. She swiveled around to look at him.

"I might ask you the same thing." Come to think of it, it was a little offensive that he'd abandoned her the entire afternoon.

He raised his brows in surprise. "I've been at the party," he returned levelly. "The last time I saw you, you were headed for the garden with Monheno."

The matchmaker turned around with interest at the mention of Monheno's name. "El jardin con Monheno!" She clapped her hands together with obvious delight. "El jardin es muy linda. Es muy ro-man-teek."

Savanna gritted her teeth and jumped down from the wagon. This was getting worse by the minute. She needed to leave before her foreman got the wrong idea about her and Monheno. She smiled at the matchmaker, excused herself as politely as she could, and walked around the wagon to Brandt.

"I am *not* interested in Mister Devilla," she said under her breath as they walked away.

"Glad to hear it." The twinkle in his eyes said he didn't believe her.

"Don't be flip," she snipped. It was maddening to have a man, a member of her staff, making such ridiculous insinuations about her. "I am not the slightest bit interested in Mister Devilla. I find him a curiosity, that is all." It had to be the biggest lie she ever told.

"How's that?" He scoffed as he said it.

"I am curious about who he is." She could hardly tell him she found Monheno Devilla fascinating—exotic—exciting. "He hardly seems to be what he claims."

"And what's that?"

"A rancher."

Brandt shrugged noncommittally. "That's true. He's got a place down on the fork's bottom, a small spread—nothing like the Del Sol." He looked across the rodeo grounds at Monheno. "That can't be his only income, though. He gambles money like he's never wanted for it."

Just like her father. "Is he a native?" She wasn't certain why she wanted to know. "He speaks with no accent at all."

Brandt tipped his hat back thoughtfully. "Not sure. He's been here long as I can recall, but I only came out from Texas five years ago. I heard a . . ." he paused, turned red, and cleared his throat, then went on, ". . . lady say once that he had ties to the old families—that there were Devillas in the valley years back."

He crossed his arms over his chest, chewed at the side of his moustache, and looked her in the eye. "You're awfully curious for someone who isn't interested."

That told her it was time to change the subject. "It must be coming close to dinner time." She glanced up at the waning sun.

The foreman gave her a knowing look, then started to grin. "Dinner time is any time at a Californio wedding," He clicked his boot heels together and offered her his arm. "At these affairs the food and wine never stop."

Her stomach rumbled and her mouth started to water. "Lead on." She nodded dramatically. "I will trust you to guide me through the trials of the local cuisine."

"I'll do my best." He ushered her away from the rodeo grounds toward the patio. "Though I have to confess, I've been living with these Mexicans so long I've come to eat like one, but I'll try to point out the hot stuff."

They strolled slowly toward the hacienda, making their way through the milling crowds leaving the rodeo. Near the dance floor, they passed Señor Baca and the bride, the first time Savanna had seen her all day. The bride gave Brandt a long stare, then turned away haughtily, and smiled at her father.

Savanna looked from the bride to her foreman speculatively. Monheno wasn't the only one with secrets. "Brandt?" She should probably mind her own business.

"Yes?"

"Why did you come to this wedding? I can't help but notice that you and I don't fit in here."

"I used to work for the Roho," he reminded, then with a guilty smile, "In the past, I consid-

95

ered asking for the hand of the bride, if you really want to know." He chuckled behind his moustache. "But I discovered I wasn't the type to be married—at least not to her." He glanced back over his shoulder at the girl. "I imagine she asked me here today to show me what I was missing. I didn't want to spoil her big day by taking the opportunity from her."

Savanna felt completely ridiculous for having asked. That definitely wasn't any of her business. "I see." she muttered.

"La Comida," he said as they stepped onto the patio, where a huge open-air buffet had been set. Not far away, several cooks worked over a huge brick stove cooking giant pots of beans and Mexican stew and slowly turning a spitted pig. On the long tables lining both sides of the porch sat a menagerie of brightly painted pottery dishes, some with fruit grown at the nearby San Domingo mission, some laden with slabs of charcoaled beef, others holding puffy loaves of wheat bread, olives from San Diego, and huge stacks of tortillas. At the end of the table stood two vats of wine—one pale and one crimson—along with enameled wooden cups.

The serving girls giggled at Savanna as she made her way down the line choosing mostly meats, breads, fruit, and other harmless items. By the time she reached wine vats, her plate still looked empty. Brandt's, on the other hand, was full.

Skeptically, she looked at the plate. "Do you always eat that much?"

He chuckled. "I don't get lined up for a spread like this every day."

"We don't feed you on the Del Sol?" She cocked a brow and gave him a one-sided smile as he helped her to a cup of wine.

"I can't complain about the food on the Del Sol," he admitted as they left the patio. "One thing . . ."

She didn't hear the rest of what he said. Her eyes caught Monheno, back on the dance floor with the pretty girl from that morning. He was smiling and telling her something, his face animated as he spoke. She turned her ear to him and snuggled closer, dark eyes cutting narrowly to Savanna. The looked of wicked triumph on her face was disgusting.

Mortified, Savanna jerked her attention back to her plate. Good Lord, the woman thought she was competing for Monheno! Heaven help her, rumors were probably running rampant.

Coming to the Baca-Garza wedding was a mistake. She should have considered that Monheno might be there. Being in close quarters with him wasn't doing her reputation any good. Well, she could remedy that. She'd just stay away from Monheno. By the time the wedding was over, everyone would know there was nothing between them.

Brandt was still eating sometime later when Señor Baca strode onto the patio. A bulky, middle-aged Californio, he wandered through the tables in a gait that looked mildly inebriated. He bellowed and sloshed wine from the rim of his cup as he greeted guests on his way back to the vat. Watching him go, Savanna smiled. There would be no more perfect time to talk to him.

She pushed her plate aside, excused herself, and stood up. Passing the dance floor, she garnered another seething glare from Monheno's girl, now engaged with another dance partner. She ignored it and headed for the wine vats, where Baca was engaged in a scathing rebuke of his serving men.

She waited for him to finish before she approached him. "Señor Baca," she said as she came up behind him.

He turned around, smiling, seized her hand before she could back away, and placed a kiss somewhere between her wrist and elbow. "Miss Storm." He didn't sound as inebriated as he looked. "How good to finally meet you."

She gave him her most winning smile. "And you," she returned. "I must compliment you on this lovely wedding. Your daughter is a beautiful girl."

That was the right thing to say. He grinned broadly. "Why thank you." Wine sloshed out of his cup and nearly hit her shoes. "I trust you are enjoying yourself."

"Very much so." How was she going to lead into the problem with the Sombras? She had to do it quick. He was already starting to wander away. "It . . . is a welcome respite from our troubles on the Del Sol."

"Troubles?" He didn't really seem to be listening, but was looking over her head instead.

"With the Sombras."

That got his attention. He snapped his eyes downward and looked dangerously sober. "Is that so?"

Her hopes crept up. "Yes. They have come around twice now demanding extortion money."

From somewhere in the crowd, the bride called for her father. It was now or never. Her time was running out.

"I was hoping to enlist your aid, and the aid of other neighbors," she pressed on. "It is my feeling that we can defeat the hoodlums by standing as one."

He smiled and patted her arm like she was a naughty kitten caught in the yarn. "Much better that you learn to leave things the way they are." He slipped past her as he said it. "You won't find anyone here willing to take up that battle."

She stood in his wake, her mouth hanging open with shock. What was wrong with these people! They talked about this filthy blackmail like it was nothing, like it was right! Were they all that cowardly?

The disappointment was crushing. What hope had she now? Yet she had to think of something.

She wandered to a shadowed bench on the patio and sat down, staring out at the lawn as the sun set and servants lit torches. The music and celebration increased in volume as the hours passed. Wine flowed, people danced, sang, disappeared into the shadows in pairs. She leaned back into the shadows and tried to ignore it.

Exhaustion finally forced her to confront the problem of sleeping arrangements. She most certainly could not sleep there on a bench in the darkness. With the Californios, that seemed to be perfectly acceptable. They were laid out, or had fallen out everywhere—on the patio, in the lawn, in the gardens. It was the most vile display she'd ever seen in her life. No wonder the good folk of the East wrote of the Californios as drinking, gambling, gaming heathens.

It was her good fortune to find a servant to get her bag from the buggy and direct her to a guest bedroom. She couldn't help looking for Monheno and his evil-eyed señorita as she passed the dance floor, but he was nowhere to be found. She could only imagine where he was and what he was doing.

The thought of it kept her awake even after she found her way to a bed.

As the hours passed, she lay sleepless and fully clothed. She didn't change into her nightdress for fear some drunken guest would burst in on her in the middle of the night.

The sun was nearly up before she fell into a nervous, fitful sleep. Her dreams were haunted. In a whisper, she said his name, the sound of it clinging to her lips like poison—"Venenoso."

# Six

"Savanna," he called her name. He knew her name! "Savanna," she heard him again, his voice soft against her cheek like the whisper of a faint breeze—but cold like ice.

"No!" she cried. "No! Leave me alone!" In hopes of bringing help, she called the name of her attacker, "Venenoso! Venenoso!"

"Miss Storm," the sound of another voice seemed so far away she barely heard it. "Miss Storm," it came again, dragging her from her nightmare. She opened her eyes wide, sat up in bed, heart thundering wildly.

A stranger leaned over her in the pre-dawn dimness—a young man, perhaps only a year or so older than herself, with wide grey eyes and thick coal-colored lashes that made him look almost like a boy. He wasn't looking at her, but toward the window. She followed his gaze just in time to see the curtain flutter to a stop. Had

101

someone been there? The thought crawled down her spine like an icy spider's legs.

"You had a bad dream," the stranger whispered. "I heard you scream as I was walking by."

She blinked at him in complete bewilderment. Where was she? Why was a stranger in *her* house—in *her* bedroom?

"I am Tito Baca." His explanation spiraled her back to reality. "This is my sister's wedding."

She glanced around the shadowed room and remembered where she was. Pushing her hair back, she rubbed her tired eyes. "I wasn't . . . having a nightmare," she whispered. "There was someone here." And she knew who. The fluttering curtain proved he was really there.

Tito took her hand kindly, looked understanding and sympathetic. "No." He patted her hand. "It was only a dream. Perhaps from the wine."

She shook her head and leaned back against the pillow. She didn't dream Venenoso up on one glass of wine, but she was too tired to care about him, or the Sombras, or the fact that a strange man sat at her bedside. Maybe there was something in the wine, after all . . .

"I suppose," she whispered. "Thank you. I'll be . . . fine now." Her words were slow and clumsy as sleep drifted back over her like a heavy blanket. She surrendered to its warmth, its comfort, took long, slow breaths. Dimly, she heard the curtains rustle again . . .

It was well after dawn by the time she awoke. Wearily, she sat up in the bed and looked around the room. It swam and blurred before her eyes as she blinked them into focus. What was wrong with her? She felt like she'd had a dozen glasses of wine instead of just one.

Moaning, she drew her knees up and let her head fall forward. God, she hoped this wedding was over today. She couldn't take another night like last night. Were there really people in her room or did she dream it?

She wished she could just pack her things and go home this morning, but Brandt had warned her that once she got to the wedding she should stay for the duration. Leaving would be an unforgivable insult to the Baca hospitality. She didn't want that. She had enough enemies in this valley already. Maybe she could just hide in this room until it was all over.

She rolled her eyes at the thought and threw her legs over the edge of the bed. Servants would be coming soon to make the bed. Besides, she had more neighbors to talk with. Perhaps everyone didn't share Señor Baca's opinions about the Sombras.

She stared absently at the window as she walked across the room. The heavy velvet curtains were closed this morning, but she could remember them fluttering in the breeze last night. Did Tito Baca close the window or did someone else do it?

She reached absently for her overnight bag. A cool, uneasy feeling slid over her as her hand slipped inside. She looked down at the bag. Why was it open? She hadn't opened it last night. It was closed when she went to bed. Had someone . . .

She took her things out one by one—her nightdress, her pale peach day dress, her riding outfit, her brush, and mirror. Nothing seemed to have been bothered. Maybe she *had* opened the bag last night.

She tried not to think about it as she changed into her riding outfit and brushed her hair. She'd probably opened the bag and forgotten about it. Who would come into her room and go through her bag? What could anyone hope to find in there?

A knock at the door made her gasp and spin around. Slapping a hand to her chest, she sucked in a breath.

"Just a minute." Lord, she was nervous as a cat. What was wrong with her this morning? She swallowed her racing heart and went to the door. Her foreman was on the other side looking even worse than she felt.

She knew it wasn't proper, but she threw the door open wide for him and stumbled across the room to a chair. Laying a hand on her throbbing forehead, she rested her elbow on the vanity and rolled her eyes up at him. "Please tell me we are needed at home."

He leaned against the edge of the dresser and crossed his arms over his chest, shaking his head. "Remember what I said yesterday."

Unfortunately, she did. There was no possibility of going home early. She let her hair fall forward to hide her face. "How long do these affairs usually continue?"

He hesitated. "Three days."

"Three days!" She peered at him from the corner of one eye. She'd never survive that long. She'd never survive one more night in this room with strangers and ghosts slipping in and out at all hours.

He laughed sympathetically. "This morning won't be too tough," he encouraged. "Things stay pretty quiet until noon. Most people will be riding or picnicking in the woods. Care to make an escape before the rowdies come to?"

"All right." She was definitely not in the mood for any raucous wedding guests. These Californios were completely insane. "I guess I'd better put my things away. I'll only be a minute."

"I'll go out and saddle the horses," he said as he walked out the door. "I'll meet you around front."

She closed the door behind him and leaned wearily up against it, letting her eyes fall closed. Two more days! She didn't know if she could make it. She already felt like she could sleep for a week. The trip across New Mexico on the stage was nothing compared to this.

Looking wearily at herself in the mirror, she picked up her pale blue hat and put it on. The rounded straw brim wasn't as broad as her bolero's, but at least it would keep the sun out of her eyes. It conveniently matched the embroidery on her deep blue riding outfit—Esperanza's doing. She was the only maid Savanna ever knew who could match three outfits to one hat.

She tied the ribbon under her chin, pushed her hair back behind her shoulders, and put the rest of her things back in her bag. She buckled the fasteners, frowned thoughtfully at the bag for a moment, then grabbed the handles and picked it up. Best that she store it back in the buggy for today. If there was someone going through people's bags, she didn't want them looking in hers, not that there was anything valuable inside. She didn't own anything valuable anymore. She'd sold almost every piece of real jewelry she had, even the ones that came down through her mother's family. Sentiment was an unthinkable luxury when you were facing the poor house.

The heavy bag bumped clumsily against the tops of her riding boots as she lugged it down the empty hall and out the side door to the veranda. She growled under her breath impatiently as she hoisted it into the buggy box and clamped the lid shut. In the buggy next to hers, a man groaned and muttered a protest at the noise, and she hurried away, embarrassed. She didn't want to know what was going on in that buggy, or in the shadows of the bushes around the garden. There were people asleep everywhere, wrapped up in woven blankets like colorful cocoons, probably still drunk from the night before.

She stared down at her riding boots and headed for the front of the house. Hopefully Brandt was there with the horses by now.

Her horse was there standing next to a tall blood bay, but her foreman wasn't. Saddled and ready, Nantucket was munching oats from the hand of Monheno Devilla. Monheno looked disgustingly crisp, considering he was still dancing when she went to bed. Dressed in a clean white shirt, dark grey breeches, and tall black riding boots, he looked like he'd had a good night's rest. That irritated her almost as much as finding him there in the first place. "What are *you* doing here?"

He was unabashed by her untidy greeting. "Your foreman was—detained." His note of regret sounded false. "He asked that I escort you to the paseo this morning until he can join us."

"The what?" She stalled, looking for an excuse. Where was Brandt, anyway? Was Monheno telling her the truth?

"The picnic," he translated. "We should go, or all the best spots will be taken."

The winsome smile on his face made her suspicious. "Who else is coming?" She snatched Nantucket's reins out of his hand.

"Who else do you see?"

"Alone?" She widened her eyes in shock. It figured he would be the type to suggest something so lewd. "But that wouldn't be . . ." God, she sounded like a prude!

"What?"

She squirmed uncomfortably, looking down at Nantucket's reins in her hands. "Proper."

He laughed. "Perhaps not in England." He took the reins from her hand and looped them over Nantucket's neck. "But a true Californio would think nothing of going to a picnic with a good friend."

She slanted him a scathing look. "We are *not* good friends."

He clamped a palm to his heart. "You wound me." He didn't sound hurt at all. "I thought we were."

She just kept glaring.

He shrugged and grasped Nantucket's reins as if to lead the horse away. "Well, if you're too afraid . . ."

She shot her hand out and grabbed the reins away. "Of you?" she exploded. She wasn't afraid of him, really . . . just . . . well, there wasn't a word for it. She tapped a finger to her lips thoughtfully, then pointed it at him. "Promise you'll behave like a gentleman."

He swept both hands back and gave her a gallant bow. "Absolutely." But he was smiling when he said it.

She batted at his hands when he reached for her waist to help her onto her horse. "I can do this myself, thank you," she said curtly, and mounted before he could offer any more help.

He mounted his own horse, and they started down the drive. "And how did you find the rodeo?" he asked as they rode through the stone archway marking the end of the hacienda driveway.

She glanced up at the archway to keep from looking at him. "It was very entertaining." She was going to show him just how cool, how proper she could be. "I think I enjoyed the calf penning competition the most."

"I'm a fancier of the cutting myself." He gave her a wry look, as if he noticed she *hadn't* mentioned his display of horsemanship. "The Baca put on quite a display. His are some of the best cutting animals around, but they would be better without his bulk aboard."

She clamped a hand over her mouth, scandalized, then started to giggle. "It *was* rather comical." It wasn't kind to talk that way about their host, but she couldn't help picturing him clinging to his horse like an overstuffed potato.

Maybe it was after-effects from the wine, but she found herself laughing harder than she had in months as Monheno went on to describe Baca's wild ride. He leaned back in his saddle and laughed with her. His deep, rumbling laugh was charming, infectious like his smile. Her ribs ached and tears spilled from her eyes before he was finished.

"Oh please, no more," she pleaded finally. "I'm afraid I will rattle apart if I laugh one more time."

He reined his horse up near the side of a clear-running spring. "I'll grant you a reprieve." He looked out at the sparkling water, not at her. "We've reached our picnic spot."

She reined Nantucket in and looked around. The buggy road was nowhere in sight. How long ago had they drifted away from it? How long had they been riding? She hadn't even noticed. It was like she was hypnotized. She could repeat each word Monheno said—could describe each subtle expression of his handsome face, replay the deep, warm sound of his laughter, but she couldn't remember a thing about the country they passed. The last thing she remembered was the arch at the end of the driveway . . .

"Climb down." He dismounted and reached for her reins. Nantucket pinned his ears and snapped, and Monheno pulled his hand away just in time to save his fingers.

Savanna looked at her mount in shock. He'd never bitten anyone. "I'm sorry." She wasn't really. Nantucket was a good judge of bad character. "I guess Nantucket is getting protective. I'm the only one who rides him."

He stayed a safe distance away. "I heard that story. The way they told it in the Cantina, no one on the Del Sol will ride him. They say he is crazy."

She shrugged and climbed down. "People said I was crazy when I left London." Among other things. "That didn't make it true." Who on her staff was spreading her business around, anyway? She couldn't help wondering if Monheno heard the one about her dashing out onto the veranda in her nightdress.

"Well," he grinned, "you'll forgive me if I don't hold your horse." He stepped back and clasped his hands behind himself.

She heard a nervous giggle rush from her lips. Why were her hands trembling all of a sudden? "Of course." She slipped Nantucket's reins over his head and tied him to a nearby tree. "I wouldn't want you to get hurt."

He took the picnic from his horse and untied the red blanket that wrapped it "Thank you." He spread out an abundance of wine, cheese, tortillas, and apples. "Lunch?"

She crossed her arms over her swirling stomach and wandered a few steps closer to the picnic blanket. "Nantucket's a good horse," she heard herself say nervously. "I've been very pleased with him."

He sat down on the blanket and motioned for her to do the same. "Why don't you ride one of those fine palominos?" he asked. "They were once the trademark of the Del Sol."

She looked into the misted woods around

111

them as she sat down on the edge of the blanket. "I sold them."

He made an almost inaudible sound that made her look over just in time to see a peculiar look on his face. In an instant, it was gone behind his mask. "Why did you do that?"

She lowered her brows and focused an intense gaze on him. "They were not functional." Why did he care if she sold a string of useless horses?

Monheno looked at his pretty companion for a minute before he answered. "Does everything have to be?" How could someone so beautiful have so little appreciation for beauty? "They were a pleasure to look at. Sometimes beauty is its own value."

She frowned, her pretty lips molding into a stubborn line. "Not for me," she said flatly. "Not for me."

Anger boiled up on the back of his neck. "You have the sentiments of a true American." He couldn't hide his contempt. Americans came west like a thousand crawling lice, stealing things, destroying things, sucking the life out of the land.

"I *am* an American." Her violet eyes hardened to a steely grey-blue.

That surprised him. "I thought you were British." He swirled a hand in front of his lips. "The accent."

She rolled her eyes and threw up her hands. "Good God, I'm tired of hearing about that! It is true that I have lived in London for some years, but I was born an American."

He let the subject drop. He wasn't here to fight with her, although she was charming when she was angry. He could think of better things to do.

He motioned toward their waiting meal. "Shall we eat?"

She looked adorably suspicious. "Shouldn't we wait for Brandt?"

"Brandt?" He'd forgotten about that little lie. "No, I think he'll be a while."

He could tell the brief slip didn't get by her unnoticed. She stood up at the edge of the blanket and braced her hands on her slim hips, eyes narrow strips of violet beneath heavy lashes. "He isn't coming, is he?" She leaned forward and glared at him. *"Is* he?"

He didn't feel the slightest bit guilty. "No," he admitted. "In fact, I suspect he's still wandering around the hacienda wondering where his picnic partner and her mount have gone."

Her gaze turned deadly. "What!" She took a threatening step forward. "You mean you just left without telling him?"

He stood up—just in case she decided to do something violent. "More or less." Savanna Storm had to be the stiffest woman he'd ever met, but also the most fascinating. "But you see, I was doing a lady a favor."

"And *what* lady was *that?"*

Now he couldn't tell her the truth about that.

She really would think he was a cad. Arranging a liaison for a bride on her wedding day wasn't exactly respectable. "A lady who shall remain nameless," he said slyly. "She was, you might say, interested in retaining the company of Mister Wade for this morning, and she implored me to help her." He threw his hands up and tried to look innocent. "Call me a fool, but I can never refuse the request of a lady."

She stiffened visibly. "Well, in that case," she said, clenching her hands in front of her like a school marm, "I'll request that you take me back to the hacienda."

It was exactly the response he would have expected from such a proper young lady. "And spoil such a lovely morning?" Interesting, she didn't kiss like a proper young lady. There was definitely much more to her than met the eye. "Surely, you wouldn't want me to do that?"

"I would," she glared at him, her face flushed with anger.

"Would you?" He stepped across the blanket, smiling at her. The lady was protesting a little too much.

She didn't back away. "I would." Her lips parted on the heels of the words.

He couldn't have kept from kissing her if he wanted to. He couldn't even say why exactly. Something about her just . . . fascinated him, made him want her.

He parted her lips and tasted her . . . so sweet. She didn't resist, but returned his kiss with the same passion he saw in those violet eyes. He felt her hands slide over his chest, small, warm, over his heart and caught it. He parted from her and looked down into her hooded eyes.

"Are you certain of that?"

Savanna felt his words brush past her like an August wind—searing, passionate.

"No," she whispered, and she wasn't. She wasn't sure of anything except that she wanted him to kiss her again.

That hint of amusement was gone from his face—replaced by a dark, smoldering look. "What do you want, Savanna?"

She felt her hands tremble against his shirt. She couldn't answer, and he knew it. To protest would be ludicrous, to comply wanton. Yet she had to do something. They were together, alone . . .

"I want you to act like a gentleman," she heard herself say, "as you promised."

The corners of his lips twitched upward, rose into a devilish grin. He kissed her chastely on the forehead and let her go. "As you wish." He sat down on the picnic blanket and leaned comfortably back on one elbow. If the kiss affected him at all, he didn't show it.

Meanwhile, her legs were dissolving into marmalade, so she sat demurely on the other corner of the blanket. Why couldn't she catch her breath? She reached for the cup of wine he poured her and took a huge swallow. She needed something to calm her nerves.

He cut a long slice of cheese and handed it to her. "For how long?"

She didn't look at him, but watched the colors swirling on the surface of her wine instead. It was swirling like that in her stomach, too. "How long, what?"

She could feel him smiling again. "How long must I be a gentleman?"

She ran a finger along the rim of her enameled glass, then looked at him over the rim. "Until this wedding is over."

The heated look in his eyes said he would never make it that long.

But he did. He behaved with perfect decorum all that day, long into the evening as he danced with her at the wedding feast, and into the next day as the guests made ready to leave. The worst part of it was that it disappointed her.

He was perfectly collected, cool as a pillar of stone, while she melted every time he touched her, even looked at her. She even agreed when he asked if he could call on her the following Thursday. She wanted him to kiss her so badly she ached even after she told him goodbye and returned home.

Del Sol house seemed cold and empty when she came in. She walked to her study and looked slowly around. Everything was the same, why did she feel like something was missing now? Like *someone* was missing?

She rubbed her hands up and down her arms to warm the feeling away. Silly. Foolish. She had more important things to think about. The bad news of six more lost crewmen had assaulted her the minute she rode into the stable yard. That left the sheep men with too few to guard the herds, and it put Brandt in an impossible position. The cattle had to be moved to upland pastures during these summer months or they would never be fat enough for sale in the fall. But herds couldn't be moved without men . . .

She sighed and wandered across the room to the arched veranda doors. Drawing them open noiselessly, she stepped out into the evening breeze. The fresh, sweet scent of honeysuckle wrapped around her, drew her to the railing. Sliding her hands over the cool wood, she let her eyes fall shut, rolling her head from side to side. She was too exhausted to think about this today . . .

The sound of voices drifted on the air like a puff of smoke. Female laughter, girlish laughter, bubbled over the honeysuckle. Who was that? After all of the trouble with the Sombras, there were no women here except for her and Esperanza.

Curious, she stood back from the railing and walked down the veranda. Stopping at the corner of the house, she listened. Nothing. Perhaps she didn't hear it at all. Perhaps . . .

Perhaps Waddie was entertaining a girl! Her eyes snapped open and she stopped in her tracks. There they stood behind a wall of overgrown shrubs that would hide them from the bunkhouse—the two of them clasped in each others' arms, the girl throwing back her dark head and laughing. She slipped out of his grasp, threw an arm over her head and danced a gleeful little swirl in the dust, then giggled again before he recaptured her.

They came together in a kiss, and Savanna flushed. Why was she watching this? She took a silent step backward before they could see her. It was none of her business if Waddie had a girl. He was a sweet young man. He deserved for some decent young lady to love him. Of course, decent young ladies didn't meet their beaus behind hedges in the thick of the evening.

The girl's laughter tinkled in her ears again. Why did it grate on her mind and sound vaguely familiar? Why did she seem to know it?

It hit her as she was walking up the stairway to her bedroom. She stopped, shook her head and started up again. Surely Waddie's girl was not the same one who hung like a leech on Monheno Devilla at the wedding—although the girl was young enough for Waddie.

"Good Lord, Savanna, listen to yourself," she scolded under her breath. "You sound like an ornery old cat ready to claw someone's eyes out." She shook her head at herself and went on into her room.

She found her bath already prepared. Esperanza again, bless her. Somehow she always knew. Wearily, she slipped from her skirt and then slowly unbuttoned the small pearl buttons on her blouse. Slipping it off tiredly, she tossed it on the bed. The breeze from the veranda doors kissed her bare shoulders as she stood in her chemise, and she walked to the doors to push them closed behind the curtains.

Voices outside caught her ear. Perhaps Waddie and his girl had changed locations. She stepped back behind the curtain, covered herself with it and peered around the door.

The yard below was dim with the last shadows of the descending sun, but she could see two men standing in the shadow of a spring house not far away. Who were they? Why were they standing in the shadows like they were hiding something? Were they two more men planning to sneak away from the Del Sol's employ? If she lost two more men, there would be no hope. She had to know what was going on.

She slipped back into her clothes and blew out the lamp. Lowering herself to her knees, she crawled silently back to the balcony, and slipped through the curtain carefully. Her knees scraped faintly on the tile as she slid to the railing and peered over. They were still there. She could hear their conversation now, but they were speaking Spanish. She listened, even though she couldn't understand, and watched their animated movements. They were making plans . . .

Her heart caught as one stepped out of the shadows and turned her way. He was masked!

A Sombra! She glanced back at the second man just in time to see him duck away from the building and stride off toward the bunkhouse like he belonged there. One of her men!

It came together in her mind with the clarity of lightning. One of her men was working with the Sombras—at least one, perhaps more. The bandits weren't just shadows in the night, they were living under her nose, able to sabotage the Del Sol at will.

Brandt was looking at her like a second head
had popped from her shoulder. "Are you out
of your mind!"

## Seven

Brandt was looking at her like a second head
had popped from her shoulder. "Are you out
of your mind!" As if to humiliate her further,
he started to grin.

Savanna leveled a stubborn gaze at that smile,
wishing she could wipe it from his face. It was
one thing to be argued with, but it was quite
another to be patronized. "You said you haven't
enough herdsmen, so I've solved the problem.
Between myself, Manuel, Jose, and the men that
are left, you should have enough to take the
Rocky Branch herd out." She motioned to the
two Mexican youths who stood behind her looking somewhat confused but also eager for a
chance to be promoted to the cow crew. Both
ducked behind her like nervous kittens as
Brandt lowered a finger at them.

"I'm not having those two mutton punchers
on my cow crew! If there's one thing I got no
respect for, it's a sheep herder!" He paused long

enough to suck in a huge breath of air, then aimed his finger at her. "And as for you, the cow range is no place for a lady. We're apt to be gone for three, four days."

She threw up her hands in exasperation. Damn him for going against her here in front of everyone. The last thing the men needed to see now was chaos. "Manuel and Jose both ride well enough to work cattle." At least, they said they could. She hoped it was true or she was going to end up looking like a complete fool. "And they have experience herding."

"There's a hell of a difference between lightning-quick steers and those range maggots." He waved a hand toward a far-off herd of sheep. "And the cow range ain't no place for a *lady*."

She narrowed her eyes beneath the brim of her hat and leveled a stare that would have set a grizzly bear's knees to trembling. "I am perfectly capable of chasing after a flock of cattle." She knew something sounded wrong as soon as she said it. Did cattle come in flocks?

He puffed two chuckles, then burst out laughing. "Well, I guess . . . you're not . . . giving in." He was so out of breath he could barely speak, his blue eyes sparkling with tears. "Would you rather ride in front of the flock or behind it?" He heehawed again and started toward his horse. "Doesn't matter. Steers of a feather flock together." Mounting his sorrel gelding, he trotted off toward the herd. "Hey boys, flock 'em up and move 'em out!"

Her face burning, she turned back to her newly promoted cowhands and gave them a curt nod that sent them scurrying to their horses. Irritably, she stalked off to the barn where Nantucket waited saddled, but safely hidden in his stall. Brandt would probably blow his cork completely when he saw her riding Nantucket. Unfortunately, with nearly half of the remuda lost to the Sombras, there was nothing left that wasn't lame or wind-broken. She could only hope Nantucket had gained some sense since his last terrible encounter with cow work.

One look at her cow crew as she rode to the herd told her they weren't pleased to have her or Nantucket along. They moved away from her like she was a leper, and grumbled among themselves. She couldn't catch every word, but the meaning was clear. Women and mutton-punchers were bad luck, and her horse was a hell-spawn. Well, let them talk. They didn't know it, but she was listening—watching them for any indications of who might be working with the Sombras. If the infiltrator was on her cow crew, she would find him out sometime during this trip. She had only to watch and listen.

They glared at her from beneath their hats as Brandt called them together to dole out the assignments.

Only Waddie spoke to her. "I see you're ridin' Nan." He rubbed his bruised ribs and looked worried.

She nodded. If anything happened to her as

123

a result of riding the gelding Waddie would blame himself. "He's the only mount left that's fit for the trip," she whispered. "And, besides, I've ridden him all over the valley and haven't had a bit of trouble."

Waddie nodded, still looking unconvinced. "Just be careful not to git him in a bind. Don't git him penned in betwixt the cattle. That's when he goes crazy, and don't . . ."

She sent him a warning look that stopped him.

He flushed and glanced down at her saddle. "Are you sure you can ride all day in that thing?"

Despite her trembling hands, she smiled back. Confidence. Composure. How could she expect anyone else to believe in her if she didn't believe in herself? "All day and all night and all day." She hoped. She'd never ridden longer than a few hours in her life. "I'll take an English rig over those of yours any day of the week."

He shrugged. "Guess that'd be your choice, ma'am." His name came up in the assignments and he paused to listen. "But you wouldn't catch me in one of them things if it was ten degrees below freezin' hell outside and that was the only way to git to a fire." He blushed. "Oh, excuse me . . . freezin' heck."

She laughed and shook her head at him as he rode away with the others to take his position around the herd. She waited until Brandt was alone before she rode over to him. He glared at her mount, his face turning angry red.

"What do you want me to do?" She tried to sound matter-of-fact, all business.

He gave an irritated snort. "Go back to the house."

She tipped her chin up and shook her head.

"In that case," he shrugged toward the herd. "Fall in behind em about twenty foot and ride drag. Try to keep 'em—flocked up, but don't push 'em into a trot."

He spun his mount around and trotted away, shaking his head and grumbling under his breath. When he reached the front of the herd, he swung his arm over his head and called to the crew. "Come on, boys, let's move 'em out!"

A little shiver of excitement tickled up and down her spine as the herd milled up and moved slowly forward. This would be a great adventure—like she read about in the tabloids. This new life was difficult, but at least it wasn't dull. It was full of adventure and spice. Through all those years in London, she missed her freedom, and now she had it back.

A half day later, she was finding out that freedom came with a price. She was also figuring out why her foreman looked so pleased with himself when he told her to ride behind the herd. Dragging along in the hot dust and sweaty stench of the herd was by far the worst job available. No doubt Brandt thought she couldn't take it. No doubt he thought she would run for home after only a few hours.

That made her all the more determined to stay. They could tease and humiliate her all they wanted, they could make her get off and *walk* behind the herd, they could stake her naked to an ant hill, but she wasn't going home.

Unfortunately, her body didn't agree. She hadn't ridden all day since childhood, and every joint in her legs was screaming for relief by the time Brandt brought the herd up for a midday break.

The tired herd milled easily in the mid-afternoon heat, and the drovers hurried off to rest in the shade of a small grove of trees. She followed them, noting with satisfaction that her two makeshift herders were working out well. Both were fairly skilled riders, and Jose was good with a lariat rope.

"Where'd you learn to rope like that, son?" Black Jim asked as he dismounted his horse and loosened his cinch.

"I rope de dead tree stump when de sheeps grazeeng." The boy looked at Jim with obvious admiration.

Black Jim grinned, his teeth white against his brown face. "'Well, you ain't a bad hand, son, and don't let any of them boys tell you different. You stick to it and you'll be a cowman one day." He started off toward the woods. "If any of them gives you trouble, you just come and tell Black Jim, y'hear?"

Savanna smiled at her two new cowhands and reached up to pull Nantucket's saddle off. She was going to make Brandt eat his words yet.

He passed her on his way to the woods. "No need to unsaddle." He gave her a self-satisfied smirk. "We won't be here for long."

She ignored his presence and continued with what she was doing. "Don't worry." She forced a sing-song voice. Her backside felt like anything but singing—or perhaps it was only singing a different tune. "I can have him tacked back up before the rest of you can get the cinches knotted on your rigs."

Her jab at their western-style saddles drew a collective guffaw from her cowboys, and one of them called out, "Yeah, but can you tie a steer on that thing?"

She shrugged as she walked to where the rest of them were sitting and sat down herself. "Reckon not." Her accent made them all laugh again. "But can you jump a fence without getting stabbed in the stomach by your saddle horn?"

That made them all laugh so hard the nearby steers skittered away.

She nodded triumphantly and took out the small lunch Esperanza packed for her. It was better than the hardtack and dried beef the rest of them were eating, but their envious glances didn't make her feel the slightest bit guilty. If they were in the desert and she had the only canteen, she wouldn't give a sip of water to the lot of them. She smiled at them and bit into a fresh slice of bread. Let them eat cake . . .

She felt almost invisible as they joked back and forth about the events of the morning, laughing away the tension that kept them tight as fiddle strings all morning. Driving such a big herd with only three points, seven flank riders, and two drag riders was dangerous, and everyone knew it.

"Yeah, they been a pretty lazy flock so far." That from the usually quiet Hal Calfort.

She shot him a murderous sideways glance. Good Lord, couldn't they think of anything else to joke about? There were so many new terms to remember, how was she supposed to keep them all straight? Besides, she had a hundred more important things to think about than whether animals came in a herd or a flock. She had a hundred more important things to be doing right now than driving cattle, but the steers had to be moved now. Besides, this trip might help her find the infiltrator.

Her mind drifted slowly away from the conversation—to where it always drifted, Monheno Devilla. What was that strange power he had over her? How could she be so angry with him one minute and kissing him the next? Impossible! How in the world did he coax her into it?

The truth was, she enjoyed her picnic with Monheno Devilla—enjoyed telling him about Africa. She liked the way he seemed so interested in what she had to say. She'd never been with a man who listened so raptly to her. It was a wonderful sensation.

She liked listening to him, too. He knew so much about Mexico and the giant Mayan and Aztec cities there, now abandoned for centuries. He had to be an educated man, he was so full of knowledge.

The worst thing was that her favorite part of her picnic was the part where he *wasn't* being a gentleman. She could hardly stand to admit that, even to herself. The truth was, she was sorry she hadn't let him kiss her again. That kiss in the woods haunted her. *What do you want, Savanna?* She could hear him asking that, could feel his kiss now as if it were happening all over again. A tingle shot down her spine and stirred her stomach.

May I call on you on Thursday . . . if I promise to be a gentleman? He asked her that as they parted. Those raven eyes held hers and she couldn't say no. Today was Thursday. What would he think when he came to Del Sol house and found her gone?

A guilty feeling slid over her like a cool shadow. She should have sent a message telling him not to come. She knew, of course, why she hadn't. If she sent a note, he would have asked what other day he might come to call. She would have had to answer. By leaving a note for him at Del Sol house, she was running away from the question.

That wouldn't solve the problem forever and

she knew it. Sooner or later, she would have to face Monheno Devilla and tell him it simply wouldn't be proper for her to see him anymore. She was, after all, an unmarried lady with no guardian, and he was a man of very dubious reputation, particularly where women were concerned. If they spent time together, people would start to talk.

Perhaps her note would make him angry enough that he wouldn't come back again, and then the matter would be settled. Her heart sank to her feet even as she thought it. Why did she feel like she was losing something? Monheno Devilla wasn't hers. She didn't want him to be. So why did she think of him constantly? Why did she see him, feel him when she ate, when she tallied her books, when she rode, when she sat alone in Del Sol house, even when she slept?

Dear God, was she falling in love?

It didn't matter. She wouldn't let herself fall for a man like that—or any man. Her father was handsome, suave, exotic, all the things Monheno was. It didn't make him a good man. He ruined her mother's life and finally killed her. Marriage was a trap, especially to a man like that.

Monheno could try all he wanted. She'd be no fool. When it came to men, she had a chunk of ice in her heart so solid even a blaze like Monheno couldn't melt it.

But that ice didn't keep her from worrying about him the whole rest of the day as they mounted up and moved the steers on. It didn't keep her from wondering what he said when Esperanza gave him her note, and whether he was angry. It didn't keep her from thinking about where he might be as they milled the cattle up for the night and made camp.

Cow camp wasn't much for luxury, but she was too exhausted to care. Wearily, she sat down to the supper the cook prepared in the mess wagon. She wasn't quite sure what the meal was—there was some talk about it being rattlesnake stew—but she suspected it was venison. It didn't matter, she could eat horse meat as long as it was hot. Horse meat wouldn't be much different, anyway, because the stew tasted like salt, pepper, and sage.

Across from her, Brandt eyed her with something suspiciously like unmitigated glee. The other men gave her a wide berth. She probably looked somewhat less than social. She hesitated to even imagine the picture. Her hair had fallen from its braid and now hung in loose, dirty tatters on her shoulders. Her face felt as though it had an inch of dust caked to it—and it probably did. Her body ached so badly she could hardly move, but it hurt to sit still also.

Even with all of that, she still wasn't sorry she came. Today she saw miles and miles of wild country—country which belonged to the Del Sol, and she was more determined than ever to keep it.

"You still think you want to join the cow crew?" Brandt smirked from behind his plate.

She raised her chin defensively and shrugged back her dirty tresses. "I'm not sorry I came. I've been through worse." That was a lie—she couldn't even imagine worse. Nothing in her years on the pampered London social set prepared her for this. "I suppose you thought you'd be rid of me by giving me the worst job on the crew."

"I suppose," he laughed a little, shaking his head at her. "But now I can see now you're stuck like a fly on the grease bucket."

She chuckled a little at his analogy. She probably looked about as attractive as a fly on the grease bucket. "We all do what we have to." It was as simple as that. The Del Sol had a need, and she intended to fill it. If tomorrow the orchard workers walked out, she'd be on a ladder picking apples—whatever it took to get through the dry season until the money came in.

He frowned and leaned forward a bit, his eyes catching the firelight, "Seems to me it'd be a hel—pardon—heck of a lot easier just to give Venenoso his money and let the Del Sol get back to normal." She stiffened, and he slammed a fist against the ground. "Damnit, woman why do you have to be so stubborn about this? They're going to have their way. They're going to win. You're going to lose, and by the time it's all over there won't be enough left of the Del Sol to put back together."

Exhaustion and anger flared into a dangerous brew inside her, and she gave him a heated stare. She didn't need his criticisms when she was doing all she could.

"Paying them is not an option, because . . ." she snapped her lips shut. Perhaps she should just tell him the truth. But if he knew there was no money, even he might decide to leave, and she could not afford to lose him—the ranch could not afford to lose him. He was the backbone of the Del Sol, and without him, it would crumble. "Because they want a lot of money, and I won't be blackmailed."

"You're a fool." The words were harsh.

"Maybe so, but the Del Sol is all I have, and I'll do whatever is necessary to keep it." She looked away to hide the tears prickling in her throat. Blinking them back, she pretended to finish her dinner. She didn't look up as he got to his feet and went back to the mess wagon.

She set the plate aside and wiped the corners of her eyes, swallowing hard to keep from bursting into tears. Strength. Faith. She couldn't remember the last time she wanted so badly to cry—or the last time she wished she had someone to hold her like a child and tell her everything would be all right.

Maybe Brandt was right. Maybe everything she was doing was in vain. Maybe it was already too late to save the Del Sol, but what else could she do? She had nothing else.

She stared toward the fire where what was left of her cow crew now lounged against their saddles. How would she pay them when the end of the month came? The sale of the palominos paid them for last month—but just barely. There was still at least one more month to go before any revenue could be expected. Perhaps she could secure a loan . . .

The sound of music took her thoughts away. She looked up to see Black Jim near the fire with his guitar. She'd often heard him play on the bunkhouse porch.

The sweet notes washed past her like a breeze and into the night. Standing up slowly, she returned her plate to the mess wagon, and then went to the fire to listen. If anyone thought she was out of place there, they didn't show it. She stretched her aching legs out in front of her, leaned back on her hands and gazed up at a million stars.

"He left from the cattle, to town he was
   headed,
Headed to town, some drink for to find,
I found him in the morning, laid there by
   the streetside
Shot in the breast and I knew he would die,"

She listened absently to the sad tale of a misguided young cowboy mortally wounded in a bar room fight. Her mind drifted away for a while then, and came back as he ended the song.

"So we beat the drum slowly and played the
   fife lowly

Tears we did weep as we bore him away,
For he was our comrade, brave, young, and
   handsome,
We prayed his forgiveness on that judgment
   day."

As if to emphasize the finality of the song,
the painted snake rattles hanging from his guitar keys swayed, hissing an eerie sound that ran
up and down her spine.

The listeners grew quiet—as though each were
thinking about the sad tale. Jim livened up the
tune on the guitar, and elbowed Brandt. "Give
us a tune, there, boss."

The foreman cleared his throat grandly, and
started to sing, his voice deep and melodious,

> "My Spanish gal was a lovely miss,
> Sweet as dew when she was mine,
> Twas a year I spent with her,
> Down below that border line."

Around him, the cowboys chuckled apprecia-
tively, as though they were all privy to some inside joke. It probably had something to do with
his ill-fated love affair with the Baca daughter.

The music continued as the air around them
grew cold and misty. Finally heads started to
nod around the fireside. Black Jim finished a
last song and everyone got up to head for their
bedrolls.

Raymond Devine, the oldest member of the

cow crew was the last up from the fire. "Keep an ear tuned toward your horses, boys," he called. "There might be Indians about tonight."

Several of the men scoffed as if they weren't overly concerned, but Savanna stopped in her tracks. Indians? Raymond Devine would know if anyone did. Rumor was that he helped run the Comanches out of East Texas.

She'd read all sorts of stories about wild savages long before she came to America. She'd even hoped, in a perverse way, to see some while traveling west, but she was sadly disappointed. Benjamin, the halfbreed Hopi on the cow crew was the closest thing to an Indian she'd ever seen.

Was she really going to see Indians now? What if Indians were seeing *her*? She shivered and looked off toward Nantucket's picket line. If the men were going to check their horses, she should check hers also. She couldn't be part of the crew if she couldn't take care of her horse.

Outside the circle of the firelight, the night was so dark she could barely see where she was walking. The moon, which would be nearly full, hadn't yet risen. If there were Indians out here she was liable to stumble over one. If an Indian chased her, she wouldn't have the energy to escape.

She stopped, looked over her shoulder toward the camp, and wrapped her arms around herself uncomfortably. Please, God, don't let there be any Indians out here. I'm not ready for Indians tonight . . .

She wasn't used to being outside alone after dark. It was eerie to know there was no house or barn nearby. She never liked the dark anyway, had always slept with a lamp. If only there were some light out here . . .

She gritted her teeth and walked on to Nantucket's picket line. She found him as she left him—picketed and hobbled, happily munching the last of his grain. Leaning close to him, she patted him on the flank, sending a cloud of dust into the air that made her cough.

She startled a few of the cattle. She heard them bellow and scamper away.

"Miss Savanna?" The sound of a voice made her heart bound into her throat.

A few paces away, she could see Hal Calfort, the night guard, on his horse. She could barely make out his face as he leaned forward in his saddle and squinted at her.

"Ma'am? What are you doin' here?"

She lowered her hands casually to her sides and swallowed her heart back into place. "Checking on my horse." She tried to sound like she knew what she was doing. "I heard there might be Indians about."

He tipped back his hat and gave a long, low laugh that sounded remotely like the gasp of a dog choking on a bone. "Why, someone's been pullin' your leg, ma'am," he drawled. "There ain't nothin' around here but mission Indians—hasn't been for years."

"Oh." She couldn't think of much else to say. She felt ridiculous. She was going to strangle Raymond Devine. "Well, I guess I'll go back then." She turned around and headed back toward the camp.

"D'ya want me to walk with ya?" he called after her.

"No, I'll be all right," she lied. She wished she could have him guide her back, but she couldn't be a liability. "Thank you, Hal." She fixed an eye on the mess wagon lamp and started back, grumbling under her breath. Raymond was going to pay for this.

He was bedded down with the rest of the men by the time she stumbled back to the fire. She heard him chuckle in his bedroll as she took her blanket from the wagon. She threaded her way through the sleeping men until she reached the sound, then swung back a boot and kicked at his blankets.

"Oooffff!" he bellowed.

She grinned to herself and moved on. "My goodness," she chirped. "I must learn to watch where I'm going."

"Don't go too far," one of the other men called, his voice cracking with laughter. "Indians might get ya."

"Nah," she recognized Black Jim's voice this time, "Indians be more interested in that flock a' cattle."

138

"Well, there's also snakes," someone else went on.

She closed her ears to it. She was determined not to listen. They were just trying to frighten her, and it wasn't going to work.

She laid her bedroll out a short distance away. Sitting down atop it, she pulled off her boots and pushed the top of one into the top of the other to keep insects from crawling in—or snakes . . .

A plan crept into her mind, and she smiled to herself. Two could play at this game. If it was jokes they wanted, jokes they would get . . .

# Eight

Revenge is sweet. She bit her lip and tried not to giggle. She couldn't give her plan away now—not after she woke early and constructed it so carefully.

She rode Nantucket a short distance away and waited impatiently. Surely the men would be getting on their horses soon. A giggle slipped past her lips as Brandt called to them to mount up. They'd have a surprise when they did, and she couldn't wait to see it.

As she hoped, Ray Devine was the first one to his horse—a skittish sorrel cayuse that was notoriously feisty. He always humped up and bucked a few times when mounted first thing in the morning. She just hoped he went true to form today.

As soon as Devine started into the saddle, she knew she wasn't going to be disappointed. The sorrel started sideways as soon as Ray put a foot in the stirrup.

Devine jerked up the reins and hollered. "Stop that you oar-headed mule!" Impatiently, he swung his foot over and slipped it into the far stirrup.

The horse jigged to the side nervously, then rolled his eyes and snorted like he'd never seen a rider before. An instant later, he sprang straight into the air as if perched on a giant spring. Devine flew a foot out of the saddle and bellowed like a wounded goat when he slapped back down. The horse jumped into the air again, blowing and snorting wildly.

A new sound, an unmistakable sound, rattled above the commotion.

"Snaaake!" somebody hollered. Cowboys and horses flew in all directions as the sound of snake rattles surrounded them.

Devine's horse flew into a rage, bumped and crashed through the line of running cowboys and spooked horses, then spun around and started back again. Devine flew out of the saddle, slammed back down, flew up, slammed down, flew up, landed on the horses's tail end, and sailed through the air like a cannonball. He hit the ground with a thud, popped back up, and started running, looking wildly around his feet for rattlesnakes.

Savanna backed Nantucket a little farther away and laughed until tears streamed down her cheeks. Revenge was absolutely delicious. She'd never in her life seen anything so hilarious! The snake dance more than vindicated her for their jokes on her yesterday.

She wiped her eyes and looked at the men, hopping about like wild Indians, and the crazed sorrel, turning to make another pass through the crowd, six brightly painted snake rattles still flying from his saddle. They looked better there than they did hanging from Black Jim's guitar.

A blurred movement caught the corner of her eye, and she looked into the distance to see a rider approaching at a slow, easy lope. Even through the haze of tears in her eyes, she knew that blood bay horse, and the rider. Monheno Devilla. How could it be? What was he doing here? Was something wrong at the Del Sol?

Her laughter caught in her throat. She reached up and wiped the tears from her dusty cheeks, then pulled her hat off and straightened her hair.

What should she say? Should she welcome him? Her mind spun with possible greetings—everything from frosty rebukes to gracious welcomes. Why was he there?

A grin creased his face as he slid his horse to a stop beside Nantucket. He glanced at the chaos below, then suspiciously at her. "A little cow camp fun?"

She couldn't help it. She burst out laughing again, and finally choked out, "All . . . in the interest of . . . fair play."

He tipped his head back and gave her a look like he was seeing her for the first time.

She caught her breath. "Why, Monheno, don't look so surprised," she tried to sound honey-sweet. "I can play their game just as well as any man."

He chuckled. "Better, it seems." He looked back down at the ensuing disaster in camp. "Now tell me, how did such a demure young lady manage to cause all that trouble?"

"It was easy," she confessed. Things below were beginning to water down. They'd soon figure out what happened. "I equipped Devine's saddle with a snake rattle while he was eating breakfast."

The men below were clearly figuring things out.

She wiped the tears from her eyes with the back of her glove. "The thing is," laughter pressed her throat as Devine unraveled the snake rattle from his cinch, "I didn't know it would work so well." She burst out laughing as Devine raised the snake rattles above his head and shook them at her.

"I imagine one of those Indians put it there," she called. The shocked expressions of the men made her work all the more worth while. This was the high point of her cattle drive—of her whole trip west—perhaps of her life.

Monheno laughed with her, a thick, genuine sound that covered her like a warm blanket. "They're impressed," he observed. "You'll have them in your hip pocket now." He sounded a

143

little disappointed, and she cocked a quizzical brow at him. Why was he here, anyway?

"What are you doing here?" She tried to sound as though she wasn't elated to see him, but it didn't work.

A devilish twinkle rose in his eyes. "Happened by?" He raised his dark brows to see if she would swallow it.

"Hardly likely." She surveyed the empty land around them incredulously.

He sagged forward in his saddle, looking falsely wounded. "You're right," he admitted. "I rode all this way through the dead of night just to see you."

"But why?"

"I couldn't wait until you returned to see you again." The words slid off his tongue like quicksilver.

A hot rush came over her, made her feel like she might swoon. How was a woman supposed to resist that? "How . . . how did you find us?"

He lowered one brow like he couldn't believe the question. "Several hundred head of steers don't exactly move without a trail." He waved a hand toward the herd, then leaned against his saddle horn and caught her eyes. "If you were trying to hide from me, you should have chosen another way."

She shook her head numbly, unable to withdraw her eyes from his. She wished there weren't a half-dozen cow hands staring at them. She wanted him to kiss her. What a terribly improper notion! One look at Monheno Devilla filled her with improper notions. She'd been with many a handsome man in her life and never had that problem before. Perhaps the wild life in America was eroding her morals . . .

"Well, I'm afraid I really haven't time to visit." It was a silly thing to say. "We have to get the herd on to other pastures and we're a few hands short, so I'm afraid I'm being kept quite busy." She fidgeted nervously with the reins, staring at her fingers. "We all are."

As usual, her lukewarm reception slid off him like water. "I can see that." He slid his hat back, making the string of small silver conchos hanging from his stampede string jingle like bells. "Well then, you shouldn't mind a little extra help from a well-meaning neighbor."

Shock held her speechless for a moment. Monheno Devilla offering to help? Not likely. "You mean to ride along with us?" She wasn't sure whether she hoped he would or hoped he wouldn't.

He acted like the notion was a great surprise to him. "Well, now that I've been invited, I'd love to." He scratched his chin, made a great show of thinking about it. "Um-hum . . . yes, I can think of nothing I'd like better than spending a few days helping you . . ." a long pause, and then, "drive your cattle."

She was so caught by his devilish smile, she barely heard the words. Letting him go along would be foolish, reckless. He wasn't here be-

145

cause he was interested in her cattle. She knew it. He knew it.

"Well, if you're serious . . ." When was he ever? "We could certainly use your help." Stupid. Foolish. Insane. Why was she doing this? She knew why he was here. As much time as he spent gambling, he probably didn't know one end of a steer from the other.

That turned out to be the one thing about Monheno Devilla she misjudged. An extra-long day on the trail proved him to be a skilled hand with cattle, and even better with a rope than Black Jim.

As for herself, she had finally done something right. Her little prank on Ray Devine changed her crew's attitude dramatically. She seemed to have won their respect. They stopped teasing her and started letting her help, even though she was still riding drag. Even Ray Devine spent a few minutes teaching her how to swing a lasso. It wasn't hard, all in the wrist, sort of like croquet.

"If you're gonna do much ropin'," Devine said as he rode off, "you're gonna have to quit ridin' that pimple and get yourself a real saddle."

Monheno thought that was funny. He got quite a laugh out of it until she finally turned a murderous gaze on him.

"Why are *you* laughing?" Riding behind the herd with him all day had put her nerves on edge. She couldn't concentrate. Wherever she looked, there he was. When she wasn't looking at him, she could feel him watching her, could feel those smoldering eyes following her.

"No reason." His voice was like silk. "I was thinking that the very proper Brit I met in town a month ago wouldn't be caught dead chasing after steers."

She wasn't sure whether to feel offended or complimented. Was he calling her prim, or was he saying she'd come a long way, or did he mean she was no longer a proper lady?

"Oh, you think not?" Why did she care what he thought? "Well, I'll have you know I didn't spend all of my time in London making needle-points and drinking tea. I also learned how to break a horse and handle a rifle." She didn't add that those were completely forbidden activities.

Monheno resisted the urge to smile. She had the most seductive pout, underlip jutting out just slightly. It was incredibly tempting. "Yes, you're quite a hand with both." He wanted to kiss those beautiful lips . . .

He barely heard her foreman give the milling call. "Mill 'em up, boys, mill 'em up."

Ahead, the point riders turned the leading cattle back into the herd. He and Savanna pushed the trailing cattle forward until the herd came to a standstill. Hungry and tired, the cattle settled quickly down to graze and drink from the small creek nearby, and the drovers moved off toward the mess wagon.

147

He watched them go, then turned to his pretty companion. She wasn't watching him, but looking out at the cattle, thinking probably. She was always thinking, planning, worrying—not the kind of woman that usually caught his attention. What did he find so fascinating about her? Why was he here when he had a dozen other things to attend to?

Maybe because she needed someone to save her from her own foolishness. She'd already come after the Sombras with a rifle. It was only a matter of time before she made the mistake of firing a shot. He . . .

She turned those bright eyes his way, and he lost the thought. Violet, like an evening sky, they stared into his as if to read his mind, as if to touch his soul, as they did in his dreams. He glanced toward the nearby hills to break the spell. Women always were his downfall.

She followed his gaze, her face curious, suspicious. An idea lit in his thoughts, and he turned his horse toward the hills. Any second now she would ask . . .

"Where are you going?" Her brows drew together in the center of her forehead, and she tossed a long strand of golden hair impatiently over her shoulder.

He looked sideways at her without turning his face, grinned just enough to make her suspicious. "Come along and find out," he taunted.

Savanna frowned and glanced nervously over her shoulder at the departing herders. What was

Monheno up to this time? "But . . . the sun is almost down." It wasn't really, but she wasn't going to be taken in this time.

He followed her gaze to the crew, headed for camp. "They have plenty to do for a while," that quicksilver voice again, flowing over her, beckoning her. "They won't miss you, and if they do, they'll only think you've gone off to tend to—personal needs."

She blushed fiercely. "With you?" she scoffed. Why were her hands sweating on the reins? "I doubt that is what they'll think."

"They won't know if we leave right now." There was a glint of the devil in his eye. "Look, they're all turned the other way. We can be over the top of the hill before they notice." He met her eyes and held them, sent her heart fluttering against her chest with his challenge. "Come, Savanna, show some of that wild abandon you're so proud of. I promise you won't be sorry you came."

He spun his horse around and sent the animal charging toward the crest of the nearest hill.

She grasped Nantucket's reins to keep him from following. She had only a split second to make her choice. The men would reach the mess wagon any minute, then they'd turn around and see her . . .

Her heart rushed into her throat, and stopped. She couldn't breathe, couldn't think. She couldn't go through with this.

But she couldn't stop herself. She spun Nantucket around and charged after him. This wasn't wild abandon, it was insanity. In a moment, she was beside his big bay, racing over the crest of the hill and down the other side.

At the end of the valley, the passage narrowed until they couldn't ride abreast. She pulled up her reins and let him move ahead. The trail worsened, turned rocky, and led up a bolder-strewn slope. She pulled Nantucket to a trot, but ahead, Monheno guided his mount through the maze at lightning speed, following a trail he seemed to know by instinct.

Finally she had to let her horse go to keep from losing sight of him. The trail flashed by around her, clattered under Nantucket's feet. Wind whined in her ears, high, thrilling, and blood pulsed through her body like a whitewater tide. One missed step and they'd fall into the canyon below. This was crazy! Was Monheno out of his mind?

He stopped finally and her mount almost ran into his.

"Are you insane?" The words rushed out of her mouth breathlessly. "Why in God's name did you go so fast?" She reached back and re-covered her hat from the stampede string around her neck.

"For the excitement." He grinned. "Tell me you didn't find it . . . exciting."

She had the distinct feeling he was talking about more than their harrowing trip up the rocky trail. "You have a strange sense of excitement." She would not be lured into his trap this time. She peered up the trail. "Why are we here?"

He gave a throaty laugh and rested an elbow casually on his saddle, leaning toward her. "Savanna," he admonished, his eyes smoldering like two coals about to ignite, "Where is your sense of adventure?"

His charm dragged a smile from her. "Someplace about ten miles back down the trail." She was only half joking. Every muscle in her body was reminding her she'd already spent a long day in the saddle. She shouldn't have let Monheno lure her into his little adventure.

He took up his reins and sat back up in his saddle, "Let's see if we can't revive it." He spun the big bay around and walked on down the trail, rounded a bend and disappeared.

She gazed after him for a minute, considering turning around and going back. With a sigh, she moved Nantucket forward after him.

What she saw when she rounded the bend stunned her. The path opened into a small, lush valley green with thick grass and dotted with dancing pink flowers. On the far end, a high rock cliff face stretched toward the sky. A waterfall gurgled from a portal in one end, tumbling carelessly down into a bright pool on the valley floor. It was beautiful, but it wasn't what held her breathless.

The fragrant air caught in her throat as she stared at the massive rock cliff. It was painted like a giant artist's canvas, decorated with perhaps a dozen majestic figures—Spaniards in old-fashioned armor mounted on dancing horses. At the feet of the silent procession walked strange animals—alligators, lizards, mountain lions, monkeys, colorful birds, several other creatures she didn't know. All stood far larger than life, so gigantic that, even from fifty feet away, she could only look at one figure at a time.

A haunted, eerie feeling crept over her as she rode closer. Nantucket nickered, flicked his ears nervously, and tried to turn back. She forced him on toward Monheno, a dwarfed dark figure in front of the masterpiece.

"Where did it come from?" she whispered as she came to him beneath the shield of a giant Spaniard. "Who painted it?"

He turned his face up to the painting. "Indians," he told her. "It is hundreds of years old—painted when the conquistadors first came to this country."

Savanna couldn't take her eyes off it. Looking from one intricate detail to the next, she tried to imagine the undertaking of painting it. "It must have taken years," she whispered more to herself than to him. "Why did they paint it?"

"They were trying to understand something they feared," he replied softly. He leaned close to her, as if he wanted to see the mural exactly as she was seeing it. "The conquistadors were new to them, frightening gods. The Indians painted them here to gain power over their evil spirits. See, they surrounded them with their own spirit animals."

"It's fascinating." She twisted sideways in her saddle and suddenly realized how close he was. Close enough to kiss her. "Why were they afraid?" She wasn't thinking about the Indians anymore, or the painting. She was thinking about how handsome he was, and how much she wanted him to kiss her.

Monheno almost didn't hear her question. It was hard to concentrate on the words. He watched her lips part ever so slightly and her lashes lower sensuously over the deep violet of her eyes. "People are always afraid of things they've never known." He leaned closer, and in a breath against her waiting mouth, added, "But they shouldn't be."

She barely felt his lips touch hers at first—was only faintly aware of the feeling of his tongue tracing the outline of her lower lip. Tentatively, she responded to his coaxing, shivered as wild sensations shot through her.

Blood raced hot through her body, made her feel heady and feverish as he ran his hands slowly over her shoulders. He drew her closer, pressed her body against his, slid his fingers down her arms. She straightened, trembling as his hands slipped around her waist, touching just below her breasts, burning through her thin cotton shirt and chemise.

She drew in a sharp breath against his lips. No one had ever dared be that familiar with her before—she'd never allowed such an infringement of the rules. But here—here in this wild place there were no rules to follow . . .

Her hat tumbled soundlessly from her head, golden curls spilling from it as she leaned closer, absorbed by the fire of his kiss. She wanted to stop time right there—to linger in the excitement of a man for whom she felt such feverish desire.

Nantucket stepped sideways and she slipped from his arms. Embarrassed, she glanced up at Monheno. What must he be thinking of her! If Monheno felt embarrassed at all, it didn't show in his dark face. He smiled one-sidedly beneath lowered eyelids.

"Useless beast." He kicked a long leg over his horse's neck and slid to the ground.

She glanced down at Nantucket and blushed as Monheno walked to her and lifted her down from her saddle. She couldn't protest if she wanted to. Her voice was lodged behind a lump in her throat.

He offered his arm. "Let me show you the waterfall."

She nodded dumbly and tried to blink away the dizzy whirling in her head. Every muscle in her body throbbed rebelliously from some combination of fatigue and passion as she allowed herself to be led along like an addled pup.

When they reached the waterfall, he stood looking at it for a moment and then turned to her, a smoldering in his ebony eyes. She hoped he planned to kiss her again, and her lips parted unconsciously with the thought.

He didn't disappoint her. He took her in his arms again and tasted her lips, then moved slowly, featherlight along the curve of her chin. His breath tickled her ear as he drew her hair back, allowing him access to the pale velvet of her neck.

Her heart raced against her chest as his fingers slid aside the collar of her blouse, let him taste her, set her skin on fire. Slowly, fingers and lips descended lower to feel that thundering heart. He slipped open the buttons of her blouse, and the warm breeze flowed over her skin like water. Unconsciously, she let her head drop back, let a soft moan escape her lips as his touch brushed lightly over her breast. The nipple hardened, pressed against her chemise, yearning.

She felt him lift her into his arms then lower her into the soft grasses. Fragrant, slightly moist, they wrapped around her like thousands of sensual fingers coaxing her fears away. This was perfect, right . . .

A warm breeze dashed across the valley, pulled droplets of mist from the waterfall, tossed them over her like tiny diamonds in the waning sunlight. Eyes half-closed, she watched them glitter against her skin as his strong fingers touched her, dark against her pale skin.

She shuddered again as he collected the drops beaded at the top of her chemise, pressed the finger to his lips and tasted the moisture. He slid the chemise straps from her shoulders gently, kissed her, tasted her, drew the chemise down to expose her breasts.

Pleasure spiraled through her, carried her away from thoughts of protest. She could think of nothing but the softness of the grass, and the cool feeling of the spray, and the growing blaze of desire within her.

Dangerous sensations split through her like wild lightning as his tongue traced the outline of a breast—slowly, slowly moving toward the nipple, taunting it to hardness. She gasped, gripped the grass beneath her as he sucked her nipple into his mouth.

"Savanna," she heard him say her name, whispered like a line of poetry. "Savanna."

Somewhere in the fog of her thoughts, she realized he was speaking to her, his breath a faint stirring against her cheek.

"Savanna," he said again. "Open your eyes, mi corazon."

Slowly, she dragged her lashes up, looked up through the mist of passion. "Don't," she whispered, putting a trembling finger to his lips, knowing that any moment the spell could be broken. "Please don't . . ." She didn't know what to· ask for—how to ask him not to shatter the beautiful feeling that enveloped her. "Please don't stop."

She closed her eyes to guilt. There was no room for guilt—only for the realization of how much she wanted him to love her, of how much she wanted him to touch every inch of her.

He claimed her with a kiss, and she slipped back into the soft throws of passion—like drifting into a feather pillow. She shivered, trembled, exploded as he slipped her chemise down, his lips advancing as he drew the filmy fabric back. She slipped her arms free, let them fall to the ground over her head.

She writhed with impatient desire as he unbuttoned her skirt waist, his tongue tracing down the flat expanse of her stomach.

She lay exposed to his view in the soft grass before he rose to remove his own clothing. She stole a quick glance from beneath heavy lashes, daring to look no lower than the strong, solid muscles of his chest, and the flat, rippled cords of his stomach. He was magnificent, took her breath away.

She closed her eyes again when he came back to her, his body warm against her own, the very slight smattering of raven hair on his chest tickling her erect nipples. Her own heart pounded in her ears, thundered wildly as his strong hands ran up and down the length of her body. Could he feel it? It seemed like the very earth was vibrating beneath her.

A flicker of fear ran through her as his fingers moved over her legs and then between them to part her slim thighs. Slowly, tauntingly, he stroked toward her knees, made her quiver.

The trembling raced through her body as his

fingers drew closer to her womanhood. She gasped his name. Her body swayed to the rhythm of his touch, parted to welcome him over her. She stiffened as his manhood pressed against her, hard, insistent. He soothed her with soft sounds, coaxed her, caressed her, drove her wild until she raised her hips to meet the press of his manhood.

The pain of his entry lasted only for a heartbeat. He held her tightly in his arms until it subsided, whispered to her, then moved slowly within her. He kissed her again, and she joined his rhythm, gasped as he tasted her neck, her shoulders, her heaving breasts.

His rhythm intensified, built, fanned a strange, urgent tightening within her. She writhed against him, desperate for release, sought to bring him deeper within her. A cry burst from her lips as her soul exploded. She clung to him, met his last thrust, felt pleasure thunder through her, leaving her hot, then cold.

He held her for a long while in silence, her head cradled under the crook of his chin. Finally, he scooped her up and carried her to the inviting pool of water. Laughing, she swam with him until the waning day finally forced her back to reality. She blushed with new embarrassment as he walked from the pool. She averted her eyes as he slipped into his clothing, then glanced up as he gathered hers.

Standing at the edge of the water, he smiled. "Your clothes, my dear." He held them just out of her reach. "Though I prefer you without them."

Embarrassment and shame rushed over her like a cold wind. He was mocking her, laughing at her for surrendering her virtue to him. Oh God, how could she have been so foolish? What had she done? How could she have begged him to continue?

"I thought a cad like you didn't extend a lady such courtesies." It was a ridiculous statement considering what had happened.

He had the gall to look shocked at first, then he chuckled and offered a hand to help her from the water. "Perhaps I'm not the cad you thought I was."

"And perhaps I'm not the lady I thought I was." She batted his hand away and got out on her own. Her ears burned like they'd been set afire, as she snatched her clothing away and put it on. "Please take me back now."

"Savanna," he caught her arm as she started away, spun her around to face him, and drew her back into his embrace. "You are every inch a lady. Which is why you make me every inch a gentleman . . . well, almost."

She stared stubbornly past his shoulder. "A gentleman would come calling for me at my home, and wouldn't have such . . . unsuitable intentions." She didn't mention that she welcomed those intentions only a short time before.

He released her and stepped back, holding his hands palm up to show that there was nothing in them. "Now how do you know what my intentions are?" He cocked a brow confidently. "Perhaps my intentions are to marry you."

The statement seemed to shock even him. He fell silent for a moment, lost his composure, then regained it and gestured toward the horses. "We should go."

# Nine

Perhaps my intentions are to marry you. The words, his own words, repeated in Monheno's head as they rode back to camp. What made him say that to her? He'd said many things to many women, but never that.

From under the brim of his hat, he looked over at her, silent, pale, unmistakably angry. What was she thinking? Was she wondering if he meant it?

He stopped his horse just out of sight of the camp. "Go on in." They were the first words he'd said to her since they left the valley. "I will join you later." It would be best if her crew didn't see them coming back together.

Savanna kept her gaze fastened to her hands on the reins. "Yes," she heard herself mutter. She didn't know what else to say, how to act. What did a woman say when she'd willingly let herself be despoiled?

Shame and outrage burned into her cheeks.

Damn him! How could he sit there so cool, so silent after what he did to her, after what he took from her? How could he make false promises of marriage as if that would repair the damage?

How do you know what my intentions are? The memory burned through her mind as she left him and rode into camp. She knew exactly what his intentions were. She knew exactly what kind of man he was—a smooth-talking rake, a gambler just like her father. She knew now how her mother could have gone so wrong, how she could marry a man who would take her from her family, squander her fortune, eventually cost her her life. She never understood how a gentlewoman, well bred, intelligent, and beautiful could fall for a worthless rake like her father.

But she'd never known the allure of a man like Monheno Devilla, either. She was falling into the same trap. She couldn't let it go on. She wouldn't. She would get the help she needed from him and forget they ever met.

Tears prickled in her throat as she dismounted Nantucket and tied him to a tree. She swallowed hard to keep them back and started toward camp. The men barely seemed to notice as she walked in and sat down among them. They were occupied with finishing their meals, or were lying back against their saddles dozing. She took a plate from the cook and avoided the glances of the few who looked up at her. Could they see what she had done? Did it show?

162

Her stomach churned painfully as she picked at her meal and then set the plate aside. Pulling her knees in toward her chest, she gazed into the fire. Where was Monheno now? What would she say to him when he returned? How was she supposed to act? Surely everyone would suspect . . .

Mercifully, Monheno saved her the worry by not returning until most of the hands were in their bedrolls for the night. By the time he came back to the fire, only she, Brandt, Waddie, and Black Jim were still there.

"Cattle Call," he recognized the tune Jim was absently plucking out on his guitar.

Jim nodded. "Heard the night herder singing it, and the tune got in my head."

Brandt glanced off toward the cattle. "Speaking of which, it's about your turn out there, Waddie. Holler at Devine on your way out and tell him he's your relief at midnight."

Waddie nodded, brushing back his mop of black hair with one hand and setting his hat on with the other. "Yes sir." He stood up and gave a nervous tip of his hat to Savanna. "If you'll excuse me, ma'am."

"She'll excuse ya', boy," Jim prodded. "Now git to it." He grinned white against his dark face as he watched Waddie go, then turned his attention to the guitar again.

"There in the valley,
   Where sweet roses grow

163

> I am reminded
> When the winds blow,"

Savanna watched, listened, let his deep voice wash over her like a calming wind. She felt almost peaceful . . .

Dark eyes tugged her away, and she looked up to find Monheno watching her with that smoldering gaze.

> "And when the night calls
> Soft as a dove
> I am reminded
> Of the one that I love . . ."

She imagined Monheno was smiling, though she couldn't see him well enough to tell. Was he thinking about the words to the song—could he possibly be in love with her?

"Well, mornin's comin' fast," Brandt's voice disturbed them both, and they snapped their eyes to him. "Guess I'll turn in."

"Yup," came Jim's agreement, and he stood up also. "Best git some shut eye. I'm gonna need a good night's rest to git healed up from Miss Savanna's little joke this mornin'." He chuckled to himself, shaking his head as he walked away, "My pappy's ears if that weren't a prize!"

Savanna giggled to herself despite her black mood. "All of you deserved it."

Monheno shook his head and gave her a tsk-tsk.

She delivered him a cool, impartial shrug. "They've been haranguing me for too long now. Besides," she lowered her voice so they wouldn't hear, "if it brings their loyalty in the fight against the Sombras, it was worth it."

He poked a stick into the fire, and sent a cloud of sparks crackling into the air. "Still not giving up on that?" He sounded disappointed. "It's a futile struggle."

She raised her chin stubbornly. Did he really think she could be diverted with a few false words of love? "Nothing has changed about that." She couldn't believe she was having a conversation with him at all. Only hours ago they had been . . . "I intend to defend myself." She wasn't talking about the Sombras anymore.

"I see," he stood up and came around the fire, squatting down beside her. "You asked once for my help."

"And you wouldn't give it." She could feel her insides turning to oatmeal.

He nodded, leaned close enough to kiss her, but kept his hold on her eyes. "But I am saying yes now."

She stared at him in shock. Was he serious? Was this his way of paying retribution for what he took from her? Or was fighting the Sombras only an excuse to pursue her?

Even if it was, she couldn't afford to refuse his help. "Thank you." If he thought he could find his way back into her arms, he was wrong. She would take his help, and that was all.

He touched her hair and a warm tingle fluttered through her. Unconsciously, she parted her lips, leaned closer to him. She wanted him . . .

She jerked away and scrambled to her feet. What was she doing? Where was her mind? "I'm . . . I'm going to bed," she stammered. "Good night."

She didn't give him a chance to stop her. She just hurried to the mess wagon, grabbed her bedroll, and marched off to a secluded spot to sleep. She didn't look back at the fire to see what happened to Monheno. She didn't want to know. She didn't want to think about him.

But she couldn't help it. As she drifted into sleep, his kiss assaulted her, his touch set her skin on fire. A painful yearning burned in her private center. Her breasts ached for his kiss. Her heart . . .

She woke in the morning with his name on her lips. A dark, sick feeling slid over her as soon as the word touched her ears. Had she joined hands with the devil yesterday? Was getting Monheno's help really worth the price? Today, they would leave the cattle and go back to Del Sol house. What would happen when they got there? Had the Sombras made an appearance while they were gone?

She didn't see him during breakfast, nor as the crew saddled their horses and got ready to

166

leave. She found herself hoping Monheno changed his mind and left. It would probably be for the best.

But her heart fluttered when he rode up on his big bay. A smile rose on her lips, and she wiped it away, but not before he saw it. He smiled back and slid his horse in beside hers.

"Good morning." He sounded like he hadn't a care in the world. He probably didn't. He was the victor, not the victim.

She steeled herself against his smile. "Is it?"

He gave her a disappointed look that made her want to tell him she was sorry. "Savanna." The way he said it sent a quiver up and down her spine. "We need to talk."

Hot crimson rushed into her cheeks, and she looked around to make sure no one else was close enough to be listening. "I don't want to talk." She didn't. She didn't want to talk about what happened, or even think about it. "Unless it's about the Sombras."

He sighed, tipped his hat back, and scratched his forehead. "As you wish."

"I want to know what you think would be the best course of action against them." She straightened in her saddle, trying to erase the tingling in her thighs, the memory of his touch. "You seem to know a great deal about them."

He lowered a dark brow. "I know enough to tell you not to go against them."

She clenched her teeth to keep from screaming at him. Two days on the trail and one evening in his arms had her at the end of her rope. "That is not an option," she ground out. "If you've changed your mind about helping me defend the Del Sol, please just tell me now."

He gave her a long, piercing look, his free hand drumming on his saddle impatiently. "I'll stay with you at the Del Sol until this is over."

Until this is over? She frowned. When would it be over? When the Del Sol was safe? When the Sombras were defeated? Or when he got what he wanted from her?

"Thank you." She bit the words out crisply. "I will have things to see to when we get back. Please ask my housekeeper for anything you need. She can show you to the guest house."

She kicked Nantucket into a trot toward the front of the group, leaving him behind. She couldn't stand to be near him another minute. It was torture. Just looking at him brought back his touch, his kiss. Just hearing him say her name made her tremble inside.

Her nerves were frayed like old cord by the time they reached Del Sol house. She didn't wait to see that his horse was stabled, or that he found his way to the house. She didn't even explain things to her foreman and the others. She just left Nantucket in the care of a stable boy and hurried away to the house, to a hiding place as a summer storm flashed on the horizon.

She didn't feel safe until she made it up the stairs to her room. Her bath was waiting, as usual, and beside it sat a tray of wine and cheese. Esperanza had already cut the first slice and poured a glass of wine. She dragged off her dusty riding clothes, lit a lamp against the growing darkness, and slipped into the welcoming water. Soothing, comforting, it swirled over her waist, tickled at her breasts, reminded her . . .

She sat up and grabbed her wash rag impatiently, washed her hair and scrubbed herself until her skin stung. If only she could wash his memory away as easily as the dust. What was he doing now? Was he settling into the guest house just a short distance away? How could she bear having him so close?

Lightning flashed outside, and she glanced toward the window. Thunder rolled across the hills of the Del Sol like a warning drum. A shiver ran down her spine, and tears popped into her eyes. She lay back against the tub and closed her eyes, letting the tears slide down her cheeks. What was happening to her? What was wrong with her? Why couldn't she control this?

She felt afraid and small again, like when she was a child in Africa. Africa, where the days were so long, so hot, so filled with fear. How endless those days seemed, like each one lasted a week. How afraid and alone she was in that big house with only her mother sick in bed, and her father prowling the halls, ranting, slamming into things, drunk. *Hide, Savanna, your father's coming* . . . She crouched in the dressing closet, tried not to hear his footsteps coming, tried to shut out his voice. *The child is a nuisance. It's time she went away to boarding school.* . . . Time she went away. . . . It's time . . .

The faintest clinking of glass drove the memory away. She raised her heavy lashes and rubbed the fog from her tired eyes.

"So you've decided to wake after all." Monheno's voice.

Monheno's voice! She snapped her eyes open like shutters. "I—" She choked and sank deeper into the water. How dare he come into her room! "What are you doing here?"

He toasted her with a glass of wine. "You said to make myself at home."

"I said to settle yourself in the *guest* house." An unwanted blush burned into her cheeks, rushed down her neck, and into the bath water.

His eyes followed it speculatively.

She bit her lip to keep from melting under that gaze. Slowly, with determination, she reached an arm out of the tub. "Would you please toss my dressing gown to me?"

He gave her that infuriating smile and reached for the garment. "I'll do better," his voice was thick and deep. "I'll bring it to you."

She dipped a hand into the water and splashed it at him as if shooing away a fly. "N-no need." She reached for the garment, but he held the hem just out of reach. Damn him. How did he always do this to her? "Oooooh, give me that!"

"Come here and get it." He raised a menacing brow and held the garment out to one side like a toreador tempting a bull.

She gave him a look that could have fried eggs.

He smirked and surrendered the garment into her hands. "As you wish." He sounded disappointed.

She eyed him with distrust as she stepped from the tub and fumbled with the gown. Damn him! What was he doing here? Did he really think she would fall into his arms again?

She wrapped the gown around her and tied the sash impatiently. It clung, almost sheer to her dampened skin. Nervously, she crossed her arms over her chest to hide her hardened breasts as he turned to face her.

"What are you doing here? I assume Esperanza prepared things for you," she leveled a double-barreled glare at him, "in the *guest* house."

He raised his hands and seated himself in a heavy velvet chair beside the fireplace. "I couldn't stay away." He looked thoughtfully at the mahogany chair arm and ran a finger along the carving of a rose. Taking a match from the hearth, he struck it against the dark curve of wood and lit the lamp on the darkened hearth.

New light blazed into the room, and he looked up at her, desire smoldering in the black depths of his eyes. "Did you really think I would?"

"I don't know what I was thinking." What in the world could she have been thinking—inviting him to stay here? Was she out of her mind?

"This will never be acceptable unless you stay in the guest house." And out of my bed.

He only smiled one-sidedly and rested an arm casually over the back of the chair, leaned comfortably into one corner—like a cat coaxing a mouse. "I think we need to talk."

She took a sip of her wine, tried to look authoritative and self-assured. Her fingers trembled until she couldn't hold the glass steady. She clutched her free hand to it to keep from spilling the crimson liquid. "It isn't proper." She looked down at the glass, brought it to her lips again, tipped it up and emptied the entire thing without a breath. That wasn't proper, either, but she didn't care.

He laughed softly—a deep, warm laugh that made her stomach churn. His eyes captured hers as he stood up, reached for her. The wine glass slipped from her fingers, but he made no move to catch it. He swept her into his arms just as it shattered against the stones beneath her bare feet.

"The glass . . ." she glanced at the shattered remains, like snowflakes in the amber lamplight, then looked back at him. Broken glass was nothing compared to the danger in his eyes.

"It's too late," he whispered.

"Yes." She could see the reflections of broken crystal in his eyes. "It is."

It was too late for her heart, too late to protest as he carried her to the broad bed. Wordlessly, he pushed aside the sheer silk curtains and laid her in the center.

She raised her heavy eyelids to look at him, her body trembling, head spinning. She felt intoxicated—either from the wine or him. She raised her lips to kiss him, let her fingers twine into the jet curls of his hair, over his shoulders, down his strong back. She drank in the scent, the feel of him, his body against hers, his clothing taking dampness from her skin. He kissed her cheek, smoothed her hair back and breathed her name against her ear, told her how he wanted her as he untied the dressing gown and slid it away.

He raised to unbutton his shirt, and a sliver of cold, damp air slid over her. It smelled of rain and lightning, dangerous things, violent things. She closed her mind to it and reached for him, slid her hands over the strong cords of his forearms. His skin was smooth, warm with passion, melted against her own as he lowered his body to hers.

He awakened her with slow skill, taunted her, bent his dark head, and drew searing trails down her neck, over her shoulders, toward her breasts. She gasped as he flicked her hardened nipples lightly with his tongue, his fingers combing through her hair, carrying it with him as he caught her breasts in his hands, raising them to his kiss.

She moaned as his fingers ran over her body like warm oil—lighting her skin on fire where they had been, making her tremble where they had yet to go.

"Savanna," he whispered. His voice seemed far away, but she felt his breath against her stomach. "I wanted you from the first moment I saw you."

She tossed her head desperately as his lips caressed her thigh. "Please . . ." She couldn't bear it a moment longer. "Please come to me."

She clung to him as he moved over her, raised her hips against the pressure of his manhood, cried out at his first thrust. Need and desire flamed within her, stretched tighter and tighter, closer to some torturous breaking point. She arched against him, matched the slowly increasing rhythm of his love, but he would not be hurried.

Release burst within her, shattered her, and she cried out softly. He held her, slowed his stride, then increased it again, driving her back toward that peak of ecstasy. His release came as she found hers. She cried out his name. She clung to him and he wrapped her in his arms, his heavy breaths rustling her hair as he rolled onto the bed and carried her with him.

She curled against the warmth of his strong chest, exhausted. Lightning split the darkness, and thunder rattled the silence. She nestled closer as his hand slid up her back and around her shoulders. She felt safe, wonderful, content . . .

The sounds of the storm awoke her sometime

late in the night. A crash of thunder snapped her upright in the bed. *Run and hide, Savanna, your father's coming home. . . .* Her mother's voice whispered in her ear, made her look around the darkened room. No one there. She let out her breath and wiped the dampness from her brow. Why was she reliving that last night with her mother now?

The covers rustling beside her told her why. Monheno Devilla. She'd fallen for him again.

"It's only the storm." He sounded like he hadn't been asleep at all. He laid a hand on her shoulder, warm, gentle, ran it down her arm and took her hand. "Go back to sleep, mi corazon, morning is still a long time away."

She jerked her hand away and combed it, trembling, through her hair. Tears pressed into her eyes, and she looked away. The fog of the wine was gone now. There was no hiding from what she'd done.

"No." If only she could make it all untrue. "You have to leave."

"Savanna." His voice caressed her with gentle reproach, as if she were overreacting.

"No." She wouldn't be soothed. "You have to go." Quicksilver tears spilled from her eyes and fell warm and salty over her cheeks.

Monheno felt his heart tighten painfully in his chest. He didn't want to hurt her. He didn't want to make her feel taken advantage of. But he couldn't help himself. He couldn't stop himself from thinking about her, from wanting her and coming after her.

He trailed his thumb along the dampened curve of her chin. Just looking at her made him feel passionate, possessive. He pulled her into his arms and kissed her trembling lips, tasting the bitter salt of her tears.

"No tears, mi corazon." He drew her back to the bed, cradled her against him as if she were made of glass. He didn't want to break her. He wanted to make her whole again. "No need to cry when we have finally found love. Save your tears for those who go a lifetime without it."

Savanna closed her eyes tightly against a new rush of tears. His talk of love only made her heart ache worse, like it was breaking. If only she could see his eyes, tell if his words were true or only easy lies. She couldn't bear this ache.

"What if the Sombras come?" she whispered.

He laughed the idea away softly, his fingers stroking the length of her hair. "They won't." He kissed the top of her head, then rested his chin there. "They wouldn't dare."

He was gone when she woke in the morning. She silently thanked him for his mercy in that. She didn't know if she could face him in the sting of daylight, and the thought of Esperanza seeing him in her room was nauseating.

She dressed, combed her hair, and started toward the door. Her fingers trembled on the latch, then she drew them away. She couldn't do it. She couldn't face him, or anyone else. What if everyone suspected? What if everyone knew what had happened?

She threw herself into the chair by her veranda and grabbed the copy of *Kaloolah* from her dressing table. Maybe if she stayed here for a while, everyone would be gone about their work by the time she went downstairs. Maybe Monheno would be gone with them.

The book did little to take her mind off her problems. *Kaloolah* was a poor choice of reading material. It was about Africa, and Africa reminded her of her mother. She laid it on her lap and stared out at the yard. Was she repeating her mother's mistakes? Was she falling into the same trap that took her mother's life? She saw no sign of her father's violent nature in Monheno. When he held her, he seemed gentle, caring. Was it all a mask to lure her in? Was that how her mother fell?

The muffled sound of Esperanza's laughter floated up from the downstairs. She set the book down and walked to the door, cracking it slightly. Spanish voices floated up the stairway, then more laughter—Esperanza's and Monheno's.

Irritation scratched up her backbone like a fingernail. What was he doing down there in *her* kitchen, saying God-knows-what to her housekeeper? It was infuriating! How dare he insinuate himself into her household as if he lived there! What would people say?

She would have to ask him to leave. There

was no other choice. Sombras or no, she couldn't have him around. Her reputation could not bear it, and neither could her heart. She would rather face Venenoso again than continue this game of cat and mouse. At least Venenoso could only take property. Monheno Devilla was robbing her of her soul piece by piece. It was no good to sell her soul to one devil to avoid another.

He was gone from the kitchen by the time she got there. Esperanza was still red-faced with laughter.

"He ees in el jardin, I theenk." She chuckled and shook her head. "El Devilla ees so charm-eeng, eh?"

Savanna bit her lip to keep from saying something that might give her away. She just thanked her housekeeper and headed for the garden. The garden? What was he doing there? The garden was trashy and overgrown from years of neglect. No one went there.

She found him sitting among dozens of newly planted rose bushes, rose bushes she never purchased. At the far end of the garden, *her* peons were busily clearing years of overgrowth to plant more. She stood on a carpet of fresh mimosa clippings and watched them in amazement, then looked back at Monheno.

His eyes seemed far away as he gazed at the scrappy-looking starts. He smiled, swept his hand across the garden as if picturing them fully grown, then his smile faded. There was a private sadness in his face that made her step back. What was he thinking?

He looked up vaguely, as if he heard something. A smile touched his lips again. He nodded as if in response to whatever he heard, then propped a foot up on the marble bench where he sat. Resting an elbow on his knee, he leaned back and watched the roses.

Her determination melted like ice cast into a flame. He looked so gentle, so much like he belonged there, so much like the man who drove her body mad with passion, then carefully cracked the shell around her heart with tenderness. What was she to do? She hadn't the time nor the inclination for love, yet here it was with its grip so tight around her heart she could hardly breathe—and in the form of a man so much like her father.

But there was no tenderness in her father. Her father had no time for planting seedlings. Yet, here was Monheno, apparently restoring her rose garden. *Her* rose garden. Irritation scratched up her spine again. It wasn't his to restore. In fact, it was a luxury the Del Sol could ill afford right now.

She took a few steps backward, then rounded the bend in the path more noisily.

He looked up as if he wasn't surprised to find her there. "Come to check the progress?" A smile played on his lips, as if he knew what her reaction would be.

"To halt it," she replied stiffly, and tried not

179

to look around. The garden was beautiful, even in its present transitional stage. "The Del Sol has . . ." she paused, ". . . has no need for a rose garden at this point."

He swung his propped leg down and let his boot fall heavily on the stone path. "Consider it a gift." He swung a hand to the garden as if creating it by magic. "From someone who thinks that beauty in itself gives things value," he met her eyes, "to someone who doesn't."

She shifted her eyes to keep him from seeing how the remark stung. It made her sound like an ogre.

She took a deep breath and brought up her real reason for being there. "I have been doing a great deal of thinking." That was true enough. She clasped her hands in front of herself and forced herself to look up, not at his eyes, but past them. "And I have decided it would be best if you left." She nodded definitively. "Yes, it would be best for both of us."

"Speak for yourself," he chuckled like her words rolled off him like beads of oil. "I think it would be best for me to remain right here. Home is where your heart is, after all."

Anger split through what was left of her composure. He was making fun of her, toying with her, pointing out how easily he captured her.

"Don't mock me." Her lips trembled with a thinly veiled mixture of shame and anger. "It is bad enough that you've made me the fool. There, you see, I've admitted it! Now you can go home and be satisfied there isn't a woman in the world you can't conquer."

Saying the words stung even worse than the fact they were true. She bit back tears, raised her chin and regarded him through narrow eyes. "That is what you wanted in the first place, isn't it?"

Monheno didn't answer her at first. She was right in a way. In the beginning he was out to conquer—up to his old games again, but now he had more in mind. When he had made love to her, it wasn't a matter of conquest—of victim and victor; it was exchange of love—one heart traded for another. How could she be so blind to that? Didn't she feel it at all? What had happened to her to make her so afraid to love?

"Hardly so. What I wanted was your heart, and in return I give you mine." He stood up, took a step toward her, caught her narrowed violet eyes. "That, my dear, is the truth."

She tossed her golden hair stubbornly. "The truth is that you don't even know me." She was wrong about that. He knew more than she thought. "Nor I you. How can you talk of love? It is ridiculous. We are practically strangers."

Strangers? A smile teased his lips, and he let his eyes drift possessively over the curve of her breasts, then back up. "We're hardly strangers, you and I." He caught her hand in his, stared down into those haunted eyes, wounds open there for him to see. "I know you, Savanna. The problem is that you don't know yourself."

# Ten

She started to tell him she knew her own mind perfectly well, that she didn't need him to tell her what was in it. But one look into his eyes, those dark smoldering eyes, made her forget. Was it possible to be drawn to a man more each time you looked at him?

"And there is still the problem with the Sombras," she barely heard him speak, "or had you forgotten that?"

Forgotten that? Of course she hadn't, but the threat of bandits seemed small next to the assault he was waging on her heart.

She pulled away and ran a trembling hand through her hair. Why was her own body, her own mind betraying her? Why was she being tormented this way? Why didn't God just strike her down with a thunderbolt and be done with it?

"What is it that you want from me?" She had to know. She had to understand why he was playing this cruel game with her heart.

"I've already told you," he returned without hesitation. "I want your love. Why are you so sure I'm after something else?"

"Men like you always are." She flushed and stared at the hem of her dress. What sort of a woman did that make her? What sort of a woman took a man into her bed because she needed something from him?

She glanced up to find him not wounded, but smiling slightly. Was he laughing at her, or merely proud of his dubious reputation?

"And how is it that you know so much about men like me?" He came closer again, close enough to touch her, but he didn't. "Surely you don't associate with cads and scoundrels as a regular practice? I'd hate to think you weren't the proper young British lady you've pretended to be."

"This isn't about me," she snapped. How dare he toy with her after what had happened between them! How dare he stand there smiling and practically admitting he was a womanizer!

The smile faded. "But it is." He looked deadly serious. "The only problem between you and me is in your mind—in your damned unbendable ideas of what things should and shouldn't be, and of what people are and aren't." There was a calculated sparkle deep in his eye, like he was maneuvering her toward a trap. "You said yourself you hardly know me. How can you possibly know what kind of man I really am?"

How did she reply to that? If she disagreed, she was admitting she knew him well enough to truly be in love with him. If she agreed, she was confirming she didn't know him well enough to know whether she loved him or not.

She leveled an accusing finger at him. "You are trying to confuse the issue." And doing a good job of it. She couldn't even remember now what the issue was.

"Which is?"

Of course he would say that. She threw up her hands and rolled her eyes skyward. "I don't know." She truly didn't anymore. "But I'm telling you now, Monheno Devilla, I'm no prize to be won. As I told you before, I haven't the time nor the inclination for a man. I've seen what marriage is like, and I want no part of it."

He cocked a quizzical brow, and allowed an evil twinkle to show in his eye. "I haven't forgotten your vow of spinsterhood." His voice was deep, compelling. He captured her in his arms and looked down at her confidently, as though nothing she could say would sway his course. "But promises like that are made to be broken."

"Not by me." She pressed her hands against his chest and wiggled out of his arms. She'd had enough of this sparring match. "Stay here and tend your roses, Monheno Devilla," she muttered as she walked away. "I hope they pay you back in thorns."

She hurried back to the house and went to her study, closed the door behind her and shut the veranda doors. She was hiding again, and she knew it. It was shameful, ridiculous. She was letting him make her a prisoner in her own house. But she did have books to see to. At least her time in hiding would be well spent.

She didn't venture out until supper time. She was almost surprised, disgustingly disappointed when he wasn't at her dinner table. But she didn't have the energy to wonder where he was, nor the time to worry about it. Her thoughts were occupied with the fast-approaching problem of how to pay next month's salaries. Even as she ran over the figures in her head, her gaze drifted to the window. It was almost dark. Where was Monheno, anyway . . . ?

"Oh, Savanna!" She growled, gathering up her tally books and heading up to her bedroom. She slammed the door behind her, locked it, then felt foolish and unlocked it again. She'd not hide behind locked doors in her own house. If Monheno came to her room, she would tell him straight out they had some things to settle, and not in the bed, either. She'd tell him if he really loved her, he would move away from the Del Sol and court her properly. She'd say . . .

With a sigh, she went back and locked the door again.

She opened the tally books with good intentions, but the sight of them made her stomach turn over, and she lay back against her bed pillows wearily. Perhaps it was time to quit trying to make an old dog get up and dance—perhaps the Del Sol really was dead, and it was time to give up on bringing it back to life. If she sold everything, she might gain enough money to go back to London—or to purchase a small plantation in Africa. It was something to think about . . .

The feeling of the tally book slipping from her hands awoke her. She reached for it out of reflex before she realized it was being lifted, not falling. Blinking sleepily, she watched Monheno take the book and set it on the night table. From the look of it, he had been riding hard. His jet hair was blown back into unruly curls, and his clothes smelled of the nighttime dew.

"Wha . . .?" she hovered between asking him where he'd been and demanding he leave her bedroom. She'd locked the door—how could he possibly get in? "What are you doing here?"

The glint in his eyes told her why he was there, as if she couldn't have guessed. He sat down on the edge of the bed like he belonged there.

"It doesn't matter." She pressed her hands to the bed and scooted away from him. "If you think I'll make the same foolish mistake again, you're wrong."

He chuckled—a habit she was coming to hate. "I've been called a lot of things." He looked disgustingly comfortable on the edge of her bed. "But never a foolish mistake." He scratched his chin as though musing on the words. "I'm not sure I like it."

186

"Stop toying with me!" She'd had enough. "I don't know how you came in here, but I want you to leave!"

"Do you?" He leaned a little closer, caught her gaze. "Look me in the eye and tell me that."

"You . . ." She wavered, and he came close to her—or did she come closer to him? "Damn you." The words felt strange on her tongue. "This isn't a game."

"And I am not a gamester." His face was earnest, but his eyes held shadows, like dark rooms with things hidden within. "At least not the kind you think I am." He touched the curve of her chin, a tender gesture that made her heart stop. "I would never gamble with you, Savanna. You are a prize too valuable to risk."

Her heart clung to those sweet words like a lifeline. It had been so very long since she felt precious to anyone. For almost as long as she could remember, her life had been a string of impersonal acquaintances and hired companions. A century had passed since anyone cracked the shell around her heart—or even really tried. Without it, she felt naked, like that little girl hiding in the closet again, frightened, vulnerable.

His lips brushed hers and the spark was instant. She fell into his arms, surrendered to the consuming blaze.

His lovemaking this time was different from the last—slower, more deliberate—as if he so quickly learned each of the things that pleased

187

her the most, and was using each to its fullest advantage.

Something else was different, too. There were sweet words to touch her ears—words that told her again she was precious—words that confessed a desire for her that began the first moment he saw her. Words that said he was as much a prisoner as she—that said he loved her.

Something awoke her again in the middle of the night. She stared at the gently blowing bed curtains, luminous in the moonlight, and listened. Only the faint barking of a dog at the bunk house. Perhaps it was just the stifling heat and humidity that stole her away from sleep. For several minutes, she lay perfectly still, nestled in the crook of Monheno's strong arm, her head resting on his gently rising and falling chest.

She never dreamed it would feel so wonderful to have someone. She never imagined that a man's arms could make her feel so complete. Never in a million millennia would she have predicted she'd lose her heart to a man so like her father.

Perhaps she should have fought harder. Perhaps she should still be fighting, but what was the use? He had her heart on a string, her soul in his hands. All she could do was face it and try to make some order of things. When morning came, she intended to do just that.

Whatever his intentions were, she would find them out in the morning—no more of this tempting and taunting and bickering. If they were going to be together, then so be it, but it was going to be proper—there was that word again. If he was any kind of a man, he'd make his intentions honorable—which meant, of course, marriage.

Marriage! The word tied her stomach so tight it hurt. She didn't want to be married—she'd never wanted to—yet what choice did she have? Her heart wouldn't give him up. Wasn't marriage preferable to this sordid liaison?

She slipped from his arms carefully, leaving him sleeping. Giving him one last glance, she parted the curtains, slid from the bed, then let them fall noiselessly back into place. She walked unsteadily toward the open veranda door. The heat tonight was stifling . . .

She scooped her blouse off the floor and slipped it on, then sat down in the chair by the veranda door. Laying her head back, she let the cooling winds wash over her. But the night breeze couldn't clear her mind. Her very soul felt as though it were being invaded by Monheno's presence.

The heat, the closeness of it was unbearable. She grabbed her skirt and boots and put them on. Perhaps a walk or even a ride. The moon was full. She would be able to see well enough. It was bound to be cooler outside.

She glanced one more time at him sleeping, then tiptoed across the floor, her boot heels clicking faintly on the polished tile. Her hand settled on the door knob. Locked. How did Monheno enter? She took the key from the shelf by the door, stared at it for a moment, then turned it in the lock.

She froze as the tumblers clicked, glanced back toward the bed, but no sound came from behind the curtains. Placing her free hand against the door, she drew it open without a sound, stepped into the hall, and closed it behind her.

The light of a full moon poured through the windows, illuminating the stairway as she went silently down and out the kitchen door. Outside, the veranda was as bright as at sunrise, a faint breeze blowing, carrying the scent of honeysuckle. She drank it in, letting the breeze wash over her and lift her moistened hair from her neck.

She wandered off the end of the veranda and into the rose garden. His rose garden. The air smelled of fresh soil, and newly trimmed trees and bushes. The gardeners had cleared nearly the whole thing, all except for one small corner, where the honeysuckle and climbing roses still hung from their trellises in overgrown tangles.

She clasped her hands behind her and strolled toward the miniature jungle, watched as the eerie play of moonlight and shadow painted the brambles into a mass of claws and talons.

A shudder ran through her—a strange cold feeling the old African maid of her childhood called the touch of death. She couldn't stop herself from moving closer. Her feet ground on the cobblestones, strangely thunderous in the silence. Why did she feel like she shouldn't be there?

Something glinted through the brambles as she stood at the edge of the tangle—something grey-white and vaguely shiny. She reached over the brambles, wrapped her fingers around, started to pull them back. A thorn pricked her finger, and she drew back with a gasp.

Something rustled in the brush, and she jumped back, then spun on her heel and hurried back down the path. She could look at whatever was there in the daylight. An eerie feeling prickled her skin, and she hummed to herself to break the silence as she trotted up the steps.

The song froze in her throat as she rounded the corner of the house. Someone was there! If she hadn't been so shocked, she would have reacted more quickly and kept the spark of recognition from her eye as he turned around, kept from saying his name to prove she knew who he was.

"Tito Baca?" She clamped her hand to her mouth as soon as she said it, realizing her mistake. They were standing almost exactly where they were the last time she saw them—the night she learned one of her men was consorting with the Sombras.

She panicked, froze. Tito Baca was one of the Sombras. Now she had seen him and he knew it. If she screamed, would the men in the bunk-house hear her. What if Tito had a gun?

She launched herself toward the house, bolted on legs that wouldn't seem to move fast enough. Dear God. Dear God, I don't want to die . . .


The sun was already high in the sky, stream-ing through the windows like it was noonday. How could she have slept so late? Why were the dogs barking outside? They should have been out with the sheep long ago . . .

She opened her eyes, stared up at the windows on the far wall, and reality crashed in on her like a cannonball. Those were not her windows. She wasn't at home. She remembered . . . Tito Baca. Had she been shot? Was she at the doc-tor's house?

She looked from the leaded glass windows to the rest of the room. Rainbow spears of light danced like pixies over the dark tiled floors and heavy, carved Spanish furniture, splashed over the bed and touched her hands. She gripped her fingers to her reeling head and tried to sit up.

"Sssshhh, don't try to move." Monheno's voice—something familiar. It made her heart stop thundering. Nothing could be wrong as long as he was here . . .

The events of the night before flooded back to her like pictures frozen in a book. She sank back against the pillow and closed her eyes to

# ENJOY ALL THE PASSION AND ROMANCE OF...

*Heartfire*

## ROMANCES from ZEBRA

After you have read HEART-FIRE ROMANCES, we're sure you'll agree that HEARTFIRE sets new standards of excellence for historical romantic fiction. Each Zebra HEARTFIRE novel is the ultimate blend of intimate romance and grand adventure and each takes place in the kinds of historical settings you want most...the American Revolution, the Old West, Civil War and more.

## SUBSCRIBERS $AVE, $AVE, $AVE!!!

As a HEARTFIRE Home Subscriber, you'll save with your HEARTFIRE Subscription. You'll receive 4 brand new Heartfire Romances to preview Free for 10 days each month. If you decide to keep them you'll pay only $3.50 each; a total of $14.00 and you'll save $3.00 each month off the cover price.

Plus, we'll send you these novels as soon as they are published each month. There is never any shipping, handling or other hidden charges; home delivery is always FREE! And there is no obligation to buy even a single book. You may return any of the books within 10 days for full credit and you can cancel your subscription at any time. No questions asked.

**Zebra's HEARTFIRE ROMANCES Are The Ultimate In Historical Romantic Fiction.**
**Start Enjoying Romance As You Have Never Enjoyed It Before...**
*With 4 FREE Books From HEARTFIRE*

# TO GET YOUR
# 4 FREE BOOKS
## MAIL THE COUPON BELOW.

# FREE BOOK CERTIFICATE

*Heartfire Romance*

# GET 4 FREE BOOKS

**Yes!** I want to subscribe to Zebra's HEARTFIRE HOME SUBSCRIPTION SERVICE. Please send me my 4 FREE books. Then each month I'll receive the four newest Heartfire Romances as soon as they are published to preview Free for ten days. If I decide to keep them I'll pay the special discounted price of just $3.50 each; a total of $14.00. This is a savings of $3.00 off the regular publishers price. There are no shipping, handling or other hidden charges. There is no minimum number of books to buy and I may cancel this subscription at any time. In any case the 4 FREE Books are mine to keep regardless.

NAME

ADDRESS

CITY _____ STATE _____ ZIP

TELEPHONE

SIGNATURE

(If under 18 parent or guardian must sign)
Terms and prices subject to change.
Orders subject to acceptance.

ZH0294

# GET 4 FREE BOOKS

Heartfire
Romance

HEARTFIRE HOME SUBSCRIPTION
SERVICE
120 BRIGHTON ROAD
P.O. BOX 5214
CLIFTON, NEW JERSEY 07015

```
AFFIX
STAMP
HERE
```

sort them out—her walk, the brambles in the garden, Tito Baca, the Sombras. She had been shot. That was why her head was throbbing.

Her blood raced at the thought, and her heart pounded in her ears. She didn't hurt anywhere except her head. Could a person be shot and not feel it? Maybe she was shot in the head. "Monheno?"

"Yes?" He sounded distant. Was she falling away again?

She sucked in a breath, and gathered her courage to ask, "Am I going to die?" It didn't seem like such a bad alternative. God, her head was throbbing.

"Not unless clumsiness is lethal." He was laughing—laughing!

She opened her eyes in shock and horror. "How can you be so callous when I've been shot?" How dare he make a joke of her suffering! If she died, she was going to come back and torment him until the end of his days.

"Shot?" He chuckled harder. "You haven't been shot, Savanna, you ran into one of the columns on the veranda and put yourself out." He leaned over her, gave her forehead an appraising frown. "It's a nasty lump, but I think you'll live."

She wished she had been shot. Dear Lord, how embarrassing—ran into a column . . .

"Where am I?" The doctor's house, no doubt. She hoped he wasn't drunk this time.

There was a strange look in Monheno's ebony

eyes when she looked back at him. Was there something wrong she didn't know about?

"Where am I?" she repeated. Foreboding swept over her, and left her so cold she pulled the coverlet closer to her neck. Why was he looking at her like that? What was that dark, humorless stare, like he was a stranger.

"You're safe," he replied evasively. "For the time being, however, I'm afraid you'll have to consider yourself a guest of the Sombras."

Sombras! The word exploded in her mind, chilled her body like ice. What was he saying? What did he mean? She watched in disbelief as he stood up. Something in the way he was dressed was familiar—something in the way he stood now reminded her of someone she had seen only once.

She'd been a fool not to spot it sooner. "Venenoso." The word ripped her heart from her. "You bastard, you're Venenoso."

His manner changed—almost looked remorseful, then turned hard again. He made no attempt to deny it.

"But how . . . ?" She didn't know what to ask. How could you pretend to love me? How could you steal from your neighbors and friends? How could you be so devious? How could you have gotten away with it? How could you unlock my heart only to break it? All the questions she wanted to ask, but all of the answers too painful to hear.

Aching, she turned away from him, closed her

194

eyes against the pillow as tears slid from beneath her lashes and rolled down her cheeks.

She heard him turn, his boots cross the floor, the sound of the door opening, then closing, and finally the sound of the lock turning, making her a prisoner. Then she was alone, and the pain intensified as she considered what he had been to her—her dearest love, now her most bitter enemy. How could anyone be so cruel?

Part of her longed for him to return, to explain, if he could, why he used her so—what she did to deserve such a terrible punishment. Another part hoped she never saw him again, unless it was to bring his black heart to justice.

She thought about it throughout the day, thought about him and the way he made her feel, thought about trying to escape. She tried the leaded-glass windows, but they were nailed shut, and far too high to jump from anyway—unless she wanted to die. They offered no clues to her location, except for the far-away sounds of horses and cattle.

The house was silent as a tomb. She sat for nearly an hour listening for the sounds that should have accompanied such a grand house—the movements of servants, the opening and closing of doors, the voices of occupants. Nothing. She was there alone. Where was Monheno? Was he coming back for her?

Monheno. She wavered between anger, heartache, and indignance each time she thought of him. Was he really Venenoso? If he was, how many people knew about that? Certainly the Bacas and the Garzas. Were they laughing at her as they watched Monheno lure her into his web? Who among her own men knew his identity? Waddie said he'd seen Venenoso once. If Venenoso and Monheno were one and the same, why didn't Waddie tell her? It didn't add up, but she didn't want it to. She wanted him to walk through that door and tell her it wasn't true.

What did he intend to do with her? Neither he nor Tito Baca could afford to have her go to the authorities with what she knew . . .

The sound of the lock turning shattered her thoughts. She stiffened in her chair, and fought the urge to run to the far side of the room. *Run and hide, Savanna, your father's coming home . . .*

She wouldn't be that frightened little girl in the closet. She wouldn't. Strength. Courage. She had to be brave. She narrowed her eyes, fastened them on him as he opened the door.

His gaze bored into hers as though he saw right through her front. "Still here, I see?"

"I had little choice." How could he be so cruel to her? Did he have no feelings for her at all? "But, as you can probably imagine, I won't be staying any longer than is absolutely necessary."

"And how long might that be?" He closed the door, clasped his hands behind himself and rocked back on his heels casually.

She forced her composure to hold. "Not much longer, I hope." She wanted to fall at his feet

196

and beg him to tell her this was all a mistake. "Because the sight of you makes me ill."

He winced visibly. Finally a reaction. At least she was landing blows. She stood up as he crossed the room, wanting to face him on even ground.

"Here is the problem as I see it," she'd been rehearsing the speech all day. Why were the words running from her like traitors now? She looked away, then back, but not into his eyes. "Neither you nor Tito Baca can afford to have me go to the law with what I know, nor can I afford to sit here in your prison while you rob me blind." She tried to sound as though she were in a position to bargain. She wasn't. All the chips were on his side of the table. "You commit to leaving the Del Sol alone from now on and to returning the livestock you have stolen from me. In return, I'll tell no one what I know."

She wasn't sure her conscience would let her keep that bargain. How could she sit back and allow her neighbors to be robbed when she had information that could put away the Sombras once and for all? But how many of those neighbors were involved in this?

He seemed to consider her offer, then gave her a tilt of brows that told her he hadn't considered it at all. "Such an impersonal bargain," he remarked, "and not a word of . . . more personal things?"

Unwanted color burned into her cheeks. How

could he bring that up now? "I've come to terms with that already." She hadn't. She never would. "You've done a very good job of making me a fool—how nice for you. I hope you enjoyed it. As for the physical *matter,*" she spat the word, disgust making it bitter, "I can see, after some thought, that as I do not intend to marry, it was of no great loss. I have no one to save myself for anyway." Just saying it made her heart break. She hoped that somewhere in his wicked soul he felt just one one-hundredth of the pain he had caused her.

Something in the depths of her eyes, some little detail of her expression, something in the way she held herself, must have betrayed her. There was an unmistakable spark of under-standing in his eye, and then that smile again. She knew he'd glimpsed all of the cards in her hand.

"Well, my dear, I'm afraid I can't take you up on your offer. You see, too much hangs in the balance for me to merely trust it all to your word that you won't tell what you know." He took a step closer—slightly menacing, slightly compel-ling, and reached out to brush her hair back from her face. "Besides, letting you go now would mean giving up on that . . . matter," he imitated her tone, even the expression on her face when she had said the word, "that I took such pains to pursue, and I'm not about to do that."

## Eleven

She recoiled from his outstretched hand like it was a snake. Did he really think she would come to him again, after what happened, in view of what he was?

"The day I let you touch me again, Monheno Devilla," she leveled a gaze that could have turned him to a pillar of salt where he stood, "will be the day they need wool socks to keep warm in hell."

He gave her a knowing shrug, turned to leave, looked sickeningly confident. "We'll see, won't we?" He stopped at the door and glanced back over his shoulder. "Feel free to move about the house as you like, but don't try to leave. I wouldn't want one of the dogs to mistake you for a trespasser."

She shivered at his meaning, or at something in the tone of his voice, then squared her shoulders with determination. "I'm not afraid of you."

He cocked a quizzical brow. "I should hope

not." His face was deadly serious, his eyes two flat bits of slate, no sparkle. "Don't try to leave the house."

She watched him go, shivering despite the uncomfortable heat and closeness in the room. A terrible sense of foreboding chilled her skin like ice—like the one that came over her the day her father's letter came to her at school—the letter that changed her life with the sloppy, drunken strokes of a pen. There would be no more money for school, it said. She should come to California to live. She ignored the letter, made an excuse to Miss Culpet about her tuition. Fortunately, her father died before he could force her to join him.

At least she hoped he was dead. She never saw his body. She made no arrangements for a funeral. She just received his death certificate along with a letter from the sheriff in Oro Grande. Died of a gunshot to the head. Case ruled self-defense. Did Monheno have something to do with that? Did the Sombras kill him, perhaps when he ran out of money to pay their tithe? Did Monheno order it?

Her stomach rose into her throat and she swallowed hard. Was Monheno hiding those terrible secrets the whole time he was with her? When he was laughing, joking with her? When he was making love to her?

Tears burned her tired eyes like lye. She wiped them away impatiently and headed for the door. She couldn't think about it any longer. She couldn't stay here. She had to get away from this place, from him, from her own breaking heart before it tore her in two.

She moved cautiously through the door, peered into the hallway. No one there. No sign of a guard. One hand on the doorframe, she leaned out to look around before stepping onto the heavy crimson carpet that lined the long hall. Nothing there but a row of polished mahogany doors like hers. Was Monheno behind one of them? Was someone else? Was she being watched right now?

She took a deep breath and went through the door, letting it close behind her. The faint click of the latch made her gasp, and the sound echoed down the silent hall. She froze, listening. Silence. She was alone.

She wandered the house for nearly an hour, moving from room to room, each one elaborately furnished in heavy Spanish-style furniture, but with walls eerily bare. Most of the rooms smelled dusty and stale, closed. The furniture, though fine, was faded, but not worn, as though time, rather than use had ravaged it. The windows and doors were nailed shut, all except the front door, which was locked. Scrappy-looking red heeler dogs prowled outside. They looked menacing, but not overly alert. Maybe if they fell asleep later, she could get one of the windows open.

She found no one in the house, yet, the more she moved about, the more evident it became she was not alone. Footsteps echoed down the empty halls, doors opened and closed, locks turned—always from the other side of the house, like someone was moving from one end to the other without her seeing. Once she even thought she heard singing—a man's voice in Spanish. When she stopped to listen, it was gone.

The fading daylight finally forced her to search for a lamp. The huge empty house was getting more and more eerie by the minute. She didn't believe in ghosts, of course. No, of course not. There was no such thing.

If there was such a thing as ghosts, they could read her mind. When she walked back into the dome-ceilinged entry hall, a lamp was waiting, already lit. Too much of a coincidence for her liking. *Was* someone reading her mind? Or was Monheno trying to drive her out of it?

She shuddered as she picked up the lamp. Who touched it before her? Who lit it? She steadied it and went to the windows to look out the front of the house. No sign of anyone coming.

A door slammed upstairs. She jumped and the hurricane glass fell off the lamp, shattered at her feet. Her heart lurched painfully against her chest. She froze there and listened. Did whoever, or whatever, was in the house hear the glass break?

She shivered and backed away from the broken glass. If someone was coming, she didn't want to be here. Shielding the lamp with a hand, she turned and hurried down the hall to a small library at the end. She lit every lamp in the room, then sank down in a chair and wrapped her arms around herself. She couldn't stand being alone in the dark like this! She couldn't!

She grabbed a book from the table and tried to read it. It was no use. If she didn't get out of this dark house, she was going to lose her mind.

A sound in the hall made her jerk her head up. Her heart raced and her hands dampened on the book. She stared into the dark hall, caught a fleeting glimpse of a man passing— someone portly, perhaps not much taller than herself, elaborately costumed in what looked like a uniform. His face was hidden in the shadows of the hallway, but she had the distinct impression he was looking at her. A moment later, he was gone, and so were the sounds of his footfalls.

She ran to the doorway, stopping just short of it and peeking out into the hall. Nothing moved except shadows from the row of lamps now lit in the hall. Who was that? Why was he sneaking around lighting lamps?

"Well, I see you've found a good book."

She whirled around to find Monheno in the other doorway. For an instant, she was glad to see him, glad not to be alone. The feeling faded like smoke.

"I've been attempting to while away my hours of captivity." More like attempting to keep her sanity. "I must say, your hospitality is somewhat lacking. I haven't had a thing to eat all day, and there isn't a scrap of food in that kitchen big enough to feed a mouse."

"My apologies." He gave her a polite half-bow, setting the book down on the desk as he did. "I've had other things to attend to. I'm not usually one to neglect my guests."

"Your prisoner." She regretted her words almost immediately. They hardened him until he looked like a stranger.

"As you like," he bit out. "If you'll follow me, we're serving prison rations in the dining room."

She gritted her teeth and followed. Starving to death wouldn't help her escape. Neither would making him angry. She'd have a much better chance if she could convince him she was resigned to his plan, whatever it was. If she could win his confidence, he might slip up . . .

She glared at his back as she followed him through the darkened halls to a private dining room. Like the other rooms, it was only half-finished, as if no one had ever used it.

"Is this your house?" She modified her glare and smoothed her tone of voice as he helped her to a chair. "Do you live here?"

He gave her a suspicious sideways glance as he sat down across from her. "Yes and no." He took the wine bottle and poured them both a glass. "This is my house." He glanced toward the doorway behind her back. "But I don't live here. It's haunted."

She swung her head around to look over her shoulder.

"Now, Savanna," he admonished. "Surely you don't believe in ghosts."

"Well of course not." She felt foolish, but checked the corners of the room anyway. "Does anyone live here? It seems so . . ."

"Unfinished?"

She nodded. Why did he bring her here, anyway? Because no one would ever find her? She picked up the wine and took a sip—just a tiny one. The last time she drank wine with him, the results were disastrous.

He lifted the lid from the serving platter, set it aside, and leaned back in his chair. "Ladies first."

She chafed at the smile on his face, but took a small helping of roast and peas. It was probably laced with arsenic, and this was how he planned to do away with her.

"You were telling me about the house," she pressed. The more she knew, the better her chance of escape. Maybe he would reveal something that would tell her where she was, how far away from the Del Sol, how far from town—anything.

He gave her a questioning look, "I was?" He took a bite of roast and chewed it thoughtfully. She hoped it *was* laced with arsenic.

"The house is nearly a hundred years old, but it has never been lived in—only maintained as you see. It was built, they tell me, by a Spaniard for his lady love. Unfortunately, the lady died before the house could be occupied, and the Spaniard didn't have the heart to live in it or to tear it down. So here it stands."

She widened her eyes. Was he telling the truth? Was the Spaniard one of his ancestors, the tragic story the saga of his own family? "But what happened to the Spaniard?"

He gave her a one-sided grin, a devilish one. "I don't know. I came by the story, and by the house, third hand." He raised his glass, toasted her, and took a small sip. "In a poker game."

She crossed her arms over her chest and sank back in her chair. "I should have guessed."

He served himself another helping and set the platters aside. "You have a healthy dislike for gamblers." He said it like he was talking to a stranger, like there was nothing intimate between them. "Which is odd, considering your father was a fairly good one."

That was the first time she'd heard her father called fairly good at anything. "You knew my father?" Did Monheno have something to do with his death?

"I did." Did his eyes harden, or did she imagine it? "He was an interesting man to sit across the table from."

She leaned forward, placing both palms on the table. "You needn't find something nice to say about him." Hatred welled up inside her, made her rash. "My father was the devil's bastard, as are you. He never did a thing for me in my life and I'm well rid of him, as I will be of you."

He looked vaguely surprised. "Well, I never liked him either, and I never expected to be so . . ." he paused, gave her a long, melting look, ". . . fond of his daughter, but here we are, back to the real matter at hand."

She swallowed hard. She shouldn't have been so quick to tip her hand. She had to control her temper. "Yes, we are." Better to let him make the next move.

Minutes ticked silently away as his eyes bored into hers, searching her, stealing her secrets, making her weak and feverish. "It seems that you and I have a problem."

The words twisted her heart into a knot. He'd said them to her before, in her bedroom, wearing a mask. He was Venenoso. Why was she so slow to recognize it?

"You see," he was saying. He laid down his fork and turned his palms up helplessly. "We can't have one newcomer spoil what has taken years to build. You know how it is with bandits—if we let one person get away, then pretty soon people hear about it." He gave a sigh of mock-exhaustion. "And then we have to work like dogs to get everyone in line again. Surely you can understand our position."

Her temper bolted like a runaway horse. "You

are despicable!" She stood up so suddenly her chair toppled behind her and clapped against the floor like thunder. "You talk about this as though it were some sort of joke! Don't you realize you're stealing from people—taking what they've worked honestly to earn? Doesn't that bother you in the least?" She suspected not. "You're bleeding this valley dry while the rightful owners of it struggle to keep their heads above water."

That disgusting smile left his face, and he stood up, his raven eyes blazing as bright as two flames. "The rightful owners?" he scoffed. "An interesting term for squatters such as you, considering that I and a few others are the rightful owners of this valley."

Her mouth dropped open in shock at the note of conviction behind his words. He said it as though he believed it, and his eyes, which usually held the hint of a good joke, were deadly serious now. Yet he could not be right. She couldn't be certain about the other ranches, but she owned the Del Sol. She had the papers to prove it.

"You are very much mistaken." Moisture trickled down her back, made her skin prickle. "The Del Sol is mine. It is the one thing my father didn't gamble away before he died. It is the only thing I have left, and there is hardly money to pay those who work it—certainly none to give to thieves."

Monheno stepped back in shock. Was that

true, or was it a clever scheme to win her release? The Del Sol had always been a rich holding. Was it possible all its wealth could really be gone?

"Interesting." He looked deep into her eyes, saw fear mixed with self-righteous fervor. "Your father must have been an even worse gambler than I thought."

She shrugged impatiently, narrowed those stormy eyes at him. "Be that as it may." She stood steady as a rock, unwavering. "The Del Sol will never have enough money to pay bribes to thieves such as you."

He nodded, relieved. So the Del Sol wasn't bankrupt after all. It was just her own stubbornness that had made her hold out against the Sombras. He hated the fact that her lie wounded him.

"Well then, my dear." She winced when he called her that. "Let me offer you a bargain."

She nodded, probably hoping he would take her up on her earlier offer and let her go. He laughed under his breath. Hardly. He had something much more . . . advantageous in mind. There was only one acceptable way to end this—his way.

"If by tomorrow night you can still tell me I was in the wrong, you'll be free to go. If, on the other hand, I can convince you I was in the right, you will stay with me for another week." He hoped a week would be long enough. Her life, possibly his own, depended on it.

She traced the outline of her crimson lips with a fingernail thoughtfully, slowly, seductively. He felt a tug in his groin. He wanted to take her to bed right now—tell her the truth and convince her to be done with this foolishness. He wanted to love her, not fight with her. But he had to prepare himself for the possibility he might not be able to win her back. If he couldn't, he'd have to send her away . . . far away, where she couldn't be found.

"Do you agree to the bargain?" He prodded.

"Yes." She pressed her shoulders back confidently, making the cotton blouse outline her rounded breasts.

He clenched his fist against the edge of the table and dragged his eyes away. He had to show a little self control here. "Then it's settled." He sat back down and picked up his fork again, but food was the farthest thing from his mind. "Second helpings?" The only thing he wanted a second helping of was her.

"Thank you." She tipped her chair back to its feet and sat back down. "I think I will."

He smiled into those stormy violet eyes. *I think you will too.*

Savanna forced herself to look down at her plate. That smile made her feel as pliable as a sapling, ready to bend to his will. But she wouldn't do it. She couldn't let herself. What was behind his confidence? Did he have something up his sleeve?

It didn't matter. An act of heaven wouldn't

convince her he was in the right. Unless he went back on his word about letting her go, she'd be leaving tomorrow. But that still left tonight . . .

He finished the last of his meal and set his napkin aside, then swilled the last of the wine from his glass. She picked her own up and glanced at it in surprise. Nearly empty. The pressure of sitting here with him was getting to her. She shouldn't have drunk so much.

He set the glass down with a clink. "Well, what should we do now?"

She forced herself to look at him. "Clean house." She stretched a hand across the table, palm up. "Have you a gun I can oil?"

He chuckled, a deep, throaty sound that went straight to her stomach. "No. Would you like to sharpen my kitchen knives?"

"Very much."

He glanced toward the door again, a strand of jet hair falling over his dark forehead. "How about a walk in the garden?"

"Will there be man-eating dogs there?"

"Yes."

"Good." She stood up. "Show me the way."

He rose from his chair, came around the table, and extended an elbow to her as if they were in cordial company. She laid her hand on the sleeve of his shirt and looked down at her fingers, pale against the tan cotton fabric. Just touching him— that one simple touch—brought desire rushing back into her body. That faint, insistent tingle

211

deep within her beckoned, burned through her stomach and thighs.

She bit her lip and shut it out. He was a liar, a thief, her enemy. She wouldn't surrender to this again. She was going to the garden to size up the dogs, to find an escape route in case he went back on his word tomorrow, nothing else.

The evening air was crisp, the yard bright with moonlight when they stepped out the door. She took a deep breath, clearing the scent of dust and age from her lungs. It felt good to be out of that eerie house.

A dog ran forward, and Monheno brushed its head absently before waving it away. "Fickle creatures." He nodded toward the dog. "Half of the time they've got their teeth into my heels, and the other half they're looking for affection." He glanced at her and gave her a wink. "A little like women, come to think of it."

Outrage boiled into her throat and spilled out her lips. "I never lied to you. I never tried to steal from you. I . . ." Tears ached in her chest. "I never used your heart and threw it away."

Monheno felt those words tug at his soul. "Savanna." He touched her hair, almost silver in the moonlight, and stopped walking. "I may not have told you the truth about who I was. I had my reasons—you'll know them tomorrow, but I never toyed with you. When I said you had my heart, I told the truth. If circumstances hadn't taken such an unfortunate turn, we would still be together now." It was true, every word from his heart, but she shrugged it off and pulled away.

"You mean I would still be your fool." She hid her eyes, but her voice was razor-sharp, her words filled with bitterness.

He caught a moon-bright curl as it fell over her cheek. "A fool for love." He did love her. He knew it, whether he wanted to or not, whether it was convenient or not, even if it cost him everything he had worked for.

She jerked back like he'd stung her. "I do not love you." She tipped her chin up and met his eyes. "I never did, and I certainly never shall."

He knew better. She was melting like a candle before his eyes, burning like he was. He could see it in the way her lips parted after she spoke, in the way her breasts hardened against the fabric of her blouse, in the way she smoothed her hair behind her shoulder.

He captured her in his arms, but she kept her own crossed like a barricade against him. "Never say never, mi corazon."

Savanna's thoughts reeled. "Don't call me that," she spat. Why were her knees turning to jelly now! Good God, she couldn't let him do this to her again. "I'm not your love."

He laughed deep in his throat and gave her folded arms a complaining look. "That isn't what the words mean." Fire leapt in his raven eyes, making her feverish and dizzy. "Mi corazon is 'my heart.'" He brushed a kiss across her lips.

She felt them tremble, an odd reaction for someone who didn't love him.

He traced her trembling underlip with his thumb. "Now, if I said 'mi amor mi corazon,' then you'd have cause for complaint." He breathed the words against her lips, kissed her again, then added, "Assuming, of course that you weren't my love."

She pressed away from him in a halfhearted protest. "I don't speak Spanish."

"Of course." He smiled, warm, seductive, irresistible like his kiss. "Spanish is a tongue for lovers, and, as you said, you are no man's love."

She didn't have to wonder how to reply—whether to confirm or deny it. His lips possessed hers in the instant of silence that followed.

He parted her lips, tasted her, made her mind spin like a whirlwind. She reeled against the circle of his arms, slid her hands over the strong cords of his chest, around his neck, pulled him closer. Protests rang through her mind like thunder. This was wrong, insane. He was a liar, a thief. He broke her heart, and here she was in his arms again. She had to stop herself.

But she couldn't. She melted against him like honey as he smoothed the hair from her ear, nipped the tender lobe. Tiny shivers tickled up and down her spine as his fingers slid into her hair, followed it to her waist.

He hardly seemed like a cruel thief now. He was gentle, warm, like the man who cradled her in his arms when she awoke in the middle of

214

the night, like the man who soothed that frightened little girl in the closet. No jokes, no sly smiles, no smooth words. This was the man who stole her heart. He was back, and her heart was his again.

She pressed closer to him, lost herself in his kiss, his touch. He circled her with his strong arms, driving her ghosts away.

Monheno tasted her lips again, felt desire tug at his loins. It wasn't right to lure her in like this. It wasn't what he planned. He wanted to win her back through love, not passion. He wanted to make her know he loved her, to gain her love in return.

He wanted to make love to her. He parted from her, and whispered her name. He liked the way it sounded, the way it felt. He knew now more than ever he could never release her—that he had to hold her somehow, but not against her will. He would have to convince her to stay. Love was too precious to give up for pride or power or money. He had all of those things, but love he'd been too long without.

"Mi amor, mi corazon," he whispered as his lips trailed down the velvet curve of her neck.

His words of love swept the protests from her mind. Not even the tiniest voice in the darkest corner of her mind told her to stop him. Every inch of her flesh quivered with desire, burned with need.

His hands slid, fingers outstretched, from the curve of her waist, pulled her against his insistent hardness. Her blood raced with anticipation, rushed like a whitewater tide in her ears.

She clung to him willingly as he lowered her into the grass, damp with moon-bright drops of dew. They glittered around her like jewels as she gazed up at the moon, a lovers' moon, waning a little, and a touch crimson with a misty halo around it. Oh, how she wished it would never set, and the sun would never rise tomorrow.

# Twelve

Daylight was a cruel master. She glanced at the other side of the bed. Empty. At least he was gone.

She pulled the covers up over her head and tried to shut out the persistent rays of sunlight streaming through the high leaded-glass windows, tried to shut out the memory of what happened in the garden. There was nothing cheery about this morning. Once again, she was waking up to the gruesome recollection of what she had done the night before. Once again, it involved Monheno Devilla.

Who was it that said things always looked better in the morning? Sometimes, they looked a lot worse. She did it again—fell into his arms like a star-struck fool—and for what? Physical attraction? Sweet words? How many times had she been told in her life nothing ever came of those two things? What kind of a fool was she?

It didn't matter. Their bargain still stood.

She'd not be spending another night in this strange house with him. There was no way he could convince her his thievery was justified. After last night, she was more sure than ever that she had to get away from him—far away.

"Oh, Savanna Storm, you are the biggest fool!" She threw the bedcovers aside and swung her legs over the edge. From the chair beside the bed, she took the royal blue skirt and pale blue top and pulled them on with little enthusiasm. She was sick of looking at them! They smelled like fresh grass and wet dew, and faintly like Monheno Devilla. Looking at them reminded her of him taking them off her body, of her being his willing fool.

"Stupid, stupid, stupid!" She took the hairbrush—the same one Monheno used the night before to comb the stems of dew-dampened grass from her hair—and threw it against the wall. Damn him! What was she thinking last night? What was wrong with her mind that she couldn't control her own body? Maybe that bump on her head did more damage than she knew.

She stared at the brush as it clattered to a stop on the floor, pictured it in his hand. How long did he sit there on the bed with her, gently combing the grass from her hair?

What a strange sensation it was, being with him like that, comfortable, natural, as if they belonged together, as if they were . . . married? He claimed he'd brushed his sisters' hair often in the past. Sisters! Lovers more likely. He'd probably had more women than she could count. He probably still did. For all she knew, he could be with one now. When did he leave the bed? Last night as soon as she was asleep? This morning before she awoke? Where was he now?

She walked to the dresser, braced her palms on the top and looked into her own eyes. What was wrong with her? Why was she standing here thinking about him with other women and feeling *jealous*? She hated him, despised him. After today, she hoped never to see him again. What was he going to say to her today? What could he possibly say?

She smoothed trembling hands over the front of her skirt and started toward the door. Best to get this over with. The sooner she rejected his lies, the sooner she could go home. She glanced back at the mirror one more time, steadied herself, then grabbed the door handle and jerked it open.

From the hallway, he almost fell on top of her. She took a startled step backward and gasped in shock. He stumbled forward, flailing his arms to get his balance. She backed against the door-frame. That wasn't Monheno.

"Wha . . ." she stammered. That wasn't Monheno at all. That was the man she saw in the hall yesterday. Something in his face was vaguely familiar as he stared boldly at her through haughty eyes made even darker by the greyness of his unkempt hair. His dress was almost as strange as the expression on his face. He looked overly formal, clothed in breeches and a faded blue waistcoat trimmed with deteriorating gold braid. The suit was odd and many years out of date, like something an actor might wear in a play.

"Who are you?" She finally found her tongue. "And why were you listening at my door?" God, what if he was listening there last night also? What if he was watching them in the garden?

"Allow me to introduce myself, milady." He had a thick Spanish accent, but he spoke slowly, so the words were clear. "I am Adolfo Devilla, Grandee de Espana."

She gave an unconscious curtsy. Something about him wasn't exactly right. He seemed . . . touched in the head. Grandee de Espana. Grandee of Spain? What was he talking about? Was he dangerous?

"F-forgive my rudeness," she stammered. "I didn't know there was anyone else here." He called himself Devilla—a relative of Monheno's, no doubt. Something in his features reminded her of Monheno. How perfect that insanity ran in the family.

"Oh, I live here," he was saying, this time with almost no accent at all. He drew his waistcoat together with both hands, took a broken loop of faded gold braid and secured it over a non-existent button, then nodded at it with satisfaction as it fell open again. "When I am not on my ship." He looked up like he suddenly realized again she was there. "Which," he studied his boot toes intensely, "I must," then looked slowly up to the wall, "attend to now."

He turned away as though he had forgotten her presence altogether, took a few steps, stopped without turning back and added, "We shall talk later, after the ship is secured at anchor."

She didn't reply, but hurried into the hallway in case he was violent as well as insane. Something inside the room clicked, like a door closing, and she peered back in. Empty. She inched just inside the room and looked around. It was completely vacant. A ghost? Monheno said the place was haunted. She spun around to find someone very real blocking the door.

"Monheno," she breathed with relief, for getting all his crimes, at least for the moment. Even a thieving scoundrel was better than a ghost.

He looked at her for a moment like he was confused, then started to smile. "I see you've met the Grandee."

She shivered from head to toe and leaned against the doorframe for support. "The . . ." So it wasn't a ghost after all. "But who . . . ?"

He gestured toward the room behind her, looking vaguely apologetic. "That is my uncle, Adolfo Devilla, but we more often call him The Grandee—which is as he prefers. He never actually was a Grandee. In fact, he's never even been to Spain, or on a ship for that matter, but it's

The Grandee, nonetheless." He leaned a little closer, like he was going to tell her a secret, then stated the obvious, "He's a little touched in the head."

She gaped at him in complete confusion.

He whirled a forefinger at his temple for emphasis. "His biscuits aren't all baked—he's one egg shy of a dozen—one brick shy of a load—his hens aren't all in the coup—he's . . ."

"All right!" she snapped, giving him a nasty little smile. "It's nice to know insanity runs in your family. At least *that* you came by honestly." For an instant, just for the blinking of an eye, she thought she had struck a nerve, but then it was gone, and he smiled perfectly.

"Then I'm forgiven." He extended an elbow to her. "Good. We have a great many things to do today."

She pushed his arm away petulantly and crossed her arms over her chest. "I'll follow," she grated out from between clenched teeth—teeth she wanted to sink into his neck. One more day. One more day and she would be free of Monheno Devilla forever. She had only to convince him he could not alter her convictions against him, and she would be free.

Monheno raised his eyes and offered up a little prayer to Mother Mary and Saint Jude. Joking and baiting her wouldn't put off what had to be done today. Today was his last chance. He needed it to go well. He was going to have to do something equivalent to moving mountains.

Still, no fair judge could hear his case and refute it. Savanna, while emotional, was fair. She would have to admit what he did was just, and then she would stay with him another week. Then he would have seven days to convince her he loved her and that she should marry him. The Lord built the world in less time. But then, he didn't have the wrath of Savanna Storm to deal with.

Savanna clenched her fists over the folds of her skirt as she followed him down the stairs to the dining room. The hour of judgment was at hand. She had to be strong, determined. She had to stand up to whatever lies he told her. She had to win her freedom now, this morning. Her heart couldn't stand another week of this torment.

He said nothing, just took three age-yellowed documents from the sideboard and unrolled them onto the table. She listened calmly as he told her what the documents were—two Spanish land deeds dated 1740, and an ancient map of the valley that bore the seal of the king of Spain. Her heart sank as she looked at it. There was the river, the mission at Oro Grande, even the painted mountain where she and Monheno had made love. There were the gigantic land grants of the Bacas and Garzas, and others. And there in the center, right where the Del Sol now lay, were the land grants of the Devillas, the name circled with a bright graphic of the sun that matched the one carved in stone on her fireplace. She stretched her fingers out and touched the name to make sure it was real. The Del Sol once belonged to Monheno's family? How could that be?

Her fingers trembled on the brittle, aged parchment. She couldn't speak. She couldn't think. It had to be some sort of trick.

"Your family once owned the Del Sol?" she choked.

He rested his hands heavily on the polished wood, looked at her across the table. The gravity in his ebony eyes made her hold her breath.

"My family *built* the Del Sol. For two-hundred years, Devillas have been born in that house, and buried in that soil. My mother is buried in the corner of the rose garden you let go to ruin. That was her garden." He looked down at the map, then back up, the wounds open in his eyes. "So you see, what I take from the Del Sol, I do not steal," he looked deadly now, "because the Del Sol is mine to begin with."

She stood staring at the map, collecting her thoughts. Her legs went soft beneath her and her head spun dizzily. She was going to faint.

"But my father won the Del Sol in a poker game." She was so ashamed to use that defense she couldn't look at him when she said it. But if he was fool enough to wager something so precious in a game of cards, perhaps he deserved to lose it . . .

He gave a rueful laugh. "Do you really think I am that much of a fool?" He slammed a fist against the map. "The Del Sol was lost when your government reviewed the legality of the original grants. Your father claimed the Del Sol by petitioning with falsified paperwork. Had I been here, I could have prevented it, but I was not."

Tears welled up in her eyes and dropped onto her fingertips, then ran onto the edge of the map. "Oh dear God," she whispered. Now, the only thing she had left in the world wasn't hers either. Her father had left her truly penniless.

Anger boiled in her stomach like hot lye, rose into her face and made her feverish. Damn him! Damn him for ruining her life and her mother's. Damn him for locking her away in a boarding school so he could take what was hers. Damn him for making her that frightened little girl in the closet.

"Damn him." She sank down in a chair, covered her face in her hands to hide her shame. "I should have known." She should have seen it coming. She should have known the only thing that came from her father's hand was torment.

She pulled her hands away from her face and looked levelly at Monheno. "I want you to tell me if my father is really dead." She had to know. She had to be certain he was gone from her life forever, at least from her future. Her past would be tormented by him forever.

He looked surprised at first, then narrowed his eyes suspiciously. "Yes, he is."

Relief spiraled through her first, and then a

strange sense of grief she didn't want to feel. "Good." She hoped he could hear her from hell. "Did you kill him?"

He didn't flinch, didn't bat an eye. "Yes. It was self-defense. He tried to shoot me in the back."

A rueful laugh slipped from her lips. "How perfect. That is exactly the end he deserved." She saw Monheno's eyes widen with shock, but she didn't care. "I hope he suffered."

Monheno stepped back from the hardness in her voice and the bitterness in her eyes. He'd never seen her look like that, not even when she talked about Venenoso. What did her father do to her to make her hate him? She said once that he killed her mother. Was that true? Was that why she wished him an agonizing death?

"It was quick," he said flatly. "He asked for you in the end." He remembered those final moments. You never forgot seeing a man die, especially when that man tried to kill you, then begged for your help. "He asked that I take care of you when you came here."

She laughed again, a thin, vindictive sound. "I wasn't coming. I didn't set out until I received notice of his death."

"I see." He wasn't sure what to say. "He didn't know that."

She leveled a cool gaze filled with hatred. "I wish he had."

Savanna looked down at her hands, clenched white with anger in her lap, impotent anger.

Once again, she couldn't strike back at her father. Once again, she was helpless.

She heard Monheno come around the table and felt him take her hand. "There is something else you should see."

She couldn't look at him. "I need no more proof." There was no reason to go on with this any longer. "You've proven the Del Sol is yours, and as for my father's deathbed concern for me, you needn't worry. If you'll take me back to the Del Sol to get my things, I can take care of myself."

He leaned down to catch her eyes. "That wasn't our bargain."

She dropped her mouth open in surprise. How could he even bring up that insane wager now? "I still do not agree with your actions," she defended. "Even my father's treachery doesn't excuse your going outside the law to terrorize the people of this valley."

He looked completely unaffected, entirely confident. "There is more you need to know." He pulled her to feet. "I haven't finished making my case."

She held her tongue and followed him outside to the stables. His bay was saddled and waiting, and beside it, was one of the palominos she had sold. Seven more stuck their heads out of the stalls as she walked up.

"My palominos," she muttered.

He handed her the mare's reins. "*My* palominos," he corrected. "My family brought their ancestors from Spain, I could hardly let them be sold to the highest bidder."

Shame made her flush. It must have been hard for him to watch her lay claim to the things his family treasured. She mounted up and followed him out of the barn, thinking of him in Del Sol house, in the rose garden. What a fine actor he was, concealing the fact that he once lived there, that his family had lived there for generations. What fine actors all her neighbors were at the wedding, watching her with him and keeping silent. Who among her own employees knew who Monheno really was? Brandt? Waddie? Esperanza? Did they just not know, or did they betray her?

She fixed her gaze numbly on the road ahead. Thunder rumbled somewhere in the distance, reminding her of the night they came home from the cattle drive. She'd been falling in love with him that night, thinking in the back of her mind about marriage. All the while he was playing her for the fool. Why?

"Why didn't you just come to me with the facts—or to the law?" She glanced at him, then stared ahead again. "Why did you have to try to romance Del Sol away from me?"

From the corner of her eye, she saw him straighten. "Is that what you think?"

"That I know. When I would not yield to your thievery, you used . . . other methods." She blushed fiercely. "It should have occurred to you that I might yield to the truth."

He reined his horse closer, so close his knee brushed hers, sending a hot shiver through her body. "It should occur to you that I am after more than the Del Sol."

She clenched her fists on the reins and forced herself to look at him. "I suppose that is why you found it necessary to break into my bedroom in the middle of the night to steal from me." He looked surprised, and she nodded triumphantly. "Oh yes, I know that was you! And I know you are Venenoso."

He shook his head and smiled deviously. "Hardly," he laughed. "I'll grant that was me in your bedroom, but I was only there for your own good. I assure you I am not Venenoso. Had he been in your room, you wouldn't have escaped the encounter with your . . . virtue intact."

She gasped. "There for my own good!" she exploded. "You were there for your own profit!"

His face went stony. "I was there to stop you from making more trouble with Venenoso, who was ready to solve the problem by having you killed."

She widened her eyes and drew back in horror.

He leaned closer to her harshly. "Did you think he wouldn't? What did you think this was, a game?"

She realized in an instant how foolish she'd been to go against the Sombras. Her stubbornness again. What was she thinking? "It doesn't matter now. It's over. I'll be leaving as soon as you show me the road home."

He looked vaguely wounded, then turned away from her and pulled his horse up. "We'd better walk from here." He dismounted and tied his horse up, then reached for hers. "No noise."

A shiver crawled over her shoulders and down her spine as she dismounted and followed him into the trees. Where was he taking her? What could possibly be out here in the middle of nowhere? What did this have to do with his reasons for taking the Del Sol?

She trotted to keep up with his long strides until she was breathless. "How much farther is it?"

"Not much." He didn't look back. His tall, sinuous form moved easily through the trees ahead of her—in and out of the shadows, almost like he would disappear.

He slowed finally and she saw the light of a clearing ahead. He crouched down, motioned for her to do the same. She got to her knees and followed him through the last of the underbrush. What was out there? What did he . . .

He parted the brush and she looked into the clearing. There was a camp there, more of a small village really, built of canvas, log and chink, mud brick, adobe. People, mostly ragged and unwashed, walked in and out among the buildings—women carrying heavy burdens of washing or water in tightly woven baskets, children following, men, for the most part, sitting idle in the shade.

"Who are they?" she whispered. Why would so many people be living in this ragged camp?

He answered as if he were waiting for that question. "They come from different places." She couldn't see his face, but there was empathy in his voice. "Some were once wealthy patrons living on ranches in the valley. Others didn't live much better than this before."

"But why are they here?" And why did he bring her to see them? Why was she hiding in the bushes like . . . a thief?

"They're here because they have nowhere else to go." He looked at her, his eyes accusing. "They are here because people like your father stole their homes. This is Venenoso's camp. These people fight alongside him to regain what rightfully belongs to them."

She said nothing. If she did, she was certain she would choke on her own shame. She had been so certain Monheno was in the wrong—that Venenoso was the worst kind of criminal. Now suddenly she was the thief.

"But the Sombras ride against all the ranches in the valley—not only the ones with American owners, but the old Spanish ranches also."

He gave her a look that made her wish she could turn into a snake and slither away. "Only for appearances," he said flatly. "They are never made to pay. They ride with the Sombras also—like Tito Baca."

231

She only nodded dumbly, his words sinking through her like heavy black oil, making her feel unclean. She should never have come west to lay claim to what her father left behind. She wanted no part of him before he died—she shouldn't have gone digging through his gold afterward. A sick feeling rose up from her stomach. Clamping her hand over her mouth, she pressed back out of the brush and ran for the horses. She didn't want to think anymore. She didn't want to see anything else. She just wanted to go home, to leave California and forget all this ever existed.

"Savanna, wait!" She heard Monheno's hushed call, but she didn't stop. She grabbed her horse's reins and climbed aboard, turned him toward the road and kicked him.

Tears blurred her eyes as he ran, and she wiped them away. Bargain or no, she was leaving—now. She couldn't face Monheno again. She couldn't face the truth.

Lightning flashed overhead and thunder rattled the ground as the palomino charged down the road. Around her, the woods grew darker, thicker, and the path waned like it would end altogether. Oh God, did she go the wrong way? She glanced over her shoulder. No sign of Monheno. Was he following her?

The path narrowed. Branches slapped her in the face, tore at her clothes, tried to pull her from the horse. She closed her eyes, bent low over his back and hung on. A voice raised over the crash of her horse's hooves. Thunder exploded, once, twice, three times. Not thunder. Shots!

The horse stopped suddenly, threw her against his neck and nearly unseated her. She grabbed frantically for the reins as he rose onto his hind legs, and pulled hard to bring him under control. He reared again, and she saw why. The ground was crumbling under his feet, rocks falling off the edge of a darkened canyon where the path ended.

She released the reins and let him fight for his footing. He screamed, scrambled away from the edge, struggled back to solid ground and stood there heaving. Grabbing the reins, she looked down at his legs for damage but found none. Her heart started beating again but then stopped in her throat.

"You make work for us." A thickly accented voice said from behind her. "Now we will have to keel you ourselves."

She spun the horse around to find three men behind her. Venenoso's men. A gasp passed her lips, and she backed the horse away a few steps. The shots she heard were aimed at her!

"Let me pass." Her voice was a thin ribbon. Nervously, she looked around. No escape. The cliff barred her from behind and the men from the front. The front rider raised his pistol and pointed it at her, taking deadly aim.

"No." She gasped.

He gave her a hard look, then nodded.

"Stop!" Monheno's voice boomed past her and echoed through the canyon. The men lowered their guns and turned their horses as he rode up from behind them.

"El Devilla," the leader muttered, eyes widening like he saw a ghost.

Monheno's eyes were cool like two bits of stone. "Let her pass."

The leader shook his head. "She has seen de camp."

Monheno pushed his horse past them, edging their nervous mounts out of the way. Extending a hand, he motioned Savanna away from the edge. "Tell Venenoso I will see to it."

Savanna didn't wait for an answer. She urged the nervous palomino forward and prayed as the men looked back and forth at one another, hands twitching nervously on their guns. The click of a hammer shot down her spine as she moved past them to Monheno.

"El Devilla," the leader spun his horse around, "I *weel* tell him." It sounded like a threat.

Monheno motioned silently for Savanna to continue on. "Do that." He bit out, then turned his horse and followed her.

Savanna held her breath until the men were well out of sight.

Beside her, Monheno sat cool and stiff like a statue. His eyes were midnight-dark when he turned to her. "Your word is about as good as your credit."

She winced and stared down at her horse's plodding hooves. She did give her word—another week if he could prove he had been in the right. He proved it. He also just saved her life, but she couldn't bear another week of his torment. Her heart would never survive it.

"Let me go." The words choked her throat like splinters of glass. She didn't care about her word. She couldn't keep it.

"I couldn't if I wanted to." His voice was razor-sharp, meant to wound, she could tell.

She raised her eyes imploringly. "Let me go." She hated herself for pleading, hated the tears rushing into her eyes. "You've proven your case to me. I won't go to the law. Just let me go."

He shook his head, his broad shoulders a hard, unbending line. "You'd be dead as soon as they found out," he said steadily. "Your performance back there just assured that."

Her heart sank to the bottom of her stomach and sat there like a cannonball. You'd be dead . . . Would the Sombras really come after her? "I'll go away," she pleaded. "I'll go where they can't find me, back East, back to England."

He smiled bitterly. "Anywhere but here with me?"

The way he said it, the look in his eyes took her aback, held her silent. He looked hard, angry, but wounded also. He looked hurt for the first time since she'd known him.

"You don't understand," she tried again. How could she explain that the price of his games was too high for her? How could she tell him he twisted her heart every time he looked at her, touched her soul every time he laid a hand on her? How could she make him see?

He sighed and looked at the path ahead. "I understand." His voice was like acid. "But I still can't let you go." He looked back at her, his mask replaced. "A bargain is a bargain, Savanna. Is a week really so long a time?"

# Thirteen

She took the chair across from him and stared down at her hands in her lap. Food, not maps filled the dinner table this time. The smell of it made her stomach turn.

They'd been playing this game for hours since they came back from the ride—her being silent, him acting like she was his guest not his prisoner. Nothing she said could convince him this was a futile effort, that he should just let her go and be done with it.

She looked at the food with little enthusiasm as he passed the platters to her. Was he telling the truth when he said Venenoso would kill her if she tried to leave? What was to prevent Venenoso from coming here and killing her now?

". . . and don't starve yourself."

She realized he was speaking. She reached out half-heartedly and took a scoop of brown beans. This game was insane. She wasn't his lover. She wasn't his guest. She was his prisoner.

"Savanna," he admonished. "Surely you can do better than that." He moved the platters closer to her.

"Must you harangue me about everything!" she spat, looking up murderously. "I may be your prisoner, but I suppose I can eat as I like! Or is your controlling my every move part of this insidious bargain also?"

He had the gall to roll his eyes toward the ceiling and think about it.

Damn him and his games! She slammed a fist on the table, sending her entire place setting an inch into the air.

He glanced at it with raised brows. "No, I suppose not." And then that damnable mask of a grin. "You know, next to laughter, anger is your most fetching emotion."

It was all she could do to keep from assaulting him with her dinner fork. She gripped the handle and pictured the tongs wiping that irritating grin off his face. The idea made her smile back at him.

Glaring at him, she plunged the fork into her ham and shredded it brutally into pieces. It was a poor substitute for his face.

He raised his wineglass and looked at her over the rim.

A tingle burned through her stomach and into her thighs and she looked down at her plate "Who . . . who prepared all of this?" She stirred the pile of beans back and forth and considered flinging a forkful at him. Oh, God, why was she having these feelings now?

"You don't like it?" he asked as though the walls had ears and he didn't want them to hear.

She shrugged. "I just wondered . . ." she looked up to find him glancing around the room as though he expected to see someone else there, "who prepared it since there is no staff."

He leaned across the table and crooked a finger to bring her closer. "The food is brought in, but The Grandee will tell you Edwardo does all the cooking."

"Who is Edwardo?" So someone was bringing the food in. Perhaps that would be her chance to escape.

"The galley chef."

"Where is he?" He was close enough to kiss her—so close she could see the minute flecks of brown against the blackness of his eyes.

"In The Grandee's head, I'm afraid." He raised a palm in a helpless gesture. "Actually, he has an entire crew there."

"And you pretend to see them?" Why was she sitting here conversing politely with him? "Isn't that dangerous?" Silly question. Everything about Monheno Devilla was dangerous.

"Hardly," he assured her. "He's as harmless as a church mouse, but we try not to press him with the truth. It's upsetting for him. He lost his wife and five daughters to cholera during the rush of forty-nine, but he doesn't remember it. Since then, he's been sailing the high and dry seas, so to speak."

She nodded. She understood how grief could lead to a weakened mind. A stillbirth started her own mother toward insanity, and death . . .

She put away those thoughts and met his eyes, saw grief there for a moment before he hid it. Did his own family die from cholera too? Was that what happened to his mother? Was that why his voice was solemn and low last night when he mentioned his sisters?

She didn't ask. She couldn't afford to. She couldn't let herself feel sympathy for him. Already, desire was kneading in her stomach, making her heart race, making her meet his eyes when he looked at her.

Monheno caught her gaze and held it, or it held him. A tugging ache pulled at his loins, but he ignored it. It was the tug in his heart that worried him. He'd had more lovers in past years than he could count—the loss of loved ones made you search recklessly for someone new to love. That empty space inside him was so vast, so painful, he'd been desperate to fill it.

He wanted the Del Sol back because he was trying to heal that wound on his soul—trying to blot out his guilt for not having been there when his mother and sisters died. He'd joined hands with Venenoso to get it, to regain for everyone the things that belonged to them. Now he had the Del Sol back, and the wound was still bleeding.

He looked deeper into her eyes. He was in love with her. After what happened today in the woods, Venenoso would know it. If he wasn't already wondering why Monheno intervened so many times on Savanna's behalf, he would know now. Venenoso was like a snake, coiled and ready, always striking in the weakest spot. If he struck Monheno, it would be through Savanna. He had to keep her close, to keep her safe . . .

She parted her lips seductively, driving the thoughts from his head. "Monheno." The word was soft, thick, almost a caress in itself. Her eyes were smoky with passion and desire. "Please, just take me to bed."

Savanna flushed as the words tumbled from her mouth. Did she really say them? What would he think? It didn't matter. She couldn't help herself. Sitting there with him in the lamp light, looking into his eyes as they turned dark with need, brought her alive with desire. Her blood was racing, burning through her body like lightning. He would have her sooner or later anyway. Why endure the torment of resistance?

He led her down the darkened hallway and up the stairs to a grand bedroom where the lamps had been lit and the bed turned down. She stopped just inside the door and looked around the room. "Are we alone?"

He nodded. "Quite."

A shudder passed through her, and she looked around the dark corners of the room—corners where ghosts, or strange uncles could be lurking. "Turn up the lamps," she whispered.

His eyes widened questioningly. "Up?"

She nodded and he moved around the room raising the wicks.

She stood uncertainly between the door and the bed until he reached for her hand. Even that simple touch made her skin quiver. She yielded as he pulled her closer—almost close enough to kiss her. She stood looking into his eyes—those bewitching, intense devil's eyes that had held her spellbound even the first day she had met him.

"Savanna," he started to speak again.

"No, don't," the words rushed breathlessly from her mouth and she raised her fingers to his lips. Slipping into his arms, she replaced the fingers with a kiss. No more false words of love . . . no more.

He drew her closer, slid his hands, fingers outstretched, down the curve of her back and over the swell of her buttocks, pressing her against his hardness. Her blood raced as he moved slowly back up, caught her shoulders and looked down into her eyes. His grin was devilish.

"I might enjoy . . ." he ran a finger along the neckline of her blouse, ". . . watching you disrobe yourself for a change." He traced the finger over her breast, then turned and walked into the small dressing room on the other side of the bed.

She stood gaping after him in shock, an offended gasp dropping her underlip. He was toying with her! How dare he! If he thought she would play the temptress for him he had another think coming . . .

That thought flew from her as he reappeared from his dressing room minus his clothes. His powerful body was a picture of male perfection, strong, flawless, smooth cinnamon skin. She watched him cross the room, transfixed, let her eyes drift slowly down his strong neck to his chest, now crossed confidently with muscular arms. She drifted slowly past them to his tapered torso, his strongly corded stomach with just the faintest line of hair that led to . . .

"Oh!" She slapped a hand to her mouth and blushed furiously. She'd never looked at that before! A lady wasn't supposed to.

"Your pardon, have I offended you?" She could feel him smiling, but she couldn't look at his face. Her gaze was fastened to the heart of his indiscretion.

"I never!" was all she could think of to say.

"I should hope not." The muscles of his stomach twitched with laughter, making his hardened member do an erotic dance.

"Oh my goodness!" She gasped without realizing it. Her eyes were still magnetized to . . . it.

She watched it cross the room as he went to the bed. He laughed deep in his throat and she forced her eyes away. What he must think!

He didn't look like he was thinking of much

of anything as he settled himself on the bed. Without a hint of decorum, he propped a pillow behind himself, crossed his long, sinewy legs at the ankles, then raised his arms and twined his fingers comfortably behind his neck.

He nodded toward the bed beside him and raised a dark brow suggestively. "Care to join me?"

She blushed from head to toe. He was laughing at her, laughing at how inept she was in an area where he was so skilled. Well, she'd show him!

"I think I shall." She tipped her chin up, lowered her lashes coolly, and moved her fingers to the top button of her blouse. They were shaking so badly she could barely manage the simple task. She worked open each button, then left the blouse dangling while she unfastened the hooks on her skirt waist. Strange, he was so much better at removing her clothes than she was.

Desire quickened in Monheno's loins as he watched. Was she taking so long on purpose? It was driving him crazy, watching her stand there half dressed. It was all he could do to keep from going and helping her. She let her skirt fall finally and slipped out of her blouse, then stood there in her chemise like she might shrink into the floor.

Savanna swallowed hard. She wasn't going to faint. She wasn't. She wouldn't give him the satisfaction. She had come this far. She couldn't let him get the best of her now. She tossed her hair back and slipped off the chemise, drew it slowly, she hoped seductively, over her hips, past her breasts, over her head and tossed it onto the floor. Goose bumps prickled over her skin as she stepped toward the bed.

"Darling." He was still wearing that infuriating smile. "I'm as much a one for adventure as any man, but you might leave your boots at the bedside."

She dropped her gaze in complete shock. Boots. Two of them. On her feet. How completely idiotic! She stood on one foot, jerked a boot off and sent it flying at him. He ducked and she fired the second one, which he caught. Leaning over, he set it calmly beside the bed.

"Now that's enough of that." He extended a hand toward her. "Come to bed."

She pursed her lips and stayed just out of reach. "I've changed my mind," she said softly, seductively, her mouth and tongue caressing the words, and her lashes fanning over her half-closed eyes.

He darted across the bed, caught her hand, and yanked her down, pinning her under his weight. "I think not." The humor was gone from his eyes, and he looked wild as the devil. "I think you've tortured me long enough."

Tortured him? He was torturing her. Every inch of her flesh cried out to be touched, tasted, caressed. She sighed in contentment as his mouth drew a simmering trail down the side of her neck. He moved languidly to her breasts, slid his hands up to mold them into his mouth, then let his fingers travel slowly down her stomach.

Dimly, she heard music—the soft, lilting notes of a piano and the far-away tones of a voice . . . a woman's voice, she thought. A ghost? The spirit of the woman who died before ever living in the house?

Perhaps it was only her own imagination. Monheno's strong hands moved over her thighs, and she imagined all sorts of things . . .

He parted her legs gently, his fingers slipping within to tease at the soft nest of golden-brown hair. She burned, quivered with desire, and he trailed his lips slowly down her stomach, tasted the skin of her inner thigh, drew near the heart of her passion. She gasped in shock, then in pleasure, let her head fall to the side, and grasped the pillow. How could one man know so many things about love?

His taunting turned slowly to torture. She grabbed him in desperation, but he rolled to the bed beside her, and drew her on top of him. She opened her eyes in shock as he gripped her buttocks, lifting her into position over his hardened shaft.

"N-no!" she stammered hoarsely, pressing against his chest. This was immoral, unthinkable!

"Sssshhhh," he soothed, his raven eyes liquid with passion. "There is nothing to be frightened of, just let me show you, mi corazon."

Her fear melted like dewdrops before fire as he lowered her over his manhood, filling her, sending streaks of lightning throughout her body. She relaxed, let his hands instruct her in the rhythm until she learned it herself. His touch moved upward then, over her back and then to her breasts, his thumbs teasing roughly at her hardened nipples as they moved up and down to the newly learned pulse of their love.

She arched backward, drew even greater pleasure, gave him greater pleasure also. He groaned, his touch on her breasts growing pleasurably rougher, more demanding. She bent her head forward, and saw through her parted lashes the thing that had so offended her before, appearing and disappearing beneath her own body. The sensuality of it fired her. She cried out as she felt him lean up and take her nipple again in his mouth. It was more than she could stand. Her body tightened exquisitely in release, then brought the warm evidence of his also.

She fell to his chest, exhausted, unwilling to be parted.

Monheno wrapped her tightly in his arms and buried his face in the softness of her hair. "Mi amor, mi corazon," he whispered, kissing her lightly on the cheek. She came to him this time, of her own free will. Perhaps he had finally softened her iron resolve not to love. Perhaps there was some hope after all.

Savannah sighed against his chest. She didn't want to love him, had never wanted to, but here she was. She couldn't deny what she felt was love. Her heart felt full and warm.

Hours passed as she lay beside him, her head resting against his chest, her ears listening to the slow rise and fall of his breath. She stared into the flame of the slowly dying lamp on the night table. The others had burned down already, this one would follow soon enough.

She hadn't slept without a lamp since childhood. Strangely, it didn't bother her now. She felt safe and protected for the first time in years. She couldn't hear the voice of that little girl in the closet, didn't feel that nagging fear that had haunted her for years.

A new fear nagged in its place. What if this new peace, this new love didn't last? How was it possible for her to feel so strongly for him but also feel so uncertain? She'd always imagined love to be a certain thing—reliable, like tea at two o'clock every day. Marriages were planned, sometimes for years in advance, and love was something that was learned, like you learned to like tea whether you cared for the taste or not . . .

He stirred in his sleep then and chased away her thoughts like a pack of unwelcome hounds lingering on the stoop. No more thinking. She would let the week play itself out and see what happened.

She'd barely fallen asleep when the dogs barked outside. Beneath her ear, she heard

Monheno's heart quicken and she felt his arm tense around her.

"Is something wrong?" Her pulse hurried into her throat, parched and swollen from sleep.

He slipped away from her and cool night air rushed over her skin. "Ssshhh." He sounded fully awake, anxious. "No. Nothing."

She sat up in bed, holding the covers around her breasts. Chills crept up and down her spine. Something was wrong, she could hear it in his voice. She could see it in the way he left the bed and jerked on his trousers and boots, not like he was sleepy and confused, but like he was angry and worried.

Fear balled up in her throat until she could barely breathe. "Where are you going?"

He didn't answer, just buttoned his trousers around his bare waist as he crossed to the door. He stopped with his hand on the latch. "Stay here."

*Stay here.* The words whispered in the clap of the door as he closed it behind him. She watched it shudder to a stop, then turned up the last flickering lamp, sat there, and listened. Silence. Where was he? What was happening?

Her heart's nervous pounding forced her from the bed, and she slipped into her clothes. She couldn't stay here in this dark room hiding, wondering, afraid.

She hurried to the door on silent bare feet, clicked it open a crack, and listened. Nothing. Holding her breath, she peeked into the hall.

249

No sign of him. The hall was dark except for one lamp at the end.

Wrapping her arms around herself, she headed toward it, blood racing, heart thundering at the base of her neck. The dogs outside stopped barking. Did that mean the trouble was gone? Or did that mean the trouble had come inside? The thought grabbed her by the throat like icy fingers.

She stopped by the lamp and looked back. Was someone watching her? Her heart froze until a sound at the bottom of the stairs started it beating again. A door closing? Was Monheno down there?

Taking a deep breath, she tiptoed down the stairs, then stood at the bottom clutching the banister. The hallway was quiet and dark as pitch except for a sliver of lamplight from the door cracked at the end. She slid one hand soundlessly along the wall and moved closer to it.

"Something to drink?" Monheno's voice.

She hurried through the shadows, her heart racing until she could barely hear the rumble of another man's voice. Who else was in there? Was Monheno talking to his uncle?"

". . . until now, my friend." She caught the end of a sentence. "I think we have a little something to discuss." She didn't know the voice. It was hard, cold, slightly threatening.

She edged closer to the door, almost close enough to peek in the crack. Who was in there?

What would happen if they found her outside? She slipped a hand over her thundering heart as she edged one eye and then the other into the light.

"No need for discussion at this point." Monheno turned from a table at the far end of the room, two glasses of liquor in his hands. "And particularly not at this hour."

An evil chuckle drew her eyes to the second man as Monheno stepped forward and handed him one of the glasses. He was seated in a chair, his back to her, his enormous frame dwarfing the delicate piece of furniture. His black, broad-brimmed hat, trimmed in fine expensive gold braid, hid all but the corner of his chin. Thick cords of long silver hair fell from beneath it and spread over his shoulders and the chair like intertwining serpents.

"You always preferred to keep farmer's hours, Monheno."

Something about that voice scratched along her spine like the cold point of a blade.

Monheno took a sip of his drink, his eyes slightly narrowed, his posture falsely pleasant. "I always preferred to be a farmer."

The other man laughed, a vicious sound like a dog's growl. "So I am told." He took a sip of his own drink. "So now that you have what you want, you have turned on me."

Monheno eyed him for a moment, then looked straight toward the door. Savanna slapped a hand to her mouth and drew back. Did he see her there?

"You are sadly misinformed." If he saw her, he gave no indication. "I have done nothing to betray you. I have done my best to solve the problem without bloodshed."

The other man scoffed and jerked his wine glass up. Liquid sloshed over his dark hand as he pointed a finger at Monheno. "By taking her on a tour of my backyard?"

Tour of my backyard? Venenoso! She should have known just by looking at him, even if she couldn't see his face. This was Venenoso. The realization made her blood run cold.

Monheno looked at the door again, this time more intensely, like he suspected she was there. "I thought it best."

Venenoso sprang out of his chair like a cat, silver hair flying around his shoulders. "Let me tell you what I think is best." His voice was low, but tight like stretched rawhide. "I think it best that I take her with me now and see to this problem myself."

Savanna gasped beneath her hand, terror quivering through her muscles, screaming for her to run, but she couldn't. She stayed rooted to the spot with morbid fascination.

Monheno glanced momentarily at Venenoso's glass, then looked back to his eyes and smiled. "We came to an agreement as I recall." His voice was as smooth as fine whiskey, but animosity kept the muscles tight in his bare chest and arms.

With lightning speed, Venenoso swung his hand out and sent the glass sailing across the room. It shattered against the far wall with a deafening crash.

"I have no more patience for your agreement." He stood face to face with Monheno and touched the knife at his belt threateningly. "Perhaps I will just have my men come in and show your guest to the door." He scratched his chin and looked narrowly toward the ceiling. "Where might we find her? In your bedroom, perhaps?"

A murderous look crossed Monheno's face, but was quickly masked. He grinned and raised his hands. "Precisely why I'd prefer you leave her be."

Savanna swallowed hard to stop the offended gasp rising to her lips. She knew what he was doing—trying to save her life. If Venenoso brought men in here now, there would be no way Monheno could stop it. Monheno was trying to diffuse the situation before it exploded like a cannon ball.

Even so, the thought of them conspiring together made her blood boil. How close were they, anyway? How much did Monheno have to do with running the Sombras?

Seconds ticked by with painful sloth as she waited for Venenoso to answer. What if he refused? She could tell by the look in Monheno's eye, he would never let her be taken. But if he fought . . .

Monheno raised his hands palm up at his sides and grinned. "Of course, you can see my position, amigo," he pressed.

Venenoso bent forward at the waist, leaned closer to Monheno. His hair fell back over his shoulder so she could almost see his face. "As usual, it has to do with a woman."

"As usual." Another grin.

"And you insist on keeping her alive?"

"Of course."

Venenoso sighed and took a step backward, closer to the door, close enough that if he turned around, he could reach out and grab her by the neck. She stepped back unconsciously and waited for his answer.

"Very well." He sounded calmer now. "You and I will make another bargain, Monheno, but this time the terms will be mine."

Monheno nodded, then glanced toward the door again like he heard something. Slowly, deliberately, Venenoso followed, cocked his head to the side, listened, then started to turn around.

Fear struck her like hot lightning, and she scrambled away from the door, turned and rushed back down the hall and up the stairs. She slammed the bedroom door and leaned against it, catching her breath. Did they see her? Were they coming? Clutching the door handle, she listened and waited.

An hour seemed to pass before she heard boot

254

steps echo down the hall. An instant later, the door handle moved under her fingers and she jumped back, spun around to face the door.

"Monheno," she breathed as soon as he appeared in the doorway.

He stepped inside and closed the door, then lowered a brow and looked her up and down. "Going somewhere?"

She glanced down at her clothing and shook her head like a guilty child. "I was starting to worry," she stammered. "I just thought perhaps I should go downstairs and look for you." Did he know she saw him with Venenoso?

He gave her a long, suspicious look like he knew, but then shrugged. "No need to worry." He sat down on the edge of the bed and started to pull off his boots.

No need to worry? The lie scraped over her like a steel brush. How could he even tell such a falsehood? And so smoothly?

"What was wrong?" she pressed. Would he tell her the truth or another of his easy lies?

"I had a visitor." He said simply, as he set his boots on the floor and reached for the button on his trousers.

She flushed and averted her eyes. What a good liar he was! He did it without batting an eye, with a smile on his face that turned her resolve to marmalade.

She lowered her brows incredulously and stared at her bare toes. "A visitor?" What was the bargain he made with Venenoso?

She heard him climb into bed. "Yes, Savanna, a visitor." The razor-sharp impatience in his voice made her jerk her head up. She'd never, ever heard him take such a tone with her. It hurt even through her anger.

She met his eyes. They were tired, red, worried. She resisted the urge to offer comfort as he extended his hand to her.

"Stop pressing me, Savanna," he said flatly, "and come to bed."

# Fourteen

Monheno gritted his teeth and stared out the window at the morning sun. It was bright and promising . . . and just about to be doused by a bank of brewing purple storm clouds.

Buttoning his shirt, he glanced over at Savanna. Her eyes were just the color of those clouds, and filled with venom. She was angry with him about last night, of course. She knew he was hiding something. In fact, she knew him better than he wanted to admit.

It was a strange feeling to have someone see right through him—something he'd never experienced and didn't like. Usually women were easy to win with a well-placed compliment, or a smile, or kiss. But not this woman. And she lay teetering on the far edge of the bed all night just to prove it.

He couldn't tell her what happened last night, of course. If she knew the bargain he had made with Venenoso, she would never go along with it. She would probably come after him in his sleep with one of his kitchen knives just to keep from it. So now his problem was to convince her to go along with Venenoso's bargain . . . without letting her know she was going along.

It was either that, or let Venenoso kill her. He watched her stomp a foot into her boot, and considered it. Not a bad idea . . . then he wouldn't have to tolerate any more of this stubbornness.

She smoothed her hands over her hips and wiped that idea right out of his mind. He couldn't let her be killed. Unfortunately, he loved her.

"Breakfast?" He tried to sound pleasant, as though nothing was wrong between them.

"No thank you." She looked like she wanted to make a breakfast of him, and not in a way he would like, either.

"A walk in the garden?" Or maybe just a wringing of her pretty neck.

She glared at him, crimson washing into her face and down her neck to the buttons she was just fastening over her breasts. "No thank you." Again.

That answer was starting to wear on his nerves. He tucked his shirttail in and started toward her. "Good, then we'll go for a ride."

She tossed back a heavy length of sun-bright hair. "No thank you."

He grabbed her arm and pushed her toward

the door. She gasped in offense and hurried to finish her buttons.

"It was not a question." He'd had enough. He was usually a patient man, especially with women. Having five sisters taught him about the ebbs and flares of female personalities, and how best to handle things, but Savanna was an unfair test. She was expert at getting under his skin.

She made an offended sound in her throat and tried to pull away. He squeezed a little harder to hold her.

"Let go of me!" she spat as he threw open the door and escorted her down the hall. "You're hurting my arm."

He knew better. "I might just break your arm." The urge was getting stronger by the minute. God, she could drive him out of his mind quicker than a rattlesnake could swallow a rat.

She glared at him, her chin tipped up obstinately as he led her down the stairs. "It is time we stopped this foolish charade, Monheno." She narrowed her eyes at his hand on her arm. "I want you to let me go home this instant."

He blinked at her in disbelief. Where did that come from? What did it have to do with last night? Just like a woman to think everything was connected.

"People will be looking for me," she insisted, almost like she was trying to convince herself.

He rolled his eyes in exasperation. "No one will be looking for you."

She dropped her mouth open like he had insulted her. "Of course they will," she gasped. "Do you think my staff won't notice I'm gone?"

He couldn't help chuckling. His way of taking care of her staff was almost a stroke of genius. "I'm sure they would be if you hadn't left that note. But given that, they undoubtedly think you are having a wonderful time shopping in San Francisco." Savanna stared at him in complete shock. What was he talking about? "Shopp . . ." she muttered. "I left no note." He made an infuriating flourish with his free hand. "Of course you did, don't you remember?" She narrowed her eyes murderously. "I did no such thing."

He tapped a finger to his temple like something just occurred to him. "Hummm, well you must have done it after you knocked yourself unconscious."

She realized suddenly what he meant. "Youuuu . . ."

He slapped a hand, spread-fingered, to his chest. "Me?"

She tried to jerk away again as he led her out the door and down the path to the stable. When he wouldn't let go, she cocked her free arm back and swung it at him. He caught it just before it would have made satisfying contact with his chin.

He stopped walking and held her there, her arms imprisoned, then jerked her up against him. Her traitorous flesh ran from the battle instantly, burning against his.

She met his eyes, and that was her undoing. Every inch of her melted with the desire that tormented her all night in his bed. She raised to meet his lips as he lowered his head to kiss her, taste her, claim her. He parted her lips and drove within, drew her out, and she responded without meaning to or wanting to. He released her arms and smoothed his hands over her back, pressing her closer to him, sending shivers of desire shooting through her stomach.

She was trembling when he pulled away. Slowly, she dragged her heavy lashes up to look at him. How could he do this to her so well—every time? It was absolutely maddening.

"You said we were going riding," she muttered, but riding wasn't what was on her mind.

"Ummmm." He brought his fingers up and stroked them over her hair. He didn't look like riding was on his mind either. "We are."

She gathered all her resolve and issued a challenge. "Then we should go." She wasn't going to let him lure her into bed again—not this time.

He nodded, his eyes warm and smoky. "We should . . . unless you're afraid it will rain."

"No." She glanced at the building line of thunderheads not far away. "I'm not afraid."

She listened to the far away thunder as he led one of the palominos from the stall and saddled it. *I'm not afraid.* That couldn't be farther from the truth. She was afraid—afraid of what was happening to her, afraid of what he was doing to her. She had no way of stopping it, or controlling it, or even understanding it at all.

She rubbed her forehead tiredly as he saddled his bay and led the horses to her. He tried to give her the reins to the palomino, but she reached for the bay instead. "I want the *bay*." She said flatly. "The palominos give me a headache with all their prancing." And she had a thunderous one already.

He looked reluctant. "I can't say I care much for them myself."

She rolled her eyes and snatched at the bay's reins. "Why did you buy them if they aren't of any value?"

He gave her that slightly disappointed, slightly bewildered look, like she was speaking a language he couldn't, or didn't want to understand. "They are of value for their beauty alone," he said quietly.

She rolled her eyes and jutted her jaw out in complete exasperation. "That is the most foolish thing I have ever heard." And it was. "Sometimes, Monheno Devilla, I question your sense." Actually, she questioned it all the time.

He grinned and shrugged. "That isn't much threat to me since everyone in this valley questions yours."

"Do tell?" She jutted her lower lip out in indignation. "Well they are probably correct about that. If I had my sanity before I came to California—and I'm not even certain about that—I've certainly lost it since I met you." That was the truth. She could only imagine what those she left behind in England would think if they could see her now. Scandalized wouldn't even begin to describe it—perhaps mortified was a better word.

He laughed at her, then leaned close and gave her a quick kiss. "No worry for me," he lifted her onto the palomino before she knew what was happening, "insanity runs in my family, but what is your excuse?"

She gave a wry one-sided smile as he mounted his horse. "It's contagious."

He tipped his head back and laughed, the sound of it mingling with a far-away clap of thunder. "Your problem, Savanna Storm, is that you worry too much about what other people think."

She gathered her reins and moved her horse out beside his. "Don't you?" Stupid question. He had the worst devil-be-damned attitude she'd ever seen.

He caught her eyes. "Never," then looked away toward the thunder clouds. "Though I wish at times in the past I'd given in a little."

The tone of his voice, the look in his eyes intrigued her. "Times in the past?" She wondered if he would answer.

He nodded, but seemed far away.

She moved her horse a little closer. "What times?"

He gave her a long dark look as they moved the horses into a slow walk down the overgrown lane.

Just when she was sure he wouldn't answer, he did. "If I'd been here as my family wanted, my mother and sisters would be pruning the roses in that garden on the Del Sol, not lying buried beneath them. If I'd been here to defend my claim against your father, the Del Sol would never have been lost." His eyes turned grey with pain, like the storm clouds. "So you see, I have a few reasons to regret my independence after all."

She could have shot herself for opening such a wicked box of memories—some of which included the one of how her father stole the Del Sol. "I'm sorry." What else could she say? "W-what happened to your family?"

He turned back to her with a look that ripped her heart from her chest and made her draw back at the same time. She didn't want to feel such empathy, such a terrible rush of emotion for him.

"Do you really want to know?" he asked, an open wound in his eyes.

She nodded. "Yes. I want to know."

He searched her eyes, as if searching for her real intentions, then finally answered. "Cholera," he choked on the word, drew a long breath. "I left the Del Sol years ago—you know how boys are about working with their fathers. By the time I came back, he'd died in an accident, but I still wasn't ready to stay. In the fall, I left the Del Sol in the care of my mother, five sisters, an aunt, an uncle, two cousins, two nieces, and three nephews."

He sighed and looked off into the distance again, off into the past, she supposed. "There were so many children in that old house you couldn't move without tripping over one. So many voices . . ." She saw him swallow hard. "In the spring, I came back to bury them all, except for the Grandee." He gave her a long, piercing look. "Is it any wonder he lives in a world of his own making? He, at least, stayed to face the tragedy."

Sorrow flowed into her like bitter wine, sorrow that came from his eyes, from the way he held his shoulders, from the memory of him sitting in the rose garden that day. "Monheno, you can not blame yourself for cholera." She reached out and touched his arm, wondering what else to say. "You must remember they are in a safe place now." She withdrew her hand, feeling inadequate. She'd never been able to handle death herself, who was she to council him?

He braced his hands on the front of his saddle and leaned closer. "And do you blame yourself for the death of your mother?"

She gasped in shock, a hand flying to her mouth. How could he know her secret pain, the thing she'd never told anyone?

He met her eyes and seemed to read the question there. "I heard you talking to her in your sleep."

Tears rushed into her eyes, and she blinked

265

hard to keep them away. "I don't want to talk about my mother," she whispered, and then changed the subject. "Would it upset you to tell me about your sisters?"

He shook his head, a sad look coming into his eyes. "Those girls were joy itself." He gave a wry smile. "That is when they weren't defeating me in races or stealing my favorite horses."

She nodded tentatively, and resisted the urge to smile at the picture. How could he talk so easily about those he had lost? Why did he want to? She never wanted to talk about her own beloved mother after her death—it only made the loss hurt more.

"Maria was the eldest of my sisters—a year older than I," he began, his gaze wandering into the trees beside the path. "She was married and had two sons and a daughter. After her came Malea, who was a year younger than myself, and, we thought, too young to have already born two children, but she eloped and married when she was fifteen. She was always too serious for her age though, always mothering the younger ones, and she couldn't wait to grow up and start having children of her own. Then there was Blanca, who was almost two years younger. She was given to books and studies." He smiled, glancing back at Savanna, "A little like yourself."

She resisted the urge to sneer at him. They were talking about the departed, after all.

"A year behind Blanca was Marta. Marta was

plain, but had the sweetest soul. She loved horses. She would spend all day long at the paddocks, and she trained many an ornery colt—much to my mother's horror, of course. Those palominos were her pride and joy."

Savanna looked away guiltily at the mention of the palominos. She wasn't only stealing from him when she took over the Del Sol, she was treading on the graves of his loved ones.

"And the littlest was Elena, who was just becoming a woman." He took in a deep breath and chuckled warmly, his gaze somewhere far away in the trees, in the past. "To me, she will always be a chattering five-year-old clinging to my pant legs like a burr."

She smiled, picturing little Elena. The way Monheno talked about his sisters made them seem as though they were still alive. She could picture each one of them—small feminine versions of him, each with the same raven hair and thick, coal-colored lashes.

A familiar loneliness crept over her, made her feel empty and hollow. "It must have been wonderful growing up in such a big family."

"Ummm." He looked back at her, the mists clearing from his eyes. "We Spanish believe in big families. You've no brothers or sisters?"

She shook her head, frowning regretfully. "No, I had none." How nice it would have been to have someone else to cling to. "I think my mother's life was so unhappy she could not bear the thought of bringing another child into it.

She had a stillbirth not long before she died. It affected her mind, I think." Those long, frightening days came rushing back to her, those days she hadn't let herself think about in years. She stared down at her fingers and pictured her mother's hands, pale, grey, silent against the bed covers. "She never cried for that baby. She just lay there and wasted away. I think she was relieved not to leave the burden of two children behind."

She heard Monheno's saddle creak as she shifted. "But where was your father?" His voice was hard and critical.

Bitterness flowed through her like lye, burning her skin, her stomach, her eyes. "My father stood above her bed and tormented her day after day until she died." She looked up at him through a haze of tears and saw horror and anger in his face. "My mother would hide me in the dressing closet when he came home. I would crouch there and listen to him wish her dead, until finally he had his wish."

Monheno just stared at her in complete shock and disgust. The picture of her mother and father, of a Savanna, a little blond-haired angel, crouched in the darkness formed in his mind. It made him sick, then angry and outraged. How could any man, even a man like Carver Storm, do something so heinous? How could he torture his bedridden wife? Make his own child so afraid she hid from him? What else had happened that she wasn't telling him?

He watched quicksilver tears spill down her cheeks, and finally understood her—all of her. He understood now about the nightmares, the times she whispered for her mother in her sleep, the way she spoke with such hatred of her father. He could see now why she didn't want to marry, why she didn't want to be close to anyone. How could she learn to love and trust when she had been tortured by someone who was supposed to protect her?

She looked slowly back down at her hands. He watched her not knowing what to say. How could he know what to say? He never had anything but love in his family—never saw anything but closeness and caring. Even in the years he fought with his father, he knew his father loved him, he knew he was always welcome at home, knew he would always be safe there.

He watched her hair sway back and forth across her shoulders as she bent her head and wiped her tears impatiently. No doubt, she'd curse herself later for telling him all of this. She didn't want him to know about her, didn't want him to be close to her. Why was that? Because she didn't trust him, or because she was falling in love with him too?

The sky split suddenly with a resounding crash of thunder, and Savanna jerked her chin up in shock. Her memories flew away like a flock of lurking crows.

"Oh no," she muttered. The forest path had

turned from midday to dusk. "I think we'd better start back."

Monheno glanced up from the corner of his eye. "I have a feeling we're doomed to get wet." The idea seemed to appeal to him. He smiled devilishly.

That grin filled her mind with images of sodden clothes—sodden clothes which would, of course, have to be removed. Her skin tingled, but not from the first drops of rain.

She bit her lip and kicked her horse into a trot. "We should hurry."

His horse moved into a trot beside her. "Why, Savanna?" His eyes had that smoky look, and she knew what it meant. "This is your namesake, after all."

Only he would have thought of that when they were about to be drenched by a summer squall. "You'll have to enjoy it without me." The wind whipped the words from her tongue. "I hate storms!"

The sky tipped over like a bucket, sent down a curtain of water as she kicked her horse into a blind gallop. Behind her, she could hear Monheno's bay charging a close second.

He caught her just as they rounded the last bend in the trail and slid up the overgrown drive to the barn. Abreast, the horses clattered into the aisle way, pushed by a clap of thunder and a burst of wet wind.

Savanna jumped down from her saddle and stepped back. She held her arms out to keep her chilly clothing from touching her any more than necessary, and looked down at herself with disgust. Bending forward, she slung her heavy hair over her shoulder and wrung the rainwater from it with her hands.

"This is positively disgusting!" Her clothes were covered with spatters of black mud. "Good Lord!" She slung the hair back and stood up. "I'm soaked to the bone."

"Ummm." He leaned casually back against the wall, one long leg crossed over the other. "So you are." The tone of his voice, deep, sexual, conveyed his meaning.

She raised her eyelashes slowly, rolling her eyes in irritation. "And I suppose you are merely going to stand there and watch while I freeze to death?"

He ran his gaze downward, and she crossed her arms over the fabric molded to her hardened breasts. "Stop that!"

"I beg your pardon?" He brought outstretched fingers to his chest. "Stop what?"

"Stop looking at me!" Her knees started to shake, but not from the cold.

"But you were talking."

"You know very well what you were doing!" She pointed a schoolmarm finger at him, and shook it back and forth—*shame, shame*.

"I was looking at you."

"That's right!" she said victoriously.

"But you were talking to me."

"You weren't looking at my *face!*" She advanced on him with the finger still armed and dangerous.

A crash of thunder blotted out her choice words—all except the last two, ". . . love you!"

"Why thank you, my dear." A crocodile grin and a wicked glimmer in his raven eyes. "I love you, too."

He silenced her outraged gasp with a kiss, then grasped her shoulders and held her on her unsteady feet as he parted from her.

"Run along to the house, Savanna," his voice was thick with restraint, "before you catch your death of cold . . . or something worse."

She came to her senses and stepped back, her stomach fluttering like a leaf in the breeze. Swallowing hard, she turned to make an escape, but not before he snaked a hand out and gave her a playful pat on the behind. An offended gasp rose to her lips, but she forced it back and glanced evilly over her shoulder as she hurried from the barn.

Rain buffeted her in the face as she left the barn. She ducked her head and pressed through it, wrapping her arms around herself against the cold. Thunder rolled overhead like a wild herd of horses dashing across the clouds, and lightning flashed like the crack of a whip.

She shivered and hurried to the door, jerked it open and slipped through just before the wind blew it shut with a crash. The noise crashed through the empty house like a cannon in a tea shop, and she winced at the sound. It was enough to wake the dead.

The clatter of hurried footsteps at the end of the hallway made her heart lurch. She looked up to find the Grandee there, looking quite frantic.

"Dios Mio, are we under attack?" His hand went to the rusted sword hilt protruding from his scabbard. He jerked three times but only managed to remove it a few inches.

"No, no," she choked. Was he speaking to her or some imaginary crew member from his imaginary ship?

He didn't answer, but gripped the hilt with both hands and pulled until his face went red.

"It was only me coming in." She stepped back in case he planned to use the sword on her. "The door slammed with the wind."

"Oh." He looked a little disappointed, then reversed his efforts with the sword and tried to put it back in again. "Well, I didn't mean to alarm you. This storm has the whole crew on edge." He looked up and down her wet clothing. "My dear, you shouldn't have been on deck. You could have been swept overboard."

"You're quite right." She managed not to smile as she said it. "But I wanted to make certain the ship was doing all right in the storm."

She noticed his look of surprise, and then of pleasure.

"You see," she went on, making use of the jargon she learned on the sea voyage from England, "The. . . um . . . mainsail looked to me to be . . . getting a tear."

"A tear?" He gave up on the sword and just left it hanging halfway out. Running a hand through his grey hair with concern, he paced a few steps to one side and then to the other, then he stopped and looked back at her. "Dios Mio! I shall have to see to this!"

"Oh, it has been repaired already." She didn't want him going out in the storm for no reason. "Your . . . first mate saw to it straightaway."

"Mr. Caldeon?"

"I think so." She smiled. He was, doubtless, the most charming insane person she'd ever met.

"Caldeon isn't the First Mate." He shook his head grimly, looked at the wall, then followed an invisible line to the ceiling. "He is my Second Mate. The first mate is Deleon, but he is lazy and a drunkard. No doubt, he is ill in his cabin just now—the man can't stand a storm." He shook his head and rubbed his chin, which was in need of a shave. The idea seemed to occur to him as he rubbed the whiskers. "I must do something about Deleon."

With a nod, she agreed, "Oh, most definitely." A draft made her shiver and she decided to make her exit. "I'll leave you to your men while I go change."

He looked back at her and smiled—a warm, gentle expression that looked completely sane. "Oh, of course, my child." He patted her on

274

the head with a sympathetic hand, as though she were a drowned dog. "How inconsiderate of me to keep you waiting here when you are drenched and cold. I think the cabin boy has prepared a warm bath in your quarters. Please, go along before it turns cold."

She nodded and headed toward the stairs. Hopefully the bath wasn't another figment of his imagination. A warm bath was exactly the thing she needed.

She found it waiting in a long copper tub in the bedroom she shared with Monheno. In the fireplace, a small fire burned to keep away the unusual chill from the storm, and on a table beside the tub sat a bar of perfumed soap, a small jar of scented oil, and a single red rose.

Someone thought of everything. But who? Could it really be The Grandee? It hardly seemed likely that he could manage all the household chores on his own. There almost had to be someone else.

She shook the thoughts away with a shiver. No use picturing ghosts again. There wasn't any such thing, and if there were, they probably didn't do housework.

Even so, she glanced around one more time before she stripped away her sodden clothing and laid it on the hearth. If she was lucky, it might be dry enough to wear after the bath. If not, she'd figure something out when the time came. Right now, the invitation of the warm water was irresistible. Perhaps the imaginary crew had an imaginary seamstress who would sew clothes for her.

The water was deliciously warm after her chilly afternoon ride. Heat prickled through her as she slipped in and lay back, letting the water wash over her stomach and tickle her breasts. With a sigh, she wet and lathered herself, then scrubbed her body clean until her skin was pink from the effort. It felt wonderful to be clean again.

She leaned back against the tub just to enjoy it, and let her eyes fall closed. Something about baths always made her sleepy. She couldn't let herself fall asleep, of course. Monheno would be back any minute, and it would be better, safer, if she wasn't lying nude in the tub when he arrived.

The very thought made her flush, and she climbed hurriedly from the tub. The door rattled, and she gasped, looking desperately around for something besides the wet towel to cover herself. Nothing in reach. She stood frozen, waiting for him to come in, but the handle never turned. Finally, she slapped a hand over her eyes and let out her breath. It was probably just the house settling.

What was wrong with her, anyway? Why was she jumping at every little noise and shadow? Why was she so afraid Monheno would come in and find her this way? He'd certainly seen her in the nude a time or two before, and last night even at her own invitation. God! What in the world possessed her to do that? Where did she think this was all going to lead? Marriage? A life together? Surely not. Surely she wasn't a big enough fool to believe that.

But she knew she was. She didn't want to admit it. She didn't want to even see it in herself, but it was true. She could feel those unwanted pictures forming in her mind. She could see evidence of it in the fact she'd told him secrets about herself she'd never told anyone.

The walls crackled again, and she jolted back to reality. Nervously, she rifled through the chest at the foot of the bed and found one of his shirts. The mirror cast her reflection back to her as she held it up in front of herself. Hardly appropriate, but better than nothing.

A flush prickled her cheeks again as she slipped the white cotton garment on. The sleeves hung over her hands, so she rolled them up, then surveyed herself in the mirror. Shaking her head she uttered a "tsk, tsk," under her breath. Good-Lord-and-all-the-saints, if her friends in London could see her now! They would faint with shame, every one.

She should be crippled with shame herself, half naked in his bedroom, and in his clothing for that matter. Instead, she was tingling all over, anticipating his arrival, the look in his eye, his touch. She shook her head at herself and picked up the rose on the dressing table. Its sweet, soft scent drifted up to her as she climbed into the bed and pulled the covers over her bare legs. Strange that she should be so tired when it was only afternoon. Something about dark, cloudy days made her lazy and leaden.

She leaned back against th pillows and looked at the rose absently. It was beautiful. Perfect. Fragile. Who left it here? Where was Monheno? He should have been back a long time ago. It couldn't take long to see to the horses . . .

Monheno found her asleep in the tangle of covers when he entered the room. Had she done it on purpose, she couldn't have arranged a better picture. He closed the door behind him silently and just stood there watching her, her golden hair spilling around her like a halo, her long lashes fluttering against her cheeks, her full lips slightly parted like she was waiting to be kissed. She looked like an angel, something precious, almost too perfect, like the rose in her hands, fluttering gently with each breath.

Desire quickened in his loins, and he shook his head at himself. It didn't matter what he was thinking about, looking at her put his mind on only one thing. It was ridiculous to be so unable to concentrate. Women had always been his downfall, but not like this. He'd never lost his mind over one.

He chuckled and went to the tub, then took off his clothing. The water was cold, but he supposed he needed that to cool his raging blood, so he climbed in and washed away the scent of wind and rain.

His head was a little clearer by the time he

climbed out and dried himself. Even so, he didn't look at the bed as he tossed a few more sticks of wood onto the fire to bring it to life again. They were going to need it tonight. The storm showed no signs of stopping. Though it was still afternoon, the thick clouds made it look as though dusk had already come.

He stood for a moment and looked at the driving rain, rubbing his forehead tiredly. At least that would keep Venenoso and the rest of them from his doorstep tonight. Tomorrow might be another story, and if not tomorrow, the next day, or the next. The bastard wouldn't give up until their bargain was sealed, and if Monheno couldn't keep up his end, Venenoso would strike—not at him, at Savanna.

He turned and looked at her sleeping in the bed. What if Venenoso grew impatient in the meantime? Savanna's life was hanging on a fickle thread that might be sliced any moment. All he could do was watch for shifts in the wind and take her out of there if trouble came—if he could get her out. Venenoso had spies everywhere. Getting Savanna away might be impossible. He made a mistake not sending her away before she figured out so much about the Sombras. Now she was almost as far into this mess as he was. *Throw your hand in with the devil, you'll end up in hell. Monheno.*

She shifted, took a heavy breath, and whispered something in her sleep. It made him smile despite the dark thoughts, and he started toward the bed. This would turn out the way he planned for it to. One way or another, he would convince her to go along.

He slipped into the bed, leaned back against the pillows and looked at her hopefully. Maybe she wasn't asleep after all. She didn't stir, so he shifted, making the bed frame squeak and rattle. Still no sign that she was waking. He bent closer and looked under her dark lashes. One glimmer from those violet eyes, and he'd make love to her.

She only stirred a bit, rolled onto her side, and snuggled closer to him for warmth.

He groaned and crossed his arms over his chest. Even in her sleep, she chose to torture him.

# Fifteen

He was lying there in torment when she moved like she was waking. Pulling the covers up to his waist, he hid his need and lay back against the pillow, half-closing his eyes so he could watch her. He did that often—watched her when she didn't know he was looking. It was refreshing to catch a glimpse of the real person behind her stiff appearance. The only other time he saw that person was when passion swept away her disguises. She didn't really know he was watching her then either.

Savanna rolled the stiffness from her neck and started to climb from the bed. A slight movement in the covers stopped her, and she turned to look. Monheno. She knew he was there, really, had felt him in her sleep, and could smell the faint, manly scent of him now.

How handsome he looked, dark face smooth in the uneven grey light, sensuous lips relaxed into something that was neither a frown nor a

281

smile, thick lashes moving just a bit against the solid line of his cheekbones. Was it any wonder she was falling in love with him? Was it so terrible anyway? If she hadn't stumbled onto the Sombras that night at the Del Sol, she would quite possibly have married him. Was that what he had in mind when he came to live with her at the ranch?

She could picture it in her mind—the two of them married, happy, spending their days working the Del Sol together and their nights lost in passion. It might have come to pass if she hadn't fallen upon his connection with Venenoso.

Did that really matter? What was really hurt except her pride? This war between the white squatters and the old Spanish settlers had nothing to do with her now. She had come innocently into the wrong side of it, but that was over now. What was really to stop her from seizing the moment and settling down with Monheno?

He moved, and she jerked her eyes away, flushing. She didn't need for him to catch her watching like this. If she was feeling different about him, if she was softening toward him, she had to keep that to herself, at least until she felt more certain. She jumped as his hand stroked up her back and caught her shoulder.

"Don't run away quite yet." His voice was clear, not like he'd been asleep at all.

"I . . . I wasn't," she stammered, her skin burning where he touched it, her mind simmering with lewd thoughts. "I was only going to light the lamp before it's too dark." It was a lie, of course. She was running away to avoid the pictures forming in her mind, the desire flaring in her stomach.

"You promise to return?" he opened his eyes halfway and peered up at her suggestively.

She flushed down to the neck of the shirt and beyond. "Of course." Something in her quivered at the thought. She wagered dollars to dimes he would be making love to her before the blush could cool.

The shirt tickled around her legs as she climbed from the bed, lit a sliver of kindling from the fireplace, and touched it to the wick of the lamp by the bed.

He tossed the covers back and patted the mattress beside him. "Finally."

She stood back, her pulse racing. "I was only gone a moment."

"Seemed longer." His raven eyes twinkled suggestively. He extended a hand toward her, his fingers moving in mid-air as if to pull her closer.

She placed her hand in his. A shiver raced through her as his fingers closed over her, and her heart bounded up until she could barely breathe.

She gave willingly to the pull of his hand, slipped into the bed beside him and met his lips as he bent to kiss her. Boldly, she slid her hands over the hard cords of his chest, felt them bunch beneath her fingers, felt his heart hammering.

The memory of their lovemaking the night before lit her on fire, and pulling off the shirt, she raised up to move on top of him. He caught her wandering hands and pressed her back into the pillows, then raised on one elbow and looked down at her.

"Why such haste, mi corazon?" The question was thick and deep, washed over her like warm water.

She could only manage a slight sigh—half of disappointment and half of anticipation. Sweet torment was ahead, and she knew it. Satisfaction would be long in coming.

He traced a single finger along the moist line of her lips, down her neck, toward her breasts. Anticipation and agony hardened her nipples as he circled around one breast, then the other, slowly moving toward the sensitive peaks. She gasped and let her eyes fall closed. He bent his head and kissed her shoulder, drew a searing trail around her breasts, circled them with his tongue and pulled one into his mouth.

Thunder exploded outside, and lightning flashed through the dark room. She fluttered her eyes open, then closed them again as a wave of ecstasy swept over her. She abandoned herself to it, heard some words of nonsense she couldn't even understand as his breath feathered her stomach. The muscles trembled, tingled as he slid his hands lower, parted her legs, ran his hands along the outside to her knees, then back up her inner thighs.

She clutched the bedcovers and writhed closer to his touch, but he circled lazily on the edge. His lips tasted the curve of her waist, and she arched closer. This was torture, torment. She couldn't bear it.

She cried out his name as he parted her and touched the moist center of her womanhood, taunting her. Need tightened inside her, made her raise her hips against his touch, made her gasp as he found the bud of her passion. The familiar, torturous tightening built within her, made her cry out again, and reach for him.

He came to her, entered her with a driving thrust that sent release spiraling through her, then held her as she gasped in waves of pleasure. Whispered words of love touched her ear as he kissed her again, then teased roughly at her breasts with his tongue. Her desire swelled again as he moved within her, slowly, with long, even thrusts until she raised her hips against him and slid her hands over his back, aflame with need.

She matched his increasing speed, cried out as he drove to his own climax, and brought her to shattering release. Gasping, she clung to him in the aftermath, ran her hands along the dampened muscles of his back, felt the faint tremors of passion there.

He whispered in her ear that he loved her, then rolled away and gathered her against his chest. She swallowed her own words of love, and nestled into the crook of his arm, silent. His sigh rustled the hair on the top of her head, and he let his hand fall from her shoulders to the bed beside her.

Was he disappointed? Did he expect to hear her admit she loved him in return? She closed her eyes and tried to press the questions from her exhausted mind. She didn't want to wonder if he meant it, to wonder if this was wrong, to think about what would happen tomorrow.

Midnight was striking when she awoke to a raging hunger. Rolling over, she found Monheno already stepping from the bed and pulling on his trousers.

He glanced up at her and smiled. "Hungry?"

She smiled and blinked misty eyes at him. "How did you know?"

"You were making strange noises in your sleep." He leaned over the bed. "I left in self-defense to find you something to eat."

She had a nagging feeling he was headed somewhere other than the kitchen before she saw him, but she pushed it aside. "A wise choice." She rubbed her stomach through the bedcovers. "I could eat a horse."

"Dios Mio, the palominos better run for their lives." He started toward the door, then stopped as he opened it and shot back a grin. "I shall return."

Giggling, she grabbed one of the small pillows from the bed and tossed it at him. It hit the door just as it closed behind him, and she sank back against the bed, hugging the covers around her. The room seemed cold with him gone, dark and frightening. Sounds seemed to be everywhere, close by and far away.

She hugged the covers tighter and tried not to think about it. Why, when she was on the edge of happiness, did she always ruin it for herself? Why was she always looking for disaster around every corner? Didn't she deserve happiness as much as the next person? Who was to say she couldn't find that happiness with Monheno Devilla?

She looked up with a smile when he returned. Just looking at him made her feel warm, confident. He seemed so sure this was right, so determined to be with her.

She leaned over the side of the bed, and fished for the shirt discarded there earlier, but found herself face-to-face with two large bare feet instead—feet which kicked the garment from her reach.

"And what are you doing?" he asked.

She glanced up at the bottom of a huge silver tray. "I was . . ." She flushed with embarrassment and pulled the sheets up a bit over her breasts. Why did his brazen gazes still make her blush like a school girl? "My shirt," she said simply, and leaned to reach it.

*"My* shirt," he corrected, kicking it further away. "And you may not have it." He moved away with a haughty swagger, the arching mus-

cles of his thighs sliding gracefully beneath his black trousers.

Unconsciously, she wet her lips with her tongue, then, realizing it, flushed again and sat up. "Well surely you don't intend that we eat in the . . ."

"Nude?" he finished for her, then waved the tray under her nose. "And if you make one move toward that shirt, you'll not get a bite from me . . . at least not a bite of food."

She stiffened because he imitated her accent when he said it. "Don't do that."

"Do what?" He looked at her as though she'd sprouted horns, then set the tray down and started to remove his trousers.

"Imitate me." She jutted her lower lip. "I would appreciate your not making fun of my accent."

"But I like your accent." He sat down in the bed and arranged the tray between them. "It makes you unique."

"An ugly duckling is unique," she protested. "I've no desire to be unique."

The scent of fresh bread tickled her nose, and she lost interest in the argument. The food looked delicious—sliced sausages and cheeses, strawberries and cream, white and dark bread with butter and two types of marmalade, and some little round Mexican cookies she couldn't remember the name of.

"You *are* unique." If he was more interested in the food than in her, it didn't show. His jet eyes fixed on her with such intensity they forced her to look up just as she was about to settle on a slice of bread.

"Only because I am a foreigner." A tingle ran up her spine, and she looked back down at the platter. How did the conversation manage to turn from food to her anyway? "I promise you, I am not a bit unique where I come from." Who cared? All she wanted was a slice of bread anyway. Snatching up a slice, she took a ravenous bite.

"I suspect that is not true." He was toying with the stem of a strawberry—just toying, not eating, and still watching her as though there were something he wanted to know. The look made her nervous, not that she had so much to hide. He knew about her father, and that meant he'd seen most of her family's dirty linen already.

"What is it that you want?" Wasn't he going to eat? "You're looking at me as though I'm some sort of two-headed toad."

He laughed at the analogy. "Hardly." He slipped the strawberry between his lips and chewed it thoughtfully. "I want to know more about you."

"I think you know me quite well." Did she need to point out that they were sitting completely naked in his bed having a picnic together in the middle of the night? Did she need to remind him how they shared the twilight hours of the day? If that didn't constitute knowing someone, she didn't know what would.

"I know what I see." He took another strawberry—one so plump and red it was almost double. "But, you see, it's a little like this strawberry. I may know what it looks like on the outside, but until I bite into it . . ." he demonstrated in a most tempting way, "I have no idea what is inside."

"I seem to recall some tasting you have done already, and not just what was handed to you," she pointed out. "But you should be careful, Monheno, your strawberry may be rotten in the core." She squirmed uncomfortably. After so many years of taking pains to conceal her past— the truth about the shameful state of her family's affairs and finances—she couldn't help being disturbed by his probing.

He laughed. "I'd like to judge for myself." He gave her a look that said he would be hurt and disappointed if she refused.

"I told you about myself before." Hadn't he heard enough?

"You haven't told me how things came to be so bad between your father and mother." He looked concerned, almost loving. "She must have been a wonderful person because I know you don't favor your father."

She grimaced at the memories—still painful after all the years passed. She didn't want to talk about that, didn't want anyone else to know about it. But wasn't love a complete opening of one's soul? Perhaps this was a test of whether she really loved him, or was merely caught up in the physical pleasure he gave her.

"My mother came from a good family, one of noble blood and a good name." She stared down at the tray and felt her stomach swim. "She was the only child of my grandfather and grandmother, so there was a sizable fortune to be settled on her. That, I suspect is what caused my father to woo her." Long-forgotten memories of her mother flooded into her mind. "You see, my mother was not a pretty woman. She was . . . frail, I guess you'd say, and somewhat plain, and shy, which is no doubt why she was so blinded by the attentions of a smooth young American like my father."

Her fingers trembled as she peeled the crust from a slice of bread. It hurt so to remember how badly her mother was tortured—how much she suffered. Was she falling into the same trap herself?

"She loved him so. She would have done any-thing for him, but he didn't care a whit for her. He dragged her from one continent to another—from one scheme to another in spite of the fact that she was sick."

Tears filled her eyes and flowed down her cheeks—the first tears she had shed for her mother in years. Somehow, that grave in Africa seemed closer now, almost as if she were there again, looking down at her tiny shoes as the dust fell over them and mingled with tears to make mud.

"He squandered away everything she loved, used other women before her face and laughed when she protested. He refused to take her back to her family though she begged it of him. He drove her to an early birth of my brother—a still-birth, and then he tormented her until she died."

She looked up at Monheno through the blur. "I suppose you can see why I wasn't remorseful over his death. I would dance on that man's grave if I knew where it was."

He smoothed a hand over her hair. "I can see why." His voice was heavy with emotion. "You can't blame yourself for any of this, Savanna. It isn't right to let your father's cruelty keep you alone for the rest of your life."

She took a deep breath to gain control of herself before speaking. Now was no time to fall apart. "Marriage was my mother's death."

He slid his hand down and held hers. "All marriages are not that way," he whispered. "Marriage was my mother's life, and my father's. They loved each other beyond reason, more than they loved themselves."

She raised her chin, determined not to fall into his trap. "They were fortunate. Not all marriages are so blessed."

One look into his eyes melted her determination like a pillar of butter, and truth spilled from her mouth. "How can I not be afraid? My mother was so dear, but she ruined her life by falling for the wrong man. I don't want to be blind, like she was. I can't bear the thought of ending up as she did. I want to make my own way in the world . . ."

She clapped her hands to her ears to shut out the whirlwind of conflicting emotions, then rubbed her eyes impatiently and looked back at him. "I swear to you I have not a cent to my name—nothing except the Del Sol, which rightfully belongs to you, anyway. Please, if the prospect of riches drew you to me, tell me now.

He pulled back from her, his eyes the angry grey-black of storm clouds. She jerked away in anticipation of a blow—an old habit cultivated by her father when she was very young.

When he spoke, his voice was level, but strained. "Is that what you think?"

Guilt made her sick inside. "I don't know." She reached out and took his hand, looked pleadingly into those angry, hurt eyes. "Make me believe."

"Savanna." He softened visibly. "I've no great need for money. Your father may have stolen the Del Sol, but in its absence I've made myself a comfortably wealthy man, although through means of which you wouldn't approve."

"Gambling."

He nodded. "That is so, but that is also where my similarity to your father ends."

She searched his eyes for any sign of easy lies, but found none.

"I love you, Savanna." He brought her hand to his chest and pressed her palm over his heart. "Whatever unfortunate circumstances have come between us in the past, I love you now, Savanna, and I want to marry you."

She couldn't reply. The words she wanted to say choked like a lump of ice in her throat.

He set the tray of food on the dressing table and gathered her in his arms, kissing her as he lay her back on the bed.

"Don't answer tonight," he whispered. "Think about it until morning."

She closed her eyes and pressed closer to his comforting warmth. He was right. Things would be clearer in the morning. Right now she was exhausted, upset, filled with grim memories of her mother and her own childhood.

Monheno slid his hand along her arm, smooth like silk, and took her hand in his. His cards were on the table now. There was no more chance of turning back. It was strange to be lying open to a wound, vulnerable. He'd never been in such a position before.

But he'd never wanted anything, anyone, as much as he wanted her. He loved her. He wanted her with him, always. He wanted to fill the empty places in her soul and have her fill his. He wanted to give Del Sol house happy voices and little children again, to sit on the veranda and watch the sun fade, to listen to songs for lovers . . .

Morning sunlight pressed Savanna's eyes and

she rolled away from it, touched the empty pillow beside her. It was still warm, but he was gone. Startled, she sat up and looked around the room. He was gone already, but where? Why would he wake and leave the bed so early when such an important question hung between them? Did he regret asking it? Was he trying to escape the answer?

She closed her eyes and pressed back against the pillow. What was she going to say? In the quiet room, she could still hear his words from the night before.

I love you now, Savanna. I want to marry you. His words. Did he mean them? She could still hear them just as he said them—softly, honestly, his handsome face solemn, his eyes as deep and warm as a summer night.

Pictures of a future painted themselves in her mind. The two of them together bringing the Del Sol back to its former grandeur, filling the home with life and giving it the laughter of new children. It was all so perfect, as though someone planned it. She thought she didn't need love, that she could be happy alone, but he knew better.

She rolled onto her side, grabbed Monheno's pillow to her and hugged it tightly. She could still smell him there and she breathed it in with a deep sigh.

I want to marry you. The words replayed again. She would marry him, just as soon as he wanted. Then they could leave this dingy old house and return to the Del Sol. The staff could be told her trip to San Francisco was an elopement, and none would be the wiser. It would spark a scandal, but only a small one, and in the end everyone would forget about that.

Actually, sooner would be better for a wedding, given the fact that they had already shared the marital bed. She could be carrying his child. That was a possibility she'd not allowed herself to contemplate before. It took more than a few times in bed together to conceive a child, didn't it? Her own mother tried for two years to conceive her, and four for her stillborn brother. It couldn't happen in one month, could it?

A child. His child. Their child. She wasn't exactly sure how she felt about it. She'd given up the idea of having children of her own when she had decided not to marry. Now, the thought of it made her feel a little strange, a little frightened. What if her own marriage turned out as badly as her mother's ill-fated match? Alone, she could escape that terrible consequence. She could go away, or there was always the scandalous possibility of divorce, but with a child involved, she would truly be tied forever. Could she bring a child into the same unhappy world she was born into? Was it even possible that this wonderful beginning with Monheno could turn into something so sour?

Her happiness from only moments before faded to a nondescript sense of gloom. She lowered a hand to her stomach, spread her fingers over the smooth expanse of bare skin. Was it possible? Wouldn't she know if she were pregnant? Didn't a woman automatically know? Having lost her mother when she was so young, she wasn't really certain. Such feminine facts were not exactly curriculum in school. But surely she would know . . .

She tossed the bedcovers aside and climbed impatiently from the bed, crossed the room, and stopped for a moment to look at her naked profile in the long mirror. She didn't look any different—no larger around the waist. It hadn't been so many weeks since her time, had it? Mentally, she tried to count, but she couldn't quite remember. Two? Three? Four weeks?

Something shiny caught her eye, and she turned to notice for the first time a cranberry-colored dress hanging over the door of the wardrobe. Stepping closer, she ran a hand over the fabric. Silk. She smiled in admiration. She couldn't remember the last time she was able to afford a silk dress. She gave it up long ago in favor of less extravagant fabrics. Then she gave up buying new dresses altogether.

She took the dress down carefully and held it in front of her, then gazed into the looking glass. It was truly beautiful, its creases and folds shimmering a subtle shade of berry pink. Beautiful, but hardly appropriate for such an early hour.

A glimmer of color from within the wardrobe caught her attention, and she threw open the doors. A dozen dresses and riding outfits hung there, all fashionably patterned—almost too fashionably for California—in lavish fabrics with beautiful braids, beadwork, and embroidery for trim.

She carefully laid the silk dress back over the wardrobe door so she could take the other outfits from the closet one by one. Each was more beautiful than the next, and she lingered over one and then the next like a child torn between two lollipops.

More precious than the clothes was the way they made her feel like a queen, spoiled, pampered, loved. Each of them showed some small touch that told her they had been selected for her alone. Some weren't things she would have chosen, but looking at them now, she could see how they would be becoming to her figure, or hair color, or skin tone. Perhaps Monheno knew her better than she knew herself.

She chose the last dress she set her eyes upon, a day dress of white cotton with small pink rosebuds woven into it in a shimmering silk thread.

In the bottom of the closet, she found an assortment of underthings, a discovery which made her blush. It was more than a little embarrassing to think of Monheno selecting camisoles, and pantaloons, and petticoats for her. For a man, he'd chosen well, though the underthings were finer than those she was accustomed to.

She dressed and took the hairbrush from the

dressing table, then combed her hair slowly as she watched her reflection in the mirror. She looked like a different person, a little more like the person she wanted to be, a little less like the person circumstances had forced her to become. In such finery, she could almost pretend her father had not gambled away her station in life, that those sad days never existed at all.

Perhaps she didn't regret her introduction to reality after all. If her father hadn't squandered away everything, she would have still been sequestered from the world in a stuffy boarding school, or perhaps by now married to one of the pompous upper-crust beaus she knew.

She sat down on the edge of the bed, and leaned back on her palms, contemplating that existence. No. She didn't regret her journey into life at all. She had been hiding away for years, comfortable, stale, stagnant. It was fortunate that fate finally forced her to shake the dust from her wits and make her own way. Only then did she find her own spirit and learn her true potential. She was as smart and as capable as any man. One of the most wonderful things about Monheno was that he didn't seem to resent her for that. The more spunk she showed, the more he loved her. He was different in so many ways from any man she'd ever known . . .

A sound in the hallway drew her attention from her musings, and her eyes bolted toward the closed door. Her heart thumped into her throat, and she swallowed it back into place.

"Good Lord, Savanna," she scolded "you've a fantastic imagination."

She tried to put the thought of the ghosts out of her mind. There were no ghosts, only one crazy old man and a whole shipload of imaginary crew members—imaginary.

Another sound from the hallway struck her heart, and she stood up from the bed with determination. She wasn't going to be afraid. She was just going to go to the hall, look out, and see what was making the noise. Maybe it was Monheno coming back.

She took a deep breath, stood up, and started toward the door.

# Sixteen

Her fingers trembled as she grabbed the door handle. She rolled her eyes and jerked it open. What was wrong with her?

The noise turned out to be the Grandee standing a short distance away, his hands clutched over the sides of a picture on the wall. He looked over his shoulder at her as if she startled him.

"Oh, my dear." He smiled at her. "You gave me quite a start." He turned back to the picture and tipped it to one side, then the other. "The current tends to make them crooked. I find myself spending a great deal of time straightening these pictures."

She lowered a brow and looked up and down the hallway. Not one other picture in sight. "I see." What were a few nonexistent pictures compared to an imaginary ship and crew?

"I am glad to see you've found your sea legs again so soon after the storm." He finished with

301

the picture, still crooked, then turned to her and smiled. "You are quite a sailor for an English woman."

She giggled. "Oh, I wasn't afraid. I have complete confidence in your crew."

He nodded, clasping his hands behind his back and looking proud. "As well you should, though I suspect they are at their best because we've royalty aboard."

"Royalty?"

He looked shocked. "Why yourself, of course."

She drew back in surprise. What was he talking about now?

"I must apologize for not having been aware of it on our first meeting, but my nephew has kindly informed me of your true identity." He took her hand, and patted it soothingly, his dark eyes kind beneath the thick silver hair immaculately combed today. "Tsk, tsk, don't look so frightened, Princess, I completely understand your need to travel in disguise. Your secret, and the secrets of the crown of England are safe with me."

She blinked twice before it sank in that she'd been crowned Princess of England. How could Monheno tell the old man such a ridiculous lie? "I trust you implicitly," she assured him. "It is your nephew of whom I am not certain."

He drew back in surprise, releasing her hand. "Would you care for some tea? My cook has just laid a fresh pot in the library."

She nodded a little reluctantly. Even Adolfo Devilla's company was preferable to being along in the old house. Where was Monheno, anyway?

He offered an elbow, and she placed her hand on it lightly, noticing he had discarded the faded blue waistcoat for a fashionable one of light yellow-gold with black braided trim.

She followed him along the hall and down the stairs. A movement caught her eye when they reached the downstairs hall, and she turned in time to see a woman come from the dining room doorway—not a ghost, but a woman. Savanna watched over her shoulder as Adolfo Devilla led her away down the hall. The woman turned slowly around, a serving tray in her hands, and looked levelly at Savanna.

Savanna knew her instantly. The woman from the dance, the same one that was laughing with Waddie in the shadows at the Del Sol. So she was the one bringing the food here. Had she been here all along, or did she just come in and out as needed? How was she connected to all of this?

A sickening possibility rushed into her mind. Instantly, she pictured Monheno and the woman at the cantina in town, at the dance, laughing, talking, in each other's arms. She acted comfortable, possessive, like she was . . . his lover?

Her stomach flipped over and her heart sank. She didn't want to think about it, but she couldn't stop. Was she the reason Monheno disappeared for long periods of time with no explanation? Was he with her? Did they meet right here in the house while she was in another room?

Blood drained from her face, making her feel dizzy and cold. Could she possibly be so wrong about Monheno? Could all his promises be lies after all?

Adolfo turned the corner into the library, and Savanna followed him in numbly, her head spinning, her stomach rising into her throat. She barely noticed as Adolfo helped her to a chair and brought over a tea tray from a table beside the door. He set it down on the low table in front of her and picked up a note left on the tray. With a frown, he read the printing on the outside and handed it to Savanna.

She looked down at it through stinging eyes as he clumsily poured two cups of tea.

"We usually have someone to do this." He wiped up the spillage from the tray. "Sugar?"

She nodded.

"One lump?"

She nodded again.

"And cream?"

Again, a nod.

"Thank you," she muttered as she opened the note.

The writing, she guessed, was Monheno's—a careless scrawl she would never have expected from someone so precise with spoken words. My dear it said, Expect me back within the hour. I hope to find you in my bed . . . The rest was too embarrassing to read under the watchful eye of Adolfo, so she folded it away in her hand.

"This matter of my nephew," Adolfo spoke as though he'd run the words through a dozen times in his mind. "It distresses me that you feel you cannot trust him. Monheno is a good man. He would never betray you in a matter of honor." He paused and squinted toward the ceiling. "In a matter of love, however . . ."

She jerked her eyes up from her teacup. Did Adolfo know what she was thinking? Did he know she saw the woman in the hall? She swallowed hard and forced herself to speak.

"In . . . in a matter of love?"

He looked completely sane now—sane, and perhaps a little sad. "His honor in matters of love is not nearly so good as he might like it to be. He is something of a fool for love, that boy— always gone head over his heels for one woman or the next."

She sank back in her chair and swallowed hard, the tea cup trembling in her lap. Adolfo's words, the woman in the hall, Monheno's smooth nature. It all added up to something she didn't want to hear, couldn't bear to believe.

He leaned forward and set his cup on the table with a clank that shook her to the bone. "Do not let yourself fall prey to his promises, my lady. He may convince you—he may convince himself even—that he is in love, but with him these things are passing. I have seen him steal the hearts of a dozen women—all of whom he thought he loved, but, as you can see, none of them are with us now."

Except one. Monheno couldn't even give up his other women long enough to be with her. She glanced toward the door, her hands shaking so badly the tea cup tipped off the saucer, shattering on the floor.

Her soul shattered with it. She drew in a rattling sob and threw her hands over her face. Was it true? Perhaps this was more of Adolfo's raving. How could she know? But still, there was the woman in the hall.

She felt him trying to comfort her, but she ignored it. Oh, why didn't he tell her earlier, a day ago, two days ago, before she lost her heart so completely, before she laid all her dreams at Monheno's feet?

"Please leave me alone," she whispered, shrugging Adolfo's hand away from her shoulder. She didn't want to be near him now. She didn't want to be near anyone.

"I . . . I will check on you . . . later." She heard him get up and walk out the door.

Left alone, she lay back against the settee. She felt weak and sick, like a rag wrung until it was tearing in the middle. She shouldn't believe Adolfo. She knew she shouldn't. He was out of his head, and even if he were sane, how could he know what was in Monheno's mind? Monheno loved her. She knew it. She was the one looking into his eyes when he said it. She knew the words were from his heart.

She needed to find Monheno, to go to him and tell him what the old man said. To have him ease her fears with soft words and kisses. She knew he had many women in the past. Why should she be shocked to hear it said aloud? That didn't mean he didn't love her. That didn't mean he wouldn't love her forever.

She wiped her eyes impatiently, and stood up, smoothing the white cotton day dress, his token of love to her.

He would probably be back in their room by now, waiting, as his note said, to love her again. She gathered her skirts and strode from the library. They should talk this out, at least. She loved him too much not to take that chance.

By the time she reached the stairs, she was running, dashing toward shelter from the storm. She took the narrow steps two at a time, holding her skirts up almost to her knees.

Her breath caught in her throat as she reached the upstairs hallway. She had to be wrong about him. She just had to. She stopped and smoothed down her skirts, brushed back her hair, and wiped her eyes again. It wouldn't do to go rushing in there in tears. He would only say the things he thought she wanted to hear. She had to be calm, rational. She had to think of exactly the right questions to ask.

She walked down the narrow hall, rehearsing the scene in her mind. She'd start by thanking him for the clothes—Thank you for the beautiful dresses, my love . . . and, by the way, do you buy dresses for women often?

She clenched her hands together and stared down at them. A swaying mass of cranberry silk made her jerk her gaze upward and stop. The woman from downstairs, coming from Monheno's bedroom, looking very much like she belonged there, and wearing the cranberry silk dress. Her silk dress.

The woman didn't turn at Savanna's startled gasp, but took the time to close the door carefully first. Slowly, deliberately, she drew up her skirts and swiveled around, smiling beneath catlike raven eyes.

"M-my dress." The words choked from Savanna's throat, and she raised numb fingers to her lips to see if they were moving: What did the dress matter now . . .

Raven eyes sparkling, the woman smiled in a mocking apology. "He has torn mine," she lamented, wrapping slim fingers around the low neckline of the gown and pretending to rip it across the bosom. A smile spread across her dark face, and she laughed quietly. "He ees sooch a demanding lover."

"L-lover . . ." Savanna strangled on the word. It burned her tongue like scalding oil. It ravaged her soul like fire. All this time . . . all this time while he had been with her, he had been keeping a lover. It was true. Oh God, it was true.

"Oh, si, si," she chirped. "I have always been his woman." She stepped away from the door, flouncing the silk dress, and stopped only a few feet from Savanna. "He has ask me to marry him. He loves me so good . . ."

Savanna stumbled backward, clutching her skirts, then spun about and dashed down the stairs to the library.

Slamming the doors closed, she leaned back against them and let tears flow unheeded down her cheeks. How could he? How could he use her so cruelly, wrest her heart from her only to break it? Was property so important? Was money so important? Was conquest?

"Why?" she asked the walls, or the ghosts, her voice broken—dewy tears trembling on her lips. No answer, and she cried harder, times they had spent together spinning in her mind. "Oh, Monheno, why?"

She sank to the floor and sobbed, then sat clutching her knees to her chest as time passed, and morning crept into midday outside. Finally, she couldn't hide there any longer. She had to find him, to face him, so she went upstairs to the bedroom. No one was there, so she poured water into the basin and washed the tearstains from her cheeks.

Finally, she laid the washcloth down and looked at herself in the mirror. She looked better. The cool cloth reduced the puffiness around her eyes. He probably wouldn't know she'd been crying. That was best. When she told him she never wanted to see him again, she wanted him to think it was because she didn't love him, not because she caught him at his games. She hoped it wounded him just a little bit to be spurned.

She laid the brush down again, her fingers lingering for a moment on the carved "D" inlaid on the handle. Devilla. She hoped she never heard that name again as long as she lived.

She squared her shoulders and headed toward the door. If Monheno was somewhere in the house, she would find him. She would get this over with, and one way or another she would be leaving tonight.

She found him in the dining room, seated at the end of the table, his attention turned to a piece of paper in his hands. Probably a note from some other lover.

"Savanna, my dear." He stood up. "I thought I might have to come after you."

*My dear.* How could he call her that! How could he stand there and be cordial after being with another woman only hours ago!

"No," she said simply. She couldn't give any advanced hint of her intentions. She wanted him to feel shocked and scorned like she did. "I'm sorry if I held you from your luncheon."

"For you, I would gladly wait." Words spoken with his usual smoothness. "But being away has left me with a hunger for something other than food."

She stiffened, and he lowered a dark brow with concern.

"I'm sorry I left you alone for so long, but I had business to attend to."

Business to attend to. Business! The snake! How could he stand there and lie like that? "Oh, I wasn't . . ." She stopped short of commenting about having met an old friend in the hall outside his bedroom. No need to give him any clues.

"I wasn't lonely." She corrected herself flatly, lowering her lashes coolly.

Despite her efforts, she could see that he sensed something was wrong. "Good." He served a plate of stew for her and then himself.

She sat down and ate without a word, forcing each bite into her swirling stomach.

After a few minutes of strained silence, he slammed his glass down with a resounding clank. "Savanna, what the hell is wrong?"

She took a long drink of her wine before answering. "Nothing is wrong." She forced herself to look him in the eye—the same stare she practiced in the mirror. "I think it is time that we talked."

"Talked?"

She folded her hands in her lap where he wouldn't see them trembling. "I know I committed to stay here with you for a week, but I do not think there is any point in continuing this any longer. I have already admitted to the justness of your claim to the Del Sol, so I think it is time you let me go."

For once in his life, Monheno was at a loss for words. Did he hear her right? Was this the same woman who gave herself totally to him last night? "I think not," he countered, still in shock. "There are still five days left to our bargain."

She stood up hotly, gripping the edge of the table like she wanted to tear two fistfuls from the wood. "You can keep me here for five days or five thousand, Monheno Devilla, and I still will not agree to marry you! I don't love you now, and I never shall."

Monheno rocked back in his chair, stunned by the blow. For a heartbeat, he couldn't breathe—couldn't do anything except sit there. How could she mean that? How could he love her so much and she not love him at all?

"Savanna," he stood up and went around the table to her, but she backed away.

"Please don't touch me." She put her hands up in front of herself to ward him off. "I don't deny that I am attracted to you physically, but I do not love you. It is too cruel for us to prolong this, don't you see?"

He shook his head. He didn't see. All he saw was that he loved her more than life itself and all she felt for him was physical attraction? The thought made him feel sick inside, wounded. Over the past days, she had showed him what he was missing in his life. She proved he could love again—that he needed to love, and he needed her.

In his mind, he wrote the rest of their lives like a storybook. Now she was asking him to put the book back on the shelf and forget it. Maybe she could rewrite their ending so easily, but he couldn't.

He'd been on the reverse end of this paradox before. He never realized what a blow it was from the other side. "What if there is a baby?"

Savanna swallowed a gasp of alarm. "There is not." If there was a child, she would cross that bridge later—alone.

"I see," he said flatly, staring into her eyes like he didn't believe her. He looked disappointed, so hurt she wanted to run to his side and offer him comfort.

"Let me go." She had to get away from him before she lost her resolve.

He stood up and walked to the fireplace, rested a foot on the hearth and stared into the darkened pit. "Go to your bedroom, Savanna." His voice was as hard as slate. "You won't be leaving today."

She started to protest, but he waved her away angrily. "Go."

Monheno heard her go, and he stood staring into the ashes, cold, dead, the way he felt inside. In his thoughts, he replayed the past days and nights. Weren't they happy despite the unfortunate circumstances surrounding the Del Sol? Didn't they share their thoughts, their bodies, their love? Could it only be a physical obsession for her?

He could remember times when physical attraction made him think he was in love. Maybe that was the case with her, or maybe she knew all along she didn't love him. Maybe she was acting all along, hoping to win her freedom.

He grabbed the iron stoker and threw it into the fireplace, slammed his fist into the mantel, and leaned against it.

"Damn." He pushed back from the mantel and spun around. His coat caught the rack and sent the fire tools clattering onto the floor. "Damnit, I'll forget I ever met her." He kicked the tools across the room and headed for the door.

Savanna heard the slamming door rattle through the empty house. Moments later, she looked out the window and saw him ride from the stable. A crash of lightning rained an eerie glow over the flowing folds of his black cape and the sleek lines of his blood bay mount. The gelding's hooves struck lightning of their own as they collided wildly with the cobblestones in front of the stable.

He was out of his mind leaving in such a storm. The afternoon outside was as dark as evening. No doubt he was headed to the consolation of his lover's arms. The thought of the woman stung her anew. Were they really to be married? Or did he propose marriage to every woman he took to his bed?

He had looked so devastated when she said she didn't love him. No doubt it was all a very good act. If he was bruised at all, it was only his pride. His little Spanish miss would soothe that.

She spun away from the window, flew to the wardrobe, grabbed the new dresses and slung them onto the floor. Damn him! How could he do this to her! How could he torture her this way by making her stay?

Well, she wouldn't. One way or another, she was getting out of this house and away from him. She couldn't bear this torment any longer, couldn't face any more of his falsely hurt looks, or smooth advances. She had no resistance to him physically. Just the sight of the bed she shared with him was making her weak.

She hurried to the door, grabbed the handle and pulled, but nothing happened. Locked? How could it be? She never heard it click. Who could have locked it? Did Monheno follow her up and lock the door? Would he do that to her? Trapped, impatient, she rushed to the window, grabbed it with both hands and pushed it up. It creaked and groaned in protest as she braced her shoulder under it and pushed until the opening was wide enough to slip through.

Damp, cool air slapped her in the face as she pushed her shoulders through and leaned over the sill. It smelled of thunder, and lightning, and approaching rain. She glanced up at the swelling thunderheads and then down at the wet rose garden below the window. No trellis or tree to climb down. If she jumped to the cobblestone path below, she would probably break her legs, or her neck.

She slipped back inside and stood in the cool

breeze, drumming her fingers on the sill. There had to be a way. She had to find a way. She had to be gone when he returned—before night came and he came back to his bed, to her.

She paced the room for an hour as thunder roared closer and lightning flashed overhead. The grey light outside faded with evening, and she moved nervously back to the window. If she found a way out, she could stand the storm if she had to, but how would she find her way in the dark? How would she find her way at all? What if she wandered back into Venenoso's camp by accident? Monheno said Venenoso had men everywhere in this valley. What if they found her before she could get away?

She could travel at night once she found her way to the main road. She could take one of the horses from Monheno's stable, sneak back to the Del Sol for the last bits of remaining money and jewelry in her purse, then leave—go where even Venenoso's wicked grasp couldn't reach.

She had to find someplace where she would be free of Monheno forever—where he could never find her if he decided to try. Where? She didn't have many options given the state of her finances. If she went back East perhaps she could secure a position as a governess or a tutor. She was educated, after all.

She tried to imagine herself as a governess for some wealthy family, but she couldn't. The thought of returning to a life so stuffy, so civilized was unbearable. This western freedom was in her blood, and she no longer wanted a life of musty houses and afternoon teas.

There was more to the west than California—the thought came to her in a sudden flash. Why couldn't she go somewhere else, perhaps secure a position as a school teacher? There had to be a need for teachers in any number of frontier towns. Didn't she see at least a dozen bulletins posted in St. Louis when she first came out West? If she returned there, it would only be a matter of sending a letter of her qualifications to some of those townships. Surely at least one of them would offer her a position and pay her fare out West.

The plan sent a shiver of anticipation through her, but at the same time made her stomach sink with dread. It was appealing, exciting almost, but frightening also, and heartbreaking. She wanted that life with Monheno, the one she dreamed of for longer than she cared to admit. Leaving was a final admission that it would never be.

She tried the door again, then went back to the window and tapped a finger impatiently on the glass. Somehow, she had to find a way out of here. Maybe she could find something she could use to trip the lock.

She hurried to the dresser drawers, threw them open and searched through them, then went to the vanity table and pulled open the center drawer. The contents made her pull her hand back. Monheno's things—cuff buttons, a carved bone comb, handkerchiefs, a cloak clasp, and a decidedly feminine hat pin. She swallowed hard and reached for the pin. It was probably his lover's. The sickening vision of his hands removing it crossed her mind.

She laid it aside and dug in the back of the drawer. Nothing else . . . except . . . Her hand settled on something cold, and she brought it out. A small knife, his initial inlaid on the handle. She turned it over in her hand, then closed her fingers over it. Better than no protection at all.

She grabbed the hat pin and opened it, then bent the sharp end back. It was the only thing she'd found that might possibly trip the lock. In a way, it would be poetic justice to use it for her escape. If she managed to get the lock open, she'd leave the pin dangling right there so he would know how she did it.

She pressed her ear to the door for a moment and listened before she knelt down by the lock. No sounds outside, not even the usual settling of the house. Everything was strangely quiet. Too quiet. Almost as if the house were listening for something.

The click of the pin against the brass lock echoed through the silent room as she slid it in. She paused for a minute, listened again. No sign that anyone heard. Perhaps the noise wasn't as loud outside.

She gritted her teeth and went back to work. The pin scraping and the lock clicking seemed loud enough to wake the dead, but she kept trying anyway. She could only hope there was no one else in the house.

The pin slid upward without resistance, then hooked on the bolt. She closed her eyes and said a prayer as she moved it upward. It slipped off the pin and fell, and she let out her breath, then tried again, but with no success. She stretched the bunched nerves in her neck and repeated the process again, again, again, until finally the lock slid open with a resounding click. An amazed, triumphant gasp passed her lips and she leaned against the door, catching her breath and listening. No sound of anyone outside.

She picked the knife up from the floor and glanced at the clothes now scattered around the room. She wanted to cut each one to shreds, but she forced herself to select a riding outfit instead. She'd never make it far in the day dress and slippers. At least in a riding outfit, she could mount alone, walk or run if she had to, and maneuver quietly in the brush if she needed to hide.

Her trembling hands could barely manage the buttons on the front of the day dress as she slipped it off. She growled in frustration, and pressed it over her hips with only half of them unbuttoned. If this plan was going to work, she had to get out of here now. Monheno would surely be coming back soon. She'd be lucky if she didn't meet him in the hall or at the stables now.

She tried not to think about the new pantaloons and riding outfit as she slipped it on, tried not to picture him selecting it, him hanging it in the wardrobe this morning while she slept. It wounded her and galled her at the same time to be forced to take even this one thing from him. When she got back to the Del Sol, she would sneak away with at least some of her own clothing and leave these things behind.

Her boots were damp and sticky from the day before. She groaned and strained to wiggle her feet into the wet leather, then finally stomped the floor impatiently. It echoed through the quiet room like . . . like the sound of horses running?

Her heart raced up with her next breath. Horses! More than one, on the lawn outside. Was it Monheno? Who was with him?

She raced to the window, then looked down at the garden and courtyard below. Four horses slid to a stop and pranced nervously on the cobblestones. It wasn't Monheno at all. She couldn't see the faces below, but the colorful silk bandanas around their necks told her who they were. Venenoso's men.

# *Seventeen*

The sound of the door opening shot through her, made her spin from the window. Her heart thundered, then froze as the door creaked open. The hair bristled on the back of her neck and she stepped back against the curtain, clutched the knife in her hand. Would she be able to use it if she had to?

She gasped when dark eyes peered around the door at her. The woman from the hall. Monheno's lover. Her fingers tightened around the knife. Rage boiled up in her and made her want to use it, but she held back, just stood there fingering the blade behind her back.

The woman slipped from the dark hallway into the light, and the hair bristled on the back of Savanna's neck. Something in her expression was different. The vicious look was gone, replaced by one of fear accented by ghostly pallor.

She stepped hurriedly into the room and closed the door behind her like she was being chased. "He ees come for you," she whispered, then pointed to the window. "he ees come outside."

Savanna glanced over her shoulder, her pulse quickening. Did this woman mean to take her down to her jailors? If so, she was going to have a fight. "I won't go."

The woman shook her head and hatcheted her hands in front of herself. "No, no." Her words were hurried, breathless. "I weell help you leave before they come."

Savanna lowered one brow and laid a hand over the racing pulse at her neck. "Help me leave?" She repeated. Something in this didn't seem right. Why would this stranger, who made no secret of her desire for Monheno, want to help her? She seemed more like she would turn Savanna over to Venenoso and then dance on her grave.

The woman's eyes darted around like she expected someone to appear in the room with them any moment. "Yes. Hurry." She gripped the front of her dark cotton skirt nervously. "They will keel you."

Savanna took a step forward from the curtain, then stopped, uncertain. Should she go? What if this woman was lying, leading her into a trap? But what choice did she have? There were four men outside and Monheno was gone. They could come in and take her any moment, take her to Venenoso.

Any chance was better than no chance. She

took a step toward the woman, who rushed forward and grabbed her hand anxiously.

"Come."

Savanna followed her away from the window. "Where are we going?" How could they possibly get by the four men outside? The woman shook her head.

Savanna pulled her hand away and stood in the middle of the room. She slipped the knife discreetly into her pocket and crossed her arms over herself. "What is your name? Who are you?"

The woman moved forward a few steps to the wall. "Daniela." She didn't look back, but ran her hand over one of the panels in the wall instead. "I am Daniela." As she said it, she slid one of the panels open like a door.

Savanna bent forward in amazement. A secret door! No wonder the Grandee could come and go from all parts of the house like magic. No wonder she heard footsteps passing but could not place the source.

Daniela hurried to the night table and grabbed the lamp, then lit it from the dying coals of last night's fire. She glanced at Savanna, but didn't meet her eyes as she moved back to the passage.

"I can show you this way." She bent over the lamp and slipped through the panel. "Come through, and help me make it close."

Savanna fingered the knife under her skirt and moved toward the dark passage. She had some protection with her at least, even if it was small.

Footsteps echoed in the hall as she ducked through the passage.

Daniela set the lamp on the floor and helped her slide the panel back into place. It squealed like a reluctant hog, and Savanna pulled her hands away. Surely, anyone in the house could hear that noise.

"We must make it close." Daniela's voice was an insistent whisper. "No one can know where we've gone."

Savanna gritted her teeth and helped slide the squealing panel closed. By the time it clicked into place, her ears were ringing and her heart was beating at a furious pace.

"What if they heard?" she whispered.

Daniela shook her head and picked the lamp up. "No one will know."

*Please, God, don't let them hear.* Savanna prayed as Daniela steadied the light and started down the passage. Savanna blinked against the darkness for a moment as she watched her go. The passage was small, barely tall enough and wide enough for Daniela to pass through, and black as pitch except for the circle of lamp light.

She hurried to catch the fringe of lamp light, her boot heels clicking loudly on the hollow wooden floor. Blind in the darkness, she stumbled over the uneven boards, and braced her hands against the sidewalls to keep from losing her balance. The last thing she wanted was to fall down in here. There was no telling what was lurking on the floor.

Daniela dashed ahead and turned a corner with the lamp, leaving Savanna groping in total darkness.

"Wait!" she cried, fear creeping over her skin like a centipede.

"Hurry," Daniela's voice echoed back, sounding far away.

Savanna braced her hands on the walls and stumbled into a run. She had to get back to that light before she lost her way, or her mind. She couldn't see anything, just blackness that strained her eyes and panicked her mind.

"Wait!" she called again.

"Hurry." The reply seemed farther away.

She turned the corner and the light came back into view, far ahead in the passage, a dim halo shone around the outline of Daniela's dashing form.

"Daniela, wait!"

No reply and the shadowed form turned another corner. Savanna shivered from head to toe and pressed her hands against the walls, feeling her way as fast as she could. Splinters rose from the rough wood and drove under her skin like tiny rapiers, but she ignored them.

Her mind spun with memories of those dark nights in the closet—those terrifying times when darkness wrapped around her like a strangling blanket. When she sat and waited for hard words and cruel hands to find her.

She forced the memories away and turned another corner. The walls fell from under her
hands, and she lost her balance, sprawled forward into a room, and hit the floor hard on her
hands and knees. Breath rushed from her in a
gasp, and she scrambled back to her feet. The
light was ahead, steady this time, not moving.

"Daniela?"

"I am here."

Savanna breathed an enormous sigh of relief.
"Wait for me."

"I weell."

Savanna moved across the dark room carefully,
feeling in front of her, one small step at a time.
"Bring the light closer," she whispered. "I can't
see."

"There ees no time." The light didn't move.
"Be careful, the floor ees . . ."

The ground gave way beneath Savanna's boot
before the sentence was finished. She gasped
and fell backward onto the ground as tiny peb-
bles clattered, then splashed into water below.

"There is a well here!" she gasped. "Bring
the lamp forward."

The light moved closer until Savanna could
see her boot at the edge of a deep pit.

"I deed not see it," Daniela breathed.

Savanna slid away from the pit and climbed
to her feet, then stepped around the well. "It's
too dark to go without the light." She grabbed
the back of Daniela's shirt. "We have to stay together."

She saw Daniela's dark head nod in the light. "Yes. It ees not far now."

Savanna thanked God and St. Nicholas for that and followed Daniela across the room and into another passage. Unless Daniela slipped out of her clothes, she wasn't letting that light get away again.

They turned another corner, and she collided with the woman as Daniela came to a stop.

"Keep the lamp." She turned around and placed it in Savanna's hands. "I weel open the door."

Hinges squealed and gray evening light peeked into the passage. Savanna let out a sigh of relief and followed Daniela out. The fresh air smelled moist and sweet as she took a deep breath of it.

Daniela took the lamp and blew it out. A horse whinnied not far away, and Savanna looked around to get her bearings. They were in back of the house, near the path to the stables. If they could get there without being spotted, they would have a good chance of making their escape.

Daniela hid the lamp in a bush and moved along the dense line of untrimmed hedge, motioning silently for Savanna to follow.

Savanna held her breath and crept along in the shadow. Just on the other side of the hedge, she could hear the Sombras's horses shuffling around. She bent low and clamped her hands over her face, fearing that even her breathing might give her away. What about the dogs? The dogs were always around the yard. If they came barking, the men would find her and Daniela immediately.

Daniela didn't go into the stable, but slid around the edge of the building instead. Savanna followed, moving through the shadows with no more sound than the faint swish of her skirt. Even that seemed like too much.

Two horses stood tied at the back of the stable, palominos she recognized from Monheno's string. She took the reins to one and climbed aboard as Daniela mounted the other. Dimly, she realized she was horse thieving, a hanging offense. The idea gave her vicious pleasure. The least Monheno deserved was to lose a few horses. If she had the time, she'd go back into the stable and turn the whole string loose.

She kept her horse close to Daniela's as they walked to the dark path, then loped until the night grew too black to see. Daniela seemed sure of her course, not worried about riding in the dark, so Savanna kept her mount close as they trotted through the darkness.

"Do you think anyone will follow?" she asked when she finally felt safe to talk.

Daniela shook her head, her raven eyes fixed on the road ahead, her face nearly hidden by her thick sable hair. "I theenk no one weel know."

Savanna let out a relieved sigh. She hoped Daniela was right, but this all seemed too simple. If the Sombras were figuring that she had escaped, why wouldn't they come after her? Why wouldn't they spot the tracks leading away from the stable and follow?

She recognized the main road when they rode onto it. Even in the dim moonlight, the remains of the original Oro Grande mission were visible. Relief rushed over her like cool water, took the feverishness from her skin. She knew how to get back to the Del Sol now. She didn't have to rely on this strange partnership any longer.

"I know the way," she whispered. "You should go. I don't want to put you in danger."

Daniela shook her head and looked at Savanna. Her eyes were cool, emotionless, but she reached out and touched Savanna's shoulder. "No. I should go weeth you. You can not return to Casa Del Sol. They may wait for you there."

Savanna pushed her tangled hair back thoughtfully. "I can go in late tonight to get the things I need. No one will see me." She didn't know what she would do if someone did.

Daniela nodded as if the plan pleased her. "I weel show you where to hide at Del Sol."

Savanna gave the plan a nod and looked ahead at the dark road. The decision was made. There was no going back on it now. She was leaving for good, without so much as a word of goodbye to anyone. In a few months, they would all forget she was ever there.

Tears pressed her eyes. Would Monheno forget her? Would he really marry Daniela, bring her into Del Sol house, into the bed where they made love? She hooded her eyes and looked over at Daniela. She was beautiful, young, probably only eighteen or so. Her long hair was flawless raven, and her skin a smooth olive shade. No wonder Monheno found her attractive.

And no wonder she wanted to help Savanna leave. With Savanna gone, she would have Monheno to herself, to marry, or whatever else they chose to do. Well, she could have him. A man like Monheno Devilla was a curse, not a blessing. She knew that well enough. Never, ever again would she forget it.

The yard at Del Sol house was still crawling with lazy evening activity when she and Daniela pulled their horses up behind a patch of brush on the hill.

"You can leave the horse here and hide there." Daniela motioned to a small adobe spring house not far away. "Go to the house when they sleep."

Savanna climbed down. "I will." She knew she should thank Daniela. The woman may very well have saved her life, but she couldn't force the words out. She knew very well why Daniela was helping her. The triumphant look in those dark eyes said it all.

Daniela nodded and reined her horse back. "I must go." She glanced around like she expected someone to be over her shoulder. "Leave before morning."

"I will," Savanna said again. And still no thank you.

Daniela reined her horse away and disappeared into the darkness. Savanna watched her go, then hid her horse deeper in the brush and sneaked to the spring house. She couldn't force herself to enter the dark interior, so she crouched outside by the wall as the noises quieted in the yard below.

The moon was overhead by the time she found the courage to start toward the house. More than anything, she wished she didn't have to return there at all. Everything about the place reminded her of Monheno, made her heart ache and her body throb.

She didn't have any choice. She had to return long enough to gather her purse and the few remaining pieces of jewelry that could be sold to raise trip fare. She could leave a note for Esperanza to send the rest of her things to St. Louis by freight.

The last light went out in the bunkhouse as she dashed across the yard and into the stable. From a stall near the door, Nantucket nickered to her.

She patted his sleek nose to quiet him. "Don't worry, we'll be leaving on a good ride pretty soon," she whispered close to his ear. Just the thought of taking him along made her feel a little better. At least he belonged to her, not to Monheno Devilla.

A dog trotted up but didn't bark as she crossed

the path to the house. She patted it absently, then hurried up the veranda steps to the study doors. They opened with only a slight creak, and she slipped into the dark room. From the hallway, dim light shone from the night lamps, and she moved carefully toward it, feeling her way around the furniture.

Her boots clicked lightly on the tile as she walked down the hall and up the stairs. There was no one there to hear it anyway. Esperanza was the only one in the house, and she slept in a room off the kitchen. At least until she tried to cross the yard again, there was little danger of her being seen.

Her things were still in her room when she took one of the dim hall lamps and went inside. Everything was in its place just as if she never left. She stood and looked at the hearth. Esperanza had cleaned it, of course. Was it really only a few days ago shattered glass lay there?

She blinked hard against memories and tears and took a small carpet bag from her wardrobe closet. It would hold the things she needed immediately, and she could strap it to the back of her saddle. Beyond that, she would have to hope Esperanza managed to send her things along.

She filled the bag with necessities, then added her purse and the very last of her jewelry, the precious pieces from her mother that she had never intended to sell. She would now if she had to.

The curtains on the bed blew invitingly as she

grabbed an extra skirt and blouse. She stretched out a hand and touched them, remembered him pushing them aside to lay her in the center.

An ache started in her stomach and spread through her. She released the fabric and turned away to make it stop. She couldn't think about this now. She had to be strong. She had to be alert and careful. She had to resist her need to love him.

She grabbed the carpet bag, slipped her pistol from the table by the bed, and went back into the hall, down the stairs, silently into the kitchen. By the light of the moon through the window, she gathered what she could, some fruit, cheese, a little bread and chip beef. She didn't dare look for more. Esperanza was sleeping just on the other side of the wall. There was no way Savanna could explain this if she awoke and came out.

The house settled and creaked as she went back down the hall to the study, almost as if it were protesting her leaving. She touched the doorframe and sighed. She felt like she was leaving home, her home, a place in which she had hoped to finally belong and find happiness. She felt right here and comfortable despite all the trouble the past weeks had brought. Now she would have to find another place, another life, one completely on her own.

She sighed and went to her desk, then slid the drawer open and took out paper and a pen. Squinting in the light from the door, she wrote her note to Esperanza, a poor explanation about sick relatives needing care, about selling the ranch to Monheno Devilla, and needing her things sent general delivery, to St. Louis. She couldn't say whether Esperanza would believe it, but she knew the housekeeper would send her things. She was always more than faithful.

The last clouds had cleared from the night sky when she stepped back outside. She stopped for a moment near the overgrown honeysuckle on the veranda railing and listened for signs of activity in the yard. There were none, and she knew she should cross to the stable to get Nantucket, but something drew her the other way instead.

# Eighteen

She wasn't sure what drew her to the rose garden, maybe the sweet scent of mimosa on the moonlit air, maybe the glitter of leftover raindrops on the leaves, maybe the scrappy rose bushes now starting to push forth leaves. Or just the memory of that day she found Monheno looking into the empty garden like he saw something there.

She set down the carpet bag and walked silently toward the corner where once there had been only a tangle of brambles. Now the headstones of the Devillas were visible, new rose bushes planted around them.

She walked toward the grave sites, straining her eyes to make out the names chiseled in the white stone. Maria, Malea, Blanca, Marta, and little Elena, just as he said. Nieces, nephews, the Patron and Patrona Devilla, all buried there just as he told her. Why did he bother to tell her about them? Why did he share these painful things with her if not because he loved her?

*Oh, Savanna, stop it!* She was fooling herself to think he loved her. If he did, he wouldn't have another woman in his bedroom. He used her as a means to an end, that was it. No matter how much it hurt, those were the facts and she was going to have to face them.

She blinked her eyes hard to keep back the tears, turned away and walked back through the garden. Would she ever feel whole again? Did hearts regrow like torn branches when they were ripped apart?

She turned away and crossed through the garden as tears pressed her eyes. The yard was quiet as she passed through, and the stable was dark and silent. She lit the lamp in the tack room and saddled Nantucket, then led him silently down the aisle. The other horses nickered quietly as she passed, and she held her breath. If one of them decided to whinny, someone might come from the bunkhouse, especially with all the trouble on the Del Sol lately.

She mounted outside the barn and walked the horse up the hill to the springhouse, then tied him beside the palomino. In the morning, she would turn the other horse loose and let him find his way down to the barn. She had no more use for him now that she had Nantucket.

She didn't go back to the springhouse, but curled up in the brush by the horses and rested

336

her cheek on her knees. Sleep teased her off and on until until dawn came.

As the sky turned from black to gray, she tied her carpetbag to Nantucket's saddle and removed the palomino's tack. He pressed closer to Nantucket as she tried to mount, and she shooed him away impatiently. The breakfast bell sounded at the Del Sol as he trotted toward the barn. Perfect timing. They probably wouldn't notice the palomino until after they finished eating.

She pulled her hat on and mounted, then turned Nantucket away from the Del Sol, touched the pistol in her pack for reassurance, and headed out at a lope. If she kept moving today, she could be in Riles City before nightfall.

She kept him at a good pace until she was a safe distance from the house, then continued at a trot until nearly an hour had passed and she was crossing over the north border of the Del Sol.

A strange, cold feeling crept over her and she gazed back toward what she left behind—houses, barns, land, cattle, all gone now. But the memories and the bitterness were still with her. No matter how hard she tried, how much she planned, or how much she tried to think of something else, she felt hollow inside, lost and afraid.

She was alone again, as always. But this time she didn't want to be alone. She wanted to be with Monheno, to still be living in that dream of the house and children, days filled with laughter and nights filled with passion.

By noon, she was exhausted, and she stopped the gelding beside a shady stream to eat lunch. Nantucket rubbed his head against her tiredly as she took his bridle off and hobbled him so he could graze.

She saw to her personal needs, then sank down at the base of one of the trees and unwrapped her lunch, eating it hungrily. It had been a long morning. At least she only had to go off the road twice to hide from wagons. She would easily reach Riles City by nightfall.

Her plan to leave the Del Sol was going well. There was no way Monheno could find her now, except in her thoughts, and with time she would drive him from those also.

Her heart sank. What if she never forgot him? What if every day from now on found her as black inside as this one? She'd heard of people pining away for love, but she never thought herself the kind of fool who would do it. She was stronger than that, wasn't she?

She finished her meal and tied the ends of the cloth back around what was left, then lay back against the tree to rest, only for a moment . . .

The sound of a horse's whinny rattled against her ears, and she sat up with a start, climbing to her feet quickly. Had she fallen asleep? Nantucket wasn't where she had left him. She ran from the shade frantically, saw him being led away by a man in a ragged sombrero.

"Stop!" She ran toward him without thinking. Her pistol! It was in the packs on the horse!

"Alto, señorita," a man's voice came from behind her, and she spun around in shock to find a second stranger holding a gun on her. He moved his horse forward a few steps. "Callarse!"

She knew the meaning of his words immediately, and she stood absolutely still. Was he going to shoot her? She could feel him thinking about it, could see his eyes twitching back and forth nervously.

He motioned for his partner, and the other led Nantucket forward, dropping the reins at her feet and motioning for her to mount up.

Her mind spun wildly. Were they letting her go, or taking her prisoner? "What do you want?" She took Nantucket's reins and moved him a little closer. If she could manage to get the gun . . .

Neither man seemed to understand her question. The one with the gun only motioned insistently for her to mount the horse.

She looped the reins over Nantucket's neck, pretended to comply, moved her hand slowly toward her pack. It was open. The gun would be just inside. If only she could get to it before he realized her intentions . . .

The man with the gun squinted and drew back the hammer. "Nada de eso." The words didn't sound like a hollow threat.

She jerked her hand back. This man was no ordinary thief. There was blood in his tone.

She fought back a shudder. "Just let me go."

He motioned again for her to mount. "Rapido!" His voice boomed as he pushed back the brim of his sombrero.

She climbed aboard, her gaze welded to his face. He was the most grotesque man she had ever seen. The severe features of his face were hardened by a thick moustache and a mottled complexion, pitted and scarred. His eyes were black as a well, and had the most pure look of hatred she'd ever seen.

They forced her back the way she came that morning. Rapid words of Spanish passed her, and she listened intently, trying to gather clues from their conversation. The only words she recognized were common ones that told her nothing. If only there weren't watching her so closely, she could try again for the gun.

She had no chances as the afternoon passed. Her thoughts drifted back to Monheno. Where was he now? What was he thinking? Perhaps he would come after her . . .

It was ridiculous, of course. No one knew where she was except Daniela. She should have been more careful, should have considered that there could be thieves on the road. Were these thieves? If they meant to rob her, why were they taking her with them? A lump sank to her stomach. What if they planned something else?

She tried not to picture the possibilities as

they rode the rest of the afternoon. Toward evening, they moved onto a wooded trail that seemed vaguely familiar . . . but why? Where were they? Had they been here before?

The truth hit her like a slap as they turned a corner and sounds drifted to her ears. She knew where she'd heard them before. In Venenoso's camp.

When the first shabby row of mud brick and log buildings came into view, she knew for certain. Her body crawled with fear as if she'd been thrown into a pit of spiders. In its wake came a crippling anger. Damn Monheno Devilla! This was his doing. When she saw him, she would claw his eyes out with her bare hands! It was her right to leave, how dare he send his bandits after her! How dare he drag her to this filthy camp like a prisoner!

Her silent protests snapped as a giant ducked through the doorway of one of the buildings to meet them. She knew by the long silver hair that he was Venenoso. He seemed taller here than in Monheno's study, a towering colossus. In younger days, he'd undoubtedly had a remarkable physique, and even at an age that had drawn heavy lines down his cheeks, he still looked strong.

His hair hung well past his shoulders, and his skin was as dark like an Indian's. But his eyes, narrow and set too close in his face, were such a pale shade of grey they almost seemed colorless. Like his name, he looked poisonous, as though he were a snake about to strike.

She drew back when he stepped toward her. A wide smile creased his face, and she shuddered, forcing herself not to look away.

"Miss Storm, I presume," he studied her boldly from head to toe. "It is an honor to finally meet my . . . shall I say . . . my nemesis?"

She shrugged numbly. His nemesis, indeed! If anything, he was hers, or would have been if that position wasn't reserved for Monheno Devilla.

"I demand that you release me." The words, which sounded like something from a poorly written novel, were out of her mouth before she could stop them.

She flinched when the snake laughed.

"What a charming accent." He looked anything but charmed. His gaze left her for a second and moved to survey the growing number of curious eyes turned in their direction. "Might I suggest that we go inside?" He stepped back and made a motion toward the door. "I wouldn't want you to freckle."

In the instant he looked away, she realized no one was watching her. With a desperate quickness, she reached into her saddlebag, and closed her hand over the pistol. She had it halfway out before a crushing blow sent the pistol spinning from her fingers and into the air. A hand jerked her roughly from her horse, dragged her through the air, then tossed her down. She hit the ground hard, air rushing from her lungs in a gasp.

She lay in a crumpled heap inside the building she refused to enter a few minutes before. Gathering her wits, she scrambled to her feet, backed away from the giant, who shut the heavy wooden door behind him.

"Shooting at your host is hardly proper behavior for a lady." That same hard edge sharpened his speech—as though he wanted to cut her throat.

"I am hardly your guest!" She drew to her full height, still a pittance next to his. Made bold by her anger, she rammed her fists into her hips and faced him head on. "You can tell Monheno Devilla he has no right to hold me prisoner any longer. In fact, bring him here, I'll tell him myself!"

He gave a false shrug of regret. "I am afraid you misunderstand. The intrepid Mister Devilla has nothing to do with this. In fact, I am more than a little displeased with him due to his deception concerning you."

"Deception?"

He laughed. Looking down at her, he stroked the top of her head as though she were a darling puppy, his fingers moving down her cheek and then grasping her chin.

He jerked up her head and forced her to meet his eyes. "Do you really think I would release you when you know so much about the Sombras—when you could easily lead the law to my doorstep? I haven't lived this long by being a fool for a pretty woman, though I am afraid I can't say the same for Monheno. I was more than a little disappointed to hear he had broken his promise to me and released you." He let go of her chin and threw his hands into the air as if in frustration. "That was not part of the plan."

"Plan?" Did he think Monheno let her go on purpose? Did Monheno tell him that?

"The plan, the plan," he wheeled his hands in front of himself like she should know what he was talking about.

She shook her head in complete confusion. "I knew nothing of a plan."

He tipped his head back as though seeing her for the first time, his mouth dropping open in sudden understanding. "I see . . ." He was obviously speaking to himself now, and then to her, "Well, you will hear about that later."

The way he said it made her turn cold to the very bone, and she bit her lip to keep from shivering in front of him. Whatever this plan was, she had a feeling it involved something very bad. Looking at the giant who stood before her now, she sensed that things were bad enough already.

He grabbed her upper arm and led her to a small room, then told her to remain there if she valued her neck. She sat on the bed in the corner and obliged. Anything was better than being in the same room with that devil.

Over the following hours, she had a great deal

of time to review his words in her mind, and to fear what they might mean. Outside, the sun descended, leaving the room dark save for the light of one candle.

Could it be true that Monheno betrayed Venenoso by letting her go? What would happen to Monheno now? She had a feeling being in Venenoso's bad graces was deadly. Only a few hours ago she was planning to kill Monheno with her bare hands. Now she was terrified he would come to harm.

There was another side, one that she barely dared to think about. If Monheno risked his life by blaming her escape on himself, didn't that mean he cared for her? Even if it wasn't love, he did feel something.

It made the memories of what happened between them a little less painful. As the pain of heartbreak lessened, another ache began to grow—an ache for the warmth and safety he offered her. Alone in the dark room, she longed to be in his arms again—to feel loved, to feel whole.

From the main room, she heard a familiar voice. Adolfo Devilla? She stood up from the bed and walked into the hall. There was no guard at the door, nor was it locked. Venenoso's threat was enough to keep her in the room, but now she had to know if Adolfo was here, and if Monheno was with him. She stopped at the end of the hallway, slipped into the shadows by the wall and peered into the main room, then stepped tentatively through the door.

At the crude split pine table sat Venenoso, his back to her, his huge frame towering above the table like it was a toy. Across from him, and facing her was, as she thought, Adolfo Devilla. He looked up when she entered, and stopped talking as though he didn't want her to hear.

"Ah, Princess." There was no sign of apprehension in his face. "Glad to see you are unharmed. My crew will be very relieved to hear of it."

Savanna stood dumbfounded in the doorway, her underlip hanging slack. He was farther out of his mind than she thought. How could he sit there calmly discussing imaginary ships when there were lives at stake—when across the table from him sat the most ruthless killer in the territory?

"Where is Monheno?" she choked.

Venenoso's shoulders tightened at the question, but he didn't turn around.

Adolfo squirmed in his chair. "He is . . ." He seemed to be searching for something to say, and finally finished with, ". . . not here."

Several minutes passed in silence. The air in the room stretched so tightly it seemed like the slightest movement would shatter it.

Finally, Venenoso stood up, and turned halfway around, a strained smile on his face. "Please, come in and sit down, Miss Storm.

You'll have to excuse me for a moment. I have something to see to."

There was a subtle hint in the way he said it that let her know the thing had something to do with her. She waited for him to leave before she moved toward the table, but she didn't take a seat. Instead, she ran to the Grandee, and knelt beside him desperately.

"You must tell Monheno not to come here. I think Venenoso plans to kill him." When he didn't respond, she gripped his arm, shook him insistently. "You have to leave! You are in danger here!"

"Oh, my lady," he said soothingly as he pried her hands from his arm and held them in his. "There is nothing to worry about here. Nothing will happen to us."

"Listen to me!" She pulled away from him. "Please, just tell Monheno not to come here."

"Fine, fine," he soothed as though appeasing a frightened child. "If that will make you happy, my dear."

"No. Listen . . ."

Heavy footsteps made her stop, and she glanced up to see Venenoso coming back down the hallway.

She withdrew from Adolfo's side. She couldn't let Venenoso suspect she had warned him. If the bastard knew it, he might not let the old man go.

"And what has the Queen of England been telling you, Mi tio?" Venenoso returned to his seat at the table. In his wake came a young Spanish girl, perhaps twelve or thirteen, with a serving tray and a water pitcher in her hands. Setting them on the table, she smiled shyly at the giant, and he reached out to stroke her glistening raven head fondly.

Savanna drew back, mortified, offended. Good Lord, how could he? Poor little thing. She was barely more than a child.

"My daughter." He laughed, turning his eyes to Savanna as the girl left. "Pretty child, don't you think?" He didn't wait for an answer, "Must have her mother's looks—can't exactly remember who her mother was . . ."

That comment was almost as disgusting as her original assumption about the girl, and she gave Venenoso a sneer in reply.

"Care for some supper?" he asked, as if he didn't notice her murderous look.

She narrowed her eyes coolly and shook her head. "No. I don't want anything from you except my release." She crossed her arms over her chest and started to leave, but a chair skidded into her path.

"You will stay here with us for now." His pale grey eyes were deadly serious, the threat in them unmistakable. Turned upward from beneath thick brows, they dared her to move an inch further away. Slowly, he swiveled his head toward her, bringing into view the long scar on his cheek, now a gruesome shade of white, twitching almost imperceptibly.

She pulled the chair back to the table and sat down on it.

"That is better." He grinned, but with not an ounce of warmth. His eyes still fixed on her, he leaned closer, and pushed the serving tray in front of her. "In your valley, I may be the devil, but here I am god. Everyone will do as I say, including you—including Monheno Devilla." A pause and another look at the tray, and then he sat back in his chair, adding, "Eat."

She fixed her eyes on the tray of food, and paid little notice as female hands set an enameled glass before her and poured an ample portion of wine. Absently, she frowned as the crimson liquid was splashed carelessly over the edge to stain the heavy table top. Venenoso needed to get better help . . .

"Anything else?" The voice snapped her head around into wicked raven eyes—eyes she recognized. Daniela! Why was she here?

With a careless swipe, Daniela tipped the glass over, then looked murderously at Savanna as if it were her fault.

"Enough!" The roar of Venenoso's voice made them both jump like puppets. He slammed his fists on the table top, stood up, and leaned across the table until he was only inches from the two women.

Snake eyes met raven ones, and he growled, "That is enough, Daniela."

To Savanna's horror, Daniela snorted and pouted her bottom lip stubbornly. "I theenk you

349

shoult just keel her," she protested. "She . . ."
She never finished the sentence. Venenoso's
enormous hand caught at her throat.

"You will leave," he ordered as though he
might break her fragile neck. He shoved her
backward, sent her stumbling into the wall. "Or
I will kill you."

He stood watching her go as though contemplating it, then smiled, shook his head, and sat
back down in his chair. "My daughter," he explained absently. "She once was my favorite." He
motioned to the tray, smiling into Savanna's hor-
rified face, "Family squabble. Don't let it spoil
your appetite."

Savanna's stomach swirled like a whirlpool as
she took a corn tortilla. She was afraid not to.
If the punishment for spilling wine was death,
she could only imagine the sentence for refusing
the food. She tipped the glass back up and
poured water from the pitcher.

The snake was watching her, she could feel
it, but she kept her eyes turned downward. Cold,
like death, the color drained from her face. She
wasn't about to give him the satisfaction of seeing it.

From beneath a veil of lashes, she sneaked a
glance up at Adolfo Devilla, hoping Venenoso's
threats had forced him to realize the urgency of
the situation. If so, it didn't show in his posture.
He was sitting comfortably, calmly scooping as-
sorted vegetables and a helping of meat onto
his tortilla. His lips curved upward pleasantly at

the edges, and he hummed a tune as he finished with the platter and passed it cordially back to Venenoso.

It dashed Savanna's hope that he might carry her message back to Monheno. He was too far out of his mind to realize the danger. Somehow, she was going to have to find another way.

Venenoso looked up from his food and said something in Spanish. The Grandee, laughing, answered him in Spanish. A jovial conversation began, and each of the men continued laughing and commenting, their words augmented with wild hand gestures. It was almost more than she could stand. Their gestures made it clear they were talking about her.

She returned their glances with bitter stares, but it didn't stop them. They started jesting about that and mimicking her actions.

Why did she ever like Adolfo Devilla? Crazy old coot. He was probably the one who told Venenoso that Monheno had let her go. Obviously, none of them knew Daniela was involved. If they did, she was quite sure Daniela would be dead already.

She finished a few bites of food, then asked to leave. Neither man answered, so she stood up and left the table, holding her breath the whole way. Venenoso didn't call her back. In fact, he and Adolfo were so involved with their wine, they barely seemed to notice her at all.

Weary but afraid to sleep, she sat on the bunk in her prison room. She had no idea what time it was—undoubtedly well after midnight, perhaps even just a few hours before dawn.

Outside in the darkness she could hear the sounds of voices, those of men and women speaking Spanish, and the far away strains of a mandolin. A dog barked occasionally from somewhere just beneath her window. That bothered her.

It interfered with her plan—a plan which began with slipping through that narrow window. Undoubtedly, Venenoso had thought it too narrow to be a route for escape, but she could slide through, albeit in an embarrassing state of near-nudity. She would have to throw her outer clothes through first and put them back on outside.

The only problem was the dog hovering beneath the great room window next door collecting scraps as Venenoso chose to fling them out. It was impossible to tell whether the animal would bark when she made her exit. If it did, she would be trapped in the back alley half-dressed, a situation which could lead to things she didn't even want to think about.

With a steadying breath, she made her decision. It was either act or be acted upon, and she was going to act. Hopefully, the dog would not.

With nimble fingers, she slipped from her skirt, blouse, and the thick split petticoat underneath. Standing in only her chemise, she prayed silently that no one would come through the open door of the bedroom.

She tossed the petticoat underneath the bed—better to leave it behind—then bundled her outer clothes and tied them loosely with her shirtsleeves.

She took one last deep breath and pushed the bundle through the narrow window. No turning back now. She blew out the lamp and candle and slipped a leg through the window. She just hoped she was right about being able to fit through.

It turned out to be more difficult than she planned. The rough split-pine frame tore through her thin clothing and clawed at her skin as she wiggled through the opening. Just when she was beginning to wonder at the wisdom of the entire plan, the wood gave a bit, and she was through, her boot touching ground on the outside. Hopping on that foot, she brought her other leg out and stood safely in the alley.

She let out a huge breath and slipped back into the shadow of the wall, then reached for her clothing bundle. Her fingers descended into empty dirt. She knotted her brows and felt around. Still nothing. Breath caught in her throat and she fell to her knees, scratched around in the darkness for what simply had to be there.

Then she heard the dog. In the light of the greatroom window, she could see him standing with his shaggy head cocked slightly in her direction, her clothing bundle dangling like a two-pound steak from his jaws.

She froze in her tracks. *Be calm.* Should she try to call the dog over and risk having him alert his master? Should she go on with her plan and try to make good her escape without the clothing?

Frantic, she stood a moment longer, watched the dog as it watched her. She took a step closer, patting her knee tentatively to call the animal.

It gave a cantankerous snort, and bounded a few paces away, its tail wagging like it was playing a terribly good joke. Five feet farther away, it stopped again and turned back, the bundle still dangling from its mouth.

She crouched down and crept close to him, her hands patting the ground in what she hoped was a coaxing fashion. This could not possibly be happening. If she caught the animal, she would kill it. God, what else could go wrong!

She shouldn't have asked. The dog moved a few paces farther away and stopped just at the end of the alleyway in a circle of torchlight.

Savanna raised her eyes heavenward. Please, God, strike him down with a lightning bolt before he can go any farther. If the situation weren't so deadly, it would have been comical.

She moved forward again. This time, the dog didn't move, just watched every step she made intently, its body crouched as though it would bolt into the street any moment. If it did, her clothes would be gone forever.

She stopped within reach, slid her hand out slowly toward the bundle.

He moved it away with a playful twist of his head.

She lunged across the empty space and closed her fingers over her pilfered clothing. The dog growled playfully and jumped into the air, pulling fiercely on the other end of the cloth.

Unprepared for the counter-move, she flopped unceremoniously from her feet and fell face-first in the dust, then clung to the clothing, trying to get to her feet as the dog dragged her forward into the torchlight.

The glow crossed over her arms, and she scrambled up to take a better hold on the clothing and gave a mighty jerk she hoped would tear the animal's teeth out.

Given the option, the dog let go, and she grabbed the bundle to her with a prayer of thanks.

Commotion close by made her realize she was within view of the street. A group of people had gathered around Venenoso's door, but they weren't looking at her. They were turned toward a rider who sat atop a lathered blood-bay horse— a rider who was looking at her as though he'd seen a ghost.

Struck by a dozen realizations at once, not the least of which was that of her own shameful state, she gasped, clasped the clothing tighter against her chest, and spun away, rushing into the shadows.

Monheno Devilla! The name rang in her

mind as she shot back down the alley. What was he doing here?

With the commotion, she'd have no chance of escape. There were too many people on the street now. What if he decided to follow her down the alley? What could be worse than being discovered almost nude by a mob of bandits?

Desperate for escape, she looked the other way down the alley, but at the end was a mud brick wall far too tall for climbing.

# Nineteen

It took her several minutes to squeeze back through the window. For a heartbeat, the frame seemed too tight. Her mind raced with chilling visions of them finding her stuck halfway through, and she struggled harder. She fell into the darkness face first, and scrambled around to find her clothes, hurried fingers trying to determine which pieces were which. From under the bed, she reclaimed her petticoat and then stood up, rushing to redress herself.

Every hook and button mutinied on her, and she growled in frustration, her hands trembling wildly. Maybe they were going to find her naked after all.

She'd glanced at the open door a hundred times before she finally succeeded. When her own panting and rustling quieted, she could hear their voices coming from the great room, and stood close to the doorway to listen.

"That is enough!" Venenoso's words. "Now sit down before I have you shot!"

"Not before I rip your head from your worthless neck!" There was so much anger in the voice she barely recognized it as Monheno's. The words were followed by another crash, as if someone threw something. Before the thunder died, a new sound tore the air. A gunshot.

Savanna ran into the hallway in horror, her heart frozen like the air in the room.

"Now sit down both of you." Adolfo Devilla. "If there is one thing I can not stand, it is to see two intelligent men behaving like a pair of boys. I will not allow it on my ship!"

Savanna skidded to a halt at the end of the hallway. Relief flooded through her like warm wine. All three of them were still standing. The gun, still smoking, was in Adolfo's hands.

She sank back into the shadows of the hall and watched as both men stared at Adolfo in shock. It was hard to determine who looked angrier, the giant bandit leader, his long silver hair strewn wildly about his broad shoulders and his grey eyes gone almost white with fire, or Monheno, his skin a shade paler than usual, his eyes harder than she had ever seen them. A grim smile twisted on his lips, as though he was thinking of what he planned to do with the knife white-knuckled in his hand.

If he was afraid of either of them, Adolfo didn't show it. He holstered the ancient-looking pistol calmly and motioned again toward the table. "Sit down." He sounded like he was talking to a pair of children. "We can discuss this like civilized men."

Monheno glared at him, his face grey with rage. He slammed his arm downward, sinking his knife blade into the tabletop.

"Stop looking at me that way, boy," Adolfo scolded. "What I did was for your own good."

"For my good!" Monheno threw his fists into the air, then let them collide with the rough table top. The impact rang through the room like a drum roll as he pointed a finger at the old man. "Stay out of my business, you crazy old fool."

"I apologize for my meddling," Adolfo looked utterly conciliatory as he took a seat with Venenoso. "What can I do to remedy the situation?" A crafty look came into the old man's eye. "Sit down, will you?"

Monheno seated himself, teeth and fists still clenched, on the end of the table opposite Venenoso.

"You can release," he paused like he couldn't find the right word, ". . . her."

Adolfo glanced over his shoulder, and Savanna sunk back into the shadows. "Savanna, you mean?"

The question brought a nod from Monheno and a gesture of protest from Venenoso.

Adolfo silenced them both with two quick hands. "But she was leaving the valley, and quite unbeknownst to you, I might add."

Savanna didn't miss the look in Monheno's eyes. "That is her right." His voice was as razor-sharp as his eyes. "She and I have no further . . . business together."

Venenoso leaned forward in protest. "She knows far too much about us." He looked angry, murderous. "You were out of your mind to think she could be released. If you were anyone else I'd have you shot for your deception."

The look Monheno returned could have burned a hole in steel. "She is no danger to us," he ground the words out from between clenched teeth. "She chose to leave. I let her go."

She chose to leave. I let her go. Savanna clamped a hand over her mouth to strangle a startled cry. Why was he lying? Was he too proud to admit she escaped from his prison?

"You broke our bargain," Venenoso braced his hands on the table and half-rose in his chair. "You were supposed to marry the girl not set her free to bring the law to my doorstep."

"I never agreed to that," Monheno said flatly. "I told you I would do what I could to keep our bargain—short of force."

Savanna felt her heart stop. A bitter fire burned through her. She started forward to tell them all she wouldn't marry Monheno Devilla if he were the last man on Earth. Venenoso's next words stopped her short, threw her back against the wall.

"Well, you will agree now." He spoke like

360

there was no room for question. Monheno started to protest, and he added, ". . . or I will send her to Mexico where a woman like that brings a good price . . . and where she cannot bring me trouble with the law."

He leaned forward, the stony set of his scarred face conveying the finality of the situation. "Take your choice, cousin. She can not testify against us if she is in Mexico, nor can she testify against her husband if she is your wife." He rolled his eyes upward and added a third option. "Come to think of it, she wouldn't be a problem at all if she were dead."

They sat staring at each other, one waiting for an answer, the other waiting for a chance at someone's throat.

Adolfo broke the stalemate. He looked completely sane as he stood up, walked around the table, and laid a beseeching hand on Monheno's shoulder.

"Come now, boy, this is only pride and stubbornness," he said softly. "You've been pining away for that girl ever since she left. It's more than plain you are in love with her."

It's more than plain you are in love with her. The words repeated in Savanna's mind as she pressed closer to the wall. Was that true? How could it be?

Monheno glared at his uncle bitterly. "The feeling is unrequited," he said flatly. "I'll not have an unwilling wife."

Adolfo stood back and patted his nephew's

shoulder. "It is not so unrequited as you might think. Had I not interfered between you, the two of you would still be together now." He looked toward the hallway like he knew she was there. "Silly girl. She should not have put such stock in a crazy old man."

Monheno shook his head and stared out the window. "She made her choice."

Adolfo leaned close to his ear, and Savanna could barely hear his words. "Don't be so stubborn, boy. You're getting exactly what you really want. You want her, you're getting her. Swallow a little pride. It won't choke you going down."

Monheno sighed. As much as he hated to admit it, it was true. Venenoso was offering him exactly what he wanted—had wanted, and still did. The truth was that he still wanted Savanna, and that he believed in his heart he could make her love him. With a hard look, he faced his cousin and nodded. Revenge could wait.

"Good, then that is settled." Venenoso gave a victorious smile that made the scar stand out on his cheek. "We'll get it out of the way first thing in the morning. I'm afraid the bride is sleeping just now."

But the bride wasn't sleeping. She was stumbling back to her room, her heart frozen and her mind numb. *We'll get it out of the way first thing in the morning. You were supposed to marry the girl, not set her free. . . . She cannot testify against her husband. . . .* The whole plan sketched itself in her mind with sickening clarity. Monheno was trying to lure her into a marriage all along so she couldn't bring the law against Venenoso and his men. Damn him. How could he do something so cruel?

She rushed to the other side of the room, and leaned out the window to check her escape route. The street was still crowded with people. She would have to wait for the commotion to die, but she would get out of here. Those people couldn't stay there all night. All she had to do was sit near the window and wait.

*I will not have an unwilling wife.* The surprise would be on him. He wouldn't have a wife at all. By the time they came for her, she would be long gone. She would lie under a rotten log in the woods and let ants crawl over her for days if that was what it took to get away.

She closed her eyes and leaned her head back. She needed rest. Two nights with little sleep was catching up with her. She would just lie down for a moment . . .

Where was Esperanza? Why didn't she draw the curtain to keep the early sun away? Who was making all that racket outside? Why were they playing music?

She shot from the bed like a calf stung in the tail. Standing unsteadily on her feet, she looked around the crudely furnished room in confusion. The memory of the night before hit her like a club. Oh, dear God, she fell asleep! Her chance to escape was gone!

She brushed back her tangled hair and tried

to think of another way out. There had to be a way out. Somehow, she had to convince Venenoso she wouldn't go to the law—that, if released, she would go so far away she could no longer be a danger to him. All she wanted was a new life. Surely she could make Venenoso see that if only she could talk to him . . .

A picture of Venenoso came into her mind and shattered the idea. She had about as much chance of mercy from him as from a rattlesnake. The man had nearly strangled his own daughter.

That left Monheno. If she could see him before the wedding, perhaps she could convince him to refuse to go through with it. There had to be some other way for her to escape Venenoso. Tonight, she could slip through the window again . . .

A sound from the doorway caught her ear, and she looked up to see the child who had served them the night before. Holding out the serving tray in her hands, the girl gave a tentative smile, her brown eyes encouraging Savanna forward.

"You should eat." Her voice bore only the slightest accent. "Today is your wedding day."

Savanna's stomach lurched as she took the tray and set it on the small lamp table. It would serve no purpose to argue with the girl. Her father might strangle her for failing in her task.

She turned back to the girl and tried to look casual. "Is Monheno here?"

The girl nodded.

"May I see him?"

The child looked confused, and worried, but then she nodded. "He is at the table."

Savanna didn't ask anything more. The poor little thing looked terrified. She probably was. If she said something she wasn't supposed to, it would probably cost her her life.

Savanna straightened her hair and clothing, then walked through the door and down the short hallway. She slowed at the end and peeked around the corner. To her relief, Monheno was alone at the table. She bolstered her courage and walked into the room, moving quickly around the table to face him.

She thought she was prepared to confront him, but when he looked up from the bottle of tequila he'd quite plainly been nursing for a while, she fell silent. She'd never seen him that way before—his eyes reddened around their dark centers, raven hair disheveled, his usually dark skin washed to a pale shade of grey-beige. When he looked at her, it was as though he was looking through her.

"Monheno?" Was he too drunk to understand?

The fog cleared, and he squinted at her. "Well, if it isn't my unwilling bride." A bitter scowl marred his face. "Come to plead for your freedom?"

She couldn't think of anything to say.

He shrugged. "I assume they told you of the upcoming nuptials."

The anger in his voice sent a shudder through her. Was he really so opposed to the idea of marrying her? Then why didn't he refuse? "I heard you last night," she admitted. "Monheno, please, don't let them do this. Venenoso won't follow through with his threats, I know he won't. You saw me in the alley. I can escape tonight."

Even through the effects of nearly a half bottle of tequila, Monheno still felt the slice of her words. So she found the idea of marrying him so abhorrent she would rather throw herself to Venenoso's mercy? What she deserved was for him to let her do it. It would be a hard landing. His cousin had no mercy.

Whether Savanna Storm loved him or not, he loved her. He would never be able to forgive himself if he didn't do what he could to save her—and what he could to have her.

"I am afraid you're mistaken about that." He didn't miss the look of disbelief in her violet eyes. What a fool she was! She was lucky she wasn't dead already.

He stood up and grabbed her forearm before she could escape, pulled her body harshly against his. "Savanna, you are nothing to him but a bit of trouble in a pretty package. If you think he would walk two steps out of his way to keep from trampling you, you're wrong. You can thank my uncle for the fact that you are still in one piece now." He seized her chin, forced her to meet his eyes. "We are all doing what we can to save your pretty hide, Savanna. I would suggest that you cooperate."

Blinded with anger, Savanna jerked her arm, trying to free it from his grasp, but he held it, tightened his fingers until it hurt. She struck back with words. "How dare you act as though you are some white knight galloping down to save me!" Her body burned with anger and passion. "I know all about your little plan to coax me into marriage so I couldn't bring the law against you. You sicken me."

"Perhaps." He smiled ruefully. "Nonetheless, I am still your intended. In fact, I think the nuptials will be taking place within the hour, so you'd best go back to your room. I hear it is bad luck for the groom to see the bride before the wedding."

She jerked her arm again, her temper bolting like a runaway horse. He let her go, bitter notes of laughter rumbling in his throat.

"You bastard!" She ran across the room. "I will let them shoot me in the street before I'll marry you."

An hour later, she stood at her own wedding. A fine time was had by all, except for the bride who was sullen and angry, and the groom who was nearly drunk off his feet.

The small ceremony was conducted in a field of wildflowers near a brook at the edge of the village, by a padre who was nearly as drunk as the groom. Under the orders of Venenoso, he didn't bother about the fact that the bride never said the traditional words of consent.

Venenoso answered for her, and she squeezed her hands over the folds of her skirt, wanting nothing more than a knife with which to cut him to ribbons.

"Take your wife, cousin." He stepped back, giving her to her new husband like an unwanted affliction. "May both of you have all that you deserve."

After it was over, his people completed the sham with a small wedding feast consisting of a stolen steer, various fruits extorted as tribute, bread, and corn tortillas. No one seemed concerned that everything there was stolen, or that the bride tried three times to sneak away, only to be apprehended and returned.

Savanna sulked at the corner of the feast table, humiliated by the entire affair, from the white cotton dress Venenoso's daughter gave her, to the sham of a ceremony, to the ridiculous celebration afterward. All of it only pointed out that she had no control over her own future.

By the time it was all over, she was so angry she couldn't even speak. Her head throbbed like someone was beating a set of bass drums inside, and her body was limp from two sleepless nights and four escape attempts. She didn't even have the energy to curse Venenoso and Adolfo when they helped her onto her horse to go home.

She didn't look back. She had no desire to remember the place, or ever see it again. She set her hands firmly on the reins and turned her thoughts to the future. How could she salvage what was left of her life? There was no possibility of annulment. She and Monheno had already shared the marriage bed. She could hardly go before God now and say the union wasn't consumated. Divorce? Could a woman get a divorce without her husband's consent? Separation? They wouldn't be the first married couple to agree to a discrete arrangement.

She glanced at him from beneath her lashes, noticed he suddenly looked sober—grave even. Doubtless, he was considering what he just did, and regretting it, thinking about how a wife was going to spoil his style of life.

"You needn't look so grim." Now was as good a time as any to broach the subject. "I think we both know this is not a real marriage."

"Meaning what?" He didn't look at her, but studied the treeline in front of them.

"Meaning we will make some sort of arrangement, of course," she blurted out. How could he be so calm, so unemotional about the whole thing? "There is the possibility of divorce, or in lieu of that, I could take up a house somewhere else."

Monheno tightened his fists on the reins, the knife twisting in his gut. She was wasting no time letting him know how much she detested the marriage. He had hoped she would at least allow it a chance. Apparently not.

"I don't like either of your options." He

couldn't keep the sharpness from his voice. At that moment, he felt cruel, ready to land a blow. "Whether you like it or not, you and I are married, and I intend that we be married . . . in every way."

She shuddered at his last words, and knew what they meant. How would she bear it if he insisted on claiming his right in the marriage bed? It would only force her to remember how much she loved him—how totally she gave herself to him before he proved himself a scoundrel. How could she go the rest of her life wondering if he left her bed to go to Daniela's?

She straightened her back. She wouldn't let him force her into this. "That is only your pride talking."

"Hardly," he muttered. "I've none left. Taking an unwilling bride is not something that makes me proud."

She looked away. He seemed so saddened, so tortured, she wanted to reach out to him, to give him comfort. She kicked that urge aside.

"Then why did you do it?" Damned if she was going to let him play the martyr. "I begged you not to."

"I don't know," his lips twisted into a sadistic smile. "I probably should have left you to the wolves, but, call me soft-hearted, I couldn't bring myself to do it."

Call him soft-hearted, indeed! She'd call him a lot worse if he said one more thing! "This is hardly the time for jokes."

Monheno looked over at her and tipped his hat back tiredly. She was beautiful, even if she didn't love him, and she was his, for better or worse. They started out with the worse—which meant better things were yet to come.

He sighed and scratched his forehead. "This is anything, Savanna, but a joke."

Savanna narrowed her eyes at him petulantly. What did he mean by that? Did he really intend to take this marriage seriously? How long would that last when a pretty skirt turned his eye?

They arrived back at the Del Sol to be greeted by a shocked staff, who grew even more shocked at the news of the marriage. It was all Savanna could do to keep from telling them the truth when Monheno assembled them to make the announcement.

She bit her lip and forced herself not to pull away when he took her hand and led her to the house. As soon as they were out of sight of the onlookers, she jerked her hand away.

"I will be retiring to my room," she told him crisply and then turned toward the stairs. She stopped when he followed her.

"Sounds like a wonderful idea to me." He gave a provocative tilt of dark brows that made her skin tingle.

"You will not be coming with me!" Even as she said it, forbidden thoughts tugged at the back of her mind—thoughts that brought a shiver up and down her spine. Bitter as she was, she couldn't keep herself from looking at him,

371

or from picturing his body intertwined with hers.

Daniela probably enjoyed it too.

"Why," he said in that disgustingly taunting tone of his, "if I didn't, what would the servants think? We are husband and wife, after all."

"In name only."

"Hardly just that." The glitter in his dark eyes made his meaning plain. "Surely you haven't forgotten so quickly, mi corazon?"

He took a step closer, reached out and caught her in his arms. He'd had enough of her useless banter. If they had nothing left between them, they still had a bond of passion. Even the cold mask she presented could not hide the evidence of that. He could see it deep in her eyes, in the way her lips parted ever so slightly after she spoke, in the way she tossed her hair back unconsciously.

She moved as if to protest, but he silenced her quickly with a kiss, took her lips insistently.

Savanna felt her body melt against his, hot, dizzy, tingling. A shiver ran through her and she returned the kiss. What was she doing?

She braced her hands against his chest and pushed away. "No," she whispered, "I haven't forgotten." A sob tore from her lips, and she dashed up the stairs.

Her vision blurred as she ran into her room and slammed the door behind her, leaning up against it as though he would try to break through. It was no use. Doors couldn't keep away the crippling tide of feelings rushing into her.

She collapsed onto the floor, her tears coming unheeded, sobs racking her body. Why did he insist on torturing her? It was only his pride that had made him insist on claiming the marriage bed. He had no physical needs thanks to Daniela. Why didn't he go to her?

She had offered him exactly that option when she suggested they live apart, but he only brushed her aside. Did that mean he never intended to go to his lover again? The thought of him sharing his bed with another—doing with another woman the things that he did with her—made her feel as though her heart were breaking all over again.

She cried until no more tears came, then locked the door and went to bed. It wouldn't keep him out if he decided to come for her. She was almost too exhausted to care. Right now, she needed to sleep, to forget . . .

Things always seemed to look better in the morning, particularly at Del Sol house. Morning brought a misty blue light up from the dewy grass to stream through the arched windows on the east side of the house. She stretched and walked over to stand in the sunlight. Her heart skipped a beat as she caught sight of him below, just under her window, in the rose garden.

He was dressed for riding in a plain, cool white cotton shirt, black pants that fit neatly over the rounded muscles of his thighs, and tall black boots with tops decorated by intricate stitching. The sunlight came from behind him, outlining strong arms and torso through the oversized peasant-style shirt. It sent a pang of desire through her.

She watched as he stopped at the graves of his family. What was he saying? What did he feel when he went there? If only she knew what thoughts were in his mind. If only she could understand why he was so determined to keep her as his wife . . .

Monheno ignored the pull of eyes on him and looked down at the cold stones that marked the lives and deaths of those he had loved. They, those six women now buried beneath a bed of roses, taught him what it truly was to love, though he didn't know it at the time. Love flowed so freely in his family he took it for granted. Now he knew its value.

"Mamacita," he whispered, "have I ruined both of our lives?" He'd pondered that question all night under the onslaught of a hangover. All he wanted was to reclaim the Del Sol and to share it with the woman he loved, fill the house with children again.

The dream was far out of reach now. Perhaps it always would be. Perhaps she would never come to love him. Their happiness rested on the possibility that she would, because they were bound to each other forever now. Divorce wasn't permitted in his church. His heart wouldn't permit living apart.

He wooed her once. He would have to do it again—over time, patiently. The tug of their passion was still there. That gave him a door through which to enter.

"Only a matter of time," he whispered to himself as he knelt down to clean a stray patch of grass away from the gravestone of young Elena. "It is only a matter of time."

# Twenty

Savanna stared at the calendar on her study desk. Fingers moving over the dates, she counted mentally, her sense of doom swelling as the count grew higher. One, two, three, four weeks. Over a month since she and Monheno came to Del Sol house as unwilling man and wife. Nearly seven weeks and all the signs were there—occasional nausea and dizziness, the slightest thickening in her waist, a swelling in her breasts. She tried to ignore the obvious, but she couldn't deny it any longer. She was going to have to face the fact that she was pregnant.

The news couldn't come at a worse time. The past week had been one of the longest of her life. Things between her and Monheno grew more and more strained as each day passed. He was incessant in his determination that they be man and wife in every sense of the word, and she was determined to resist.

Her confidence flagged whenever he caught

her eye, or touched her, or when she lay awake during the long nights thinking of him in a bed down the hall. One night she went to him in desperation, ready to admit she did love him and wanted to be his wife, if he would adhere to the vows of a husband. Then she went to his room and found his bed empty. In the middle of the night, there was only one place he could be.

It hurt so much to love someone and know he was a deceiver. She could forgive his sordid past, but she couldn't forgive his bedding Daniela now that they were married.

Now, she was confronted with a new problem. The prospect of a child changed her options greatly—destroyed most of them. With a child to support, there was little possibility of divorce. Aside from finances, there was the fact that the child deserved the best life she could provide, a life that included a father.

She had to give her own child something better than the broken, lonely childhood given her. As much as Monheno pined over those graves outside the ranch house, she knew he would love his child. If it took her sacrificing her pride to do what was right, then so be it. But she'd not allow him to keep Daniela. If sacrifices were to be made for the child, he would have to make his also.

Even as she thought about it, uncertainties spun through her mind. Did he love Daniela?

Did he need her? Would he consent to never seeing her again?

The sound of the door opening drove the questions away like vultures. She looked up from behind her small desk to find Monheno standing there, his clothing covered with dust.

"So you've finally found your way downstairs." His tone was flat, neither warm nor cold. "I was beginning to think you might be hiding from your husband."

She blushed and looked away. He hit the nail right on the head. She was hiding, but not just from him, from the facts also. She stayed in bed late that morning just to avoid facing them, not that it did any good.

"Of course not." She looked at the wall just past his shoulder. "Why would I hide from you?"

He shrugged as though it were of little consequence. "I'm glad to find you dressed for riding." His lips held a serious line, but the faintest twinkle lit in his eye. "We are going on a little trip."

She crinkled her brows suspiciously. "A trip?" Why was he being so pleasant to her all of a sudden? Last night he was so mad with her he wouldn't even speak. "But I haven't packed anything."

"All taken care of." He smiled, a sort of crocodile grin that made her even more unsure. "We'll have to leave now to be there by dark."

She started to make an excuse, but then

thought better of it and took his hand. Perhaps a trip would provide a perfect opportunity to tell him about the baby.

She tried to plan the words in her mind as she followed him down the hall to the kitchen. I am pregnant, and given that fact. . . . Considering that I am going to have your child, I think you should. . . . Our child deserves . . . Nothing sounded right. She couldn't picture saying any of those things, couldn't imagine how she was going to tell him or what he would say. What if he was angry? What if he refused to give up his lover even after she told him?

Esperanza met them at the kitchen door and handed Monheno a bundle wrapped in a clean flour sack.

Savanna glanced from the housekeeper to Monheno. They were plotting something.

She slowed her pace as they walked out the door and toward the barn. "Where are we going?"

He shook his head, obviously pleased with himself for coaxing her into the trip. "That is a secret."

She chewed the inside of her lip thoughtfully. "How long will we be gone?" That might tell her something about their destination.

"That depends on you." He led his bay from the stall and secured Esperanza's bundle to the back of his saddle, then gave the bay a cheerful pat as he brought out Nantucket. "Are you sure you don't want to ride one of the palominos?"

"No, thank you." She felt a pang of irritation. Every time he mentioned those palominos, every time she saw them it aggravated her. "I notice you aren't riding one of them either."

"True," he allowed. "To be honest, I never could stand the way they dance and jig everywhere they go. It is hard to tolerate after a while."

She rolled her eyes and scoffed at his remark. "In other words, they are useless, because the men won't ride them and you won't ride them."

He gave her a noncommittal shrug. "The men won't ride this animal either. Does that make him useless?" He slipped the bridle over Nantucket's head. The gelding looked at her from beneath long lashes as though wondering how she would defend his worth.

"But I like him."

"And I like the palominos."

It was a stalemate.

She threw up her hands and let them fall to her sides with a slap that startled Nantucket away a few steps. "But you won't ride them!"

He gave her that smile that made her feel like a terrible prude. "They are a tradition. Palominos have been raised on the Del Sol for over a hundred years. I won't be the one to stop the bloodline."

She allowed him to help her onto her mount. If she lived to be a hundred years old, she would never understand his devotion to the past, perhaps because she didn't have much of a family history to cling to herself.

She looked up and down the row of golden heads sticking out of the stalls. "We . . . perhaps we could integrate some more practical breeding into the strain."

"Perhaps *we* could."

The clatter of hooves coming at a gallop snapped them both around. Monheno dropped his reins and ran to the doorway. He slid to a stop just in time to avoid being run down by a rider on a lathered horse.

"Waddie?" Savanna's heart slammed like a hammer against her ribs. "Is something wrong?" The spent condition of the roan horse said something was.

Waddie looked at her, his eyes as white rimmed as the horse's. He jumped frantically down and ran the few steps back to Monheno. "I done somethin' bad, Mister Devilla." He grabbed off his hat and twisted it nervously in his hands. "I done somethin' real bad. I know you told me not to go back to the camp, but I done it anyway. I went there after her."

Anger turned Monheno's face grey. "Madre de Dios, Waddie, I told you to stay away from Venenoso." He clenched a fist and slammed it into the barn wall. "What happened?"

Waddie fidgeted from one foot to the other, wringing the hat in his hands like he intended to shred it. "She sent me a note to come git her.

We was gonna go away and git married . . ." He trailed off, looking down at his hands.

"I told you to forget about her," Monheno breathed from between clenched teeth. He looked like he was about to blow steam out his ears.

Waddie snapped his eyes up and nodded. "I know." He winced as though he expected a whipping with a willow switch. "But she wrote how he was mad at her, and she was afraid he was gonna kill her. S-so I went there and I was gonna take her with me, b-but he found us . . ."

"And?" Monheno turned a shade more pale.

Waddie swallowed so hard the bulge in his neck jumped like a grasshopper. "A-and I killed him. God, I didn't mean to. He come up on me s-sudden." Hat still clenched, he extended his arms to Monheno like a beggar. "I-I gotta git out of the valley. If they find me, they'll kill me fer sure."

Monheno rubbed his forehead and let out a long sigh. "Are you sure you killed him?"

Waddie nodded grimly.

Monheno took the reins to the exhausted roan. "You'll need a new horse and some money." He led the animal to a stall. "How far behind are they?"

"I don't think they come after me yet." Waddie slapped his hat on his head. "There wasn't no one there but her and me when it happened, and she run off. When I rode outta there, no one paid me no mind."

Monheno pulled Waddie's saddle from the roan and carried it back into the hall. "Savanna," he barked urgently, "go into the house and get supplies for him. There is money in the desk."

Numb, she scrambled down from her saddle, started for the house at a run. Waddie's words spun through her mind. Venenoso was dead? Shot by Waddie? Was it possible?

"Put his saddle on Nantucket," she called back over her shoulder as she ran to the house. Waddie was going to need the fastest horse he could get.

Waddie was mounted when she returned, Nantucket prancing nervously beneath him. She handed the packs up and smiled, giving Nantucket a fond pat. "You two take care of each other." Tears pressed her eyes, but she blinked them back. Dear God, she hoped nothing happened to them.

Waddie nodded, looking frightened and young, and tipped his hat. "Yes, ma'am." He fastened the packs in place. "And don't you worry, ain't no horse in the valley could catch up with Nantucket."

"I know." She smiled shakily. "You two go on now."

"She's right." Monheno stood at her side and looped a strong arm over her shoulders. "Don't stop until you're in Texas."

Waddie gathered up his reins and put his

heels to the horse, waving back over his shoulder as he thundered from the yard.

Savanna said a silent prayer for his safety. Please, God, keep him safe. He's just a boy.

"He'll be all right," Monheno said as if he read her thoughts. He gave her one last reassuring squeeze, then turned and walked back into the barn.

He came back out with one of the palominos saddled and handed her the reins.

She took them uncertainly. "Do you think we should go?"

He nodded. "If Venenoso's men come around asking questions, it will be better if we're not here. We'll take the roan with us and turn him out with the brood mares where no one will find him."

She looped her reins over the palomino's neck and climbed aboard. If he thought it best that they leave, she wasn't going to question. They couldn't do anything for Waddie now, anyway. She should have done something to prevent this disaster. She should have been there to talk to Waddie instead of hiding in her room. It was no wonder Monheno took over running the ranch the minute they returned. She was inadequate at the job. She was . . .

No. She looked back at the Del Sol as they rode up the hill. She did well at running the ranch alone, especially considering its finances. There was no way she could have known Waddie was mixed up with the Sombras. She'd been busy killing herself trying to pay the bills. It was easy for Monheno to put things in order. He had money.

It was infuriating the way he took over every aspect of the operation without a single question to her. Never once did he acknowledge her efforts or her success in keeping the ranch alive.

"Monheno?" Anger made her narrow her eyes when he glanced over at her. "Did I really do such a poor job running the Del Sol?" She could shoot herself! What was she doing asking for his approval? She knew she did well. Why did she need his approval?

"Who said that?" He looked confused.

She was looking at him like he'd lost his mind. "You did."

He looked at her like she just whipped a forked tongue out of her mouth. "I did not. Savanna, I admire you for keeping the Del Sol alive at all. I know how hard that was. What fool told you otherwise?"

"Uhhh," she stalled. The fool was sitting in the saddle with her. Now she felt silly. "But you took over running everything the moment we came back."

He laughed softly, the corners of his face lifting, his cinnamon skin catching the sunlight. "In the time we've been back you hardly came out of your room. I assumed you were glad to be rid of those duties. I assumed you wanted to keep to the house."

"I *wanted* to be *asked*," she snapped.

He met her eyes. "In that case, I apologize." The tone of his voice, deep, caressing, sent a tingle up her spine. "There is nothing I want more than to have you run the Del Sol by my side."

She frowned and cocked her head to one side.

He tossed his head back and laughed. "Hell, Savanna I'll run it by your side if that will bring you out of your bedroom."

She rolled her eyes thoughtfully. "I like the sound of that." A smile tugged at the corners of her lips.

"I thought you would."

She looked down at her hands in self defense. She had no resistance to that smile, that simmering look in his eye. Just being this close to him made her want to forget about the problems between them.

She had an idea of where they were headed long before they reached their destination. She was certain of it when they started up a familiar hillside trail. This trip up the mountain, though at a calmer pace than their last, brought back memories of their hidden valley—of the first time they made love.

In her mind, she heard the thunder of the waterfall, felt the rush of thrilling new sensations. He brought to life a part of her she never knew was there, stirred needs she never knew she had. That part of her wanted him still, and loved him still. Maybe she should trust her heart.

They rounded the last bend in the trail and came into the valley. A gasp of surprise escaped her lips, and she stopped her mount. Beside the pool at the bottom of the waterfall a camp was set, a firepit prepared, a canvas erected as a tent. Beside the pool lay a bright Mexican blanket covered with white, pink, and red roses.

"It's beautiful," she breathed. "Who did this?"

He slapped a spread-fingered hand to his chest. "I did, of course. Didn't you know I am a hopeless romantic?"

She tried to resist the tug of a smile. "I hadn't heard."

"Well, my dear," he gave a suggestive tilt of brows, "come into my parlor, and let me show you how hopeless I can be."

She urged her mount forward after his. She wouldn't bet a wooden nickel on her chances of resisting him now. Of all the things he could do to win her over, he chose the best—bringing her to this special place and going to such obvious trouble to prepare a haven for them. It was no wonder he looked tired! He must have been busy since before sunrise bringing the camp equipment here and setting everything up. How could she not be charmed by such an effort?

As they rode past it, she looked up at the cliff wall with its giant painted Spaniards and menagerie of strange animals. Perhaps those paintings really were magic. They were casting a spell on her. She felt almost as if the past weeks of trouble never existed, as if their love was new, dangerous, unspoiled.

He handed her a rose as he helped her down, and she brought it to her face gently. She drank in the sweet fragrance, and rubbed it along the curve of her chin as he led the horses away to picket them. She let her eyes drift boldly over his strong frame. Just looking at him stirred her stomach, causing hot desire to move through her. It was no wonder there had been many women in his life.

That thought made her frown just as he turned back to her.

He frowned. "Something wrong?"

She shook her head. She had to get her thoughts together before she could discuss things with him. She had to plan exactly what she was going to say.

She turned away, looking at the flame-edged clouds stacked like burning bales of cotton on the horizon. "Look. What a beautiful sunset."

He stepped closer and took her hand. "It is." He started toward the hillside, pulling her with him. "I know the perfect place to watch it."

She followed him up a rocky watershed toward the top of the hill. Breath panted from her lungs as she climbed, and black dizziness spun before her eyes. She clung to his hand and tried to blink it away. Only a month or so pregnant and already she was becoming a weakling!

Her lungs begged her to stop and catch her

breath when they reached the top. Doggedly, she followed him, her face burning with effort.

He stopped when they reached a small patch of grass atop the painted Spaniards. Alarm registered on his face when he looked at her and he put a hand to her waist to steady her.

"Are you all right?" A furrow of concern drew lines across his forehead. "You should have told me to stop."

She pushed his hand away and stepped toward the edge of the bluff. A glance down made her feel dizzy, and she moved back. "I didn't want to miss the sunset." One look at the flaming clouds made her breath catch in her throat. "It is so much more beautiful from up here."

Standing just behind her, he laughed, the soft notes ruffling wisps of hair on her cheek. "Didn't you know this place is magic?" He slipped his arms around her waist. "There is a legend the Indians tell about two star-crossed lovers who fell to their deaths here. They believe the waterfall first flowed from the tears those lovers shed because they could never be together."

She gazed into the sunset, watching the colors around the edges burn from purple to crimson to bright orange and back again. "But why couldn't they be together?" She whispered because the world around them was so quiet.

"Oh, that is a long story, but they came from warring tribes." He pulled her closer, and she leaned back willingly against him. "The most tragic part of the story is that they are separated even in death. Her soul is the brightest light in the night sky, and his in the day."

"The moon and the sun."

"Doomed to be apart forever." He sounded like an actor delivering lines in a play.

When she turned to face him, the hint of melodrama faded from his face. "Are we?"

"That is up to you," he replied softly. "I'm here, for now and always."

Tears prickled into her eyes. She had wanted so badly to hear those words—to be able to believe them, but there was still a shadow of doubt in her. Perhaps there would always be. But she would be cheating herself and their child if she didn't shed her protective armor and grab for her rainbow before it faded away. At some point, she was going to have to trust.

"So am I." Her voice quivered as she said it. "Monheno, I love you and I want us to make a life together, but I'm afraid . . ."

He laid a palm on her cheek, his thumb tracing the full bow of her lips. "Don't be," he whispered. "I have always loved you. We don't need anything more."

He lifted her chin and pressed his lips to hers, his kiss hungry, but at the same time gentle. As their lips parted, he kissed her again on the forehead, and pulled her into his arms. Together they watched the sun sink below the horizon.

With the competing light of the sun vanished, the edges of the clouds grew even more bright.

She turned back to Monheno, her senses filled with him, her body alive with desire and need. He kissed her again, more deeply, parting her lips. She met his strokes and quivered against him, passion tingling through her thighs.

She didn't resist as he lowered her into the soft grass. Weakly, she clung to him, her hands exploring the hard curves of his body through his clothes, finding them just as she remembered. Oh, how she had yearned for him! Holding him now, feeling his burning, tempting caress on the curve of her waist, down her hips and then slowly back up, was almost like living in a dream.

"I love you, Monheno Devilla." Her voice was a hoarse whisper. "I love you."

He didn't reply because he couldn't. There were no smooth phrases for what he felt now. Those simple words filled him like an empty well.

Slowly, passionately, they shed the bonds of clothing, no embarrassment between them. Consumed by love, they touched each other freely, honestly, hands and lips exploring the finest details of each other's bodies.

When he moved over her, she opened herself to him without coaxing, eager to feel him within her. As he entered her, she moved her hips upward to meet his thrust, a gasp tearing from her lips. The feeling building within her was more intense than ever before as his rhythm set flame to that secret place within her. With a sudden blast, she felt it explode and ripple through her, making her entire body quiver. As soon as the ripples died, the fire built again.

Monheno resisted the insistent pull of his own release, unwilling to have their lovemaking end. Only when desire bolted beyond his control did he thunder to his own climax.

Spent, they held each other close, watching through lazy, sated eyes as the last rims of fire faded from the clouds.

It was long after dark when they returned to their camp. Exhausted from lovemaking and the climb back down the cliff, she lay down on the pallet beneath the canvas, watching sleepily as he built a fire in the pit. It was a perfect evening. Perfect. Now was the perfect time to tell him of the baby, and to settle the one thing that still stood between them—Daniela.

"Monheno?" she said softly as her eyes drifted closed. "Will you be finished soon?"

"Ummm." The fire crackled with his words. "As soon as I see to the horses. I don't think they'd care for being left saddled overnight."

"Oh . . ." she nodded faintly. The sound of his footsteps rustling through the grass seemed far away.

She dragged her eyes open, determined not to fall asleep. Overhead, a star fell across the velvet sky. She closed her eyes again, thinking of the legend of the lost lovers. Monheno would be back soon, and then she'd tell him about the baby.

Monheno returned to the camp to find her asleep on the pallet, her golden hair spread around her like a halo, her face peaceful. He sat down beside her and watched her for a long time as she slept. It was a strange chain of events which had brought her into his life.

He could remember clearly how out of place she looked that day he first saw her on the street in Oro Grande, her beautiful face pale. It was hardly a wonder she'd disliked him immediately. They didn't meet under the best circumstances.

Why did she leave him after their time at the ghost house? He knew she loved him then. He felt it. He was sure she would accept his proposal, and then he came home to an empty bedroom. If not for Venenoso's intervention, she would be gone from his life now. Why? How did she get out of the house in the first place?

Perhaps she was afraid of settling down to married life. She said more than once she never intended to marry. He would have to prove to her that their marriage would never be the cold existence her parents' marriage had been.

Perhaps a trip—to San Francisco now, and then after the fall harvests were finished at the Del Sol, perhaps somewhere else—Africa even. Maybe going there would help her clear those ghosts from her past, lift the weights from her soul.

He lay down beside her, drawing her to him. There would be plenty of time for settling down to the Del Sol. It was more important to see that she didn't feel like a prisoner in her new life . . .

The smells of breakfast awoke Savanna. Even before she opened her eyes, her body reminded her she had neglected to eat dinner the night before. Rolling onto her stomach, she propped herself lazily with her elbows and looked toward the fire where Monheno was frying bacon and boiling coffee.

"Overland trout and range water." She used the cowboy names with a smile.

"No tea and crumpets this morning, English," he chided, looking at the frying pan. "But with all that snoring I would imagine you've worked up enough appetite to eat rattlesnake and rocks."

She climbed to her knees and crawled from the canvas. "I do not snore." Of that she was certain. She'd spent enough years sleeping in a dormitory full of girls to know.

He chuckled under his breath. "Well, then there must have been a black bear sleeping outside our canvas last night."

She came around the fire and punched him hard on the shoulder as she passed. "That will teach you to say such things about me!"

He flailed a fork in the air to get his balance and protested the abuse with a loud grunt.

She proceeded toward the nearby brush with a self-righteous nod. "What you probably heard was yourself."

"I knew there had to be a reason you left me," he called after her.

The comment hit her like a bucket of cold water. She felt the warmth drain from her body as she ducked into the brush to see to her personal needs.

His smile was gone also when she returned. "It couldn't have been me snoring last night, because I was up thinking." His expression was deadly serious. "I was thinking there is no reason for us to be tied to the Del Sol all of the time. We could do some traveling—to San Francisco perhaps, and then after the harvests are in, I thought we might even make a trip to Africa."

"Africa . . ." The word didn't register in her mind. All she could think of was what he said before that. There is no need for us to be tied to the Del Sol. Was he already seeking a way to escape their life together? Was he bored with it already? All she wanted was to settle down, to provide a warm, stable home for their child, but he didn't want that at all. He wanted adventure, and she would be the one to spoil it for him.

"Savanna?" He looked worried. The eggs crackled forgotten in the pan.

"The eggs," she muttered, glancing down. She felt like her heart was boiling in there with them, turning burned and hard. Gather your wits, Savanna. Gather your wits and think of something to say.

He set the pan in the sand and stood up, then

walked to the blanket and squatted down beside her. "God, Savanna, what is wrong?"

Her entire body trembled and quicksilver tears formed in her eyes. She couldn't force herself to look at him, though she could feel him watching her.

She swallowed hard and forced the truth out. "I can't go to Africa, or to San Francisco either." She was standing in a hangman's noose, waiting for the trap door to drop. "I can't travel anywhere, Monheno, because I'm pregnant."

# Twenty-one

"W-what?" He crumpled from his squat to sit facing her on the blanket. "But you said . . ." His sable eyes grew steadily wider. "When did you find this out? Dios Mio, why didn't you tell me? Are you all right? Good Lord, you shouldn't be riding! And that climb up the cliff Last night!" He started to grab her then stopped like she might break. "Is there anything I can do? Are you all right?"

Laughter bubbled up through her tears. She'd never seen him frantic. He looked like he might faint.

She took his hand to steady him. "You can calm yourself. I'm expecting a child. I'm not mortally wounded. There is nothing to worry about." The assurance didn't seem to calm him. He looked more worried than ever, and she flinched with new guilt. "Except that I have spoiled your plans to travel." Unless he planned

397

to travel without her. The idea made her empty stomach ache.

His next words dispelled her fears like a warm breeze. "Travel?" He acted like he couldn't believe she mentioned it. "I don't care about that. Dios mio, Savanna, my only concern is getting you home safely."

"Then you aren't disappointed?" Her heart swelled with hope. He didn't look disappointed at all. He looked ecstatic.

"Of course I'm not disappointed," he coughed. "I only suggested we travel because I didn't want you to be bored with our life before it began."

"I don't want to travel." Her smile felt as though it came from deep within her. "The only thing I ever wanted was for us to live together at the Del Sol. But . . ." She looked down at their intertwined hands, holding her breath. "B-but I want your vow that you will not see Daniela again."

Silent moments passed, and her hopes sank lower with each one, like leaves dragged under by the tide. He wasn't going to give up his mistress, even now that she told him about the baby. What chance did their marriage have given that?

"Daniela?" he choked. "What are you talking about?"

She drew back and pulled her hand from his. Dear God, he was going to deny it. "She is your lover."

"My what?" He looked at her like she just

398

sprouted horns. "What in the world gave you that idea?"

Anger boiled up in her stomach. How dare he deny it! Didn't this marriage mean anything to him? Didn't their child? Didn't last night?

"*She* gave me that idea." How could he look so innocent? "And I saw her at Adolfo's house—coming from *your* bedroom."

He lowered his brows and scratched behind his ear as if to rout the answer like a flea. "Little witch," he growled. "If I see her again, I'll break her scrawny neck."

She stiffened. "Hardly proper treatment for your mistress."

Anger sparked in his eyes as he captured hers. "Daniela was there to bring the food, that is all," he said flatly. "I won't deny I've been with a woman or two in my life, but certainly not her. I've known her since she was a child, and I never liked her then either. I'd like to kill her for what she did to poor Waddie. He's lucky she didn't get him shot."

"Waddie?" Now it was all making sense. The day she saw them in the garden. The carelessly scrawled note that didn't look like Monheno's handwriting. Daniela coming out of his room with such perfect timing. Daniela helping her escape . . . trying to make her fall down the well in the darkness. It all made sense, and she had played right into it.

She nodded in understanding. "I-I don't know what to say."

399

He ruffled the sleep-mussed strands of her hair. "Don't bother," he muttered. "She isn't worth any more of our effort."

"No." She looked into those dark eyes, forgiving eyes, loving eyes. "You won't hear of her again from me."

Their breakfast was cold by the time they returned to it. She took it without complaining. His were the best burned eggs and cold bacon she ever ate.

"A baby," he said after a while, shaking his dark head and smiling. "But when I asked you, you said there was no baby."

She looked guiltily at the charred edges of her egg. "I know." She knew he would bring that up sooner or later. "I couldn't bear to consider the possibility. I thought you had been with . . . her. I knew if you thought I was carrying your child you wouldn't let me go."

"True," he admitted. "I suppose we can thank Venenoso for the fact that things turned out after all."

She gave him a murderous glare—one that was really meant for his outlaw cousin. "I wouldn't have a word of thanks for that thief if he gave me a drink of water in the desert. He was a bastard and a murderer, and I hope he rots in hell where he belongs."

She meant it. She hoped Venenoso and her father were both sitting in the flames cheating each other at cards. Finally, there would be peace at the Del Sol . . . unless . . . a sickening thought came into her mind.

"What will happen to the Sombras now? You don't intend to ride with them any longer, do you?" She held her breath.

He looked up at the painted Spaniards, his ancestors who claimed that country hundreds of years ago. "No. The Sombras's time has come and gone. California will never go back to what it was." Sadness was obvious in his voice. "I guess I've known it for years. I think we all knew it, that is why all the good men left Venenoso years ago. The Sombras haven't been more than a band of thieves since then."

"Yet you rode with them."

"Only on one occasion recently," he gave a wicked, one-sided smile, "against the Del Sol, and I think you can verify that I did no mischief that night."

She narrowed her eyes. Was he really not a part of the Sombras? What would happen now? "Will they reband now that Venenoso is gone?"

"No." He sounded definite about that. "Strong leaders always surround themselves with weak men. If Venenoso is really dead, that will be the end of the Sombras. There is no one else to pick up the torch."

"Except you." She was almost afraid to utter the words, but she had to know. He seemed to have such a feeling for the people in Venenoso's camp. It was hard to believe he would abandon them now. "If they come to you, will you lead them?"

She wasn't sure what she would do if he said yes. She couldn't be party to stealing no matter how much she loved him. She couldn't raise her sons up to be soldiers and her daughters to be . . . like Daniela.

He shook his head. Clearly, he had thought about it already. "No," he replied. "I'll break my back to help them, but I won't reband the Sombras."

She slumped in relief. His word was good enough for her. Finally, there would be peace in their valley. Perhaps there were legal procedures they could use to help the old families regain what was rightfully theirs. She and Monheno were not without means. Aside from that, the Del Sol needed staff. If men came wanting honest work, they could be hired on. Those who didn't want to work for their money deserved whatever fate awaited them.

But she didn't want to think about that now. "Do we have to go home straight away?" She turned her most soulful look on him. "Couldn't we stay here a day or two more?"

Her hopes sank at his look of apprehension.

"But what about the baby?" He looked down at her stomach, then back at her eyes. "I thought I would ride home and bring a wagon out so you wouldn't have to go on horseback."

She stood up indignantly. "You will do nothing of the sort! I'll not have you pampering and pandering over me for seven more months, Monheno Devilla, so you'd best forget the notion. I am quite capable of riding home, and of doing everything else I have always done. I don't need you worrying over me like an old mother hen."

She tipped her chin up stubbornly and walked toward the spring pool. "As a matter-of-fact . . ." She slipped her clothes off, leaving a trail behind her as she walked to the water's edge. "I think I will start right now by going for a swim."

Monheno stood up, watching as the satin curves of her body slide into the water. Tempting . . .

"Savanna," he called.

She twisted tauntingly around in the water, pale breasts peeking above the lapping surface. "Yes?"

He chuckled. How long had he been waiting to hear that word from her lips? "Don't go in too deep."

She splashed water at him playfully. "Come in and stop me."

He didn't need any more invitation than that. He didn't need an invitation at all, in fact, but it felt good to have one. It felt good to have all the bickering and misunderstanding and lonely nights over. He didn't plan on sleeping alone again . . . ever.

He took his shirt off impatiently, then stood on one foot to remove his boots. Droplets of water splashed over the toes, and he glanced at Savanna from the corner of his eye.

She widened her eyes innocently and backed away a few steps. "Is this too deep?"

He threw off one boot and looked at her, not at her face, but at her breasts now hidden beneath the sundrenched water. "Yes. That is too deep."

Her violet eyes turned smoky with passion as she moved back into the shadows. "Is this close enough?"

Erect nipples peaked at him from just below the water's surface, and he felt his manhood harden. "Not quite." He yanked off the second boot and unbuttoned his breeches impatiently. He'd had about all the teasing he could stand.

She swished a few steps closer, her breasts and waist rising out of the water. "Is this close enough?"

He slipped his breeches off and tossed them aside, then stood at the water's edge. "Almost."

She smiled, that sweet seductive smile that made his heart warm and his body feverish. A comely flush stole down her cheeks as she walked to the shore. He could see everything above her ankles, and he took the time to look.

"That is perfect." He took her hand and pulled her from the water, drew her against him and looked down into those bright eyes.

She batted her lashes drowsily. "Perfect?" The word came in a passionate sigh as he slid his hands down ner back and over her buttocks, teasing at her golden nest.

"Ummmm," he breathed against her lips.

Savanna felt fire explode through her body as his kiss tasted her, parted her, foreshadowed things to come. She slid her hands over his chest, across the strong cords of his shoulders, into his sable hair.

It was amazing that every time he touched her she felt more passionate, more complete. Her heart swelled with love until it felt like it would burst each time it leapt against her chest. She wanted him, needed him, loved him. They would have children together, and grandchildren, and great-grandchildren—a lifetime together to share their thoughts and bodies.

His lips parted from hers and trailed down the side of her neck, made her shoulders tremble.

"I love you," she whispered. The words weren't hard to say this time. They made her feel whole.

He lifted her into his arms and looked into her eyes as he lay her in the soft grass. "Siempre, mi corazon."

She smiled into those dark, smoldering eyes. *Forever, my heart.* The words clung to her like wings, making her light, dizzy. She let her eyes close with passion as he drew a taunting circle around one breast then flicked the hardened nipple with his tongue. His hands slid up over her waist, teased her stomach, gripped her breasts, and molded them into his mouth.

She gasped, half in pleasure, half in torment. His tongue drew a searing trail along her stomach as he slowly slid his hands downward to part her thighs. Mist blew from the waterfall and tickled her feverish skin, reminding her of the first time they made love. This time she wasn't afraid.

She parted her legs willingly, yielded to the pressure as he pushed her knees upward and teased the edges of her inner self with his kiss. His fingers slid back down her legs, parted her and entered her. She writhed against him, gasped, and tossed her head from side to side in torment.

"Please . . ." she breathed.

He moved back upward, tasted her breasts again, then grabbed her and pulled her on top of him. She raised her hips impatiently and lowered herself over his hardened shaft, felt his manhood fill her, and cried out.

He slid his hands over her breasts, her waist, gripped her buttocks and guided her in the rhythms of pleasure. She threw her head back and moved against him, feeling that desperate tightening build within her.

He whispered her name, drove her harder against him, drove her beyond reason until finally her body shattered in release with his.

She collapsed against him, exhausted, breathless. The hum of the waterfall and the thundering of her own heart mixed in her ears, lulled her nearly into sleep.

Her body was leaden when they parted.

"Savanna?" His voice was thick with leftover passion.

She rolled drowsily onto her stomach and looked at him through half-closed eyes. "Yes?"

"I want there to be no more misunderstandings between us."

She looked down at her hands in chagrin. She knew what he meant. He was pointing out that she made both of them suffer needlessly over the past weeks. Pride and stubbornness kept her away from him, kept her from asking the questions that really mattered.

"There won't be," she promised.

He touched a finger under her chin. "Look me in the eye and tell me that."

She brought her gaze up. "There won't be. I promise . . . if you'll promise me something in return."

He tapped the end of her nose playfully. "What?"

"That we can stay here a few more days."

He pressed his lips together and rolled his eyes upward like he needed to consider it. "If you insist."

She nestled into the crook of his arm and listened to the slow rhythm of his heart. "And something else."

"What?"

"That you won't expect me to become a model wife overnight."

A chuckle rumbled beneath her ear. "Or perhaps never?"

"Perhaps not."

She sighed and closed her eyes drowsily. If this was a dream, she hoped she never woke up.

Two days later as they packed and rode away, she felt like she was still wrapped in the downy warmth of that dream. She stopped and reined her horse around to take one last look at the painted Spaniards. This was a perfect place, a magic place, the place they fell in love, and found their love again.

"Is something wrong?" He stopped his horse just ahead of hers.

She shook her head and smiled. "No." What a worrier he was! He'd been a nervous wreck all morning at the prospect of riding down the mountain trail. "I just wanted a last look."

"We'll come back," she heard him say, "after the baby is born."

"Good Lord, the way you fuss!" She turned her mount around and caught up with him. "You'd think you were having this baby!"

"I just don't want anything to happen to my son."

She lowered a brow incredulously. "And what if your son is a female?" She hadn't given much thought to whether the baby would be a boy or a girl. She'd be happy with either one, but fathers always wanted boys.

408

He tipped his hat back and leaned forward in his saddle with intense seriousness. "I beg your pardon, madam, but no son of mine will be a female.

She widened her eyes in shock, and he grinned.

"However, I expect each and every one of my daughters to be."

"Oh, you!" She snatched his reins and pulled them forward over his horse's head, then dropped them into the ground before he could stop her. "Just for that, I'll race you to the bottom of the mountain."

Before he could gather his reins or protest, she trotted her horse around him and headed down the trail. Glancing back, she laughed at the expression frozen on his face. If she didn't know him for a strong man, she would swear he was going to faint dead away.

He was not at all pleased by the time he found her at the bottom. "No more races please." He let out a deep breath and turned his horse toward home, shaking his head. "I am going to be a hundred years old before this baby is born. I wish I were the one having the baby. It would be easier."

She giggled and started after him, keeping to a demure walk out of respect for his nervous condition. She'd never seen a man fuss so over a pregnancy. Her father didn't care a whit when her mother was pregnant, or when she miscarried twice, or when the last baby was stillborn.

Monheno was so different from that—so devoted. How could she ever have thought he was like her father? "I shall endeavor to behave myself from now on." She moved her horse alongside his. "I wouldn't want you to age a hundred years in the next few months."

"Yes, well, keep that in mind the next time you want a horse race." His tone was stern, but he winked at her from the corner of his eye. "Or I will have to tell the staff to keep you locked in the house."

That brought to mind a question that was plaguing her. "Monheno, I am afraid of what the staff will say . . . about the baby, I mean. If they were to count . . . well, we have only just been married."

He smiled at her. "Is this the same woman who went against the Sombras in her night dress?" He asked. "With all that to talk about, do you really think people would waste time counting the months to the birth of our child? In any case, what matters is our happiness, not what the staff thinks."

"I know." He was right, of course. She was worrying about things that didn't matter. "I suppose I'm just the type to worry."

He put his hand atop hers and gave it a squeeze. "A habit you'll have to correct. After all, you are a Californio now, and we don't waste our time worrying . . ."

He said something more, but she didn't hear him. Her mind was still considering his words.

You are a Californio now. She supposed that was true. She was hardly the same prim girl who came from English boarding school such a short time before. She didn't regret the change. She liked the person she was becoming—her own person, and perhaps the one she would have always been had the circumstances of her life been different.

They rode slowly back to the Del Sol, and reined their horses in on the hill above the yard. Standing beside him, she looked down at the grand old adobe, still sturdy after the births and deaths of generations of Devillas.

Never would she have predicted the changes the Del Sol would bring into her life. Leaving it to her was the only thing for which she owed her father thanks.

"I just thought of something." She turned to her husband with a wicked smile. "I am finally rid of that awful name. I'm not Savanna Storm any longer."

"I always liked that name," he protested. "It had . . . vision."

"Humph." She shrugged. "It was dreadful, and when our child is born, we'll give him or her a normal name—something that will not be an embarrassment."

He grinned that charming grin that made her tingle all over. "When this child is born, you can give it whatever Christian name you wish, just as long as you remember the surname is Devilla."

She smiled with him, looking back down at

411

the house. "Now how could I forget that? And if I did, generations of Devillas past would no doubt come back to haunt me."

She thought of all the lives that had come and gone on the Del Sol. It was fitting that the house would again be filled with children bearing their name. "I guess you got what you wanted." She gave a wry smile. "The Del Sol is yours again, even if you did have to romance it out from under me."

That devilish spark winked in his eye. "I have exactly what I had hoped for." He trailed a finger along her shoulder, sent a shiver through her. "But then, as I told you, I am a hopeless romantic."

"Definitely hopeless." She followed as he urged his mount on down the hill toward the barn. When they reached it, she dismounted wearily, leaving the horse to a stable boy.

"Don't put him in that stall," she said as the boy swung open a door. "That's Nantucket's stall. Leave it empty."

The boy only shrugged, unconcerned, and closed the door again, leading the horses away. She turned to see her husband frowning at her.

"For good luck," she explained quietly. "At least until we hear from them." She passed by the door where so many times she'd patted Nantucket's velvety black nose. In her mind, she could picture young Waddie on his black horse, streaking across the grasslands toward Texas. "Who knows? They may be coming back to use it again."

He nodded. "I have a feeling they will." He took her hand and led her to the house. "I was wondering, Señora, if you would sit with me on the veranda and watch the sun go down?" He stole a kiss before they climbed the steps. "If it wouldn't be too scandalous, I mean."

She chuckled, "Not too," and seated herself beside him on a huge white swing.

"Oh, listen," she whispered when the reluctant swing stopped creaking. "Do you hear it? It's Black Jim."

He cocked an ear to the soft, low tones of the old cowboy singing with his guitar. "Listen." He pulled her closer, resting his cheek on the top of her head, "He's singing that one just for us. It is an old song about lovers. They call it 'Heartsong.' "

She listened, her heart floating to the soft rhythms of the song as it drifted to them through the warm, dusky air,

> "My Spanish gal was a lovely one
> Soft as dew when she was mine,
> We lived the life of sweetest love,
> Down below that border line,
>
> Midnight on the patio,
> Much too late and all alone
> She would lean close and whisper low
> Es siempre, mi corazon
>
> No sweeter words in all my years
> Have come to touch my heart and soul

As those of my Spanish love
Es siempre, mi corazon.
Si siempre, mi corazon

*It is forever, my heart . . .*